Hearts Collide: Strange Romance, Vol. 2

A Romance Short Story Series

Kristine Kathryn Rusch and Dean Wesley Smith

Hearts Collide, Vol. 2
Copyright © 2024 by Kristine Kathryn Rusch and Dean Wesley Smith
Published by WMG Publishing
Cover and layout copyright © 2024 by WMG Publishing
Cover design by WMG Publishing & Alex Hale
Cover art copyright © grandfailure/Depositphotos
ISBN-13 (trade paperback): 978-1-56146-967-3
ISBN-13 (hardcover): 978-1-56146-972-7

Due to limitations of space, expanded copyright information can be found at the end of this volume.

This book is licensed for your personal enjoyment only. All rights reserved. This is a work of fiction. All characters and events portrayed in this book are fictional, and any resemblance to real people or incidents is purely coincidental. This book, or parts thereof, may not be reproduced in any form without permission.

Contents

Untraditional Kristine Kathryn Rusch	vii
Stories by Dean Wesley Smith	ix
THE SECRETS OF YESTERDAY *A Poker Boy Story* Dean Wesley Smith	1
CUCUMBER PARTY *A Buckey the Space Pirate Story* Dean Wesley Smith	17
AFTER THE DANCE Dean Wesley Smith	29
IN THE SHADE OF THE SLOWBOAT MAN Dean Wesley Smith	41
ROSES AROUND THE MOMENT *A Ghost of a Chance Story* Dean Wesley Smith	59
THE LADY OF WHISPERING VALLEY *A Buckey the Space Pirate Story* Dean Wesley Smith	83
THAT OLD TINGLING *A Marble Grant Story* Dean Wesley Smith	99
AN IMMORTALITY OF SORTS *A Buckey the Space Pirate Story* Dean Wesley Smith	115
SMILE Dean Wesley Smith	127

SOMETHING IN MY DARLING   145
A Bryant Street Story
Dean Wesley Smith

Stories by Kristine Kathryn Rusch   153

NAME-CALLING   155
Kristine Kathryn Rusch

SOMETHING BLUE   173
Kristine Kathryn Rusch

CANOPY   197
Kristine Kathryn Rusch

ARTISTIC PHOTOGRAPHS   205
A Roz & Jack Story
Kristine Kathryn Rusch

TRAINS   241
Kristine Kathryn Rusch

MIDNIGHT TRAINS   255
A Faerie Justice Story
Kristine Kathryn Rusch

EXCEPT THE MUSIC   277
Kristine Kathryn Rusch

LOOP   313
Kristine Kathryn Rusch

MILLENNIUM BABIES   331
Kristine Kathryn Rusch

WITHOUT END   387
Kristine Kathryn Rusch

About the Author: Dean Wesley Smith   417
About the Author: Kristine Kathryn Rusch   419
The Make 100 Kickstarter Series   421
Also by Dean Wesley Smith   422
Also by Kristine Kathryn Rusch   425

Hearts Collide: Strange Romance, Vol. 2

Untraditional
Kristine Kathryn Rusch

I find it quite amusing that my section in our untraditional volume of the *Hearts Collide* series begins with not one, not two, but *three* stories about weddings. I find weddings endlessly fascinating, but the stories I tell inside them—while romantic—aren't a traditional romance with a meet-cute and a happily-ever-after ending.

As I look through the titles of the short stories that Dean and I chose for this volume, I'm not sure I see a traditional happily-ever-after ending in any of them. Oh, many of them end —not necessarily happily (one even features a death)—but with something upbeat.

Each one of these stories is memorable and each one features people who love each other or who are falling in love. You'll find a number of different genres in here, from westerns to science fiction to fantasy to something akin to erotica.

This is the first volume that features my romance pen name, Kristine Grayson. (Future volumes have more stories from that pen name.) Grayson usually focuses on fantasy romance with humor, but the story here, "Name-Calling," has no fantasy at all and the humor, while there, isn't as broad as the usual Grayson pieces.

See what I mean? Untraditional, all the way around.

So, settle in and prepare yourself for the unexpected. I think you'll be both surprised and pleased.

STORIES

BY

DEAN WESLEY SMITH

The Secrets of Yesterday

A Poker Boy Story

Dean Wesley Smith

One

From my office floating a thousand feet over the MGM Grand Casino and Hotel in Las Vegas, the city and surrounding area seemed painted in light brown. I could almost see the heat shimmering off the concrete and streets below as the record temperatures continued for a third day.

For a change I was alone in this office that I had designed to look like a booth in a fifties retro diner. All four walls were clear and the red vinyl booth sat in the middle of the room, two fake trees behind it to give it a feel of containment.

I had put in a wooden railing in front of the glass walls all the way around because it felt like I could fall off the edge of my office floor. Before I put those railings in I couldn't even walk near the edge. Just too creepy.

The place was invisible to anyone from below and there were only three ways to get here. You either had to teleport, which I knew how to do, or go through the door from my girlfriend and sidekick Patty Ledgerwood's apartment. But most of the team entered through the secret door from The Diner off Freemont Street in downtown Vegas.

This office looked exactly like a booth in The Diner, actually. We used to meet there when dealing with a problem, so when I built this office, it just felt right to make it look like the old booth in The Diner.

Most everyone on my team except Stan used The Diner entrance. Patty tended to either come with me, or use the door from her apartment.

At the moment I was waiting for Patty and we were going to head to dinner, but she didn't get off work at the MGM Grand Hotel front desk for another twenty minutes.

It felt kind of odd being here alone. Normally at least three or four of the team were with me, talking about one thing or another.

And Madge, from The Diner, was always coming in and out serving us milkshakes and burgers.

At times the room had held up to fifteen people, but Madge had had to bring chairs from The Diner for that. The booth only held eight when we crowded in, and three chairs could be pulled up at the head of the table.

Right now I sat in a chair, my feet up on the wood railing around the room, facing downtown Las Vegas.

What a view. It just didn't get any better.

I felt about as relaxed as I ever could feel as a superhero always chasing down one bad person or another. Usually I only felt this relaxed while playing poker.

Suddenly one of my faint alarms in the back of my head went off.

As a poker player, before I had become a superhero, I had

learned to trust those alarms. They warned me when I was up against another player who had better cards or who might be cheating or who was getting angry.

I called the feelings my "super powers" back then. Little did I know that many of them actually were superpowers. All I had done was learn to trust them.

This time my little voice was telling me someone was watching me.

But at the same time I knew that wasn't possible. I was in an invisible office floating a thousand feet over the Las Vegas Strip. No one could see this place.

As Stan, my boss and the God of Poker, told me one day, the office was slightly out of phase with the real world. A plane trying to land at the nearby McClaren airport could fly through the office and no one would notice.

I expect that if I saw a plane coming directly at this place I would notice.

So who could be watching me now?

And why was my little voice considering that a threat?

A God of something or other might be able to see the office.

Or maybe another powerful superhero like me.

But not many others.

In fact, no one else that I could think of.

I stood and stared in the direction of downtown Vegas. The new Rush Tower of the Golden Nugget stood above most of the buildings there, but I still had to look down on it from my height.

My little voice was telling me that tower was where the problem was coming from.

And I didn't like this at all. Not one little bit.

Two

"Stan?" I shouted upward as I always did when calling my boss. Stan appeared almost instantly beside me, also looking out toward the downtown area.

He had on his normal gray slacks, gray shirt and sweater and had his brown hair combed perfectly. He was the most nondescript man I had ever known. You could walk right past him in a hallway and never notice him, which was one thing that made him so deadly on a poker table.

I had yet to sit across from him at a poker table, and honestly had no desire to do so any time in the near future.

"You feeling it as well?" I asked as he stared at the downtown area.

"Someone's watching," he said. "And they are not blocking the fact that they are watching."

"That's why I could sense it?" I asked.

He nodded.

"Can you get a spot on the location?"

"A suite on the 25th Floor of the Golden Nugget. Corner suite. The person is staring at us?"

"Suggestions?"

"I'm going to jump us there and take us out of time," Stan said.

I nodded and a moment later we were standing in a large suite on the top floor of the Golden Nugget. The place was decorated in brown tones, with a large brown couch and chairs in an area under a large screen television.

A made king-sized bed filled another part of the huge room, with a brown comforter and white pillows. A large vanity with a marble surface faced the bed with a desk and another large flat-screened television.

Someone was in the bathroom to my right, pocket-doors slid closed.

And standing in front of the window facing in the direction of my floating office over the strip was a teenager, not more than sixteen at the most.

He was frozen, his hand holding open the drape, as was the newscaster on the television screen, since Stan had taken us out of time.

Actually, I knew how to do that as well. It was more that he had slipped us between two instants of time, but it had the affect of seeming to stop time for anyone taken out of time.

The kid was dressed like most normal teenagers with jeans and a blue tee-shirt not tucked in. His hair was cut short and he looked like he played sports because his shoulders were broad and he didn't have an ounce of fat on him.

"He's powerful," Stan said, nodding at the kid. "I can feel it."

Actually, I could as well. "Is this unusual for someone his age?"

"Very," Stan said, his voice serious.

"Can he sense us here?" I asked.

"He might be able to."

"I can hear you as well," the kid said, turning to look at us.

His face was angular and his eyes a deep black. And as he turned just about every alarm I had as a superhero went off in my head.

More than anything I just wanted to jump and run. But Stan stayed put beside me and so I did the same, my best poker face firmly in place.

"You were looking for us?" Stan asked, his voice as neutral as it always seemed.

"I was," the kid said, nodding and moving away from the window. He moved past us and sat on the couch. "Actually, I was looking for more people of my kind. Guess I found a few, huh? That your place out there floating over the Strip?"

I nodded and said nothing more. At this point, I was glad, more than glad, to let Stan handle this.

"So who are you?" Stan asked.

"Jason King," the kid said. "My mom, Bonnie, is in the bathroom. She doesn't have any of these powers I have, or at least doesn't seem to."

"Oh, I do, dear," a voice said as the pocket doors to the bathroom slid back. "I just never let you know about them."

I glanced around.

Stan still held us in a time bubble. The newscaster on the

television was still stuck in mid sentence and outside the window I could see a jetliner headed for McClarin just hanging there in mid-air. And there were no sounds coming from the city around us at all.

Yet two people had broken into the time bubble Stan had set as if it were nothing unusual. I couldn't do that and I was supposedly one of the most powerful superheroes out there.

Or maybe no one had taught me how to do that yet.

"Hi, Stan," the woman said as she came around the corner in the suite from the bathroom area.

She was attractive and thin and looked to be about the same age as all the Gods and superheroes, mid-thirties. It seems we all pretty much stopped aging at that point for some reason or another.

She had long brown hair pulled back off her face and dark brown eyes. She wore a red summer dress and was barefoot. And she was smiling, but I wasn't sure the smile was reaching her eyes or not.

"Bonnie?" Stan asked, actually sounding shocked.

I glanced at my boss. He was the God of Poker. Even when something shocked him, he never showed it. He was the master of poker faces. But right now he was showing surprise just as any normal human would.

This time the smile actually did reach her eyes. And there was more there. A love, a fondness.

"It's great to see you again," she said, moving over and taking his hands and then reaching up and kissing him on the cheek.

"But I thought... I thought..." Stan couldn't seem to finish his sentence.

"That we were dead," she asked, still smiling. "We were."

"And it wasn't a lot of fun, either," Jason said, dropping onto the couch and putting his feet up on the coffee table.

Stan stared first at Bonnie, then looked at Jason. Then back at Bonnie with a questioning look.

I was reading Stan's face. In the years I had worked for him, that had never happened. Not once.

"Is he...?" Stan asked.

Bonnie nodded. "Jason," she said, turning to her son slouched on the couch. "I would like you to meet your biological father, Stan, the God of Poker."

"So," Jason said, nodding, but not acting surprised or shocked. "He's the guy who killed us."

Three

The silence in the room couldn't have been cut with a chainsaw.

I moved silently over and dropped onto a chair near the vanity, doing my best to just pretend I wasn't here. I had no idea what was happening, what had happened between Bonnie and Stan, and not a clue why Jason scared me to death.

This all seemed way, way out of my league at the moment. I really, really, really needed someone to spend some time filling me in on the history of all this, including the history of the people I worked with. I had only been a superhero now for a short ten years. I was an open book, but it sure seemed that everyone around me had a lot of history and secrets.

"I didn't..." Stan said, shaking his head, clearly upset and clearly surprised at meeting his son.

"Oh, we know you didn't," Bonnie said, smiling at Stan. "Don't we, Jason?"

"Yeah, whatever," he said, shrugging like any teenager.

Bonnie smiled again, but this time the smile once again didn't reach her eyes.

Every alarm in my body went off again.

I focused all my powers and without saying a word out loud, I shouted the thought, *Laverne!*

Watching. Her voice came back strong in my head. *And no need to shout.*

Laverne was Lady Luck herself, one of the most powerful Gods there was. I felt a lot better with her watching this. Whatever this was.

Stan shook his head and then regained his calm poker face. "If you didn't die, then where have you been for the last sixteen years?"

"Oh, we did die," Bonnie said.

"Buried," Jason said.

I almost shuddered at the very idea, but managed to stay still, tucked off on the side in my chair.

"Buried?" Stan asked. "How can that be? I saw the cabin burn to the ground with you in it. I couldn't get to you and couldn't stop the flames."

"Did you find a body?" Bonnie asked.

Stan shook his head. "The magic in those flames took everything down to fine ashes. I killed Crystal for what she did to you."

Holy smokes. Stan killed someone?

Bonnie nodded, clearly sad. "I know you did. And I know what that cost you."

Don't ask, Laverne's voice said softly in my head before I could even form a thought about asking Stan what had happened later. *Don't ever ask him. Ever.*

Understood.

"I had crawled under the floorboards of the cabin," Bonnie said, her voice soft. "I dug down into the mud and soft dirt, but I still died. And our unborn child, Jason, died with me."

"But how?" Stan asked. Then clearly, as I watched his face, he seemed to understand something. "Osiris?"

Bonnie nodded.

Laverne put in my mind an image of a tall, thin, green-skinned man wearing a white long beard and carrying a black stick. He wore robes that seemed to shimmer in the image. *One of the great old ones. The major God of Death and of Life.*

I didn't know there were great old ones.

Laverne thankfully said nothing to that stray thought by me.

Bonnie went on. "Osiris took my remains while the flames were still hot and put me in an ancient wooden coffin in an old cemetery in Boise, Idaho. The previous resident had gone mostly to dust. In there, in that darkness, Osiris slowly let life come back into my body."

"I was born in that coffin," Jason said, clearly disgusted. "We were in that old coffin until I was five living on worms and grubs and dripping water from above."

Now I actually did shudder. There were many things about the Gods and superheroes I had come to dislike, but whatever had happened to these two topped anything I had learned so far.

Stan's face looked white and he turned away. I had no idea how he was even holding it together. His son had been born six feet underground in a coffin. And had to stay there for five years.

"It took that long before we regenerated completely," Bonnie said softly. "But we are now alive. Osiris accepted us into his world and we live in comfort there. Osiris is training Jason."

I wanted to ask what he was training him for, but then Laverne thought *To replace him as the God of Death*.

Oh.

Stan looked at his son and then bowed slightly to him. "I did try to save you. I had no idea you survived. I owe Osiris a great debt."

Jason just sat on the couch under the window and shrugged like any bored teenage kid would do.

A moment later a very tall, very green man with a long white beard appeared beside Bonnie. He wore a silk robe that shimmered and radiated power like I had never felt before.

Suddenly the suite smelled of a beach fire and rose petals.

Laverne appeared beside him and bowed to him.

Stan bowed to him and I scrambled to my feet and did the same, stunned that Laverne would bow to anyone. Wow did I have a lot to learn about the Gods and this world I played a very small part in.

I so wanted to just jump away from this, but instead I backed up as much as I could and tried to make myself as unnoticed as possible.

Jason just sat on the couch looking bored.

Osiris faced Stan. "I am sorry I could not tell you about your wife and son. I did not know if I could save them or if they would come through the process sane."

"I am very glad you did save them," Stan said.

"We cannot return to you," Bonnie said to Stan, a sadness now in her brown eyes.

Stan nodded. "I understand."

Osiris reached over and took Bonnie's hand and it was clear they were now a couple of some sort.

Stan nodded and smiled and after a moment Bonnie also smiled.

Then something happened that I am sure would give me nightmares for years. Osiris, the God of Death and one of the ancient ones that even Laverne bowed to, turned and faced me directly.

His eyes were a swirling pool of silver and black and he seemed to have a sly grin hidden in that white beard.

"Poker Boy," he said and I swore his voice seemed to echo into all parts of my head. "I have watched you and your team save this world and the gods in it many times. I now ask for your help."

I nodded and somehow said with a slight bow, "Anything you desire, sir."

"In a few years Jason will require training in the arts of discipline and control of his emotions if he is to someday rule in my place."

On the couch Jason just snorted. I did not look away from Osiris.

"When the time comes, I would like you to teach him those arts through the game you call poker. You are the best poker player in the world. Jason will require the best."

I don't think I was breathing, but I did manage to say, "I would be honored, sir."

"Very good," Osiris said, smiling and showing me a mouthful of rotted and yellowed teeth.

He turned to Laverne. "It is always an honor."

"The honor is mine, Great One," Laverne said, bowing slightly.

Osiris then turned to Stan. "I am deeply sorry for your loss."

Stan nodded and then glanced at Bonnie with a smile. "It seems that from the ashes has come some good."

Bonnie smiled back and the smile reached her eyes. And the relief that Stan understood.

Stan was letting her go.

Osiris nodded and bowed slightly to Stan. "You are as great a young god as Bonnie led me to believe."

Then Osiris, Bonnie, and Jason were gone.

My legs gave out and I dropped down onto the chair.

Laverne stepped over to Stan and put her hand on his shoulder like a parent comforting a small child.

Then without a word they were both gone and the sounds of the city outside the suite came crashing back in as they let go of the time bubble we had all been inside.

I was now alone in a plush hotel suite trying to catch my breath. I took two deep, shuddering breaths, working to slow my heart that seemed to want to pound right out of the front of my chest.

I worked to just clear my mind and relax as I had learned to do at a poker table in times of stress.

In a moment I felt better.

I stood, went to the window, and looked out the window at my office floating there in the sky over the MGM Grand. There were still almost thirty minutes before Patty got off work. She'd never believe what had just happened. Or maybe she would.

And then I realized that I had just agreed to give the adopted son of the God of Death poker lessons.

Once again I had to sit down and try to catch my breath.

And that wasn't easy to do.

Cucumber Party
A Buckey the Space Pirate Story

Dean Wesley Smith

I was dressed in my Buckey the Space Pirate costume sitting in the hallway with about twenty other people in costumes, my back against the wall in front of room 1212, when she handed me the cucumber.

"Pass it on," she said in a husky whisper.

Then she winked at me. She had the edge of her eyes taped back and black cotton glued to her eyelids in typical alien-cat fashion. The wink made her look as if she was closing her eyes from a bad migraine.

"Hell, thanks a lot," I said.

"Hopefully, it will be myyyyyyyyyyyyyyyy pleasure."

She tried to make the "my" sound like a purr, but it came out more like she was gargling.

Then, with one more migraine wink, she headed off down the hall with her tail with a big black fur ball on the end whacking people who sat along the walls.

"I can't believe it," my best friend Alex said. "You've been invited to a cucumber party."

I held the warm green cucumber up in front of me and

studied it. I wasn't sure if I wanted to know where it had been or how it had gotten so warm.

"It is kind of hard to believe, isn't it?"

I'd heard of cucumber parties before. Hell, who hadn't? They were the latest "in" things at science fiction conventions.

The first time I'd heard of one had been two conventions ago at Biggerthanlife Con.

And at Biggerthanyours Con last week, there had been rumors that people were actually thrown out of the hotel for participating in one.

I stared at the cucumber in my hand. Now I was invited. Me, Buckey, a simple space pirate, at a cucumber party.

The very idea of it made my stomach churn and my mouth water from excitement.

And it was only Friday night. The convention was just getting going. This was going to be one damn good convention.

"Can I go with you?" Alex asked and reached to fondle the cucumber.

"Look, Alex. I don't—"

"It's Hoover," Alex said, demanding he be called by his costume character name. "And I don't see why I can't go."

I looked at the cucumber and then at Alex. He looked damn stupid in his Hoover, the Jovian Fur Merchant costume. He'd tacked two of his mother's old fur coats together and it smelled of mothballs something awful. No girl in her right mind would get within ten feet of him, let alone join him in a cucumber party.

But what the hell. This was a science fiction convention. Stranger things had happened. He just might get lucky.

"All right," I said. "You can come along."

Cucumber Party

Alex brightened right up and smiled a I'm-better-than-you smile at the guy dressed like Darth Vader sitting across the hall from him.

The guy just breathed a little louder.

"You got any idea how we can find the party?" I asked.

I twisted the cucumber in my hands. "There doesn't seem to be a room number here anywhere."

Alex's smile dropped into a frown as he thought about trying to find the party. In a hotel that had over fifteen hundred rooms, if you didn't know exactly where the party was, which wing, which floor, the only thing you were going to get was sore feet.

Alex shrugged, so I held the cucumber up for the other dozen people sitting along the hall to see. "Anybody know where the cucumbers are meeting tonight?"

All the people in the hall shook their heads and looked envious, except a young girl dressed as a flat-chested elf in green tights. "There's usually a map on the cucumber," she said. "At least that's how I found it last night."

All the envious faces immediately turned toward her like they were all on the same string.

I looked at her a little closer. She looked tired. For some reason, I took that to be a good sign.

Alex took the cucumber from my hand and studied it. "It doesn't seem to be a map of the hotel," he said.

"Of course not," the tit-less elf said and looked disgusted. "If you can't figure it out, then you don't belong at the party."

I took the cucumber back from Alex and held it up so I could see it better in the hall light. Its skin looked more like the back of a frog. Sure enough, there etched in very fine lines was a map. Or what someone might call a map. It didn't look so much like a map as a spider web made by a half-drunk spider.

Definitely not a map of the hotel.

Great. Just great.

"Come on, Alex," I said and stood. "I know where it's at."

I set off down the hall in the direction of the elevators, letting Alex scramble after me. I really didn't know where I was going, but I sure didn't want to sit there and admit it to that no-tit elf and the heavy-breathing Vader.

We took the cucumber back to my room and took turns trying to figure out what the map meant.

After an hour, I had a headache and no real good ideas.

Alex figured the entire map was a code for a room number in some alien language. Maybe Martian sanskrit or Antarian stone drawing.

Fat lot of good that was going to do us, but Alex figured it was either room 816, 927, or 1419. He wouldn't tell me how he came up with those numbers and I couldn't come up with any at all, even holding the map up to the mirror.

I figured if he was wrong, we could always just walk the halls until we saw someone else with a cucumber.

Room 816 did end up having a party going on in it. A two-person party in which the man, dressed like a Doc Smith Lensman, Lens and all, didn't like being disturbed.

No one was home in 927.

At room 1419, Alex knocked. "This is the place," he said. "I'm sure of it."

I just shrugged. If it wasn't, I was going to need to go to the convention suite to get a Diet Coke and some cookies. No wonder the no-tit elf looked tired. She couldn't find the party either.

A woman with only a towel wrapped around her answered the door. She had green eyes, light blonde hair, and toenails painted bright orange. I was in love at first sight.

I pushed Alex aside, took off my white-plumed hat and bowed slightly. "Excuse us. We seem to be having some—"

"Midge," the girl said, shouting back into the room. "They're here."

"Well, let them in," a voice said from deep in the room.

The girl stepped back and let the door swing completely open.

Alex nudged me. "I told you," he whispered, and pushed past me into the room, leaving a smelly trail of mothballs.

"Oh, God," Alex said as he got past the bathroom door and entered the main part of the room.

Orange Toenails motioned for me to come in, then closed the door behind me and let her towel drop to the floor.

I don't think I've ever had my mouth go so dry so suddenly as it did at that moment. I felt like the planet Dune had been transported to the top of my tongue.

Orange Toenails had a great body. Medium sized boobs with huge brown nipples, light colored pubic hair, and a small butterfly tattoo on the inside of her right thigh.

I must have kept walking as I stared at Orange Toenails, because I bumped into Alex who had stopped just inside the room.

"Oh God," he said, again.

I glanced around to see what he was oh-Goding, even though I didn't want to stop staring at the beautiful body of

Orange Toenails and that butterfly tattoo in a place I so wanted to explore.

On the closest of the room's two beds was a long-haired woman without a stitch of clothes on. She had her legs slightly apart and I could see just a hint of Never-Never Land no one was going to have to fly to get to.

"Oh God," I think I said.

Or Alex said it. I wasn't really sure at that point.

All I know is that my Buckey the Space Pirate costume was suddenly very tight in the crotch.

Buckey Junior wanted out real bad.

"You're still dressed," the woman on the bed said softly to Alex and me.

Somehow I closed my mouth.

Swallowing was out of the question.

Orange Toenails reached for my belt and started pulling me toward the empty bed. "I'm so honored," she said. "I've never made it with a famous writer."

I started unbuttoning my shirt as she worked on my pants.

Out of the corner of my eye I could see that Alex already had his mother's fur coats off and was climbing on the bed.

"I've read all your books," Orange Toenails said.

She helped me out of my pants.

Buckey Junior saluted her.

Right about then I certainly didn't want to ask her just what the hell she was talking about. Hell, I hadn't written any books. I could barely write a term paper when I was in school.

But if this was the reception a writer got at these conventions, I was sure willing to learn.

She had my pants off and pulled me down on the bed with

her. "Just let me do all the work," she said, kissing her way past my neck and heading down my chest.

I think Buckey Junior waved hello as she got closer.

"My pleasure," I think I managed to choke out.

On the other bed Alex was saying "Oh God."

Over and over again as the long-haired woman rode his mid section like she was riding a bull in a rodeo.

I hoped for Alex's sake she didn't have spurs.

Miss Orange Toenails swung her leg up over my chest and took Buckey Junior in her mouth at the very same moment she sat down on my face.

She tasted of a cross between hotel soap and Oolong tea.

I loved it.

I might become a tea fan after this.

She ran Buckey Junior in and out of her mouth with vacuum pump skill while at the same time moving her hips on my nose in a slight circular fashion.

I tried to concentrate on letting my tongue explore the strange new world and kept thinking about going for a five-year mission, but with the excitement of the moment, Buckey Junior just couldn't hold on.

She worked at draining him dry, not letting one drop escape while I managed to find a world I had never explored with my tongue.

Then she turned suddenly around and cuddled against my chest, pressing her boobs against my side and pressing her crotch into my leg.

"That was really nice," she said.

"Yeah," I said, trying to stop the light fixture on the room from spinning. "That it was."

On the other bed, Alex let out one last "OH GOD" that they must have heard two floors up, the long-haired women threw her head back, and from my viewpoint, they crossed the line in a photo finish.

"Would you sign one of your books for me?" Orange Toenails said, looking up at me and fluttering her big green eyes.

"I'd love to," I said, "but—"

"Oh, nifty-keen," she said.

Nifty-keen? Who said that?

She jumped from the bed, grabbed a stack of books off the dresser, and set them down beside me on the bed.

Then she sat down cross-legged on the bed facing me. I could see all of the strange new world my nose and tongue had just explored.

Buckey Junior twitched enviously at the sight.

I forced myself to look down at the pile of books.

The top one was "The Edge of Planet Ten" by Aaron Frost, Jr.

Oh, no, she thought I was Aaron Frost. That's why the reception. Alex had been wrong. This wasn't the cucumber party. Now what the hell were we going to do?

I flipped the book over. On the back jacket was a picture of Aaron Frost.

I had to admit, he did look a little like me. Only a bunch older.

What happened if he suddenly knocked at the door? Obviously he had been expected. That meant he was still on the way. The best thing Alex and I could do was hit the road quick.

"Look," I said, clearing my throat. "Since you both have

been so nice to me, I've got a very special limited edition of this very book in my room."

I tapped the top book.

"You do?" Alex asked. He didn't understand what had happened, so I tried to give him the sign to be quiet.

"I do," I said. "And after this wonderful reception, I would love for both of you to have a copy, personally autographed by me. We'll just run and get those and be right back."

"You'd do that for us?" she asked, looking almost in tears.

"After this wonderful encounter, which I shall always remember, it's the least I can do. Then I can sign all of these and maybe we can have a rematch. All right?"

That sounded so weak, I couldn't believe she'd fall for it.

"Ohhhh.... That would be great," Orange Toenails said.

She bought it. I couldn't believe it.

"Why don't I just stay right here?" Alex said.

"No," I said. "I need you with me. To help me find the books. We'll be right back, ladies." I jumped off the bed, grabbed Alex's clothes, tossed them at him, then started putting mine back on. All the time I kept expecting to hear a knock at the door and it would be the real Aaron Frost with BIG friends.

I would be dead for messing with his date for the night. I had this clear image in my mind of me being stoned by Aaron Frost fans with his books as I ran naked down the hall.

"You promise you'll come back?" Orange Toenails asked.

I looked at where she was sitting cross-legged on the bed with all her charms exposed. "Of course," I lied.

Buckey Junior wanted me to take the chance and just stay for a second round. But somehow, I got my pants back on, Buckey Junior tucked safely away, and Alex out the door.

"What the hell was that all about?" Alex asked as I halfway pushed him down the hall toward the elevators.

"Wrong party," I said.

"You mean that wasn't a cucumber party?"

"Nope," I said. "They thought I was Aaron Frost."

"The Aaron Frost?" Alex asked, then shook his head. "No wonder. The lady I was with said she had a story she wanted me to give to you to read. Lucky I didn't ask her why like I was going to."

In the elevator, I punched the floor number for the bar. Damn, I needed a drink.

Two floors down, two large-chested women dressed in harem girl costumes got on. Both looked really, really nice.

Alex had grabbed the cucumber on the way out the door, so I handed it to the shortest of the two just before the bar floor.

"Room 410," I said, giving her the number of my room. "Midnight. Just the two of you."

She looked startled, then happy. "Thanks," she said and waved as I pulled Alex off the elevator before he could ask me what I was doing and spoil everything.

We'd be waiting for them with our own special cucumber party. And if this worked, I'd bring my own cucumbers to the next convention.

Maybe a dozen of them.

Maps and all.

After The Dance

Dean Wesley Smith

F rom the moon-cast shadows of the night I watch Billy pick up his gray wool sweater from the newly mowed grass of my grave.

He holds the sweater away from him, as if he has never seen it before, let alone worn it to the dance last night.

Those gentle hands of his shake, and even across the darkness of the cemetery, I can see the fear clouding his green eyes. His brown hair is mussed by the night breeze and I can tell he is about to panic and run.

I want to step out of the shadows, to let him kiss me again as he did at my parents' front door, to feel his strength against me, but I know that would send him fleeing, now that my father has told him the truth. I can't have him leave. There are only a few hours before the sun breaks over the tops of the hills and I will be forced to return to my grave. I must act before then.

But at this moment the time is not right.

I stand in the night shadows and watch him hold his sweater. He stares at it and then at my headstone.

I know the words he reads.

LAURA JANE ROBERTS
Born September 22, 1946
Died September 22, 1962

Nothing more. A simple statement of facts.

Even frightened, Billy seems unable to tear himself away from those words that are carved in the cold, smooth stone. He must love me as much as I came to love him in the few short hours of the dance.

I almost laugh out loud, but then stop. That would scare him too, so I hold my hand over my mouth and let the laugh die with the wind in the trees.

Billy sits down beside my grave, his sweater beside him on the grass.

Good. He is not going to leave yet. I can wait a little longer, until the night air chills him and forces him into my arms.

I move to a group of shadows closer to him and stand thinking about my first fall dance twenty-eight years ago tonight.

That night had started out so special.

I went to the dance with my best friend, Donna. I remember my stomach twisting with excitement. The first dance of my sophomore year. And my birthday would start at midnight.

Donna and I had planned to stay out late, until one in the morning, dancing with every boy we saw and celebrating the arrival of my birthday.

Only Donna started drinking. Rum and Coke that some stupid kid from another school gave her.

Before midnight, before my birthday had even started, she was sick. She had ruined everything.

I remember telling her I hated her, yelling at her, calling her names as she threw up time after time.

I stormed out of the bathroom and into the parking lot and the cold night air.

That's where I met Craig.

He was sitting in his blue Chevy, with the radio blaring and the windows wide open. He said he was from downtown.

Looking back now, from the cemetery, the dark shadows, and all the years, I should have known better. But I was so mad at Donna and the cloth seats of his car felt so soft and he liked the same music that I did. After all, at midnight it was going to be my birthday. I had a right to have a good time.

At eleven he suggested we go driving around.

I knew better, but I didn't want to go back into the dance and face Donna, so I said yes.

At first we only went downtown and cruised. But by quarter to twelve, he had driven out to the edge of town and pulled off onto a dirt road next to an empty field.

He stopped, shut off the car, the radio, and the lights.

The darkness seemed to scream in my ears and I was so frightened, my hands were shaking. He tried to kiss me and I wouldn't let him. I told him I wanted to go back to the dance, but he just laughed.

I started to get out of the car like my mom had told me to do, but he grabbed my arm, yanked me back, and hit me.

From that point everything was sort of fuzzy. I think he hurt me real bad with that first hit.

I remember crying and him laughing at me. A high, nervous sort of laughter that I knew didn't sound right.

He kept trying to kiss me and touch me.

Every time I tried to make him quit he hit me.

I screamed once and he hit me so hard I could taste the blood.

Looking back now I mostly remember him laughing. That and thinking about my birthday and how it was ruined.

I guess he finally hit me too hard, because everything went completely black.

The next thing I knew it was years later, the dance was again being held the night before my birthday, I was standing on my grave, looking at my own headstone, and thinking how odd it was to be dead because I didn't feel dead.

In fact, I didn't feel a thing.

Nothing.

I didn't even care what had happened to Craig. I just wanted to meet someone and dance.

Now, four dances later, Billy, my date and dance partner for the evening, is sitting next to my grave. I think he is shivering.

Maybe it is time for me to talk to him.

Maybe now he will listen if I go slow.

Very, very slow.

"Hi, Billy," I say as I move forward, my voice as friendly and as sweet as I can make it in the night air.

He jumps and scrambles to his feet, clutching his sweater to his chest. His eyes are wild and his face is twisted in fear.

I know he is about to run.

"I'm sorry about lying to you about where I lived," I say.

I stop far enough away that he does not feel threatened.

He looks around as if searching for an escape route, then back at me.

I just stand there in the seemingly bright spotlight of the

moon, looking as timid as I can, waiting, hoping he will stay without me forcing him to.

After a moment he chokes out a question. "Are you really dead?"

I nod, making my best sad expression, even though I feel no sadness. I know that's what he expects.

"But how..."

He leaves his question open. "I don't know," I say. "I really don't. I just knew I had to go to the dance, maybe to meet you. I don't know."

I give him my best lost-girl shrug. I am surprised at how calculating I can be. I could have never done this while I was alive.

He turns and points at my headstone. "Is that really you? I don't believe this."

"That's really me," I say.

He shakes his head. "No way. Someone is playing a joke on me. That's it, isn't it? This is just a big joke and you set that old man up in the house to tell me you had died. Right?"

I shake my head slowly, thinking back over the night. After Billy and I danced for hours, dream hours, he took me home. On the way to his car I asked to borrow his sweater. I told him I was cold. He took it off and gave it to me to wear. Then he kissed me, softly, and left me at my parents' house.

Down the street he remembered his sweater and went back to get it. I watched from the shadows as my father answered the door. Even after having this happen four times on the anniversary of the night I died, my father does not believe I return.

He refuses to believe.

So four times he has yelled at a boy.

He told Billy, in no uncertain terms, that I was dead and that Billy was rude for doing such a nasty thing to him. Then he slammed the door in Billy's face.

I feel so sorry for my father, but he is part of the pattern and I cannot break it.

Billy, very confused, found his way to the cemetery and to my headstone. I knew he would.

They all did.

"This has to be a joke," he says.

He glances around the night shadows and up and down the rows of headstones.

"All right!" he yells. "The joke's over."

But his call is swallowed up by the darkness and the cold light of the moon. Nothing moves.

No one comes forward.

After a moment he is forced to turn back and face me.

"I don't believe you," he says.

Again I shrug. "There is nothing I can do to prove it to you. I only have a short time. I must leave at sunrise."

"Why?" he asks.

"I really don't know. Anymore than I know how I got here. I just know. Would you stay a little while and talk?"

He glances quickly around. Then it is his turn to shrug. "Why not?"

I smile and move closer to him, to my grave.

He backs away until he sees that all I am going to do is sit down on the grass near where he was sitting. Then, slowly, he comes back and joins me, keeping his distance.

I smile at him and after a moment of studying me, he shakes his head. "You don't look dead."

I laugh softly. "I don't feel dead. I enjoyed the dance. The decorations were wonderful. Especially how they made the gym look like the insides of a space ship."

He nods. "I had a good time," he says. "But this is a strange way of ending it."

I sigh and shake my head. "I had it worse."

His face becomes serious, as if he suddenly believes that I am dead. "What happened?"

I shake my head. "It was too ugly and it no longer matters."

Of course, that's a lie. But I cannot tell him so. And I could never tell him what happened. He would never understand.

"How often do you come back?" he asks. "Every year?"

He is unlike the others. They refused to believe right up to the last moment. He is asking questions as if he truly believes that I am dead. Maybe the world is changing.

"I only go to the dance when it falls on the night before my birthday."

That is the truth. I find it funny how I can mix the truth with lies and make them both sound so convincing.

Billy nods. "That makes sense."

Now it is my turn to be amazed. He is the first one who has been so understanding. I hope he has not guessed what I have planned for him. I might not be able to hold him if he knew.

I do not let my worry show.

Instead, I turn the conversation to questions about him, about his life, about the world he lives in. The same world that was taken from me and that now I only get a few hours every few years to see.

As the others did, Billy follows my lead and gladly talks about himself.

After an hour he has relaxed.

Behind him the eastern sky starts to fill with light. My time is very short.

He notices me looking at the sky and he stops.

Then he asks the question the three before him asked in one form or another. "What happens next?"

I smile at him. "I have to go back."

I point at my headstone.

"But why did you come out in the first place?" he asks. "I don't understand."

"Because I'm lonely," I tell him. That is partly the truth.

The sun is about to top the horizon. I glance up at it and he sees me look. I think he sees the fear and the sadness in my eyes.

"My night is almost over," I say as I stand and he stands with me. "Thank you for being so kind."

He shakes his head and takes a step toward me.

They all did.

They all wanted to hold me, to not let me go.

"I have no choice," I say. I make my voice sound helpless, sad.

The sun is at the edge of the horizon.

I can feel the pull of my grave.

Now is the time.

I step toward him, gently, eyes down.

"Thank you," I again say. "You are very kind."

He steps close to me and I turn my head up as I did on my parents' front step for him to kiss me good night.

His lips touch mine.

It is a wonderful kiss and I wrap my arms around him just as the sun casts its first rays among the stones and the trees. The pull is hard, but it only lasts a moment.

Then I am back on the soft padding inside my coffin, still kissing Billy. Still holding him with my dead arms.

Still pressing against him.

I try to make the moment last.

It takes Billy a few seconds to realize what has happened.

Then he starts struggling and screaming.

His kicking messes up the crowded insides of the coffin.

He is choking because there is no air. It had all been used up years ago by Henry and Don and Brian. There is none left for Billy and I feel sad because I wish Billy would last a little longer, as Henry did.

But there is no hope of that.

My coffin is a very small bed.

So Billy realizes where he is, feels the bodies of my lovers, feels my body wrapped in his embrace, feels the thickness of the smell press over his face, feels his lungs gasp for air.

He screams and struggles.

But soon he too is dead.

I adjust his body so I can hold him and still touch the bones and dried flesh of my other lovers.

My soft coffin is now very crowded, but I don't mind. I'm sure that by the time I awake again the worms will have guaranteed that there will be room for one more.

Good night, my loves.

Sleep tight.

In the Shade of the Slowboat Man

Dean Wesley Smith

One

I was used to the sweet smell of blood, to the sharp taste of disgust, to the wide-eyed look of lust. But the tight, small room of the nursing home covered me in new sensations like a mad mother covering her sleeping young child tenderly with a blanket before pressing a pillow hard over the face.

I eased the heavy door closed and stood silently for a moment, my clutch purse tight against my chest. One hospital bed, a small metal dresser, and an aluminum walker were all the furniture in the room. The green drapes over the window were slightly open and I silently moved to stand in the beam of silver moonlight cutting the night. I wanted more than anything else to run. But I calmed myself, took a deep breath, and worked to pull in and study my surroundings as I would on any night in any city alley or street.

As with all of the cesspools of humanity, the smell was the most overwhelming detail. The odor of human rot filled the building and the room, not so much different than a dead animal beside the road on a hot summer's day. Death and nature doing its work. But in this building, in this small room, the natural work was disguised by layer after layer of biting poison antiseptic. I suppose it was meant to clean the smell of death away so as not to disturb the sensitive living who visited from the fresh air outside. But instead of clearing, the two smells combined to form a thick aroma that filled my mouth with disgust.

I blocked the smell and focused my attention on the form in the bed.

John, my dear, sweet Slowboat Man, my husband once, lay under the white sheet of the room's only bed. His frame shrunken from the robust, healthy man I remembered from so many short years ago. He smelled of piss and decay. His face, rough with old skin and white whiskers, seemed to fight an enemy unseen on the battleground of this tiny room. He jerked, then moaned softly, his labored breathing working to pull enough air to get to the next breath.

I moved to him, my ex-husband, my Slowboat Man, and lightly brushed his wrinkled forehead to ease his sleep. I used to do that as we lay together in our featherbed. I would need him to sleep so that I could go out and feed on the blood of others. He never awoke while I was gone, not once in the twenty years we were together.

Or at least he never told me he had.

I had never asked.

Two

I was hunting the night we met. The spring of 1946, a time of promise and good cheer around the country. The war was won, the evil vanquished, and the living bathed in the feeling of a wonderful future. I had spent the last thirty years before and during the war in St. Louis, but my friends had aged, as always happened, and it was becoming too hard to continue to answer the questions and the looks. I had moved on many times in the past and I would continue to do so many times in the future. It was my curse for making mortal friends and enjoying the pleasures of the mortal world.

I pleaded to my friends in St. Louis a sick mother in a faraway city, and booked passage under another name on an old-fashioned Mississippi riverboat named *Joe Henry*. I had loved the boats when they were working the river the first time, and now, again, loved them as they came back again for the tourists and gambling.

For the first few days I stayed mostly to my small cabin,

sleeping on the small bed during the day and reading at night. But on the third day, hunger finally drove me into the narrow hallways and lighted party rooms of the huge riverboat.

Many soldiers and sailors filled the boat, most still in uniform, and most with women of their own age holding onto their arms and laughing at their every word. The boat literally reeked of health and good cheer and I still remember how that smell drove my hunger.

I supposed events could have turned another way and I might have met Johnny before feeding. But almost immediately upon leaving my cabin, I had gotten lucky and found a young sailor standing alone on the lower deck.

I walked up to the rail and pretended to stare out over the black waters of the river and the lights beyond. The air felt alive, full of humidity and insects, thick air that carried the young sailor's scent clearly to me.

He moved closer and struck up a conversation. After a minute I stroked his arm, building his lust and desire while at the same time blocking his mind of my image. I asked him to help me with a problem with the mattress on my bed in my cabin and even though he kept a straight face the smell of sexual lust almost choked me.

Within two minutes he was asleep on my bed and I was feeding, drinking light to not hurt him, but yet getting enough of his blood to fill my immediate hunger.

After I finished I brushed over the marks on his neck with a lick so that no sign would show, then cleaned up myself while letting him rest. Then I roused him just enough to walk him up a few decks, where I slipped away, happy that I might repeat the same act numbers of times during this voyage. It was an intoxicating time and I felt better than I had ever remembered feeling in years.

I decided that an after-dinner stroll along the moonlit deck would be nice before returning to my cabin. I moved slowly, drinking in the warmth of the night air, listening to the churning of the paddle wheel, feeling the boat slice through the muddy water of the river.

Johnny leaned against the rail about mid-ship, smoking a pipe. Under the silver moon, his Navy officer's white uniform seemed to glow with a light of its own. I started to pass him and realized that I needed to stop, to speak to him, to let him hold me.

He affected me like I imagined I affected my prey when feeding. I was drawn to him with such intensity that resisting didn't seem possible.

I hesitated and he glanced over at me and laughed, a soft laugh as if he could read my every thought, as if he knew that I wanted him with me that instant, without reason, without cause. He just laughed, not at me, but in merriment at the situation, at the delight, at the beauty of the night.

He laughed easily and for the next twenty years I would enjoy that laugh every day.

I turned and he was smiling, a first smile that I will always remember. He had the simple ability to smile and light up the darkest place, he had a smile that I would lose myself in many a night while he told me story after story after story. I never tired of that smile, and that first exposure to it melted my every will. I would be his slave and never care as long as he kept smiling at me.

"Beautiful evening, isn't it?" he said, his voice solid and genuine, like his smile.

"Now it is," I said. I had to catch my breath even after something that simple.

Again he laughed and made a motion that I should join him at the rail gazing out over the river and the trees and farmland beyond.

I did. And for twenty years, except to feed on others while he slept, I never left his side.

Three

The smell of the room pulled me from the past and back to my mission of the evening. I looked at his weathered, time-beaten form on the bed and felt sadness and love. A large part of me regretted missing the aging time of his life, of not sharing that time with him, like I had regretted missing the years before I met him. But on both I had had no choice. Or I had felt I had had no choice. I might have been wrong, but it was the choice I had made.

Since the time I left him I had never found another to be my husband. Actually I never really tried, never really wanted to fill that huge hole in my chest and my very being that leaving him had caused.

But now he was dying and now I also had to move on, change cities and friends again. I had always felt regret with each move, yet the regret was controlled by the certainty that the decision was the only right one, that I would make new friends, find new lovers. But this time it was harder. Much harder.

I sat lightly on the side of his bed and he stirred, moaning softly. I again brushed his forehead easing his pain, giving him a fuller rest, a more peaceful rest. It was the least I could do for him. He deserved so much more.

This time he moaned with contentment and that moan took me back to those lovely nights on the *Joe Henry*, slowly making our way down the river, nestled in each other's arms. We made love three, sometimes four times a day and spent the rest of the time talking and laughing and just being with each other, as if every moment was the most precious moment we had.

During those wonderful talks I had immediately wanted to tell him of my true nature, but didn't. The very desire to tell him surprised me. In all the years it had not happened before. So I only told him of the twenty years in St. Louis, letting him think that was where I had been raised. As the years together went by that lie became as truth between us and he never questioned me on it.

He was born in San Francisco and wanted to return there where his family had property and some wealth. I told him I was alone in the world, as was the true case, just drifting and looking for a new home. He seemed to admire that about me. But he also knew I was free to move where he wanted.

I wanted him to know that.

The day before we were to dock in Vicksburg, I mentioned to him that I wished the boat would slow down so that our time together would last. The days and nights since meeting him had been truly magical, and in my life that was a very rare occurrence.

He had again laughed at my thought, but in a good way.

Then he hugged me. "We will be together for a long time," he had said, "but I will return in a moment."

With that he dressed and abruptly left the cabin, leaving me surrounded by his things and his wonderful life-odor. After a short time he returned, smiling, standing over me, casting his shadow across my naked form. "Your wish is granted," he had said. "The boat has slowed."

I didn't know how he had managed it, and never really asked what it had cost him. But somehow he had managed to delay the boat getting into Vicksburg by an extra day. A long wonderful extra day that turned into a wonderful marriage.

From that day forward I called him my Slowboat Man and he never seemed to tire of it.

Four

"Beautiful evening, isn't it?" he said hoarsely from the bed beside me. His words yanked me from the past and back to the smell of death and antiseptic in the small nursing home room. Johnny was smiling up at me, lightly, his sunken eyes still full of the light and the mischief that I had loved so much.

"It is now," I said, stroking him, soothing him.

He started to laugh, but instead coughed and I soothed him with a touch again.

He blinked a few times, focusing on me, staring at me, touching my arm. "You are as beautiful as I remembered," he said, his voice clearing as he used it, gaining more and more power. "I've missed you."

"I've missed you, too," I somehow managed to say. I could feel his weak grip on my arm.

He smiled and then his eyes closed.

I touched his forehead and again he was dozing. I sat on the bed beside him and thought back to that last time I had sat beside him on our marriage bed, almost thirty years earlier.

That last night, as with any other night I went out to feed, I had put him to sleep with a few strokes on the forehead and then stayed with him to make sure his sleep was deep. But that last night I had also packed a few things, very few, actually, because I had hoped to take very little of our life together to remind me of him. It had made no difference. I saw his face, his smile, heard his laugh and his voice everywhere I went.

I had known for years that the day of leaving was coming. And many times over the years we were together I thought of telling him about my true nature. But I could never overcome the fear. I feared that if he knew he would hate me, fight me, even try to kill me. I feared that he would find a way to expose those of us like me in the city and around the country. But my biggest fear was that he would never be able to stand my youth as he aged.

I could not have stood the look of his hate and disgust.

At least that was what I told myself. As the years passed since I left him I came to believe that my fear had been a stupid one. But I never overcame that fear, at least not until now.

I know my leaving to him must have felt sudden and without reason. I know he spent vast sums of money looking for me. I know he didn't truly understand.

But for me I had no choice. During the month before I left, comments about my youth were suddenly everywhere; Johnny and our friends had aged, I hadn't. I even caught Johnny staring at me when he thought I wouldn't notice.

Three nights before I left, one waitress asked him, while I was in the ladies room, what his daughter, meaning me, wanted for dessert. He had laughed about it, but I could tell he didn't understand and was bothered. As again he should have been.

The night I left, hidden in a pile of magazines recycled from his office, I found a book about vampires. A well-read book.

I could wait no longer and I knew then that I could never talk to him about it. I had to go that night and I did so, leaving only a note to him that I would always love him.

I moved quickly, silently, in an untraceable fashion, to the East Coast. But less than a year later, no longer able to even fight the fight of keeping him out of my mind, I returned to San Francisco under a new name and began to watch him from afar.

As with me, he never remarried. Many nights he would walk the streets of the city alone, just smiling, almost content. I paced him, watching him, protecting him from others of my kind and from the mortal criminals. I imagined that he knew I was watching him. Pacing him. Walking with him. Protecting him. I pretended that knowing I was there made him happy. Many nights I even thought of actually showing myself to him, holding him again.

But I never did.

I never had the courage.

FIVE

He stirred under the nursing home sheet and I watched him as he awoke. He opened his eyes, saw me, and then smiled. "Good. I was hoping you were more than a dream."

"No, Slowboat Man, you aren't dreaming."

He laughed and gripped my hand and I could feel the warmth flowing between us. I leaned down and kissed him on the cheek, his rough skin warm against my face. As I pulled back I could see a single tear in the corner of his right eye. But in both eyes the look was love. I was amazed.

And very glad.

I had feared he would hate me after I had left him without warning. I had feared that when I came to visit tonight he would ask the questions about my youth and how I had stayed so young, questions that I had always been so afraid to answer. I had feared most of all that he would send me away.

But he didn't. And the relief flooded through my every cell.

Even after almost thirty years he still loved me. I wanted to shout it to the entire world. But instead I just sat there smiling at him.

In the century I had been alive I had never felt or seen a love so complete and total as his love for me.

It saddened me to think that in the centuries to come I might never find it again.

"I'm glad you decided to come and say good-bye," he said. "I was hoping you would."

I gently touched his arm. "You know I wanted to when—"

He waved me quiet. "Don't. You did what you had to do."

My head was spinning and I wanted to ask him a thousand questions: How he knew? What he knew?

But instead I just sat beside him on the bed and stared at him. After a moment he laughed.

"Now say good-bye properly," he said. "Then be on your way. I overheard the doctor telling one of the nurses that I might not make it through the night and I don't want you here when I leave. Might not be a pretty sight."

I just shook my head at him. I had seen more death than he could ever imagine, but I didn't want to tell him that.

A long spell of coughing caught him and he half sat up in bed with the pain. I stroked his forehead and he calmed and worked to catch his breath. After a moment he said, "I loved it when you used to do that to me. Always thought it was one of your nicer gifts to me, even though I never understood just how or what you did."

Again he laughed lightly at what must have been my shocked look. Even after all these years, even with very little force behind it, his laugh could still gladden my heart, make me smile, ease my worries. Again this time it took only a moment before I smiled and then laughed with him.

"Now be on your way," he said. "The nurse will be here shortly and I have a long journey to make into the next world. I'm ready to go, you know? Actually looking forward to it. You would too if you had an old body like this one."

I nodded and stood. "Good-bye, my Slowboat Man." I leaned down and kissed him solidly on his rough, chapped lips.

"Good-bye, my beautiful wife."

He smiled at me one last time and I smiled back, as I always had.

Then I turned and headed for the door. I knew that I had to leave immediately, because if I didn't I never would. But this time he wanted me to go. I wasn't running away.

As I pulled the handle open to the dimly-lit hallway, he called out to me. "Beautiful?"

I stopped and turned.

"I'm sorry I couldn't slow the boat down this time."

"That's all right," I said, just loud enough for him to hear. "No matter how long or how short the lifetime, sometimes once is enough. Sleep well my Slowboat Man. Sleep well."

And as the door to his final room closed behind me I added to myself. "And thank you."

Roses Around the Moment

A Ghost of a Chance Story

Dean Wesley Smith

One

Eve Bryson died so fast, she didn't even realize she was dead for a few minutes.

The rain was pounding down hard, one of those storms that felt more like standing under a cold shower. She had on only a light cotton summer dress, sandals, and panties. No bra, so this rain was sticking her dress to her like a second skin. Not pleasant in the slightest.

Around her the heavy pine forest seemed frighteningly dark, even though the sun was hours from setting. She could hear nothing but the pounding rain against her head, matting her long brown hair into a mess down her back.

She wasn't even sure how she had ended up in the rain. A moment before she had been driving toward a dinner date at a local brewpub in downtown Portland with three friends from college.

In the years since college, the four of them had managed to get together every month or so and she loved those evenings. It took her mind off her worthless husband and even more worthless job she couldn't figure out how to get out of.

She had thought she would love high-tech work after coming out of college with her masters in engineering. But she hated it, hated the people more than anything else. Their goal wasn't to create new things, use their brains for good. All they did was try to figure out how to get ahead in the corporate game.

And just like her job, she thought marrying Simpson Smith right out of college was a good idea as well. It didn't matter that he was taking a break from finishing his degree. They had had great sex, lots of fun traveling, and planning for a future. She thought she had found a soul mate.

Maybe a soul mate for her single sock. But that might be giving Simpson more credit than he deserved.

It seemed good ol' Simp to his friends never understood that working was required to get ahead. She had no idea what he did all day while she was working, but it certainly wasn't anything to bring in money. She had a hunch he just looked at porn and played online games. She had gotten tired of asking about six months ago.

The marriage was that dead.

So for two years now she had supported him and that was going to end very, very soon. All of the rebel things she had found charming with him in college now just annoyed her beyond belief.

And all of her friends didn't like him either right from the start. That should have been a clue to her, but when a girl was in the first blush of love and sexual satisfaction, thinking with the logical brain wasn't that possible.

So she had made two mistakes right out of college. In six months, she would be out of both mistakes.

She shivered from the pounding cold rain and looked around. What had happened?

The two-lane winding road through the trees was empty. Water ran down one side, it was raining so hard.

Then she saw her wonderful little classic blue Miata off the road and down an embankment. Then she remembered. She had been thinking about how Simpson had complained that she wouldn't cook his dinner before she left. She had gotten so angry, she had been driving far too fast down the twisting area through the trees from their house in the hills to the main street below.

Far too fast for a pounding June rain.

She had slid into one corner, managed to get straightened out, and then didn't make the next corner. The last thing she remembered was the Miata heading over the bank and for a large pine tree.

She must have bumped her head. She didn't remember climbing up here to the road.

She quickly felt her forehead, looking for any sign of blood in the rain pounding at her.

Nothing.

The Miata's lights were still on and she went to the edge of the road to look down at it. It was pretty smashed up, but it wasn't that far off the road and the next person to come by would certainly see it and her.

She felt really sad she had totaled her Miata. She had bought it right out of college as well and it was the only fun thing left in her life after two years. Now it looked like she would be starting over completely.

The rain kept pounding at her and she could feel she was starting to really get chilled. It had been a seventy-degree day today. How could she be this cold?

A blue pickup, brand new from the looks of it, came around the corner, saw the lights from her car and quickly braked and pulled over onto the gravel shoulder of the road, putting on its flashing red warning lights.

The driver was a guy about forty. Maybe older. She could never tell with men in that range.

He pulled on a rain jacket with a hood as he climbed out and went to the edge of the road to look at her poor car.

She put one arm across her chest to cover what was showing through her wet dress and said to the guy, "I sure made a mess of it, didn't I?"

He said nothing, but instead quickly scrambled down the bank. When he got to the Miata, he looked inside, then shook his head and at a fast climb came back up the bank and started toward his truck.

"Why are you ignoring me?" Eve asked.

She reached for the guy as he went past and her hand went right through his arm.

And as it did, she could feel and read his mind.

All he was thinking was to get help out here quickly. And that he doubted the woman in the car was alive. Her neck was badly twisted in a way that necks didn't twist.

She watched him move to the truck and climb in and use his cell phone to call for help.

Then in the pounding rain, she moved over to the edge of the bank and once again looked at her car.

She could see now that she was still inside.

She was dead.

And she was just about as cold and wet as she could ever remember being. And she was getting hungry.

She was dead.

She was a ghost.

How the hell could she be hungry?

Two

Eve managed to find a tree on the inside of the road to give herself some shelter from the rain, but by the time the first cop arrived, she was shivering so bad, she doubted she could even walk. Was it possible to die twice, once from a car crash, another from freezing to death?

One of the county sheriffs left his car running when he climbed out in his rain slicker. So she went over to his car and tried to open the backseat car door, but her hand went right through it.

"Shit!" she shouted into the rain. "Just shit."

She needed to do something, so she closed her eyes and just pretended she was going to climb into the back seat. She wouldn't have been surprised if she had ended up sitting on the concrete, but she actually ended up in the back seat of the car.

Success. She could go through a door, but not fall through a seat. Who knew?

And thankfully, he had the heater running on defrost to keep the windows clear, so it was warm in the car.

He had a towel beside his seat and she grabbed it, coming away with what felt like a towel in her hands, but the original towel remained in position. The one in her hand looked identical.

She didn't care. Ghost towel or not, it was a towel.

Since she was a ghost, she figured no one could see her, so she stripped off her soaked dress and underwear and used the towel to dry off. Then she finally used the towel to wrap up her wet hair on the top of her head.

She twisted the water out of her underwear and slid them under her butt to protect herself a little from the cold seat. Then she twisted as much water out of her dress that she could and draped it over the front passenger seat to dry.

She was finally starting to warm up. She was naked and sitting in the back of a cop car. Under any other circumstances than being dead, this might have caused nightmares.

It still might. The evening was just getting started.

Suddenly the cop climbed back into his car. He was holding her wallet and as she watched, he pulled out her driver's license and shook his head. "Too damn young."

"Thanks," she said from the back seat.

He pushed his raincoat hood off the back of his head and she gasped. Sheriff man was about her age and a looker, with short brown hair, a square chin, and from what she saw in the rearview mirror, bright green eyes.

And she instantly noticed he wasn't wearing a ring.

She stared at him for a moment as he called in her personal

information and then sat waiting for even more information to come up on his computer screen.

She really wanted to know more about this guy. Maybe if she touched him, she could read his mind like she had done with the guy who found her wreck.

She reached forward and put her hand on his shoulder.

Only her hand went inside him and she instantly felt the sadness he was feeling at her death.

"Holy shit, someone who actually cares," she said aloud.

He glanced around, making her pull back and cover herself.

Then he shook his head and went back to studying the information coming through the screen.

"Can I make someone hear me if I am touching them? How cool would that be?"

He didn't turn around at that, so she reached forward and once again put her hand inside his shoulder.

This time she let herself try to find out who he was before saying anything.

His name was Deputy McCall Cascade. Everyone just called him Cascade.

He was exactly her age a twenty-six, liked his job except for events like this. He liked helping people and he didn't have a girlfriend.

But there was even more. He really worked as a superhero in the law enforcement area under a woman who was a low-level god in law enforcement by the name of Reanna. She reported to some gods above her, but he had never met any of them.

She had no idea what the superhero thinking was. Some sort of game or something. He was new at it, only being recruited by the gods of law enforcement two years before right after he got out of college and joined the force.

"Mr. Perfect," she said aloud with her hand still in his shoulder.

She could instantly tell he had heard that.

He shook his head, put up his raincoat hood and climbed back out into the rain as another sheriff's car arrived followed by an ambulance.

She watched for the next thirty minutes as they got her body out of the car and up into the ambulance.

She had no idea what was going on. She had never believed in ghosts or an afterlife or anything. But clearly she was living, at least for the moment, some sort of afterlife.

And she was hungry and pretty soon would need to pee. You would think a ghost wouldn't have to deal with all the real world stuff. Rules of ghostieness were sure different from any thing she had ever read.

Twenty minutes later, with her purse in his hand with her wallet back inside it, all tucked into a plastic bag with a label on it, he climbed back into the patrol car and again lowered the hood on his raincoat.

Her breath caught, if she had been breathing, which she was pretty certain she had been. He had gotten even more handsome, if that was possible.

He put her purse on the passenger seat, then waited until the ambulance in front of him pulled away and he pulled out to follow it. It seems he had gotten the duty of staying with her body.

If he could actually see her in the back seat, sitting nude on her still damp panties, wouldn't he be surprised?

Actually, she was the one sitting here that was surprised.
She had expected a great night with friends.
She hadn't expected to die.
But she supposed no one expected to die.
She actually wasn't that upset about it for some reason. But she really needed to pee.

Three

Eve had no idea why the ambulance took her body to a hospital. She was clearly dead and they weren't even bothering to run with lights. So as they pulled into a hospital loading area, she touched Deputy Cascade again.

The answer she was looking for came easily. Because she died alone and under suspicious circumstances, they had to do an autopsy. And it seemed in this area, the hospital morgue was where that was done.

"You won't find anything in my blood stream except anger and a lot of regret."

She could see in his mind that he heard her. He wasn't certain what he was hearing, but he clearly heard what she had said.

He picked up her purse and she grabbed her dress. They were parked under a canopy so she wouldn't get wet. She closed her eyes and pretended to open the door and step out of the back seat of the car.

The evening air had a chill to it and she quickly slipped her still-damp dress over her head. That sent shivers down her spine. But it was better than walking around a hospital completely naked.

She still had his towel wrapped on her head. So if there were other ghosts, she was going to make a great first impression.

Cascade was striding toward the big double doors, following the gurney with her body on it.

She ran and caught up to him, going through the wide door beside him. Inside the dim hallway smelled of antiseptic and roses, of all things.

The gurney with her body on it sort of clicked going down the smooth tile floor and she walked beside Cascade. In this part of the hospital, there sure weren't a lot of people.

But as her body turned to the right toward a service elevator, Cascade turned left and went through two swinging doors and out into a much more active and brighter area of the hospital.

Nurses and doctors were moving around, along with patients and guests. Cascade seemed to know where he was going with her purse, so she just tagged along, trying to stay out of everyone's way, since none of them could see her.

And she almost succeeded in that task except for one man who came around a corner carrying a dozen roses. He had a dark look to his eyes and wore jeans, a T-shirt, and tennis shoes.

She went right through him before she really saw him.

And as she did, she saw why he was here.

His name was Jack Nevada and he was headed for a room she and Cascade had passed down the hall. Hidden in the roses he had a syringe that he was going to inject in a woman by the name of Stephanie to kill her. It would look like a natural death.

He was a paid killer, hired by Stephanie's husband.

"Holy shit!"

Eve froze in the hallway, watching Jack Nevada stroll toward his murder victim.

"What the hell! What the hell! What the hell!"

No one heard her.

What could she do? She was a ghost. She couldn't shout or even try to stop the guy.

She glanced back in the other direction. Deputy Cascade, gun and all, had stopped at the nurse's station and was smiling at a young nurse in front of him.

Eve had to tell him, somehow.

She ran toward Cascade, her sandals slapping on the tile. She tried to stop before she got to him, but instead slid and went right inside him.

He stood up straight as she did.

"Hi, handsome," she said. "Eve Bryson here inside you in ghost form. We got a problem that you need to solve real quick!"

He nodded to the nurse and stepped back, which made Eve smile. Even under stress of hearing voices, he could stay cool. This guy really was a superhero.

"I am, actually," he said out loud.

Some guy in a white smock looked at him and frowned.

"No need to talk in your out-loud voice," she said. "I can hear everything you are thinking."

She felt him panic and she laughed.

"Yes, even the fact that you thought I was hot. Thank you, by the way."

He took a deep breath.

"So what do you need?" he thought at her.

She described the guy she had touched and what room he was headed toward and what he was about to do."

"Shit!" he said, again out loud. "Are you sure?"

"One hundred percent," she said to him. "And if you want to save that woman's life you had better get this handsome hunk of a body moving."

He touched the counter in front of the nurse. "Security to room 1003. Stat!"

He turned and started toward the room, using his mike attached to his collar to call for backup of real police.

When he reached the room, he drew his gun.

She sent him calming thoughts.

"Thanks," he said.

Then he went inside, gun drawn, leaving the door standing open for backup to come in behind him.

The killer had put the roses down near the window and had a syringe in his right hand. He was working with the woman's IV and in another fifteen seconds would have injected her.

The woman under the blanket was a very large woman. And the room smelled like she had had an accident in the sheets.

"Step back and drop the syringe and put your hands in the air!" Cascade said.

Cascade's power and authority in his voice gave Eve little goose bumps. He could order her around like that any time he wanted.

"Trying to work here," he said in his silent voice.

"Sorry," she said, laughing. "Forgot where I was."

The man with the syringe looked shocked at the deputy and gun facing him.

The man took a step back.

"No worry," she said to Cascade. "He's not armed with anything but the needle."

"I said drop the needle and put your hands on your head."

The guy finally realized he had no options, so he dropped the syringe with a light click on the tile, then raised his hands.

At that moment two hospital security men came through the door.

"Needle on the floor," Cascade said to the security. "He was about to inject this woman with it. Hired kill I'm betting."

Cascade handed one of the security men his handcuffs. "Secure his hands behind his back."

The security man did and Cascade had the would-be killer sit on the floor with his back against a wall.

Then one of the security men used a tissue to pick up the syringe.

At that point, two police officers came through the door and the shit-smelling room got real crowded real quick.

"You're going to be busy," Eve said to Cascade. "I'm going to leave you for a bit."

"You coming back?" he asked in his inside voice.

"I think so," she said. "But I'm still new at this ghost stuff."

"So where are you going?"

"You don't know?" she asked.

"Not a clue."

"I've really got to pee."

"Ghosts pee?" he asked.

"I'm going to find out for the first time very, very shortly," she said.

And with that she stepped out of his body and worked her way out of the room to find a woman's restroom. She doubted the hospital had ghost restrooms. But who knew.

Four

It took Deputy Cascade two hours to fill out the paperwork on her body and on the arrest at the hospital. He said he had caught a glimpse of the syringe in the roses when he passed the man walking in, decided it could be nothing but bad.

Eve had suggested that story, since he pretty much couldn't tell anyone he had a ghost inside him helping him.

She had raided a candy machine for a few snacks by just sticking her hand through the glass and pulling out the ghost equivalent of a candy bar. The two bars helped a little to hold back the hunger, but she was going to need a real meal pretty soon.

Cascade then had to spend another thirty minutes at his desk at the police station filling out more paperwork before he could get off work. Wow did cops have a lot of paperwork or what? She had no idea.

So as he finally stood and started for his patrol car, she got back inside him.

"How you doing?"

"I was wondering if you were still here."

"Been watching the entire time," she said. "I figured if I was inside your body, I would just be a distraction to all the stuff you needed to get done."

"More than likely yes," he said.

And she could tell he appreciated that.

"Dinner at Shari's," she said.

"Ghosts eat?"

"I need to because I'm ravished."

So fifteen minutes later they were in Shari's restaurant. She sat across the booth from him so she could see him, but she put her feet up so that they were in his lap, so she could be inside his head and he could hear her.

She told him how she was sitting.

"Kind of forward, don't you think?" he said, smiling.

Damn from across the table, she loved that smile.

"Thank you," he said, hearing her thought about his smile.

Then as the waitress came up, he ordered his regular French dip and fries and a glass of iced tea.

"I'm going to go get something," she said. "Back in a moment."

She wandered into the kitchen and there, sitting under the light ready to take out, was a wonderful chicken fried steak meal. It smelled heavenly.

She picked up the plate, feeling the heat on her fingers.

The real plate just stayed there under the light. It seemed food had a ghost component as well.

She took the plate back out to the table, put her foot against his leg and said, "I have chicken fried steak. So pardon me if you get moaning sensations as I eat. I'm that hungry."

She took a couple of bites, then realized while she was gone, he had called for his boss on the superhero side.

Just as Eve realized that, a striking black-haired woman in a police uniform came up to the table. She had to stand a good six feet tall and her uniform looked like it had actually been starched.

The woman nodded in Eve's direction and then had Cascade scoot over.

"This is Reanna," Cascade thought at her.

"Figured as much," Eve said between bites.

This had to be the absolute best tasting chicken fried steak she had ever had. Ever.

"I understand you just died this afternoon," Reanna said out loud to Eve. "Sorry for your loss, but glad you could help Deputy Cascade."

"Tell her it was my pleasure," Eve said out loud. "Ask her if she wants me to touch her so she can hear me."

"I can see and hear you just fine," Reanna said.

Then Reanna waved a hand in the direction of Cascade.

He blinked and then said to Eve, "Wow you are more beautiful alive than dead."

"Thanks," Eve said, "I think."

At that moment she realized her dress was still damp, more than likely her nipples were still showing, and she still had her hair wrapped up on top of her head in his car towel. "I got a little wet out there at the crash site."

Then she ignored the feelings of attraction she was getting from Cascade through their touch and looked at Reanna. "If

I'm a ghost, how can you see me? And how can Cascade now see me?"

"You are a ghost agent," Reanna said, her voice firm and compact, just as she looked. "You will be recruited to join the Ghost of a Chance Agency and trained by them."

"You lost me with ghost agent thingie," Eve said.

"When a person dies," Reanna said, "almost everyone just goes on into the next life, whatever that is. But for a few thousand around the world, they are asked to stay on as ghost agents and try to help people, as you two did by saving that woman's life this evening."

Eve nodded. "That did feel good."

"I have contacted the head of the Ghost of a Chance agency," Reanna said, "and they will be sending some other agents to help you train and explain everything to you."

Eve nodded, but her disappointment matched what she was feeling from Cascade.

"However," Reanna said, "after your collaboration this afternoon with Officer Cascade, I have also asked if you could be assigned to my department and you and Officer Cascade work together to solve cases."

Reanna turned to Cascade. "Would that be all right with you?"

"I would be honored," he said.

Eve could feel his excitement at the idea. And she had to admit that hanging around with Mister Handsome Superhero sounded like a great time to her.

"Would you be interested in such an assignment?" Reanna asked Eve. "You both would be a very special team, the only ghost and live superhero working together. It has never been tried. You might work with Poker Boy and his team at times as well as reporting to me. He was very interested in meeting you both once you were up to speed."

She instantly felt Cascade's excitement. It seemed this superhero named Poker Boy and his team often were called on to save the entire world.

So she had a chance to go from a worthless husband and a dead job to being someone who could help save people and work with superheroes and gods.

Not counting staying with the hunk of a man sitting across from her.

How could she say no to that.

"I would be honored," she said out loud.

Reanna smiled and nodded.

Cascade's excitement at her answer sent tingles to places she hadn't felt tingles in a very long time.

Damn, this being dead was going to be a blast.

Who knew?

The Lady of Whispering Valley

A Buckey the Space Pirate Story

Dean Wesley Smith

One

"Why is it that I don't see you in your space pirate costume anymore?" Fred asked, his voice filling the air around me but seeming to come from no one location.

I tried to ignore him and focus on my textbook for advanced economics for a final I had coming in a week.

Fred was my talking oak tree friend. I had planted him in my mother's backyard a number of years back as an acorn. He now stood almost twenty feet tall. I spent a lot of time studying in a lawn chair under his shade in the summer, considering I was in my last year of college to get a degree in business with a combined major in horticulture. Having a talking oak tree for a best friend could get a person interested in growing trees and other plants.

I knew it was kind of sad that a talking oak tree, who had a fondness for limericks, was my best friend, but it was true.

Pathetic, but true.

Fred could not only talk, but like all oak trees, he could

travel through time to where other oak trees were in the past. And if I was holding onto him, he could take me along as well, a trick that had come in fantastically helpful for a couple history classes I had been taking.

Six months earlier, he had taken me into the past and introduced me to a wonderful woman my age named Mary that he talked to as well. She lived in 1871 outside of Boise, Idaho.

We had fallen for each other instantly, as Fred knew we would.

Mary was my age of twenty-five and had been widowed three years earlier. She lived alone in a cabin surrounded by oak trees. She had wonderful brown hair that mostly she kept pulled back and large brown eyes. I was five-ten and she was five-five and we made the perfect couple, or at least Fred told us we did. I tended to agree with him on that point.

I spent a lot of time in her cabin with her. She was the love of my life, even though as far as I was concerned, she had been dead for almost a hundred and fifty years.

We were working on that problem, or we both wanted to, but mostly we just didn't talk about it. Living a few miles apart or a city apart might have been something we could fix, but living over a hundred and forty years apart seemed to be far too much.

So we just enjoyed the time we had together, thanks to Fred, and ignored the big problem.

Besides meeting and falling in love with Mary, what was nice about Fred being able to take me there was that he could bring me back to within seconds of when I left, even though I had spent a week or more with Mary. That kept me from missing too many things in this time.

And he could return me after a week in my time to within an hour of the last time I left Mary.

"Well?" Fred asked, not letting go of his question even though I ignored him the first time. "Why don't you dress like a pirate anymore?"

I closed the book and sighed. "Honestly, I dressed in my Buckey the Space Pirate costume to go to science fiction conventions to meet girls."

I had to admit, it was a good costume. Tights tucked into tall black boots, a long coat with brass buttons, a wide belt with a sword hanging from it at a suggestive angle, and a wide-brimmed hat with a big feather.

Girls loved it.

"I have gotten a little old for that now," I said to Fred, "and besides, if you have forgotten, I have a girlfriend now."

"Oh, yes, I do remember our first meeting with you in your costume," Fred said. "Something about a punt and a runt and…"

"Don't even go there," I said, remembering that date I had with a wonderful woman with a body that would never end. She and I ended up down in the park under Fred, before he was cut down and before I saved him by planting him in my mother's backyard.

Fred had decided, right at the wrong moment, as my date and I had a meeting of the bodies, to spout some limerick about the size of a certain part of her body.

She had thought it me insulting her and had never talked to me again.

Considering what Fred had said about her body part in that limerick, I didn't blame her in the slightest.

"As I said," trying to get him from talking about that night, "I have a girlfriend now."

"Well," Fred said, "not actually now in the literal sense of the word, but I understand your meaning."

"Thank you," I said. "I sure wish Mary could spend time here with me. It would make things so much easier."

"She can," Fred said.

With that, I damn near fell off my lawn chair.

Two

After I regained my balance, I looked up into the leaves of the little oak tree. "Why didn't you tell us?"

"Neither of you asked," Fred said. "You seemed very comfortable in the situation in Mary's cabin."

"How?" I asked. "How can she come here?"

"The same way you return to her time," Fred said. "If she was here she would need to stay over oak roots or under oak limbs to remain. Same rules you follow in the past."

"Would you mind bringing her here?"

I thought I could hear him laugh slightly. Fred often laughed at me. After standing around and thinking for hundreds of thousands of years, it seemed oak trees had a superiority complex.

A moment later Mary was standing with her hand against the young oak tree, looking around.

I again damn near tipped over my lawn chair again as I rushed to stand up and hug her.

"Do not move too far," Fred said. "My young roots have not expanded out to even a respectable length yet."

Mary felt wonderful in my arms.

She had on her riding jeans and a light blouse and a wide-brimmed hat. More than likely Fred had suggested she prepare for a warm summer day.

After I kissed her, she looked around, smiling. "So this is where the young Fred of your time resides."

"This and in every other oak tree on the planet," Fred said, sounding a little indignant. He did that a lot.

Mary laughed and kept staring at her surroundings.

I glanced around at my mother's backyard, seeing it for the first time in a while. The yard had a chain-link fence around it and a small shed to hold the lawnmower to one side, but otherwise it was just a patch of mowed grass with a small and snide oak tree growing to one side.

And mom's house looked like any other house along the street from the back, with a small covered back porch and a couple chairs on it.

I just hoped mom didn't take this moment to look out the window. If she did, I was going to have some explaining to do.

I pointed out to Mary what few landmarks there were in the backyard and then said to Fred, "Could you jump us downtown near where you and I met. The street there is lined with oak and Mary can get an idea of what the modern world is really like."

"That is a splendid idea," Fred said.

A moment later Mary and I were standing under a massive old oak in a large park in the center of the city.

Traffic sped past on the two-lane road that bordered the park and some thirty- and forty-story buildings towered nearby.

She took my hand and grasped it tightly. I couldn't even begin to imagine what she was feeling.

"Oh, my," Mary said, staring first at the cars and then at the tall modern buildings, "the future is a wonder-filled place."

"That it is," I said.

After a moment, she turned to face me, a look of worry in her eyes. "What do you see in a simple woman from the past like me?"

For some reason I had my wits about me at that moment. "I would love you no matter what time you came from. But do you love me because I live in this madhouse of a time?"

"Of course," she said, kissing me. Her smile when she pulled away could light up a room.

And I think I was smiling just as large and wide.

Suddenly, being born almost a hundred and fifty years apart from the woman you loved didn't seem like such an insurmountable problem.

Three

After walking along the park for a ways, staying under the large oaks, I finally turned to Mary. "I love you. If you are willing, I would much like to start talking about how we solve this living situation we find ourselves in."

"Why Mr. Buckey Pirate sir," she said, smiling at me. "Are you asking me to live in sin with you?"

"I am, my fair lady," I said, bowing slightly and pretending to tip my hat. "And a wonderful sin it will be."

"Then how can I refuse such a sordid offer," she said, smiling, "if we can figure out how to work out this confusion of two worlds."

"I may have a few suggestions on the living aspects," Fred said, his voice almost echoing under the large oaks. "Not in the matter of the sin aspect. However, if needed, I have watched many thousands of human couples in copulation over the centuries and I am sure that..."

"Fred," I said, holding up my hand. "Thank you."

Mary was blushing and laughing.

"Could we go to Mary's cabin and the three of us have a discussion?" I asked.

Mary nodded. "Yes, please."

A moment later we were standing inside Mary's wonderful log cabin tucked into a stand of oaks in 1871 in a narrow valley outside of Boise, Idaho. The valley was called *Whispering Valley* for a reason I had not yet asked Mary about.

I really loved this place with its wonderful river-stone fireplace and large overstuffed furniture, including a couch that could lull anyone into a nap.

And Mary had a featherbed in her bedroom like nothing I could have ever imagined sleeping on. Why modern mattresses had gone to firm and hard was beyond me. Mary's featherbed just almost wrapped around me and cradled me to sleep.

Of course, having Mary beside me didn't hurt that feeling of contentment.

When we arrived, the large main room of the cabin smelled of fresh bread and light wood smoke, a combined smell that I knew I could never get tired of.

Mary made us both a cup of tea from the hot water she had left on the wood-burning stove before she left to visit me. I actually, in her time, had only left her about three hours before. But in my time I had attended a few classes, spent a night in my apartment studying, and taken one test.

We sat at her kitchen table, facing each other. I told her what I had done over the last day since I had left earlier this morning.

She nodded and said, "I can now, after this short excursion into your time, finally start to visualize some of what you talk about. I hope to learn much more about your time."

"I hope you can live there with me as well, as I live here with you," I said. "Fred, is that possible?"

"Very much so," Fred said, his deep voice filling the kitchen and living area as it always did.

"I worry," Mary said. "Are we not to become a burden on you with our constant requests to move back and forth through time?"

I nodded. I worried the same thing.

Fred chuckled. "I have lived for hundreds of thousands of years. My species, which will include me, will live for a hundred thousand years into the future. I will far outlive you both and will treasure our short time together and write limericks about you both for many to enjoy into the future."

I laughed. "So that means you won't mind?"

"It will find it no bother at all," Fred said.

Mary looked at me and smiled. Then she said to Fred, "If I haven't said this lately, I would like to say this again. Thank you for introducing me to this fine man."

"You are more than welcome," Fred said.

I could almost imagine Fred bowing to Mary. If an oak tree outside of a Disney cartoon could bow.

"So what is your suggestion?" I asked Fred.

"You must learn to think as a person unstuck in time," Fred said. "I know humans have no sense of time and very little memory. So this thinking will be a strain, but I can help."

Mary frowned. She had no idea what he was talking about either.

"Would you try that idea again with a few fewer insults to humanity and a few more concrete ideas?" I asked.

"Create your home here, in this valley, to live in at any point in time," Fred said.

Suddenly I realized what Fred was driving at in his usual Fred fashion.

"Do you own this home?" I asked Mary.

She nodded. "And the one hundred and eighty acres around it as well going up the valley and on both sides of the valley. My husband's father homesteaded it and passed it on to his son and I got the land and the home when he died."

I could see in Mary's eyes that she was starting to understand as well.

"You will need to plant a lot of oak trees all over this land in the coming years," I said to her.

She smiled. "That will be my pleasure."

"And mine as well," Fred said.

"And I need to do some research on how to pass this land down in trust," I said. "So that I will inherit it at the age of 25."

"That sounds like a very logical solution," Fred said.

I could hear in Fred's voice the sound of almost pity at the poor stupid humans. And it dawned on me why.

"Of course, in my time," I said, "Mary has already set up the trust and the land is about to transfer to my name. Is that correct?"

Fred chuckled. A condescending chuckle, but I'll take it.

"Can we see what we will work so hard in this time to accomplish in a future time?" Mary asked.

"Of course," Fred said.

A moment later they were standing near the remains of her old cabin, long since crumbled to a pile of rotted logs. I could see the stones of the fireplace to one side. Weeds covered the remains.

"Now that makes me sad," Mary said.

"We can build brand new," I said.

She nodded and turned to look around.

A forest of tall, strong oak seemed to spread over the landscape and down a shallow hill and around a stream.

As far as they could see under the canopy of oak, the land remained clear and empty.

"You left forty acres unplanted down on the lower side to sell off to get money to build a dream home here," Fred said.

"Wow," Mary said, looking around. "I planted all of these? This is wonderfully beautiful."

"You both will plant these," Fred said, his voice echoing again in the shady, cool area of the old oaks.

"How will I be able to move beyond the roots of leaves of an already planted tree?" I asked.

"Look to your right about ten steps," Fred said.

We followed his instructions, but all we could see were acorns littering the ground.

I picked one up. "Is this what you are talking about?"

"It is," Fred said. "You hold in your hand the essence of the beginning of life of my species.

I couldn't believe what I was thinking.

"Are you telling me that if I carry around an acorn in Mary's time, and she carries around one in my time, we can go anywhere?"

"Of course you can," Fred said. "As long as you do not remove the acorn from your person outside of the influence of an oak tree's branches or roots. If you do, you will just return to your own time where you left."

I glanced at Mary who was looking shocked as well.

"Why didn't you tell us?" I asked.

"You did not ask," Fred said. "It is one of the great failings of all humanity, actually, to not ask the right question at the right time. I have watched the results of that for far longer than I care to remember."

"But you can remember thousands of couples copulating," Mary asked, smiling at me.

"That is a very different matter," Fred said. "And fodder for many a limerick, I might add."

"I can only imagine," I said.

"No need to imagine," Fred said. "I would be glad to share as many limericks as you would like to hear about the copulation patterns of your species. For example:

"There was a young woman from Spain,

"Whose body seemed quite plain,..."

"Fred," I said, interrupting him, "I promise to listen to your limericks but right now I think Mary and I need to get busy making sure this wonderful place comes to pass. We have a lot of work and planning to do."

"I agree," Fred said.

"And we need to get on with this planning to live in the sin offer I have been made," Mary said, smiling at me.

I pretended to tip my hat. "That my lady, will be no work at all. Only pleasure."

She kissed me and I kissed her back.

We stood there under the large oaks in the beautiful valley, holding and kissing each other until Fred said simply...

There was a young lady named Grace,
Who loved to be held in embrace.
She hugged and she tugged
But no lover remained
For her lips were on the side of her face.

I'm fairly certain Mary laughed first, even though we both knew that laughing at the oak tree's limericks did nothing but encourage him.

That Old Tingling

A Marble Grant Story

Dean Wesley Smith

One

Who knew that so much training went along with being dead. I felt like a kid again, only I didn't have to start all the way back in diapers.

But I did have to learn how to use restrooms, since it seemed ghosts had to pee and eat and everything else and for a woman having the lid up on a toilet was a critical factor. I couldn't lift a lid yet.

One of the very first lessons I learned was to check to see if some woman was in a stall before sticking my head through the stall door to see if the lid was up.

Learned that lesson the hard way. Ugly hard way. I'll never get that sight or that smell out of my memory. Four hundred pounds, almost nude, and clearly the poor woman had eaten something very, very wrong.

Rotten fish and dead animal under a bridge kind of wrong.

Luckily the poor woman didn't hear me gasp, cough disgustingly, and stumble back and through the wall and right into the men's room. Let me tell you, that morning I heard noises from the stalls in that men's room I didn't know were possible for a human to make.

A girl could get real traumatized being dead, of that there was no doubt. Jewel said when I returned to the breakfast table that I was almost ghost white. Ghost-white skin didn't match my purple hair or my bright yellow blouse no matter how dead I was.

I also had to figure out how to eat and start learning how to actually touch something physical and move it. You know, things like toilet lids. My trainers of the dead, Jewel and Tommy, said that would take me time.

As with everything else they taught me, they had been right.

After three months of training, I knew how to control live people, knew how to eat and dress with ghost food and clothing, and could get around pretty well by teleporting, just as I had as a superhero.

I was feeling pretty darned good about it all, actually.

I also had learned more about sex by being inside of people's heads than I had learned dating men and women both for over a hundred years. Wow, some folks out there really were kinky. I mean I liked to experiment and I sure enjoyed sex, but some of the stuff I saw in people's minds just made me look away.

Damn tough when you are in a person's mind, let me tell you.

My best friend of the last hundred years, Patty, who was still alive and a superhero like I used to be before a bullet implanted itself into my forehead, helped me get a nifty and large two-bedroom condo in Las Vegas on the fifth floor of the Ogden Building downtown.

Her boyfriend, Poker Boy, seemed to have more money than Fort Knox and he bought the place and all the furniture and fixtures I wanted, as well as all my clothes.

I kissed him on the cheek and told him I doubted I would ever be able to pay him back. He had just laughed.

Patty told me later that was his embarrassed laugh. Then she told me he would never miss the money in the slightest. Seems Fort Knox couldn't match his money. Playing poker and investing the money smartly over time had clearly been good for him. Besides, he figured the condo was an investment since I sure couldn't own it or sell it.

Patty had helped me shop for clothes. Ghosts could take and wear the ghost part of any clothing. But if I actually had the physical clothes hanging in my closet, I could always wear the ghost part of the outfit any time I wanted.

And no damn laundry. I just tossed the dirty clothes in a basket and a day or so later the ghost clothes vanished. They went back and joined their real part in the closet, all neat and fresh just as I bought it for me to use again.

Didn't get better than that.

So Poker Boy had given me and Patty an unlimited credit card and I now had my bedroom and a hall closet full of brand new clothes and shoes and sexy underwear, even though I doubted the sexy part of the underwear were going to get used any time soon.

The vibrator that Patty helped me buy got used regularly to cure that old tingling, especially when I happened to stumble into an attractive man or woman and read their thoughts and their likes and dislikes in the bedroom.

Those images from those people's minds made for some good before-sleep fantasy workouts with that vibrator.

Yeah, kind of being a voyeur, I know, but a ghost does what a ghost can do.

I decided to not fill my extra bedroom closet with clothes just yet. Never knew when someone alive or dead would need a guest room. So Patty and I furnished it with a large bed, wooden dresser, and a reading chair with lamp.

One thing for certain, it was great to have rich live friends when a person was a ghost. Made living a ton more comfortable. I had had a nice place in Boise before I died, but nothing like this condo.

Everything in it was ultra modern and clean and the couch and chairs in the living room were actually comfortable. I had dozed off numbers of time already watching movies on that couch.

The kitchen was enough to make me want to learn how to cook, even though I lived in a city with some of the best restaurants in the world I could get food from at any moment.

I had gotten into a habit at night for dinner of going to a new restaurant and bringing back to my place one of their specialties. Something different every night sure kept things interesting in the food department.

The view of the condo was toward the Strip and the balcony had a glass table and five surprisingly comfortable chairs. On warm evenings I usually ate dinner out there, just enjoying the feel of being lucky.

Yeah, I know, I had been killed and I was now a ghost.

Still I felt damn lucky.

Two

I was enjoying one of the sweetest-tasting peach daiquiris on my balcony just before sunset four months after I had died when Jewel and Tommy appeared.

I had yet to jump to get dinner, but I had plans on trying a barbeque plate from a place in the MGM Grand where Patty worked. She said it was wonderful.

Jewel and Tommy both had on their normal jeans, expensive shirt and blouse, and tennis shoes. Together they were the most attractive couple I had ever met. Stunning model-like looks. Tommy had those wide shoulders of a cop and Jewel was thin and trim and always looked perfectly together.

Did I mention they were also two of the smartest people I had ever met as well. Both had higher degrees and Jewel had been a medical doctor. And on top of all that, they were just flat nice people. Go figure.

"Sorry to bother you without checking ahead," Jewel said. "But we figured you would want to join us."

I took a long drink of the daiquiri as I stood. "You know me. Always up for an adventure. Where are we headed?"

"Your partner is about to join us," Jewel said.

"Damn right I want to be there," I said, laughing.

I had been hearing since almost the moment I discovered I was a ghost that I would have a ghost partner at some point joining me. I knew nothing at all about this person. No one would say a word since the person was still alive. So it had sort of been one of those nagging events coming that I had mostly just put out of my mind.

Jewel smiled. "Then let's go."

And the next thing I knew I was standing in a hot, dry desert on the shoulder of a two-lane paved road. The sun looked exactly like it had from my condo balcony, so I figured I was somewhere in the desert southwest.

"We're fifty miles to the north of Las Vegas," Tommy said.

The two-lane highway stretched off into the distance in both directions. There was not a building or a soul in sight. A slight breeze was doing some wonderful things with my nipples through my thin blouse and my long purple hair was blowing slightly around my shoulders.

I had on my evening kick-around-the-condo sweat pants and tennis shoes. I certainly hadn't dressed for this occasion.

We stood there on the edge of the road in the fading light for a good minute with nothing happening.

"We in the wrong place?" I finally asked.

Never was one for just standing and waiting. Another nice thing about being dead, I seldom had to stand and wait for anything.

Tommy pointed to the north. In the distance I could see a

single light coming toward us. That would be the first car to pass us since we got here.

Only it became clear fairly quickly that it wasn't a car, but a motorcycle. And it was moving at an insane speed.

As the motorcycle was about to flash past us, a coyote jumped up from the ditch beside the road and the motorcycle hit the creature square in the side. Neither the poor coyote, or the motorcyclist, had even an instant to react.

I watched as the motorcyclist in black leathers and black wrap-around helmet went sailing past us about thirty feet in the air over our heads.

The impact of the cyclist hitting the road was an awful sound.

The cyclist started doing uncontrolled cartwheels along the pavement.

To one side of us the remains of the coyote landed in two parts.

On the other side of the road the big black motorcycle was doing cartwheels out into the desert brush, flipping parts in all directions like a stripper shedding clothes.

I wanted to be sick.

That accident had to be one of the most horrid things I had ever witnessed.

Hands down the most violent.

Being a superhero in the real estate and hospitality areas didn't much call for extreme violence.

Three

The three of us stood there on the side of the road without talking. I don't think any of us had expected the intense violence of that accident. That cyclist must have been going well over a hundred miles per hour.

The body finally slid to a stop about a football field's distance away from us and a moment later the cyclist in all black, still wearing a helmet, was sitting on a rock to the right of the road closer to us than the body.

"That's our signal," Jewel said and led the way as the three of us walked up the road toward the cyclist.

I was working on taking deep breaths, pushing the image of that accident out of my mind so that I could focus forward. This person was supposed to be my future partner. Certainly he or she was someone who liked to take risks.

If nothing else, that might get interesting at times.

The three of us stopped near the cyclist who looked up, face hidden by the black faceplate on the helmet. Then two gloved hands came up and took off the helmet, shaking loose long blonde hair.

Sitting there on the rock, newly dead, was one of the most attractive women I had ever seen. She had deep blue eyes, high cheekbones, and a short nose.

She looked completely stunned and even with that look she was beautiful.

"What happened?" she asked, looking at us.

"You had an accident," Jewel said.

The woman shook her head and took off her gloves, tucking them into her helmet in a practiced move.

"Not likely. At that speed I would be dead. And I don't even have a scratch on me."

None of us said a word. We just let her slowly figure it out for herself.

Finally Jewel introduced the three of us.

"I'm Sally Glass," the woman said.

"Where are you from?" Jewel asked.

I was impressed at how calm and level Jewel sounded. I was still having trouble getting my heart under control from the violence of that crash and also the beauty of the woman sitting on the rock in front of me.

I was attracted to women as much as I was to men. And clearly Sally was my type.

Also, her name sounded very, very familiar.

The more I looked at Sally under those motorcycle leathers, the more I realized she was about my size and shape at five-eight. That would be helpful in getting her some clothing.

The nagging feeling I knew her kept getting stronger like a bad itch in a place I couldn't scratch.

"Boise," Sally said, pointing back north. "Wanted to spend a few days in Vegas and clear my head a little.

"I was from Boise," I said, working to keep my voice as calm as I could. "I worked real estate there among other things."

Sally nodded. "Banks and construction, among other things. And you look very familiar."

"I was thinking the same for you," I said.

Jewel glanced at me and nodded. She was about to say something when Patty appeared.

I suddenly felt very relieved that a real live person was here.

"Patty," Sally said, standing and sounding happy.

"Hi, Sim," Patty said.

The two women stepped toward each other hugged on the edge of the road.

"I was hoping to get to see you on this trip," Sim said.

The moment Patty said "Sim" I knew who this woman was. She was also a superhero in the banking side. Patty had always talked about getting the three of us together at some point, but it had never happened. Seems Sim and Patty had met about fifty years ago when Sim became a superhero.

But now we had finally met, in the middle of the desert, with Sim's broken body crumpled in a pile beside the road about fifty steps away.

"So what is this all about?" Sim asked.

"You had an accident," Patty said.

"That's what they—Oh, crap, I'm a Ghost Agent."

Sim suddenly looked like she needed to sit down again and Patty moved to Sim's right and I went to her left side and we braced her.

"You are a Ghost Agent now," Jewel said. "Tommy, Marble,

That Old Tingling

and I are all three Ghost Agents. Marble is also a superhero like you."

"I'm dead?" Sim asked. "Really dead?"

Jewel nodded and pointed to the body.

Sim looked around until she spotted her own body and then nodded. "I knew there was no way I could survive an accident at that speed. Did you see it? Must have been spectacular."

"Violent," I said, enjoying holding her up a little more than I probably should have at that moment. "And I'm afraid to say the coyote you hit didn't make it either."

Sim laughed and shook her head.

"So you hungry?" Jewel asked.

Sim frowned. "I was really hungry before all this. One of the reasons I was going so fast. And I still am. Do ghosts eat?"

"Take it from a newly-made Ghost Agent as well," I said. "We do eat and everything tastes better than you can imagine."

Jewel and Tommy both nodded to that.

Sim looked at me, then nodded. "You were killed in a double murder in an alley in Boise about four months ago. Right?"

I nodded.

"I remember when that happened and was surprised Patty wasn't more upset than she was when I heard it was you."

I laughed. "She's been helping me. Wait until you see the condo she and Poker Boy got me to live in."

"Can't wait," Sim said and smiled at me.

I damn near melted right there in the desert. Working with this woman was going to be heaven. And if she didn't like women as a sexual partner, my poor vibrator would get a regular workout.

Patty looked at me. "All right if Sim borrows something to wear?"

I laughed. "Never a problem. I think we bought me more than enough."

Patty turned to Jewel and Tommy. "How about the three of us meet you at the Golden Nugget buffet in fifteen minutes."

"We'll be there," Jewel and Tommy said and vanished.

A moment later we were out of the slight wind of the desert and in my condo.

The idea of getting to help train Sim to be a Ghost Agent over the next months had me excited to say the least. But watching her strip naked in my bedroom topped any thought of that being the most exciting.

Her body was amazingly like mine. Thin hips and small breasts. Only she was a natural blonde where I was a complete brunette when I didn't color my hair one color or another.

And we were almost exactly the same height.

I showed her how to turn on the water in the bathroom so she could take a quick shower. When she came out with wet hair and a towel around her, she looked even more stunning.

"Kind of strange how the towel still just stays on the rack in there while I dry off with this same towel.

"Everything has a ghost component," I said. "Jewel and Tommy will explain everything."

"Wait until you taste the ghost component of food," I said. "Better than anything you have ever tasted."

"I am so starved right now cardboard might taste good," she said and dropped the towel to start to get dressed.

I had to turn away or simply melt into a puddle, she was that beautiful.

And I was that horny.

The only slight imperfection she had was a scar on one hip that someday I would ask her about, but not tonight.

Later that night, as Sim changed clothes once again to get ready for bed in my guestroom, I decided seeing her naked was by far the most exciting thing of the day.

By a long ways.

Two hours later, when she knocked on my bedroom door and came in and asked me to hold her, I knew from here the days would just get better.

I had considered myself lucky as it was.

But I remembered that first night after I had died being scared and uncertain about everything. I wish Sim had been there to hold me.

But now I could hold her.

And that was all that mattered.

I had just gotten factors luckier to have her as a partner.

We fell asleep in each other's arms.

And she never used the guest bedroom again.

Dead or alive, that would have been just fine with me.

But honestly, being dead made it even better.

An Immortality Of Sorts

A Buckey the Space Pirate Story

Dean Wesley Smith

"I am very sorry for the loss of your mother," Fred said, his voice seeming to come from everywhere around the young oak tree in my mother's back yard.

The early spring day had turned out nice, just warm enough that I didn't need a jacket. The yard was still in winter growth, but I was starting to see some small shoots of green coming up. The twenty-foot oak tree showed no signs of any leaves budding yet. It wouldn't be long until they did and the lawn needed to be mowed.

Fred was my best friend outside of Mary, my wife, who Fred had introduced me to. Fred was a talking oak tree that could travel through all history into all other oak trees. He could take me and Mary with him as well, which was how I met her.

She was a widow who had lived in a small log cabin in the late 1800s outside of Boise, Idaho, surrounded by oak trees.

I was from modern times, a kid who in college used to dress up like a space pirate to impress girls at parties and science fiction conventions. That was how I got my name Buckey.

Now Mary and I were both twenty-seven and living in a brand new home we had built on her property that we had arranged in the past to come down through time for me to inherit here in my present.

Yes, I didn't exist in Mary's time and she was already dead in my time, yet we were happily married. Time travel with oak trees could sometimes get very confusing.

I always kept an acorn in my pocket and Mary always kept two acorns, one on a gold chain around her neck, another in her pocket. As long as we had an acorn from an oak tree, or were over an oak tree's roots, we remained in each other's time.

In other words, with an acorn in my pocket, I could go anywhere in her time and if she wore the acorn here, she could go anywhere in this time.

Mostly we spent our time here, in our new modern home built where her old log cabin used to stand in her time.

But Fred, the young talking oak tree I had rescued seven years before, was planted in my mother's back yard. I had nowhere else to plant it at the time.

And just three days ago we had buried my mother. She had died far too young after a short fight against cancer.

Luckily, she had lived long enough to see Mary and me get married. I had never seen her so happy. She had loved Mary like the daughter she never had.

My mother had been well-liked and the large church we used for her funeral was jammed with her friends coming to pay their last respects. She had worked most of her life as an RN, and she had loved it, working right up to a few weeks before the cancer took her.

I could not believe my mother was gone.

Mary was inside and we were just starting to clean out some of my mother's things. We had no intention of selling the house, because this back yard was where Fred lived. Mom had left me the house, since I was her only child and dad had died when I was five.

But she had wanted much of her stuff to go to different charities and Mary and I had promised her we would take care of it. But I could only stand so much, so I had gone out to sit and talk with Fred.

"Thank you," I said to Fred as I dropped into one of the lawn chairs near him and facing away from my mother's house. Three years ago I had fenced in the back yard with a tall fence and dozens more small oak trees growing along the fence so the neighbors couldn't see me sitting out here talking to the air.

Mary and I had often sat and talked with Fred, even though we could talk to him anywhere there was an oak tree, or if we were carrying the acorns.

But there was something special about just sitting with Fred, the twenty-foot oak tree, knowing he was the real Fred.

And Fred seemed to enjoy our company in person as well.

After I sat there in silence for a time, just not really thinking, trying to get the image of the funeral and all the work ahead to take care of Mom's things out of my head, Fred finally spoke.

"Your mother was a very amazing woman."

I nodded. "She was."

Then Fred said something that damn near knocked me over backwards out of my lawn chair.

"I enjoyed our conversations and travels."

I stood up, staring at the bare branches of the young oak tree in front of me.

"You talked to my mother?"

"Of course," Fred said. "Long before you were born, actually. Your father was an amazing man as well."

"You talked to my dad?"

"Of course," Fred said. "I helped introduce the two of them."

My head was spinning and I had no idea what to think.

I turned to the house and in my loudest voice shouted, "Mary!"

A moment later Mary came out the back door, looking slightly panicked.

Every day I thought of her as the most beautiful woman in the world in any time. She was five-five with long brown hair and the largest brown eyes of any woman I had ever met.

And those eyes could see right through a person.

And right now I really needed her to help me get a grip on the reality I felt slipping away.

"You all right?" she asked as she came quickly off the back porch and down to where I was standing.

"Fred says he talked with my parents."

"Of course I did," Fred said, his voice rumbling through the yard and off the tall wooden fence.

If a young oak tree could sound indignant, Fred did at that moment.

"I have always told you that you two are not the only two humans I talk with through time."

"Wow, that is wonderful," Mary said.

She clearly wasn't as shocked at the news as I was. I always considered my mother a rock-of-the-earth person, not someone who talked to time-traveling oak trees.

"I also talked with your parents, Mary," Fred said.

At that Mary leaned against me and I thought her legs were going to go out.

I got her seated in one of the lawn chairs and then I took the other before my legs gave way as well.

I sat there, holding her hand as we had done so often over the last few years in these chairs, staring up into the bare branches of the small tree.

"How come you didn't tell us?" I asked.

Fred chuckled. "As I have said many times before in different situations, you did not ask. The greatest human failing is the inability to ask the right question at the right time."

The oak tree then chuckled and again the sound seemed to echo through the spring day and around the enclosed back yard.

"Besides," Fred said, "your mother asked me not to say anything until she died and I would never go against your mother's wishes, you know. She was a smart, formidable, and very strong human. And besides, she liked my limericks."

I nodded to that. She had been strong, but not once had I ever heard her repeat a limerick. Especially one of Fred's limericks. They were often quite racy, to say the least.

It seemed that Fred got bored standing all the time in one spot and to amuse himself through the centuries, he made up limericks. In the last few years I had had printed two of his books of limericks. They were selling fairly well, actually, which made Fred want to come up with even more.

"What were my parents like?" Mary asked, her voice soft and low.

I knew she had never really got a chance to know them. They were both killed in a train wreck outside of Chicago when

Mary was ten and Mary had been raised by an aunt and uncle who brought her west to Idaho.

"They were very much like you," Fred said. "Smart, kind, loving."

Mary nodded. "Would you tell me how you started talking with them?"

"It will be my pleasure," Fred said.

Then for the next ten minutes he relayed the story of how he first started talking with Mary's mother, then her father.

Fred chuckled. "They both, to the day they sadly died, believed they were slightly daft, as your mother put it."

Mary smiled at that.

"Would you tell me how you started to talk with my parents?" I asked.

"I met your father first outside of Boston just after the Revolutionary War," Fred said.

If Mary hadn't been holding onto my hand, I would have gone over backwards in the lawn chair.

"Buckey's father was from the past?" Mary asked because I was just sitting there trying to not pass out.

"He was," Fred said. "A dashing man who fought and was injured in the Revolutionary War. He was a landowner and farmer by trade. There were many oak trees on his property and as he recovered from his wounds from the war, sitting in the shade of a giant oak tree, we started talking."

"Are those wounds what eventually killed him?" I asked.

My mother had said something along those lines, but would never elaborate.

"To my understanding, yes," Fred said. "He would have died that first summer, but I asked your mother for help and took her to him. I told them about the acorns and she got him into a modern hospital and they saved his life."

"My mother saved my father's life after the Revolutionary War?" I asked.

"She did," Fred said.

At that point the yard was spinning and if not for the solidness of Mary's hand, I am certain I would have just slid down to lie on the grass.

"They were married six months later," Fred said. "In a wonderful ceremony on his land during his time. Then they also married in this time in a small ceremony. Both ceremonies were beautiful, both outdoors under large oak trees."

I was still so stunned I flat didn't know what to say.

After a moment, my wonderful wife said, "Would it be possible for us to watch my parents' wedding and then Buckey's parents' two weddings?"

"Of course," Fred said.

And for the next hour we watched three weddings, two very historical and one in a small chapel here and now. We stood in the back, like ghosts, unable to be seen.

I agreed with Fred, all three were wonderful.

And when we returned to my mother's back yard, the grief of losing my mother had lifted.

Mary seemed lighter and was smiling as well.

"Thank you," Mary said. "That was wonderful."

"Yes, thank you," I said.

"It is always my pleasure," Fred said.

I needed to clear up one thing. "Fred, may I ask a question?"

"Of course," he said.

I was sure that if an oak tree could smile a satisfied smile, Fred would be doing so.

"My mother, my father, Mary's parents. They are not really dead, are they?"

The twenty-foot oak tree just chuckled. "The right question at the right time. You are learning. To answer your question, they do not exist in this time and place."

"But they are still alive in their own times and their own places?" I asked. "Is that correct?"

Mary squeezed my hand, clearly understanding where I was going.

"That is correct," Fred said.

"So tomorrow evening, if we threw a dinner party for our parents, all four of them," I said, "they could attend?"

"Of course," Fred said.

I glanced at Mary and she was beaming. "I am dead in this time," she said. "Yet I am here."

I was finally starting to understand.

"So over the years since my father died," I asked, "has my mother spent time with him?"

"Yes," Fred said, "if you insist on thinking in linear time. Your mother and father existed for their life spans, but that does not mean they do not still exist in many other times and places."

"Thanks to you," I said.

"I am not the only oak tree who tries to help humans understand their own abilities in time."

I started to open my mouth to ask what he meant, but Mary squeezed my hand. That would be a conversation, a question for another time, another place.

"Fred," Mary said, "would you ask our parents to join us for dinner tomorrow evening?"

"I would be honored," Fred said. "But don't you think it would be nicer to invite them yourself?"

At that, the backdoor to my mother's house opened and my mother and father walked out, hand-in-hand, followed by another couple dressed in clothing from the 1800s.

All four of them were smiling as they came down off the porch toward us.

"Mom? Dad?" Mary whispered as she stood.

I tried to stand and turn, but failed, and finally did go over backwards in the lawn chair.

But somehow, with Fred and all four parents laughing, with Mary's help, I managed to scramble to my feet just in time to say hello and hug my dead parents as Mary hugged hers.

Behind me, I heard the young oak tree sigh a happy sigh.

SMILE

Dean Wesley Smith

Day One Lunch

"I'd walk chameleon miles for one of your smiles."

Betty Spencer wiped her hands on her brown uniform and looked up over the Faster-Than-Yours Burgers and Things cash register at the nerd standing at the head of the line. He stood no more than five-six, had a face full of bad zits, and wore plaid pants.

She couldn't believe the plaid pants.

"Can I help you?" she asked, forcing on her best Faster-Than-Yours training smile. Being the best-looking woman employee, she always got all the weird men in her line. Half the time they wouldn't even look up from her chest.

And the few gorgeous men who did come in wouldn't even notice her because of the bag-like brown uniform they made her wear.

Working here was just a bitch.

"I'd walk chameleon miles for one of your smiles," the nerd

said again. Then he stuck out a stubby-fingered hand. "I'm Brad. Brad Fanthorpe. I've been in here every day this summer. I just love it when you smile."

Betty glanced quickly over her shoulder at where her supervisor stood over-salting the French fries. He might look her way at any moment. She would have to be careful how she handled this guy. She was already on the supervisor's shit list for making a pass at the cook. How the hell was she supposed to know that the cook was as gay as the supervisor and they'd been living together for the past three months.

Working here was an absolute bitch.

She turned back to the nerd, let the official work smile drain down into what she really felt, then looked him right in the eye and said, "That's nice. Now, what can I get for you?"

"Oh, nothing to eat," the nerd said. "I just wanted to ask you to a movie this evening."

The nerd smiled real big.

Betty's stomach turned just like it had the first time she had tasted a Faster-Than-Yours burger. The nerd's teeth looked like they hadn't been brushed in six months and she could smell his breath clear across the counter.

"No thanks," she said. "I'm busy. And besides, I only go out with men over six feet tall."

"Oh, no problem at all," he said. "Thanks."

He bowed slightly, then turned and walked away.

As the next customer, an overweight man with two kids moved up in front of her, Betty glanced over at her boss. He was still doing rude things to the French fries and hadn't seen what had happened.

Thank God. She got in enough trouble on her own without having some jerk cause her even more.

Working here was sure a bitch. She forced on her smile for the dirty-faced kid in front of her.

Day One Afternoon

"I'd walk chameleon miles for one of your smiles."

Betty glanced up from the order of Itsy-Bitsy Chicken Parts she had been trying to choke down for lunch. The nerd was back, standing beside her table, smiling his rotten-teeth smile.

"Remember me," he said. "I'm Brad Fanthorpe. I was in earlier."

He stuck out his hand again.

Betty ignored the hand.

"Yeah, I remember you," she said. How anyone could ever forget someone with breath like his was beyond her. She swore it was shriveling up her already tiny Chicken Parts lunch.

"Well," he said, indicating his legs. "What do you think? I'm six feet, two inches tall now. I had to buy new pants, but it was worth it if you will go out with me tomorrow night."

Betty looked at his pants. They looked like the same plaid

pants he'd had on earlier, only these still had a price sticker on one side.

She had to admit, though, he did look taller. Some sort of lifts, or maybe a trick.

"I'm busy tomorrow night, too," she said. "And besides, not only are all of my dates over six feet tall, they all look like Bruce Springsteen."

"Oh, no problem," he said. "Thanks." Again, he bowed slightly and headed for the door.

Betty picked up a Chicken Part, then dropped it back into its box.

All she had wanted was to earn a little spending money for her junior year at the University. What the hell had she done to deserve this job?

Day One Evening

"I'd walk chameleon miles for one of your smiles."

Betty had just left the employee entrance and was trying to unlock her car. She had noticed the guy standing beside the car next to hers, but she hadn't paid much attention. Now she spun and looked right into the face of Bruce Springsteen.

"Holly shit!" she said. She didn't know whether to run like hell away from him, or move closer for a better look.

She ended up just standing there and staring. And the more she stared, the more she realized it wasn't Bruce after all.

"Hi. Remember me? I'm Brad Fanthorpe."

Just like the times earlier in the day, he stuck out his hand and moved toward her.

Just like before, there was no way she was going to touch his hand.

"Well? What do you think? Will you go out with me three nights from now?"

He smiled, showing her his rotted teeth again.

"How? I mean, why— No, what I meant to say is that is some great mask."

Having a tall, Bruce Springsteen look-a-like standing in front of her was making her nervous, even if he did have bad teeth and wore plaid pants. He was just so damned good looking.

"It's no mask," he said. "I changed just for you."

"Sure you did," Betty said. Even if he was good looking, this guy was just too weird.

She went back to unlocking her car.

"No," the guy said. "I did. Really."

Betty had the car door open now. She felt safer, so she turned and faced him. Better to get it over with now instead of having him come back while she was working tomorrow.

"Is that what all this 'chameleon mile' shit is about? I thought chameleons were lizards."

"They are," he said. "They can change their colors to blend in with their surroundings. I've spent the last three years at the University working on a way to do much more than chameleons can do."

"And just how do you do it?" Betty asked with as much sarcasm as she could put in her voice. "Drink a secret formula?"

"On no," he said. "Nothing like that. It's a combination of a special cream and metaphysical techniques."

"I don't believe this shit," Betty said and started to climb into her car.

"Wait! What about the date?"

"Tell you what," Betty said. "If you can give yourself not only Bruce's shoulders and chest, but his ass, I'll go out with you. Deal?"

She slammed her door, backed out, and drove off with him still standing there in the parking lot.

What a day. They didn't pay her enough for this job. Not by a million dollars.

Day Two Breakfast

The next morning, Betty had just finished serving her last order of Pigs-in-a-Bun and was starting to clean up to get ready for the lunch rush.

Suddenly Debbie, the blonde-haired giggle machine who worked at the cash register beside Betty's, let out a scream, "It's him! It's really him!"

Then Debbie sighed real loud and slumped to the floor, giving her head a sound crack on the just-mopped tiles.

Betty looked up.

Bruce Springsteen was walking right at her.

"Holy shit!" Betty said and stepped back away from the counter.

It couldn't be Bruce.

But it also couldn't be the nerd.

"Well?" Bruce said in the nerd's voice. "What do you think?"

He held up his hands and turned around, showing Betty his ass.

"Not bad, huh?"

"Holy shit!" Betty said again as she looked him up and down. He still had on the plaid pants, but somehow, on Bruce's body, they now looked great.

Sexy.

His button-down shirt looked two sizes too small and Betty could see dark brown hair on his chest.

"How about that date now?" Bruce asked.

"You want to go out with her?" the supervisor said as he walked up and stood beside Betty. "I'm sure Mr. Springsteen tha—"

"I'm not Bruce Springsteen," Bruce said. "I'm Brad Fanthorpe."

He stuck out his hand for the supervisor to shake.

"Anything you say," the supervisor said softly as he took the offered hand and shook it as if he never wanted to let go.

Betty tore her gaze off of Bruce's chest and glanced around.

A crowd was starting to gather. All the girls were now standing behind her and some of the breakfast customers were whispering to each other and pointing.

"Excuse me, Sir," Betty said. "Would it be possible that I take my break now?"

The supervisor glanced at her without letting go of Bruce's hand. "I don't—"

"That would be great if you'd let her just have five minutes," Bruce said and smiled at the supervisor.

"Oh, of course," the supervisor said and let go of Bruce's hand. "But just five minutes."

Betty nodded and quickly ducked around the end of the counter and led Bruce to the farthest booth.

She just couldn't believe this was happening. Her eyes told her that she was with Bruce Springsteen, but her mind said it was still the nerd.

Only there was no way that it could be either.

Someone was playing a practical joke on her and it wasn't damn funny. It was going to get her fired.

"All right," she said after they were both seated. "What's this all about?"

"Just trying to get a date with you," he said. "You said you were busy the next two nights, so how about Friday night?"

"Just hang on a minute. First off, I want to know just how you did this. I mean, what kind of trick—no, I mean, who are you? Hell, I don't know what I mean."

"Don't you remember?" he asked. "I told you yesterday. I'm Brad Fanthorpe and I changed to get a date with you. You did say you wouldn't go out with me unless I was over six feet tall and looked like Bruce Springsteen. So I used the picture on his latest album to make myself look exactly like him. Neat, huh?"

He smiled and Betty could see his bad teeth.

He closed his mouth and she was left staring into Bruce Springsteen's face.

What the hell was she going to do now?

She reached across the table and touched the side of his face, then squeezed his arm.

It felt like real flesh and she couldn't see any makeup. Maybe, just maybe, the impossible was true and this guy really could change into whoever he wanted. That didn't make him Bruce Springsteen. He was still just the nerd that had come in yesterday.

Only now he was damn good looking.

"How long does this—this effect last?"

Bruce shook his head. "I don't know. For all I know, it may be permanent, at least until I change it to something different."

"Oh," was all Betty could say.

Now that she had let herself start to accept that what he was saying might be true, her mind was racing with all the possibilities. It would mean that anyone could look young anytime they wanted. It would mean that no one ever would have to be ugly. Or deformed.

It would mean that she could look like anyone she wanted to look like.

This guy's invention would change the world.

"Have you told anyone about this invention?" Betty asked.

"Just a few others," he said. "I just got it to work three days ago."

"If you gave me some of this cream," Betty said, "would I be able to change, too?"

Bruce looked puzzled. "I suppose so. It might take me a few years to train you in the metaphysical trances involved, but I suppose you could do it. I really haven't thought all the implications of this through, yet. But I suppose anyone could be taught."

His gaze held hers and then he smiled.

"But why would you want to. I think you're very beautiful just the way you are."

Betty could feel her face getting red and slightly hot. It wasn't very often that she had a man as good looking as he was compliment her, even if he had been a nerd the day before.

"Two years?" she asked after a moment of silence. "Why so long?"

"It would take at least that long to train your mind," he said. "The cream is only an enhancer. It's the mind that has the power to change the body. You'd have to learn to tap into that power and control it."

"Oh," Betty said, again. That didn't sound real hopeful. She'd never been any good at that sort of strong concentration. It usually took everything she could do just to keep her mind on one subject for an hour class.

"Now, what about the date?" Bruce asked. "I was thinking we could catch a movie."

Betty glanced around at the counter. Not only were all the girls staring in her direction, but also the cook, the supervisor, and most of the customers. They all literally looked as if they were drooling. If she didn't go out with Bruce, or Brad, or whatever his name was, there was no doubt he would have absolutely no trouble getting anyone else in the place to go.

She looked back at him. He really did seem like a nice guy. Definitely smart. Maybe after the first date, she could get him to do something about his teeth.

"All right," she said. "But how about tonight? I'm free after all."

He slowly shook his head. "I really can't," he said, giving her his Bruce Springsteen serious look that made her hot all over. "I've got a date with Judy from the pizza place down the street."

Betty could feel her stomach starting to twist. "How about tomorrow night, then?"

He shook his head again. "Tomorrow I'm going out with Ann from the Milkshake Palace. Sorry, but it will have to be Friday. Would that be all right? I really would like to go out with you. Just this once."

Just this once echoed around and around in her head as she heard herself say, "Friday would be nice."

"Great," he said and stood. "I'll let you get back to work, now. I'll pick you up here after work on Friday. Okay?"

"Fine," she said, softly.

Then she looked up at him. "Wait. Would you tell me something before you go?"

"Sure."

"You said there were only a few others that knew about your invention. Are they the other girls?"

"That's right," he said. "Why?"

"Oh," Betty said. "I was just wondering if your other dates liked Bruce Springsteen, too."

Bruce laughed and patted her on the shoulder. "Nope. Judy is attracted to men who look like Paul McCartney and Ann likes soldiers. Francis, down at the sporting goods store gets real excited over jocks, and Cathy in my chemistry class literally drools over professor types. Everyone has different tastes. Lucky for me, I can change real fast. I'll see you Friday."

He patted her lightly on the shoulder again and headed for the door with literally everyone in the Faster-Than-Yours Burgers and Things watching him.

Betty laid her head down on the table, closed her eyes, and tried to calm the jealousy twisting her stomach into hard knots.

Four other women.

Lucky for him he could change fast?

How could she have been so stupid?

His words, "Just this once" echoed around in her mind.

One date.

Four other girls.

If she wanted to see him again, Friday was really going to have to be something.

That was the answer. She would make Friday a date to remember.

She stood and headed back for the counter, already planning the evening. She'd show that nerd a move or two.

Then, maybe on their second date, she'd get him to do something about those teeth.

Something in My Darling

A Bryant Street Story

Dean Wesley Smith

Canning Boone started to suspect something was wrong with Jenny a few days after they moved into their wonderful, three bedroom ranch home on Bryant Street.

She started smiling more.

Now Jenny, with her long brown hair, her round green eyes, and her solid, some would say obese body, had always laughed and smiled at times. Usually when eating.

But after they got settled in their new home, with their new kitchen and wonderful large recliners in front of the massive television screen, she started smiling more and talking about all sorts of wild stuff.

She mentioned losing weight.

That was the first time in six years of marriage she had used the term "losing weight." He would have been less surprised if she had said she was watching internet porn.

When she said that, he froze in his recliner, a spoonful of mashed potatoes halfway to his mouth from his dinner tray.

She went on not realizing he was shocked to his core and almost unable to take another bite. She said she loved the house so much that she wanted to get fit and enjoy it more, work in the yard on the flowers, maybe even plant a garden.

Canning managed to get back to eating, listening to her go on about such horrific ideas.

Now Canning hadn't married Jenny to have her suddenly get happy and thin and active. He had married her because he loved her pessimism, her often sharp and nasty way of looking at the world, and her ability to eat just about anything.

She could match him bite-for-bite.

He had never met a woman who could. That was why he fell in love with her, actually.

And he really loved her complete lack of any desire to do the things he hated, like sports or even walking too far.

The very idea of working in a garden just made him shudder. He paid thin people to do that.

So at first, for months, Canning ignored Jenny, nodding when he needed to, making no comments, hoping they would just settle into their normal routine. But then one morning she announced she had joined a gym and would be going there in the afternoon on her break from her job at Walmart.

He said nothing and she just smiled as she packed some "workout" clothes she had bought a few days before, showing him each bit of the outfit.

He managed to not shudder at the term "workout" and got off to his government job with a kiss from Jenny and one of her now frequent smiles.

But the day was ruined and not even four times through a buffet at lunch made him feel better.

What in the world had happened?

The only thing he could figure was that it was their new

home.

Or the subdivision. Maybe the Bryant Street Subdivision had cursed her.

He laughed at that thought and didn't even ask how her "workout" went.

But then he noticed that even though their meals together were normal in time and location in front of the television, she started eating less, not finishing platefuls of food as their parents had taught them.

And one night when they were out at their favorite Chinese restaurant, she even asked for a doggy bag to take some food home.

Shocked didn't begin to describe how he was feeling.

Socked and sad.

And afraid for Jenny's well-being. Since they had moved to Bryant Street, she seemed to be changing her personality. And there didn't seem to be a damn thing he could say about it.

So like any husband in his situation would do, he ate and said nothing. But he did a great deal of nodding.

As the next months went by, she showed him new cloths she had bought and by the end of six months it was clear she was really sick because she had lost so much weight. She would cook for him and then cook something different for herself. Usually something green.

They would eat in front of the television, but she would have one bite to his ten.

That was just wrong.

Even worse, the more weight she lost, the more energy she had. And the more energy she had, the more she talked about losing weight.

A horrid fifth circle of hell as far as he was concerned.

He had no doubt she was no longer the woman he had married. She didn't even look like the same woman.

Finally he could take it no longer.

"We need to move," he said.

"No," she said, not even turning from the sink where she was washing off some sort of cabbage.

If he hadn't already been sitting solidly on one of their heavy, wooden kitchen chairs, he might have fallen to the ground. And in Jenny's weakened condition and lighter weight, she never would have been able to help him up.

"No?" he asked.

"No," she said. "I like it here, this is my dream home, and I am staying."

"You can't afford to stay if I want to go," he said, deciding to be male macho, something he never had been and didn't play well.

She turned to him with one of those horrid new smiles on her face. "I forgot to tell you, but I am now a manager at the store, and I can afford this place better than you can."

"But this isn't who you are," he said. "I loved you for who you were, not this new person."

"I know," she said, still smiling. "You loved me because I had rolls of fat, because I could eat with you and as much as you, because I was as unhappy as you are every day. That was how we bonded."

"And what is wrong with that?"

Damn he wished he hadn't asked that question, but there it was, right out there in the kitchen.

"I don't want to be that person anymore," she said simply,

going back to washing off the vegetables in the sink. "I want to have energy, look at the world in a positive way, and be healthy."

"So what happened?" he asked, almost afraid of the answer.

She motioned around at the house. "I found the house of my dreams, the neighborhood I love, and a man I love with you. I decided I wanted to enjoy it, keep the house up, work on the yard and what needs to be done to this wonderful home, not just wallow inside it."

He saw nothing at all wrong with wallowing, but he said nothing. It was as he had feared, the house, the street had done this to her.

And he was going to lose her if he wasn't careful, if he already hadn't lost her.

That thought just scared him to death.

"So what do you want me to do?"

She beamed, a smile larger than he had ever seen before, and he had to admit, it made her more beautiful.

She wiped off her hands and opened a drawer and pulled out a folder and slid it to him. "I want you to make an appointment with this counselor and just talk with him."

"About what?" Canning asked, looking at the folder like it might just turn into a snake and bite him. He had a hunch what was in that folder was worse than any snake.

"About anything," she said. "I started going to her and talking with her soon after we moved in here because I wanted to understand why I couldn't enjoy this wonderful house."

"Will she help me understand what is happening with you?" he asked.

She smiled and nodded. "If that is important to you, yes."

"It is all that matters," he said.

With that she came over to him and kissed him. She was smiling, but there were tears in her eyes.

"Thank you," she said.

There just wasn't anything more he could say to that.

So he opened the folder and the snake bit him.

It took exactly three years to the day before he finished his first marathon run. He had started off at 410 pounds and ran the marathon at 165 pounds.

Scales in their bathroom were like gods they worshipped every day, sometimes twice a day.

Jenny had finished ahead of him in the marathon run, since this was her fifth. She was waiting and cheering for him at the finish line.

She gave him a huge smile and a long hug and then kiss.

He felt great about finishing, but what he really felt great about was that they could hit the buffet after the race and he could eat as much as he wanted. That was all he could think about for the last ten miles.

He and Jenny still bonded on the food.

And once again they could eat as much as they wanted. And when they wanted.

He still didn't much enjoy all the exercise to stay at the light weight. He doubted he ever would, but for Jenny's sake, he pretended to.

And they still lived on Bryant Street and Jenny took care of the yard and her garden. He didn't care.

All that mattered to him was that he could eat regular meals with Jenny.

Bite-for-bite. She matched him and he matched her.

And finally things were back to normal for them.

STORIES

BY

KRISTINE KATHRYN RUSCH

Name-Calling

Kristine Kathryn Rusch

S uch a simple decision, really, and yet it held her up. She couldn't say she would marry Van unless she knew what she would do about her name.

LizBet leaned back on the brown leather desk chair and stared out the wall of windows. Her office was in one of the tallest buildings in Portland, not quite on the top floor, but close enough. She could see the Columbia River and beyond to the mountain ranges narrowing into the Willamette Valley. Her desk, shiny oak, still smelled as woodsy as the day she bought it. Van had once teased her that she bought her furniture because it smelled good, not because it looked good.

She doodled on her Palm, the Mac humming on the credenza to her side. *Mrs. Van L. Lyndale. Elizabeth Lyndale. Elizabeth Lyndale-Hayes. Mrs. Elizabeth Hayes. Elizabeth Hayes-Lyndale.* She drew little hearts over the "I" in her first name, just as she had done in middle school, and made the period after "Mrs." Into a small flower. Then she sighed and erased it all, and glanced at her brag wall for reassurance.

Her undergraduate degree from Vassar read Elizabeth Hayes, and so did the sign on her desk. She was just beginning to get a reputation, and the reputation came under the name Hayes. If she dropped it, she would have to start all over again.

Van had said he wouldn't mind if she kept her name, and the statement, in the middle of a romantic dinner at her favorite restaurant near the river, had left her feeling unsettled. Even though she had expected the proposal, she hadn't thought of the name thing until that moment. And instead of the resounding "yes" she had planned, she had smiled weakly and had asked a chance to think it over.

She put the Palm away and returned to the notes she had been studying for the deposition she had at three.

She would have to decide—and soon.

~

LizBet canceled lunch with Van, pleading a heavy caseload, and instead called her sister, Maggie. They met at a coffee shop near LizBet's office. The shop had rickety tables and alternative music, old signs announcing Grunge Rock concerts, and posters of the Beats that probably dated from the late fifties. At the counter, LizBet ordered a double espresso and a croissant sandwich heavy on the veggies and herbed cream cheese, then took a table near the rain-streaked window to wait for her sister.

Maggie was a dressmaker who lived near Lewis and Clark College in an apartment as funky as the coffee shop. She made a marginal living full of occasional windfalls, and she spent her free time thinking about things. She hadn't gone to college; she said, at age twenty, that she still had time to review that decision later.

She was fifteen minutes late. She bustled into the shop,

raindrops glistening on her red and orange hair. As she hurried to the counter, she waved at LizBet, and while she ordered, she pulled the multicolored tasseled scarf that was supposed to protect her from the rain off her shoulders, and tied it around her waist. Her simple black shirt and skirt suddenly became an ensemble as fresh and personal as LizBet's suit was corporate.

"I don't see why this is an issue," Maggie said as she brought her latte to the table. "Your name is your identity, and you keep it."

"Lots of women don't," LizBet said.

"Professional women do. Look at Uma Thurman and Ethan Hawke."

"They're divorced."

Maggie waved her hand. "Not because of the name thing."

"We don't know that," LizBet said, knowing she was being unreasonable. "I mean, maybe it started there and little events made it worse and worse."

The girl behind the counter brought LizBet's sandwich on a clear glass plate. She also brought a handmade ceramic bowl full of tabouli for Maggie.

"You haven't said yes yet, have you?" Maggie asked.

"No, why?"

Maggie took a spoonful of the tabouli. The scent of vinegar and onions wafted toward LizBet. "Because this is clearly an issue for you and it shouldn't be. Beta, you're not twenty-one years old. You need to figure out why you are even considering losing your identity to some man. That's what our grandmothers did. And once you decide that, then you can see me about making your dress."

LizBet cut her sandwich into bite-sized pieces. "Van isn't some man."

Maggie snorted. "Yeah, right. He's the one who showed up when the world said, 'Time to get married.' Otherwise he's no different from all the other bozos you've been with. You watch. Three years from now, we'll be sitting at this same table, and you'll be saying, 'Mags, what did I ever see in that jerk?' just like you did about all the guys before."

"No, Maggie," LizBet said. "He's the right one."

"Uh-huh. That's why you can't decide what role to play. If he were Mister Right, you wouldn't have to play any roles at all."

~

LizBet refused to let herself think about marriage during the staff meetings. She left the office at seven, stopped at Safeway on the way to her apartment, bought ice cream for dinner and rented three movies: *The Philadelphia Story, Sleepless in Seattle,* and *Adam's Rib.* She ate Chocolate Ripple Fudge out of the carton while she watched, bare feet tucked under her sweats, her cat sleeping on the embroidered pillow beside her. She found herself wondering why Spencer Tracy had never left his wife, why Katharine Hepburn never married, and how anyone could divorce Cary Grant. She asked the cat how Nora Ephron, author of *Heartburn,* could write a romance as sweet as *Sleepless in Seattle*, and why nothing was as certain in real life. And she wished her mother was alive so she could ask what it was like to spend twenty years as a missus, and still remain even passingly sane.

Name-Calling

When the movie fest was over, and the ice cream was gone, she called up Van and asked him to give her three more days.

∽

"It causes problems," Zeke said. His jeans were rolled up to his calves and his bare feet were stuck in the sand. LizBet shivered in the cool ocean breeze. Gulls circled overhead, and children ran down to the water's edge, parents screaming cautions behind them.

She usually didn't take Saturdays off, but this time she felt she owed herself and Zeke, who had been her best friend since high school, loved the beach at Seaside. He had married his freshman year in college and his wife had kept her own name.

"I mean, we're constantly explaining to people that we are married and not just living together. And then there's the decision of what to name the kids. We thought maybe we'd let half of them take her name and half of them take mine—until it wasn't an issue anymore." He paused and dug his feet deeper in the sand. His mouth twisted slightly in the non-smile that had become routine whenever children were mentioned. Zeke and Audrey couldn't have children and they were the only people LizBet know who really, really wanted them. "So it's not as trivial as Maggie says. Besides, it says a lot about who you are."

"Who I am?" LizBet brushed a strand of hair from her face.

"Yeah." Zeke faced the water. "I mean, are you the kind of woman who takes marriage so lightly that you're not willing to make any changes? I've seen a lot of marriages end because the couples are unwilling to do the compromising necessary to live together."

"You and Audrey have been together over fifteen years."

He grinned, but still wouldn't look at her. "Well, then there's the kind of woman who is so sure of herself and her identity that she allows her husband to spend Saturday afternoon on a beach with another woman. Confidence. Audrey has confidence."

LizBet's throat was dry. "Did you talk about her changing her name?"

He shook his head. "We never discussed it."

"Not once?"

"Not at all."

∽

"So what does Van think?" Dani asked as she paused before her second serve. The tennis club was nearly empty at 7 a.m. on Sunday mornings, so Dani and LizBet picked that time as theirs. LizBet's white frou-frou tennis outfit—required wear, just like gym class only upscale—stuck to her back. Tennis was out, which was precisely why they liked it. It meant they had a sport all their own.

"Van?" Lizbet wiped the sweat off her forehead with the back of her wrist brace. "He says he doesn't mind."

Dani bounced a green ball against the ground, her first preparation for a serve. "*He doesn't mind?*"

"That's what he said."

"So nice of him to give you permission." Dani tossed the ball in the air and hit it with her racquet so hard that the sound echoed in the confined space.

The ball cleared the net and bounced. LizBet swung and

barely connected. The ball wobbled crazily before tripping over the top of the net. "He didn't give me permission," she said.

"Sure he did. He doesn't mind. If he didn't mind, he wouldn't mention it at all."

LizBet picked up the ball and tossed it back at Dani. "I think he was trying to reassure me."

Dani caught the ball with one hand. "I thought you said it wasn't a problem until he mentioned it."

LizBet swallowed. "How come all my friends try to put Van in a bad light?"

"We don't have to," Dani said, bouncing the ball once before she prepared to serve. "He does it so well himself."

∽

LizBet begged off the traditional post-tennis brunch and went back to her apartment. She picked up the phone to call Van, then hung up. She had asked for three days and only used two. And she wasn't thinking very clearly. Who was she, listening to Dani? Dani had never been married. Dani thought all men were evil and out to get women. Dani believed every woman who screamed sexual harassment and believed that all men were after only one thing. Dani did not believe in shades of gray.

With a sigh, LizBet sank into her scratched pine kitchen chair. But Dani had placed her finger on the very thing that was bothering LizBet. The comment that started the whole inquiry. Her name. *Her* name, not his.

This time she did pick up the phone and hit the speed dial. Van answered on the second ring.

"How about meeting me for brunch at Capewell's?" she said, without preamble.

"What about the sisterly morning with Dani?" he said, his emphasis on the word "sisterly" making her wince.

"She beat me soundly. My mind wasn't on the game."

"What was it on?" he asked, his voice sinking into a lower register.

"You," she said, and felt odd as if she were lying. "And changing my name."

He sucked in air. She frowned. That comment could be taken too many ways. "Does that mean—?"

"Nothing," she said. "It means I'm still thinking. Look, I'll get us a reservation for 11 and I'll meet you there. Oh, and Van, the reservation will be in my name."

~

Capewell's was a new restaurant on the Columbia River downtown. It had a spectacular view of the bridges crisscrossing the city and of the buildings that made Portland feel like new money. The restaurant was fancy, and it was expensive. She wasn't sure why she chose it. It always made her feel uncomfortable—and not just because the prices were outrageous. Because, the place felt like a special place, a place she had always expected a man to propose.

LizBet arrived late. Her stomach growled, unused to going so long without food after her weekly tennis match. Van had a table down three small flights of stairs and pressed up against the window. He was nursing a cup of coffee, and had already bunched up the white linen table cloth.

She nodded to the maître d' and stood on the steps for a moment, just watching Van. He was striking in a forties movie star sort of way. His features were chiseled, his nose aquiline, his skin darkly tan. He had dark black hair, and dreamy blue eyes. When he saw her, he stood.

Old fashioned. Of course, he would give her permission. She had liked old fashioned, she thought, like Cary Grant and Clark Gable. Only the movie star Gable wouldn't have cared if his wife kept her name, and Grant would have chided her, but in a loving fashion. Hanks, Ephron's modern sex symbol, would have said nothing at all.

As Van slipped back into his seat, he glanced at her and she saw a new expression on his face: uncertainty.

He was a contractor, and had been since high school. He worked for one of the best in the city. He was a man used to dealing with men, a man whose hands bore the scars of hard labor.

He was as different from her as rain was from sunshine.

"Hello," she said.

He nodded. Then he set his coffee cup down and put his hands on the seat beside him as if he didn't know what to do with them. "I was going to order for us, but I thought I'd better wait."

"Thanks," she said. This hesitancy didn't suit him. And she had caused it.

"Look, Beta, I'm sorry—." He sighed, ran a hand through his thick hair, and glanced out the window. Then he glanced at her. "When I proposed, I didn't expect this. A hearty yes, maybe or an are you kidding? But not this. Three days of silence, of not knowing how you feel at all. And then your sister calls me and chastises me for trying to make you change your name—"

"Mags called you?"

He nodded, his lips a thin line. His hair, tousled over his tanned forehead, made him look like a three-year-old boy fresh out of school instead of a man who'd been on his own for years. "I didn't say you should take my name, Beta."

"I know," she said. "You just told me it would be okay with you if I kept mine."

"Isn't that right? I mean, it's up to you these days, isn't it?"

"It is," she said. "And I'm having trouble deciding."

"Deciding?"

"What to call myself."

His eyes widened for a moment, then he seemed to get his expression under control. "Does that mean…?"

"I don't know," she said. "I don't know why this bothers me so much. Mags says—well, forget what Mags says. Zeke says it's all about identity, and Dani says you took the choice away from me by telling me it was okay."

"And what do you say?" His tone was low. It had a thread of anger in it.

"I say I've never been more confused in my life."

The waiter set down two mimosas, then took their order brusquely as if he could tell from their posture that they needed privacy. LizBet tapped her fingernails against the crystal.

"I mean," she said without missing a beat, "it's my dad's name, not mine, and it was given to him by his dad, and his dad before him, right? And Elizabeth is my mother's name, and LizBet is what they called me to distinguish me from her, and Beta is my friends' nickname for me. I wanted people to call me

Beth in school, but no one did, except one girl who kept forgetting and calling me Liz which is worse, but really, Van, it's not like I'm deciding the fate of a nation here. I'm only deciding what to have people call me."

Van took a sip of the mimosa, grimaced, and set it down. "No," he said. "You're deciding how you want people to perceive you."

LizBet stopped tapping her fingernails. She gripped the glass's stem as if the crystal's fragility could give her support. "What?"

He spread his fingers on the bunched linen and stared at them. "I thought about this before asking you. Whether or not a woman like you would want to marry. Your mother didn't have a career, and Maggie has made certain every man around her knows that she has chosen to live her life alone because she's afraid that a companion will take it over. Then I thought about how I would feel if you asked me to change my name—" he looked up "—and I considered it, I really did, but my name is all anybody knows me by. Then I remembered how your name is on the door of your office and on the company stationary, and I figured if you married at all you would do it under the same terms as me, and so I asked, in my inept way, and I wanted to reassure you that you don't have to fend me off with a stick like Maggie does, that it's okay to be the same woman you are now because you're the one I fell in love with."

LizBet drew in her breath. If he hadn't spoken in so many run-on sentences, she would have thought someone scripted his lines for him. She could almost hear Spencer Tracy (it *was* a Spencer Tracy speech from a movie like *Woman of the Year* or *Adam's Rib*), still masculine, but confused about the changing roles, willing to play along, but not willing to give up an essential masculine part of himself. And perfect, so perfect. If this were an old movie, she would be in his arms, bunching up the tablecloth herself in her haste to kiss him.

But no cameras were rolling, and no matter how hard she tried, she couldn't be Katharine Hepburn.

"It's not you," LizBet said. She looked down, the sudden realization embarrassing her. "It's me. I'm like Mags. I don't think I can be a wife and a person at the same time."

～

The future wasn't supposed to be like this. She lay back on the warm wood, sweat running down her stomach, her skin already pink even though she had only been in the sauna for a few minutes. Her mother's generation was supposed to have fought this fight. It was supposed to be easy to be a wife, a mother, and a climber on the corporate ladder. She had a lot of opportunities growing up. Everyone told her she was equal to the boys. She knew she wasn't going to be her father's daughter, or her husband's wife. She would be a person in her own right.

A strong woman.

Who didn't need a man.

And somehow she had gone from a woman who didn't need a man to a woman who was afraid to be with one. Afraid that all the magic and promise that she had felt as a little girl would disappear when she said, "I do."

So simple and yet so hard. It wasn't as if she could just marry Van now that she made the realization. If anything, the realization made marriage tougher. She would constantly be on guard, constantly vigilant, punishing him for things that had nothing to do with him and everything to do with her past and her perceptions.

Sweat poured down her body. Her throat ached from the dry heat. Her skin was rosy. She hadn't realized that she could choose something other than the extremes represented by her mother and her sister. She could remain herself.

But only if she had a man who understood the dilemma. A man like Zeke.

Or like Van.

～

"I think it's wrong," Maggie said, her mouth full of pins. She was kneeling, pinning the hem on LizBet's white satin dress. She wanted a simple ceremony, she had said to Van, not too traditional. He had insisted that it be dressy and that a few friends be there. *I want people to know we're proud to be together*, he said. *They need to know that.* "He'll want you to stay home and make babies."

"Men and women make babies together," LizBet said. She'd been having this argument with Maggie for two weeks, ever since she had let her know about the wedding. "Besides, neither of us want children."

"And what about your political career?"

"What political career?"

"The one you would have had if you hadn't met him."

LizBet frowned at her reflection in the full length mirror. The white set off her skin, the gathered waist gave the dress a festive feel. Perfect for dancing. Even if Maggie didn't approve, she was designing a hell of a dress.

"I never wanted a political career," LizBet said.

"But Vassar—"

"Gave me an excellent education." She sighed. "Are you almost done?"

"One more pin." Maggie stuck the pin in the hem then took the remaining pins from her mouth and placed them in her tray. "Well," she said, leaning back and surveying the dress. "It's not what Mother would have wanted."

LizBet grinned. "Mother got married in brocade covered with a thousand tiny seed pearls. Have you seen those pictures? She looked like she was wearing armor."

"She needed to."

LizBet crouched down beside her sister. Pins poked her legs. "It's not a battle, Mags. I'm not trying to vanquish an enemy here. I'm just trying to share a life with another person."

"He'll change you," Maggie said.

"Oh, probably. And I'll probably change him. That's normal." LizBet stood. "Can you unzip me?"

Maggie stood also and took a step back to examine the dress. She scanned LizBet's length, then reached up for the zipper. "I still think you should wear heels."

"They hurt my feet."

"They flatter your legs."

The zipper let go and the dress's softness gathered around LizBet's waist. LizBet caught it so that it wouldn't slip to the floor. Not white lace and promises, but still a special dress that made her feel pretty. Maggie understood with her art, even if she didn't understand with her mind.

Name-Calling

"Thanks for the dress," LizBet said.

"You're welcome," Maggie said and turned away, but not before LizBet caught the shine of tears in her sister's gray eyes.

∽

Maggie gave her away, and Zeke was her maid of honor. They didn't ask her what changes she would make. Neither did Van. They figured, apparently, that she had already made her decision. And she had.

After the ceremony, the entire wedding party shuffled into the minister's office. The minister spread the marriage certificate on the desk. LizBet used Van's pen and more than the usual flourish, signed first her mother's name, Elizabeth, and then her father's, Hayes. In parenthesis, she added the name given her by the people she loved the most—Beta—not to indicate that she was second in importance, but to indicate that she was who she had always been and no one else.

She watched as Van signed his name. Then they linked fingers—two strong independent people, facing the future, together.

Something Blue

Kristine Kathryn Rusch

"Gram," Amelia said for the fifteenth time. She was hunched in the passenger seat of her grandmother's 1968 Cadillac, elbow catching on the armrest's silver ashtray. "I don't need a marriage counselor."

"Wedding," Gram said, perching her right wrist on the top of the steering wheel while she pushed up her glasses with her left forefinger. "Wedding counselor. And you do, girl. You didn't listen to me that last time."

Amelia sighed. Her grandmother would never let her forget the divorce, not because Gram disapproved—she'd been through three husbands herself—but because Gram said that Amelia had made a fatal mistake.

She had looked behind her as she walked up the aisle.

Gram had said that meant Amelia would regret her wedding day for the rest of her life. And Amelia did regret that day, more than she could ever state to her improper and fun-loving grandmother.

Gram fishtailed around a corner, honked at a ten-year-old boy on the side of the tree-lined country road, and waved. The kid, looking startled, waved back.

"You know him?" Amelia asked.

"Should I?" Gram said.

Amelia shook her head. All her life, she had lived in awe of Gram. When Amelia was a little girl, Gram ironed the curls out of her still-black hair, and wore mini-skirts showing off legs that were better than those of most teenagers. When Amelia was a teenager, Gram wore hip-huggers and floral print shirts, but eschewed granny dresses because she'd already worn them in a previous incarnation. When Amelia got married the first time, Gram had shown up at the wedding with six pierced earring holes in each ear, and new diamond studs in each.

Now Gram wore her gray curls in an above-the-ear bob and was talking about getting her eyebrows pierced. She was dating two different men: a real estate broker twenty years her junior, and a retired pilot ten years her senior. Neither man knew of the other, and Gram had hilarious stories about sending one man out the back door as the other man came in the front. Gram had nothing against extra-marital sex, even in these days of AIDS, but she did take marriage seriously.

Very seriously.

Too seriously.

First she tried to talk Amelia out of this second wedding, but since Amelia couldn't be talked, Gram was determined to make her do it right.

"Where are we going?" Amelia asked, as she peered out the window. When she had finally agreed to come along with Gram, she hadn't expected to leave Beaver Dam, let alone find herself in the middle of the Horicon Marsh. She had memories of the Marsh that dated back to when she was a little girl. Gram had been on husband #2 then, and they had lived in Theresa, just north and east of the Marsh. Whenever Amelia's folks took her there, they always stopped on the side of the road, hoping to see wild birds in the reed-filled water. Sometimes they did. Usually they didn't.

"You'll see," Gram said.

"Gram, if we go much farther, I'm going to insist on driving."

"And who, I want to know, is missing points from her license?" Gram snapped. "Certainly not the elderly woman driving the car."

Amelia sighed and sank lower in the front seat. *Yes but*, she thought and didn't say, *who has twenty-twenty vision? Who's not wearing bifocals that constantly slip to the edge of her nose? Who drives with both hands on the wheel? Certainly not the elderly woman driving the car.*

Maybe that was the problem. Gram said whatever she thought, but Amelia never spoke back to her grandmother. And Amelia was three years away from forty. It was time she spoke up.

Besides, she was beginning to get carsick from the pine-scented air fresher hanging from the rearview mirror.

"Gram," Amelia said. "If this wedding counselor is so good, how come you didn't use her?"

"I did," Gram said. "With Willard."

Willard. Well, there was no arguing that then. Willard had been Gram's third and last husband. The love of her life. Willard had been three hundred pounds of extremely nice male who had treated Gram with the respect—and caution—that any wild animal deserved. Willard had stayed with her for five years, then died of heart failure in his sleep one cold November night.

Gram never remarried.

Even though she'd had regular "visitors" from that December on.

"I want you to have what Willard and I had," Gram said into Amelia's silence.

"I do," Amelia said. "Scott's wonderful. He's the nicest man I know."

"He's the nicest man you know now," Gram said. "But you used those exact same words about Whatshisname."

"Ralph," Amelia said.

"Ralph." Gram shook her head. "You know, you should pay attention to names. They're a sign. How could you fall in love with someone named Ralph? The name is slang for—"

"I *know*," Amelia said. That joke had ceased being funny in the first month she dated Ralph. "And he was the nicest man I knew. Then. Scotty's nicer."

"Ralph was not nice," Gram said. "Ralph only pretended to be nice."

"If he only pretended to be nice," Amelia said, "why'd you let me marry him?"

"Who could stop you? Besides, you knew."

"I knew what?"

"That it was a mistake. Otherwise, you wouldn't have looked back."

Amelia sighed. Gram had a superstitious streak that was a bit surprising given her practical and adventurous nature. When she played gin, she never touched the cards until the last one was dealt, thinking that to peek beforehand would ruin her luck.

When one famous person died, she always expected two more in related fields to go because, she said, famous people died in threes. And she never went into New Age stores that carried crystals because, she said, too many crystals in one place affected her psychic energy. Amelia had always thought that meant Gram shouldn't go into jewelry stores either—and she should stay away from the salt and sugar aisles in the grocery store, but Gram never quite got the connection.

"Gram, I looked back," Amelia said, "because of you."

"Don't go into that again," Gram said.

"I did," Amelia said, "because you whispered that my train was wrapped around my heels."

"I was in front of you at the time. I didn't expect you to believe me."

"Gram," Amelia said. "My train was not wrapped around my heels."

Gram shrugged, then turned the wheel slightly with her wrist, following the curve of the road. "So my eyesight ain't what it used to be."

"Gram, that was fifteen years ago. Is your eyesight worse now?"

"No," Gram said. "It got better. The miracles of modern science."

Amelia tilted her head back in the seat. "Gram, I'm beginning to think you did that on purpose."

"So what if I did?" Gram said. "You shouldn't've married a Ralph."

"I *loved* him."

"You only thought you loved him, dear," Gram said. "Trust me, I know."

Amelia closed her eyes and gave up. She loved her grandmother dearly but sometimes there was no arguing with her. Especially when Gram's mind was made up, as it had been from the first day she met Ralph.

Not good enough for you, Gram had said.

He's the CEO of a software company, Gram, and that's a burgeoning industry. We'll be rich by the time I'm thirty.

Rich isn't everything, my girl, Gram had said. *Besides, you've got twice the intelligence he does.*

So?

So, you'll get bored. And I'll bet he's not good in bed.

Gram!

Believe me, I can tell which ones are, my girl. He'll be finished before you've started.

Gram!

Think I don't know about such things? Your grandfather—

I don't want to know, Gram.

You should listen, honey.

No, Gram. I really don't want to know.

But Gram had been right. The software company went belly-up, Ralph was a poor conversationalist, and he approached sex like it was a one-minute mile. But how was Amelia supposed to know? He'd looked good on paper, and she'd been good herself. She'd been the only girl she knew who'd been a virgin when she got married.

The first time, anyway. This time, she test-drove the model before she decided to live with it. Scott was six-foot-seven with gentle brown eyes and a smile that softened his already round face. He was not graceful, and during the first hour she knew him, he'd hit his head on the doorway into the restaurant to which they went on a blind date, shattered the crystal chandelier, and accidentally kicked over another diner's chair—two tables away. After that debacle, they decided that Scott was not meant for fancy restaurants. He was more at home—well, at home—where the doorways were high enough, the light fixtures were made of plastic, and the other diners, when invited, were used to Scott kicking them under the table.

He was not athletic, except in bed, and he was at least as smart as she was. She'd compared their IQs. And he was a successful geneticist at the University of Wisconsin—a good researcher and one of the best teachers in the department.

He was also shy, which she saw as a good point; it had prevented him from asking other women out. She wouldn't have met him at all if a mutual friend hadn't forced them to see each other.

A mutual friend.

Not Gram.

Gram was still skeptical. She didn't see any fireworks, she said. No spark. He was smart, yes, but how was he going to use those smarts? And he lacked people skills. Always a failing, she said.

A serious failing.

But he's good in bed, Amelia had said.

I don't want to know, Gram had said with a familiar tone of distaste.

You wanted to know about Ralph.

I wanted to warn you about Ralph, Gram had said. *That one was obvious.*

Well, Scott should be obvious too.

Gram had shrugged. *If the size of his hands are any indication,* she said, *of course he's—*

Gram, Amelia had said. *Don't go there.*

You're the one who mentioned it, Gram had said.

And Amelia had given up.

Gram pulled into a driveway and stopped.

Amelia had been so caught up in thoughts of Scott that she hadn't been paying attention. Now she looked at her surroundings. They were still on the highway, but just past the marsh. They hadn't reached a town yet, or if they had, she couldn't tell. The driveway Gram had pulled into was more like a gravel yard. It extended three car lengths in the front, and at least two car widths. At the far end of the driveway was a brown ranch house that badly needed paint. Two flower boxes sat outside, with dead flowers wilting over the sides. A rusted tricycle lay on its side beneath the only tree, a weeping willow that looked as if it too were on its last legs.

Gram shut off the car.

"This can't be it," Amelia said.

Gram gave her a withering look. Amelia had cringed from that look her whole life. It meant *I certainly hope you're not going to make comments like that when we're inside.*

Amelia ducked her head and mumbled, hoping Gram would take that for an apology. Actually, Amelia felt that Gram owed her an apology for wasting her day and forcing her to go to a place she had no desire to go. She could have stayed home and caught up on her soaps. Her new job in the research area of the Department of Natural Resources gave her bank holidays off, and she felt as if she were only working half as hard as the rest of the population.

She was enjoying that.

Gram opened her car door and got out, her tennis shoes crunching on the gravel. Amelia had worn suede boots, an obvious mistake in this environment. The boots had no real sole and were designed for city walking—pavement, carpeting, with plenty of rests in between.

She felt each stone in the gravel as clearly as if she'd been barefoot.

"No dawdling," Gram said as she scurried for the front door.

Amelia suppressed a sigh. She wanted to dawdle. She wanted to get back in the car, and head for the marsh. Even that would be more interesting than this place.

She picked her way across the gravel. By the time she reached the stoop, the door was already open. A middle-aged woman with light brown hair was smiling at Gram.

"Mrs. Sparks," the woman said, and Amelia was surprised to hear, not the flat vowels of the Midwest, but the clipped tones of an upper class British accent. "And I suppose this is your granddaughter."

"Yes," Gram said. She held out a hand, as if Amelia's slow approach to the porch had been intentional. "Amelia, say hello to Sophie Danner."

Amelia smiled and said hello just as her grandmother had asked. Sophie Danner was not what Amelia had expected. She had thought to see a woman of her grandmother's age and of the temperament common to most women of that generation—most women but Gram.

Sophie Danner had to be Amelia's age.

Or younger.

Sophie stood away from the door, and Gram went in, as if

she had done so a hundred times. Amelia followed, wincing at the stale smell of boiled cabbage and garlic. Sophie herself smelled faintly of sweat as if she'd been cleaning house or sitting in the sun, and hadn't had time to shower yet. She wore a faded gold t-shirt with a logo Amelia had never seen before, and blue jeans one size too small. Her feet were bare, and her toenails were painted a vivid green.

"Do make yourself comfortable," Sophie said. She cleared some papers off the red and black plaid couch, and tossed them on the floor. They covered a gray carpet that was so thin that Amelia could see the wood underneath. Sophie took more papers off the matching easy chair, and sat down.

Amelia sat too.

Gram was thumbing through a pile of pictures scattered on the dining room table. "Your latest project?" Gram asked.

"No, no. It was an unsuccessful. The wife wants me to see what went wrong, to see if the problem was in the ceremony or the man."

"What do you think?" Gram asked.

"Upside down flowers, no wedding cake, and no rings," Sophie said. "Of course they weren't going to last the year."

Amelia suppressed the urge to groan, and then wondered how she had gotten in the habit of suppressing all her reactions around Gram.

"My granddaughter," Gram said, "doesn't believe in this."

"Wedding counseling?" Sophie looked shocked. "Your grandmother told me about your turning to look at the back of the church at your last wedding. Of course it failed."

"Of course," Amelia mumbled.

"It's good you divorced him. Regret is a terrible thing to stare at day in and day out."

"I was young," Amelia said.

Sophie smiled and clapped her hands together. "Of course you were," she said. "It's amazing what we learn as we age. It's rather difficult to admit we don't control our universe, but once you've made that admission, you can slip right over it, and control the things you can control. Right?"

"Right," Amelia said, not understanding a word Sophie had just said.

"Good." Sophie leaned forward. "Let's discuss your plans."

Gram was holding a picture and peering over its edge at Amelia. In a moment of weakness, Amelia had blabbed all the plans to Gram. Amelia couldn't well lie about them now.

Not without Gram correcting her.

And Amelia had never been fast on her feet, at lying in any rate.

"I suppose you want to hear the unusual parts first," she said, looking at Sophie.

Sophie pursed her lips together. "Actually," she said, "Let's talk intent. Church wedding or civil ceremony?"

"I hardly see how that's relevant," Amelia said.

"You'd be surprised," Sophie said. "The church often counteracts superstition."

"So you recommend a civil ceremony?" Amelia asked.

"Of course not," Sophie snapped. "I prefer church. It makes my job so much easier."

"*Counter*acts, Amelia," Gram said as if that clarified the matter.

"Oh," Amelia said, sounding as dumb as she felt. "Church. Scott's parents insisted."

"His parents are still alive. Good," Sophie said.

Amelia frowned. She wasn't that old, was she? Old enough to make the groom's parents survival suspect?

"Look," Amelia said, wanting the experience over with, "why don't you just tell me what you need to know and I'll tell you what Scott and I decided. How's that?"

"Charming," Sophie said. "It'll work best for all concerned."

Gram humphed and set the pictures down. She stayed in the dining room, though, as if she expected her presence to be a distraction.

It was.

No one could ignore Gram for long.

"Tell me about your dress," Sophie said. "I do hope you didn't chose white. You were married before, and therefore you're not a virgin, are you?"

"Damn close," Gram said.

"Gram!" Amelia felt her face flush. "No, I'm not a virgin—" and her flush grew deeper as she wondered how many secrets of her life she was willing to tell this woman "—and my dress is not white, although I'm not sure how that matters."

"In this country, white is for virgin brides. But if you're not a virgin, and you wear white, someone will die before the year's out." Sophie spoke of the impending event with unearthly calm.

"Someone? Who someone?" Amelia said. "The wife? The husband?"

"Yes," Sophie said. "Generally the husband. You know that white is the color of mourning in China, don't you?"

"How is that relevant?" Amelia asked.

"She just told you," Gram said.

Amelia clasped her hands tightly in her lap. She was doing this for Gram, she reminded herself. It was one short afternoon out of her life. She was doing it for Gram.

"My dress is blue," Amelia said. "It's real simple with—"

"Blue?" Sophie said. She shook her head. "That won't do, young lady."

Now Amelia was a young lady? This from a woman about her own age. This time she did look at Gram, and let all her annoyance show. Gram shrugged and picked up one of the discarded pictures, feigning interest.

"What's wrong with blue?" Amelia asked, knowing she was opening a door that should have remained closed.

"Blue," Sophie said. "It's a sign that your lover has been untrue."

"Oh, come on," Amelia said. "How can that be? What about something borrowed, something blue?"

"Something old and something new." Sophie leaned back on the couch. "Yes, I can see how you'd perceive that as a conflict. All those things are required for the perfect ceremony, but they're generally small, you know, like a ribbon of blue through a garter. It's rather like Jimmy Carter; it gives the husband permission to have lust in his heart, but not anywhere else. An entire dress, however, an entire dress is another matter. Has Scott been unfaithful to you, my dear?"

Scott? Gentle, gawky Scott who couldn't talk to a woman he was attracted to without accidentally breaking half the objects in the room around him? Scott, who confessed the night he fell into bed with her (literally fell; he got tangled in his pants) that he'd only slept with one other women in all his forty years, and he hoped she wouldn't think him too inexperienced? That Scott?

"Of course not," Amelia snapped.

"Fiancées are often the last to know," Sophie said.

"Why in God's name would a man get married if he were having an affair when he was engaged?" Amelia asked.

"Peer pressure?" Gram said.

Amelia ignored her.

Sophie just stared at her. "There is no understanding men, is there?"

"No." Amelia stood. "There's no understanding you. Why would what color I wear at my wedding affect the rest of my life?"

"Amelia—" Gram said in her sternest voice.

"Don't lecture me," Amelia said, rather surprised at her own forcefulness. "I have a right to know. What does it matter?"

"Your wedding day is the most important day of your life," Sophie said, "and that plays a part in the power of the superstitions attached. They work. You'll see. I can even point to one in your life—"

"Yes, yes, the infamous looking back down the aisle, as if I believe that," Amelia said.

"No, although that is a good example," Sophie said. "I suspect another one influenced you even more. Did they throw rice or bird seed at you and your first husband as you left the ceremony?"

"Rice," Amelia said, feeling rooted to the spot. Why couldn't she get away from this place of perverse craziness?

"Long grain, brown, or instant?"

"I don't know, probably instant knowing our friends," Amelia said.

"Well then," Sophie said. "There you have it."

"Have what?"

"Why you don't have children."

"How do you know I don't have children?"

"Because your guests threw Minute Rice," Sophie said.

"Probably explains other things as well," Gram said.

"Gram," Amelia growled, startled to hear the same tone in her own voice as the one Gram often took with her.

Gram shut up.

"That's not proof of anything," Amelia said. "We used birth control. We didn't have a lot of sex after a while. All of those were factors."

"All of those were *results*," Sophie said.

"Of instant rice?" Amelia asked.

"Of course," Sophie said. "The tradition is bird seed to promote fertility. Many children which was the point of marriage, at least when the tradition was developed. That got converted to rice, which was less effective, and so many people throw that chemically treated stuff, which is not effective at all."

"My god," Amelia said. "Gram, are you paying this woman for this nonsense?"

"That's none of your business," Gram said. "This is a present."

"Some present," Amelia said, out loud. Then she realized what she had done, and the realization scared her. Apparently the days of stifling her responses to Gram were gone. "Do you actually believe this crap? If I wear white, my husband will die. If I wear blue, he'll have an affair. If I fail to provide my guests with bird seed, I won't have children, as if the tubal ligation I had three years ago will have nothing to do with it."

"Amelia," Gram said.

"No," Amelia said, not willing to stop, even though she knew that was what Gram wanted. "I can't believe you're perpetrating this—this—this—garbage. Marriage is about choice. It's about choices made every day, by people with guts. People make mistakes, and they live through them. Not because they wore blue at their wedding, but because they chose to. They decided to work on the marriage, they decided to stay together, they decided to continue loving each other."

"It is not that simple," Sophie said, holding up a hand.

"Is what I'm saying *simple*?" Amelia asked. "It sounds a lot harder than trying to make one day of your life perfect. I'm sorry to insult you ladies, but do you really expect me to believe I have no control over my life? That everything is governed by superstition and the simple things we do to ward off the evil eye?"

"Yes," Sophie said.

"Are you even married?" Amelia asked her. The sarcasm that came out of Amelia's mouth was an unfamiliar, at least around Gram. Amelia only used that tone at work, and then she used it with microbes that didn't belong in people's water supplies, things that she didn't expect to appear in her electron microscope.

"I'm divorced," Sophie said, head down.

"Oh, for godsake," Amelia said.

"It's not what you think," Sophie said.

Amelia looked at Gram who was standing straight as a post, the photographs bending in her hand.

"What do I think?" Amelia asked.

"That these things didn't work for me," Sophie said. "But I discovered Wedding Counseling after my divorce."

"So why didn't you marry again?"

"Because it's more likely for a woman my age to be killed by terrorists—"

"I hate that statistic," Amelia said. "Every single woman over thirty recites it like it's the damn Bible, and no one remembers that that study was disproved. The methodology was faulty."

She had yelled the last. Her words echoed in the small living room. The flush she had felt earlier returned to her face.

"I'm sorry about your gift, Gram." Then she bowed slightly to Sophie. "And I'm sorry if I insulted you. But this just isn't for me."

"It should be," Sophie said. "I haven't had a failure yet, not in 152 consultations."

Amelia sighed. The reasons for that could be a hundred fold. It might simply be that Sophie's group of clients were self-selecting for the desire to make their marriages work. It might be that they were a statistical anomaly.

It might even be that the superstitions and her wardings worked.

Amelia didn't care. She wasn't going to follow dumb superstitions, and she wasn't going to listen to a woman who hadn't made a good marriage herself.

"I'd like to leave, Gram," she said, and headed for the door. When she reached it, she turned and saw Gram give Sophie an envelope. Gram was apologizing for Amelia's rudeness as Amelia left.

Amelia went down the cracked stoop to the gravel drive. Birds flying overhead, going to the Horicon Marsh, cawed. A slight breeze blew over her, and it blew away the stale air from the interior of the house. She had never acted like that around Gram before. In fact, she rarely lost her temper at all. But she didn't like the pap this woman had been serving, and she couldn't remain silent about it.

Somehow, the silence made her feel as if she were perpetuating the beliefs.

And she couldn't. She couldn't change her plans no matter how much Gram wanted it. This was Amelia's wedding, the one she was planning with Scott. And it was her marriage, with Scott. And it was up to them to make it work. If they failed, she didn't want to hire Sophie to scan their wedding pictures. Amelia wanted a real human accounting, a way of knowing where she and Scott had gone wrong.

The door closed behind her. She cringed, then turned. Gram was walking alone down the short sidewalk. She was clutching her purse to her chest. "I'd like you to drive," she said.

"I'm sorry, Gram," Amelia said as she started across the gravel.

"Don't be," Gram said. "This had the desired effect."

Amelia stopped. "What do you mean?"

"You won't talk to me," Gram said. "You let me blather, and you smile and say, 'Yes Gram' as if I've already gone senile. Well, I haven't. And you made a terrible marriage the last time, even though you're not willing to admit it, and I didn't want you to make a terrible marriage this time."

"Sophie's ideas are not what I need," Amelia said.

"I know, and thank God for that," Gram said.

The breeze blew Amelia's hair in her face. She brushed it back with her left hand. "I thought you believed Sophie."

"Oh, I think she has a valuable talent. I think she has the ability to make people see their future marriages clearly. I think if I had brought you here when you were going to marry Ralph, you would have decided to call off the wedding."

"So you don't buy this blue thing, this bird seed stuff."

"No," Gram said. "I wore black when I married Willard, or don't you remember?"

"I remember," Amelia said. "But I don't know what it means."

"It means," Gram said, "that you're sad about the wedding, maybe even that you're doing it against your will."

"But you loved Willard."

"Of course I loved Willard."

"And you were the happiest I ever saw you that day."

"Of course I was," Gram said.

"Then that just proves that Sophie's wrong."

"No," Gram said.

"No?" Amelia asked.

"No," Gram repeated. "It means that when I came to see Sophie and we discussed the wedding, I realized how much I wanted my marriage to be successful, and how hard I was willing to work to make it go that way. Which, if you'll recall that little speech you gave us in there, is exactly what you said about Scott."

Amelia turned slightly so that her hair wouldn't keep blowing in her face. "You could have just asked me."

"I did," Gram said. "You always told me that he was a nice man and I shouldn't worry, which is exactly what you said about whatshisname."

"Ralph."

"Ralph," Gram said and shook her head. "How you could marry a name like that, I'll never know."

"Don't start, Gram."

Gram shrugged and walked to the car. Amelia hurried behind her. Gram climbed into the passenger seat and stuck the keys in the ignition. Amelia slid into the driver's side.

"You mean you went through this whole charade just to learn if I loved Scott and would work on our marriage?"

"Yes," Gram said.

"Why?"

"You mean besides the fact that I love you and want only the best for you?"

"That goes without saying, Gram," Amelia said. She pushed the seat back so that her knees weren't crammed into the steering wheel.

"Well," Gram said, "it's because you're nearly forty. If I had married Willard when I was forty—and I knew him then—we would have had thirty wonderful years together instead of five. Five simply wasn't enough. Thirty wouldn't have been either, but it would have been better—"

Her voice broke. Amelia put her arm around Gram's shoulder and pulled her close. "All I wanted," Gram said against Amelia's collarbone, "is to make sure you have a Willard in your life. Every girl deserves at least one."

"I do, Gram," Amelia said softly.

"I know that now," Gram said. She pushed away and dabbed at her eyes with her thumb. "Will you drive? I have bridge club at seven."

"Sure, Gram," Amelia said.

She turned the key and the car started, its motor humming. She took a deep breath.

"Gram," she said. "Thanks. No one has ever given me a gift like this."

"What gift?" Gram asked.

Amelia turned slightly in her seat. "I thought you said this was a present."

"The visit was and you didn't want it."

"But you gave it to me anyway."

"You shouldn't thank me for something you didn't want."

Amelia frowned. "But it turned out all right."

"Well, it did, but that's no reason to thank me." Gram pushed a button on the door, and her window came down, letting in that errant breeze.

"Why not?"

"It worked because of you, my girl," Gram said. She leaned her head back and closed her eyes.

Amelia stared at her for a moment, still uncertain about what to make of her Grandmother, even though they'd been close her entire life.

"I suppose you and Scott will want to visit me," Gram said, eyes still closed.

"Of course," Amelia said.

"Regularly," Gram said.

"Yes," Amelia said.

Gram sighed. "Then I'll have to move."

"Why?"

"Or raise my chandelier. Which will be cheaper, do you think?"

Amelia put the car into reverse. "Raising your chandelier."

"Good," Gram said. "I rather like the house." She opened her eyes. "I think you should let me drive."

"No, Gram," Amelia said.

"Then get us out on the highway, my girl," Gram said. "Time's wasting. You young people never understand how important these small moments are."

Amelia grinned. "I think we do, Gram," she said. "I think we do."

Canopy

Kristine Kathryn Rusch

They insisted on getting married in the mountains on Christmas Eve day. I drove halfway across the county to find them, adjusting my tie, wondering if I should have worn boots instead of my scuffed work shoes. Rain washed the window—hard, driving rain of a kind we hadn't seen in years—and the wipers couldn't keep up.

I found the road, a gravel driveway off a side street in a rural neighborhood, closer to the coast than I would have liked. Had I known it was this far out, I would have told them to get a license in Noti or Veneta. But I hadn't known. The registrar of deeds had set up this appointment and had assigned me to it.

She knew I had no plans.

I turned the Buick up the driveway, listened to the wheels squeal in the mud. The driveway twisted past piles of discarded possessions, mostly made of rusted metal, through some sickly looking pine trees and past a clear-cut area. At the top stood more sickly trees and a turn-around filled by two other cars.

I had to park on the slope. The Buick slid back once as if in protest, then stopped as though it had reconsidered. I opened the door and got out, finally seeing the couple, standing beneath a canopy made of green rain slickers and held up by spindly pieces of wood.

They were no more than eighteen. The boy had his arm around the girl, protecting her from the drops that got inside their makeshift tent. She wore white, but it already had mud stains. Not that it mattered. Their attention was focused on her belly, hands holding the firm protuberance, expressions filled with the awe new parents have at baby's first kick.

Stupid, risking this, because of some odd romantic idea. The baby could die, and then where would they be? In separate apartments, staring at the rain, remembering the joy they had once felt. The joy they had lost.

I ducked under the canopy. Good Christian kids, they had no idea what it meant to be married under a canopy of any kind. "Josh Stein," I said. "I'm from the clerk's office."

They looked up, not seeing me, not caring about my name, not offering theirs back. They probably figured I had it on their application—and I did—Peter Anderson and Laura Williams, good WASP names—but it would have been nice if they had offered to tell me.

"Got witnesses?"

"My uncle Dave and Aunt Lou," the girl said, waving her hand absently. "They're staying in the car."

I didn't want to hear the pain in that, didn't want to see what the kids were fighting. Beth wanted us married on Christmas Eve—under a canopy—melding our two cultures, she said, her blonde hair tickling my arm.

No one came.

No one saw.

Death conquered.

Her father at the funeral, staring at the tiny coffin. "God knows," he said, "when things aren't right."

Beth had turned away from me then, and never looked back.

"Do we need them here?" the girl asked.

It took a moment for me to understand her. She meant her aunt and uncle. I shook my head. "They can sign when we get done. That's all we need them for."

Her smile warmed me, made me forget the ice cold rain that dripped from the space between the slickers over my bare head and down the back of my neck.

"Let's get started," I said, head bowed to hide the flush. "Do you have your own vows or you want me to be traditional?"

They had their own vows. Mawkish things about forever love, and how one plus one equals something greater than three. They giggled and held her stomach, and didn't even look up when the wind almost tore the canopy from its moorings.

I said my bit, then pronounced them married with a formality that surprised me. Their kiss was rough and unpracticed despite the baby, the kiss of two kids led astray by hormones and hopes and traditions.

I looked away.

"Don't we got to sign something?" the boy asked.

"Oh, yeah." I pulled the license from the breast pocket of my suit jacket, then bent over so that they could use my back as a table. The girl's touch was light; the boy's firm and sure.

"Uncle Dave and Aunt Lou have to sign too, right?" the girl asked.

"Yeah." I tried to stand, grab it from her, but she had already taken off down the hill.

The boy shuffled his feet, not meeting my eyes. "They think

I done this on purpose, wrecked her life, trying to hold her back. But they don't know her. And I'm going to build her the best damn house, right here on this spot, and we're going to have a dozen kids, and we aren't ever going to tell them—"

He stopped, maybe knowing that he was making up a life that would never be. If they had a house, it would be prefab, or a trailer, and the kids would scream from the too-small windows. His oldest son would get defiant, like the boy was now, only this boy would never remember it, never remember what it was like to be young and in love.

Fathers never did.

The car door slammed and she trudged back up the hill, getting more mud on her too-small white dress. She handed the license to me. I shook my head. "It's yours now," I said. "Congratulations. I wish you only the best."

The aunt and uncle's car wheezed to a start, then backed away and swerved around the kids and mine to go down the hill. Lots of love. Lots of support.

The girl's eyes misted as she watched them drive away.

"Listen," the boy said. "I got some sparkling cider down at the apartment and Laura's roasting a turkey. Come share a toast with us and some dinner. It's what we can do for getting you out in the rain."

"It's your wedding day," I said. "You want to be alone."

The girl still stared at the car going down the hill. The boy's eyes had an intensity I remembered feeling once in my own.

They didn't need to be alone. They were going to be alone forever, fighting this thing. They had no glass to stomp, no cheer from the rabbi, no fake showing of support. All they had was the rain, drumming on the slickers, and a baby's kick, and a bit of childish hope.

I made myself smile. The smile wasn't as hard as I thought it was going to be. A bit of warmth had come back into my heart. Maybe Beth and I would have had a chance if someone had believed in us.

"Turkey sounds good," I said. "And we'll drink a toast." I held up an imaginary glass, my cupped fingers catching the cool water, feeling it soothe an ache I didn't even know I had.

"Mazel tov, children," I said, feeling like the indulgent uncle they needed. "Mazel tov."

Artistic Photographs
A Roz & Jack Story

Kristine Kathryn Rusch

"She looks like trouble," Roz Donnelly whispered as she dragged the heavy box of glass photographic plates across the floor of her studio, narrowly avoiding the overstuffed sofa she had placed near the fringed lamp.

Her husband Jack peeked through the red velvet curtains. "So?"

Roz slapped his fingers and he dropped the curtain, turning to face her. He was tall, his muscles rope hard, and his body lean from too many years on the back of a horse. His brown hair brushed against his collar—new and perfectly starched for the first time since she'd known him—and his brown eyes held a trace of humor in them.

"Jealous?" he asked, leaning into her.

"Of that baby?"

He shushed her. "That baby might hear you and leave."

Roz shook her head. "That baby has a plan, Jack, believe me. And we're probably its victims."

"What are you afraid of, Roz, my darling? Afraid I'll trade you in for a younger model?"

He was so close, she could smell the tobacco on his clothing.

It mixed with the scent of her own specially made soap, and something undeniably Jack. Ever since she had met him, she had been under his spell.

"If she's the model, you wouldn't last a day," Roz said. "She may be ten years younger than I am, but she's older in spirit."

He ran his thumb along her jaw, sending a shiver through her. "My cynic."

She knew he felt the shiver; his eyes crinkled as he held back a smile. But she didn't want him to feel as if he had an advantage. "That cynicism has saved you a hundred times in the last ten years. You should respect it."

"Oh, I do," he said, this time letting the smile out. "But I wonder why it appears now."

"This city has decency laws, doesn't it?" she asked.

He shrugged. "The law is not something I specialize in, darling."

"You should." She bent down and tugged at the box of glass plates. It weighed as much as she did, and she could use his help, but she wasn't going to ask for it.

She glanced up. He was peeking through the curtain again.

"Well?" she asked. "Will she be artistic enough?"

He ignored her sarcasm. "I don't think the decency laws matter anyway. No one has applied them to photography."

"It's only a matter of time, thanks to you," Roz muttered, but she did so with a smile. Her husband's schemes had allowed her to own this photography studio for two years—the longest they'd been in one place since they got married.

He hadn't said a word about moving on. But Roz was starting to feel restless. He disappeared for weeks at a time,

Artistic Photographs

following one scheme or another, but she had to stay to take portraits of people she didn't even like.

Somehow she had a hunch there was more to photography than spending her days in a musty studio, even if it did have a secret and shady side.

A side the young woman in the other room had somehow figured out.

Roz had a feeling about this girl, a feeling she didn't like. Jack had a feeling too, and he liked his. Roz couldn't tell what part of his anatomy he was thinking with. She knew her husband well enough to know that, while he never touched any other woman, he didn't mind a long healthy look.

"We've got to hurry," he said, letting the curtain drop one final time. "The girl's getting cold."

"I suppose you know that for sure," Roz said, pushing the box all the way into the corner.

"As a matter of fact, I do." He grinned at her. "So let's move it, Rosalind."

"Then pick up the damn box," she said. "I can't move it any farther."

He bent down and lifted it as if it weighed nothing. "I thought you would never ask."

He kicked the curtain open with his foot and stepped into the small theater they had built in the back of the photography studio. The theater did not hold an audience—there was no room for seats or aisles. Instead, there was floor space wide enough for several cameras, all set up at strategic angles.

The stage itself was narrow, and even though there were curtains behind it, the curtains opened onto a wall. The theater had no windows, and the front curtains were the only way into this area.

Roz had insisted on double curtains with openings in different parts so that no one would stumble onto this back area. The curtains themselves were part of a formal furniture grouping in the main part of the studio and to date, one year since they'd added in the theater, no one had discovered it.

Roz waited a moment before going in. She had to be in the right frame of mind to confront her artistic subjects. Usually when she took photographs, she asked questions, drew people out. When she took her art photographs, she never even learned the subject's name.

It was easier to deny that she had done anything if she had no idea who she was photographing.

Finally, Roz pulled the curtains apart. She let the curtains swish closed behind her before she looked at the girl. The girl was clearly an adult, although she was no more than twenty-one. She was full-breasted and wide-hipped with enough heft to suggest wealth. Her eyes were big and brown, her mouth curved in a slight smile. She hadn't put on the drape that Roz had left for her, and Jack had been right—the girl was clearly cold.

"Cover yourself up," Roz said, nodding at the drape.

"I thought the point was to take nude photos," the girl said.

"The point is to take artistic photos," Roz said through gritted teeth. That some people found the artistic photos erotic was not her problem.

The girl did not move toward the drape. She stood there in all her goose-pimpled glory, staring at Jack, almost daring him. He, bless him, was ignoring her and not because Roz was in the room. He didn't like contrary females.

Artistic Photographs

Then Roz frowned. That wasn't entirely accurate—he did like Roz—but he claimed he hated her contrary nature, even though it had gotten them out of a thousand scrapes.

Roz checked out the first camera. Jack continued to hold the box of plates, waiting for her to tell him what to do with them. She could have let him continue to hold them until he complained, but she wasn't in the mood to torture him, even if he had brought her the girl.

"Set them next to this camera," she said, "and then get me the other box of plates beneath the developing counter."

"Roz, this is enough plates—"

She turned toward him, nearly knocking the camera. "We're taking three kinds of photographs—daguerreotypes, portraits and Talbotypes. They require different plates."

And different papers and different cameras and different skills, but she wasn't going to tell him that.

"Why so many?" the girl asked.

"Some for us and some for you. It was part of our deal." Then Roz squinted at Jack. "You told her about the deal, right?"

He nodded and looked at the girl for confirmation. She nodded too, even though Roz had a hunch the girl had heard nothing about the different types of portraits before now.

The girl walked to the edge of the stage. She hung her toes over the lip. Her toenails had turned blue. She didn't look seductive or even comfortable, although she was trying.

Jack gave her an uncomfortable glance and hurried out of the theater.

Roz stuck her head through the first camera's curtain. The girl looked even more provocative when framed by the lens.

Time to talk to the girl and make sure Jack had followed the rules. Even though Roz was taking artistic photographs, she wasn't one of society's predators. She never took destitute women and photographed them—at least not on purpose. Jack had brought one or two in early on, but Roz had figured out early what he was about. Most of those women were malnourished and therefore too skinny for art photography.

Men didn't like to fantasize about women so skinny their breasts had sunken into their chests. Men liked women who were big in front and in back, women whose flesh jiggled as they moved. Roz never fit in that category either—her life (mostly on the run) had left her slender and muscled—the antithesis of modern beauty.

"So," Roz said, "Jack didn't make any agreement with you."

"He said we'd settle it later."

Roz clenched her right hand, but kept it hidden behind her thick black skirt. What he had meant was that Roz would settle it later—and apparently he had been right.

"Are you paying us?" Roz asked.

"No," the girl said. "He said that would take care of itself."

And that, ladies and gentlemen of the jury, was what Jack called an agreement. Roz shook her head.

"All right. Before we go any further...." She paused. She really couldn't take it any longer. "Put on the damn drape. You're not here to seduce me."

The girl's lower lip jutted out. "So? He's going to take the photographs."

"*I'm* going to take the photographs," Roz said. "I'm the photographer. He's just the front and the money man."

How she hated calling him that. He really was the money-slipping-through-the-fingers-like-water man.

Artistic Photographs

"Oh," the girl said and backed away from the edge of the stage. She picked up the sheer drape and wrapped it around herself, then shivered. "It doesn't cover up much."

"It's not supposed to. There's a robe behind the curtain over there." Roz gestured toward the curtain at the side of the stage.

The girl followed her direction, grabbed the robe, and slipped it on. "How come it's so cold in here?"

"It makes better art," Roz said sarcastically.

The girl sat on the edge of the stage and tucked her feet under herself.

"Here's the deal," Roz said. "For the next two hours, we will take as many photographs of you as possible."

"I thought you were only doing a few portraits."

"There are different kinds of photography," Roz said, not willing to go into too much detail.

The last thing the girl needed to know was that she had treated a ream of paper with salt and silver nitrate so that they could reprint the Talbotypes as many times as they liked—or to put it more accurately—as many times as they could afford to do.

"This is an artistic session," Roz said. "I'll put you in different poses and take as many portraits as possible. You will get half the portraits—" Technically, she would get half of the number that Roz told her were portraits, which in the past had been less than a fourth—"and a quarter of the daguerreotypes—" actually, only about one sixteenth because artistic daguerreotypes brought a large sum from soldiers heading out to the frontier. "I hope that's acceptable."

The girl was picking at her robe. Roz wasn't even sure she was listening.

"In exchange for that, we will keep the rest and sell them to cover our expenses."

"Sell them to whom?" the girl asked.

The "whom" threw Roz. She hadn't expected good grammar from a girl who wanted to pose nude.

"Anyone we please," Roz said. She wasn't going to negotiate with this girl. It would be Roz's way or no way at all.

The girl smiled. "All right."

Roz felt a shimmer of unease. She had been right; this girl *was* planning something.

"What if I tell you I only want one portrait and you can keep the daguerreotypes?"

"I would tell you not to change the deal," Roz said.

"Hell, hon, let her change the deal if she wants." Jack was coming through the curtains, the second box of plates in his arms.

"No," Roz said.

"I made my initial agreement with him," the girl said, not looking at Roz. She was smiling at Jack instead. Jack, the bastard, was smiling back.

"Fine," Roz said, uncertain whether she was more irritated at the girl or at her husband. "He can take your portraits then."

"Roz." Jack set the plates down hard. They clanked together and Roz prayed that none of them were broken.

"All right," the girl said. "I'd rather be photographed by a real photographer anyway."

"Doll." Jack took a step toward the girl. "If you want a real photographer—"

"Then Jack's your man." Roz smiled sweetly at him. "You remember how to work the camera, don't you, dear? The one you're used to is the one in the middle. Don't touch the two on the sides. The process is different for those. And the one near me is a camera obscura. It is nothing like anything you've ever used before."

"Can't you control her?" the girl snapped at Jack. She looked so fierce that Jack took a step backwards.

"Um." Apparently Jack didn't have a good lie ready. "No, doll."

"Pity." The girl pulled her robe tighter. "Well, I'm here, I'm naked, and the price is right. Let's do this thing."

Roz didn't move. "Why do you want your photograph taken like this?"

The girl stood, shook her head like a horse about to run free, and let the robe fall away from her shoulders. "I appreciate art," she said.

∽

The session took two hours. The girl was a natural. She even managed to get the drape to hang as if the wind were blowing around her—and she sustained that pose for a good five minutes.

Roz went through every one of her plates.

Jack, whose attention wandered mid-way through, took care of the three customers who came to the main studio. His voice would filter in, and Roz felt a stab of envy. She didn't want to be alone with this girl. She would rather be taking sedate portraits of matrons who believed it was time to step in front of yet another infernal machine.

Roz had asked him to put out the closed sign, but of course

he hadn't. Jack had a penchant for risks, particularly unnecessary ones. They made his heart beat faster. Risks also excited other parts of him, which Roz didn't mind.

She almost wished the girl had held his attention, instead of being such a flinty manipulative little shrew. The girl had questioned each one of Roz's orders, but performed with a smile whenever Jack spoke to her.

Jack tired of this first and left. Roz had to endure it for the entire session.

"Get dressed," Roz said.

"Are we done?" The girl seemed almost disappointed.

Roz nodded. "If I wait much longer, some of this work will be lost. I have to process these plates quickly. They can't sit."

"I thought they've come up with a new process, one that allows the plates to be shipped without being developed." The girl had grabbed the robe.

Roz frowned. The feeling that she was being used rose again. Most people knew nothing about the current state of photography. The dry plate system intrigued her, but she hadn't seen it yet.

"The process has made its way to New York City," Roz said. "It won't come to these parts for months, maybe years."

And she didn't even want to discuss the cost. The new process would require a new camera, new and different plates, and time to learn how to use them. All things she did not have.

The girl slipped off the stage, leaving her clothes behind. She held the robe closed with one hand. "I don't suppose you have a chamber pot down here."

The only chamber pot in the entire building was upstairs, in

Artistic Photographs

Roz and Jack's bedroom. She wasn't going to let that little minx in there.

"You'll have to go out back," Roz said. "I suggest you put on your clothes first."

"There isn't time," the girl said and slipped through the curtains.

Roz cursed under her breath. From now on, she was going to pick the subjects for the art photography. Jack might claim he had a better eye—and he probably did for the female form—but Roz could spot a fellow con artist a lot quicker than Jack could.

She set the last plate in the box, wondering how long it would take before she had to rescue her husband from the girl's unwanted attention. Maybe she would let Jack get himself out of it. After all, he had found the girl attractive at first.

But not in the end. In the end, he had been as disgusted with the girl as a man could be.

Roz took pity on him. He was no match for that girl, and Roz didn't to spend the remainder of the afternoon in the theater.

She was reaching for the curtain, when a female voice cried out, "What is the meaning of this?"

That voice did not belong to the girl. Roz parted the curtain ever so slightly, careful not to let the ripple make itself noticed inside the studio.

A stout, middle-aged woman in black bombazine was standing on the woolen rug. She had both hands on her ample hips and she was staring at Jack.

Roz stared at Jack too, and suppressed a grin. He looked terrified.

But the girl on his lap—the naked girl on his lap—arched

her back, shoving those glorious breasts in his face. Only she wasn't looking at him. She was smiling at the woman.

"Hello, Mama," the girl said. "Care to join us?"

"Emmeline!" the woman in black bombazine said, unwittingly giving Roz information she didn't want. "Put on some clothing."

"But Mama," Emmeline said in a voice that purred. "I can't have fun with my clothing on."

The woman's face turned red, then purple. Roz had seen people have apoplexy before. Some had even died of it. She resisted the urge to race out from behind the curtain and calm everyone down.

"Ma'am." Jack sounded panicked. "This isn't what it looks like."

"That's right, Mama," Emmeline said. "We only just got started."

"No!" Jack started to stand.

Emmeline rolled sideways, and Jack reached for her, but if he grabbed her, his hands would have landed on those massive breasts. He must have realized that because he jerked back as if he had been burned. Somehow Emmeline managed to catch herself and remain on his lap all at the same time.

"Ma'am," he said, trying desperately not to touch Emmeline, "I'm a happily married man. Right, Roz?"

Roz didn't answer. She couldn't rescue him this time. They'd lose a lot of money in plates and equipment if she did. He would have to come up with something on his own.

The girl on his lap stroked Jack's chin.

"Roz?" Jack looked toward the curtains.

Roz cursed under her breath.

"His wife doesn't seem to mind sharing," Emmeline said.

Roz cursed again. The girl was even more manipulative than Roz had originally thought.

The woman in black bombazine had turned an alarming shade of puce. She started forward. She had an umbrella in her right hand. Roz hadn't seen it before because it had been hidden behind the wide and unfashionably hoop skirt. The woman was brandishing the umbrella as a weapon.

"Roz?" Jack's voice trailed off. He seemed to realize that she wasn't coming to his aid.

He glanced around the room. Emmeline snuggled closer to him and that seemed to decide him.

Jack stood.

This time Emmeline fell to the floor, banging her elbow against the wood and letting out a string of epithets that made Roz blush.

"Ma'am," Jack said, holding up his hands to ward off any umbrella blows. "Your daughter made advances to me, just a moment ago. You see, initially, she had come in here to have her portrait taken."

"You make innocent girls take off their clothing for portraits?" The woman brandished the umbrella over her head. But Emmeline froze. Roz stared at the girl. Something was changing here.

"Um, no," Jack said, and to Roz's surprise, he was blushing. She had never seen him con anyone with a blush. She was the one who could do that. Jack's blush had to be real.

Or maybe it was simple panic. She'd never seen him panic while standing still before. Usually his full-blown panics happened on the run.

"Actually, ma'am," Jack was saying, "she came in here asking me to take an artistic portrait."

The woman paused, holding her umbrella over her head like a scythe. "An artistic portrait?"

"Yes, ma'am. You know. The kind that French portraitists paint."

"Naked portraits? You create naked portraits?"

"For married women only, ma'am. Often they take such portraits for their husbands to enjoy. In private." Jack was finally getting into the spirit of this.

Roz glanced over her shoulder at the plates. She was running out of time. She had fifty wet plates of a naked manipulative girl drying in a box behind her, wet plates that had to be developed soon or they'd be ruined forever. Thank heavens Jack had already taken another box-load of them into the development room to start the process.

"What kind of man would take naked photographs of his wife?" the woman asked.

Every man who could get away with it, Roz thought. As if that old biddy didn't know.

"Soldiers, generally, ma'am. Men who are heading out on the frontier. They need something to remember home by so…so…" Jack was casting about for a reason. His gaze darted toward the curtain. He still wanted Roz to rescue him. "So that he won't go astray."

Roz rolled her eyes, but the woman eased her umbrella down. She looked at Emmeline, who was now cringing on the floor. Roz had no idea why the truth—or the partial truth—would cause Emmeline to be frightened, but there it was.

"Is this true?" the woman asked Emmeline.

Emmeline grabbed the robe, then held it in front of her. Jack could still get a good look at her backside, although he wasn't even trying. That proved to Roz that he found the girl unappealing.

"Well?" the woman asked.

Emmeline swallowed. "I thought maybe this time Father would notice me."

Roz gasped. Jack looked stunned. The woman swooped down and grabbed Emmeline by the arm. Instead of finishing the sentence, the girl let out a loud yell as her mother pulled her upright.

"I have had enough of you," the woman said in a low tone. "You will get your clothing and get dressed. I will take care of you at home. As for you, young man—"

And as she turned to Jack, her voice rose. She still hadn't let go of her daughter's arm.

"—you will take me to your so-called art portraits and we shall destroy them. Together."

Jack's mouth dropped open. This time, he looked directly at Roz who slipped even farther behind the curtain. Her fists were clenched. All that money, gone.

"Um, ma'am," Jack said, his voice trembling. "I'm out time and money—"

"I will pay your expenses plus a handsome sum more so long as you never refer to this incident again."

Roz leaned toward the crack in the curtain. A handsome sum more?

"How much is handsome?" Jack asked.

"Five hundred dollars. In gold."

Roz clasped her hands together. They were rich!

"Over my expenses."

"Yes," The woman sounded angry. Roz prayed Jack wouldn't anger the woman further. He had a talent for ruining a good thing.

"All right." Jack almost—almost—smiled. He caught himself just in time. Roz started to step away from the curtain so that he could bring the woman into the theater, but he didn't. Instead, he went into the development room.

The man was smarter than she gave him credit for.

Roz sprinted back toward the cameras. She took the drape and tossed it over the box of wet plates (please let them last a few moments longer!), and then grabbed Emmeline's clothes. They were made of silk. Roz should have noticed that before, but she'd been concentrating on the girl's face—on that look of triumph and manipulation.

Roz hurried out of the curtains, then caught them with her free hand so that they wouldn't wave and draw attention to themselves. Emmeline was still sitting in the middle of the floor, clutching her robe. She looked like she was about to burst into tears.

Roz tossed her clothes at her. Emmeline opened her mouth and Roz put a finger over her own lips. Then she ran to the main door, opened it, and slammed it as if she had just come in.

"What's this?" she asked as loudly as she could.

"Um, n-n-nothing." Apparently, Emmeline didn't have to pretend to sound frightened.

"I come home to find a naked woman in my studio," Roz said, and then caught herself. All of her nouns and pronouns were wrong. Home was upstairs and as far as the city was concerned the studio belonged to Jack.

"Mrs. Donnelly, I'm really sorry," Emmeline said.

"Get dressed."

"Yes, ma'am."

The sound of breaking glass stopped both of them from play-acting. Anger shot through Roz. She'd spent two hours getting those portraits. The old biddy had no right to destroy them.

Emmeline bit her lower lip. Roz took a step closer to her and whispered, "Don't say anything about that theater."

Emmeline's eyes widened. "Really?"

"Really."

To Roz's surprise, Emmeline hugged her. "Thank you."

"Thank—?"

The door to the developing room opened and Emmeline dropped out of the hug as if it had never been. She grabbed her clothes and was halfway into her shift before her mother came out of the room.

The scent of chemicals followed her, and the anger threaded through Roz again. Who was this woman that she felt she could just destroy anything that got in her way?

"You are this man's wife?" the woman asked in that preemptory tone.

Roz wanted to retort with *You're this creature's mother?* but somehow didn't think it appropriate.

"Yes," she said.

"Do you know that he takes nudie photographs in this studio?"

Roz faked a blush. She felt the heat rush through her face and she whirled on Jack who was standing directly behind the old biddy and grinning.

"You what?!?" Roz made herself sound as indignant as possible.

"Honey bunch," Jack said in his best fake hen-pecked husband voice. "It was an accident…"

He continued to make up his false excuses as Roz walked toward him. Emmeline's mother grabbed her daughter, flung the dress over Emmeline's head, and then dragged her from the studio. Emmeline's shoes and stockings were on the ground where Roz had dropped them.

"…so I hope you'll forgive me, darling," Jack said with the biggest grin Roz had ever seen. He held out both hands. They were filled with gold coins.

Roz bent over to touch them. She had dreamed of holding wealth like this, but the dream had never come true.

The door opened back up and Emmeline walked in. Her dress was on backwards and her face was tear-streaked. Her mother stood in the doorway.

"You promised," she mouthed to Roz, then she bent down, grabbed her shoes and stockings and hurried out of the studio.

"Promised what?" Jack asked as the door closed.

"That I'd develop the rest of the photographs," Roz said.

Jack leaned forward and kissed her. "Roz, sweetie," he said when he was finished, "you really are the brilliant one in this relationship."

Yet that comment didn't make her feel brilliant. Jack was still up to something, and she didn't know what that something was.

When she finally got to their upstairs apartment, tired, aching and stinking of chemical washes, Jack was waiting for her in the living room.

Naked.

"Jack, I'm tired, I'm hungry, and I'm a bit annoyed at you. This is not the time—"

"Baby, I had a naked girl on my lap, breasts shoved in my face, and you were watching the entire time. Besides, that old biddy could have shut us down and instead, she made us rich. Any of those things would have excited me, but all three together...." He pulled her close. "This, my love, is an opportunity you do not want to pass up."

He kissed her, and she leaned into him, as she always did. He was right; the afternoon had been oddly erotic. She had just forgotten about it in her haste to develop those photographs.

It had always been this way with them—from the moment she saw him, she had wanted him, even though she had not understood the feelings at the time. She had eloped with him, and learned that instead of growing weaker, that pull had grown stronger.

Afterwards, they lay on the quilt on top of their bed, spent and exhausted. Roz had no idea how they'd made it to the bed, only that they had ended up there.

Jack had been right. This had been an opportunity she would have regretted missing.

"Who would have thought," Jack said, his head tilted back, eyes closed, "that Norma Trager would have had five hundred dollars in gold on her person?"

Roz blinked.

"I don't think I've ever met anyone who carried that much

money with them. Do you think she knew what Emmeline was about and planned to pay us off? Maybe she had more money. Maybe I settled too soon."

"Norma Trager?" Roz asked.

"Oh, yes. She probably has more than she needs. After all—"

"Norma Trager?" Roz's voice rose. "You knew her name?"

Jack propped himself on one elbow. "Didn't you recognize her? You're the one who specializes in the gossip columns."

He was lying. She could always tell when he was lying. His voice smoothed out and he got a slick little smile that didn't quite reach his eyes.

"No," Roz said. "I didn't recognize her, and neither did you. You knew who Emmeline was before she came into the studio. In fact, you planned this little scam, didn't you?"

"Roz, I would never plan anything without you."

Another lie, as they both knew. "This time you were scamming me, weren't you?"

He sat up. "Roz, it's not like that."

"Oh?" she said. "Then why didn't you tell me in advance?"

He slipped off the bed, moving out of her reach.

Roz pulled the quilt around her and took a deep breath. "All right," she said. "Tell me everything, so I know just how much trouble we're in."

"We're not in trouble," Jack said as he put his clothes back on. He wasn't looking at Roz, and she knew which part of the sentence he had left out.

They weren't in trouble yet. But they would be. Roz wasn't sure how, but she knew they would be.

He didn't say anything.

Roz sighed. "Damn," she said. "Now I'm going to have to

destroy a whole day's work. You could've told me before I saved the plates."

"Don't destroy them," Jack said.

Emmeline had asked her not to destroy all of the wet plates either. Finally Roz was getting to the heart of the matter.

"Why not?" Roz asked. "We can't sell them. *Norma Trager* bought your silence for five hundred pieces of gold."

"She didn't say we couldn't sell them." He looked innocent. "She just said we couldn't talk about them."

That was true. Norma Trager had said that, thinking all of the portraits of her daughter were destroyed.

"What's the scam, Jack? Tell me now or I swear, I'll find that little con artist and have her tell me herself."

"No." He looked even more panicked at that thought. "Roz, believe me, this is a good thing."

She stood and went into the living room in search of her dress. This was not a conversation to have naked.

"I do not believe," she said as she picked up her shift, "that anything you call a good thing is, indeed, a good thing."

"Please, Roz."

She slipped on the shift and dropped the quilt, then grabbed her dress. It was fine, although the buttons from the waist down had fallen off. She was lucky she hadn't stepped on any of them.

"Roz." He had come into the living room. His pants were buttoned, but he still hadn't put on a shirt. His flat and muscular chest, lightly dusted with hair, made her want to touch him again.

She turned her back on him and fingered the ruined dress.

"All right," he said. "I met Emmeline a few days ago—"

"Oh?"

"Don't start, Roz. You know I don't do that sort of thing."

She brought the dress up to her face to hide her smile. It was hard to be mad with him when he was being sincere.

"Anyway," he said, "she knew I was a photographer. She waited for me outside. She asked me if I took artistic photographs."

The girl had studied her subject. Roz picked up her stockings and her shoes, which had toppled together like drunken sailors.

"I told her I did. Then she asked me if I knew of Robert Millard. Well, who hasn't heard of Robert Millard, I said. She gave me a strange little smile and said that he was her father."

Roz set her shoes, stockings and ruined dress on the sofa, and walked past Jack into the bedroom. She made sure she didn't brush against him. If she had, she would have had to touch him, and at this moment, that would have been wrong. He had to think she was mad at him.

Jack turned and watched her, arms crossed, his muscles standing out in sharp relief against his naked skin. "I laughed. I said everybody knows that Millard has five sons and no daughters."

Roz raised her eyebrows. If Jack knew it, then indeed, everyone knew it. Jack was right; usually she was the one who read the gossip rags. He ignored them.

Although, she supposed, he knew about Robert Millard because of his wealth. Jack always knew who the richest and most influential people were in any town.

"She nodded. She said that her mother had been his mistress and when she got older, he cast her off like an old shoe. They still got money from him, but she wanted love."

Artistic Photographs

"Love?" Roz grabbed her dove gray day dress out of the closet. "She expects love from her father because she poses in the nude? This is one sick family, Jack."

"She gave up on love a long time ago," Jack said. "She really just wanted him to acknowledge that she was his daughter. She figured that if she forced the issue, he'd have to acknowledge her."

"She was going to blackmail him?" Roz asked.

"I think so. Acknowledge me or I'll tell everyone who I am." He waved a hand. "Or maybe she's just going to ask him for money. I don't know."

Roz shook her head. People did not know how to run a proper scam any more. "She's impulsive and dumb. This plan is guaranteed to get him to ignore her. Why would he acknowledge a daughter who acts like that?"

"That's why she wants me to sell the remaining photographs. I'm her leverage," Jack said. "You did make one more portrait, right?"

"Yes." Roz slipped the dress over her head, then mentally cursed the choice. It buttoned in back.

Jack came over to help her. His deft fingers brushed her shift.

"Well, I'm supposed to make sure he gets a photograph and knows who it is."

Roz slapped his hand away. "You won't do any such thing."

She turned. He was frowning at her.

"Some day you're going to have to acknowledge that I'm the brains of this operation," she said. "If you go in there with that portrait, he'll have you arrested on some kind of charge.

Pandering or something. Forcing women into prostitution. You can't do her dirty work."

"Well, she can't," he said. "He won't even let her near his bank. She's tried. He's thrown her out before."

In spite of herself, Roz was thinking about this. Dammit, Jack always did this to her. He gave her a puzzle and, if she caught him in time, she got to solve it in ways that benefited both of them.

"Jack," she said, turning her back on him again so that he could finish buttoning her. "How do you feel about the City of Kansas?"

"It's a nice city." He'd been saying that from the beginning. But he never sounded thrilled. Jack was a rover. He had only settled because of her and her studio.

"Would you be broken-hearted if we left?"

"I always want to be with you, Roz." He patted her back, his signal that he was done buttoning her up.

"I mean it." She turned again, and found herself trapped between his arms. "What if we left Missouri altogether?"

"And go where?"

She shrugged. "I don't know. New Orleans, maybe. We have a lot of artistic photographs that we haven't sold. And if we pack up our equipment, we might be able to start anew somewhere else."

His eyes lit up. "But you like it here."

"Not really," she said. "The locals aren't that interesting. Everyone else is just passing through. Besides, I'm getting tired of taking portraits of matrons and their broods. I'm not cut out for the working life."

"I could have told you that, babe," he said, brushing her lips with his.

"I had to learn it for myself," she said.

"I trust you have a new plan?"

"No," she said, "but I'll have one soon."

∼

Roz wasn't a crusader, and she really hadn't liked Norma Trager. The woman pretended at morality when in reality she had been some man's mistress and borne him a child out of wedlock. Of course, Roz might have misjudged her. A woman usually didn't want her daughter to make the same mistakes she did—and Emmeline Trager was on the road to making if not the same mistakes, then some that were even worse.

But there was one thing that Roz really liked in a man and it was the one thing that Jack had. Loyalty. He loved her, he respected her, and even though his eye wandered, his heart didn't. She was the center of his life.

As it should be.

Obviously, Richard Millard had no center to his life. Casting off a mistress was one thing (and not really one that Roz approved of), but casting off a child was another thing altogether.

If Roz could get him to acknowledge his daughter, then her work was done. If she made a small profit in the bargain, she wouldn't complain.

So that was how she found herself outside the First Pioneer Bank of Missouri, wearing a new gray morning dress and a hated corset beneath it. Her hair was in a bun at the back of her skull, and that bun was hidden beneath a black lace net. She wore gray gloves on her hands and gray boots on her feet.

She looked as prim and proper as she could, considering that inside the thick embroidered bag she carried was a portrait of Emmeline Trager in the nude—a portrait that Roz had carefully constructed to be as…artistic as possible.

She took a deep breath, knowing that anyone watching would think her nervous. What she was trying to do was work herself into a state and time her blush so that she looked angrier and more grief stricken than she was.

Since the third man in a row held the large oak door open for her, Roz decided it was time to go inside. She nodded at the man, thanked him in a tone that perfectly imitated Norma Trager's sounds of indignation, as she stalked through the door.

Men seemed to have a finely tuned sense of when to avoid a woman. The bank's customers moved out of her way as if she were Moses and they were the Red Sea. The town's newspaper editor watched her from his position near the polished table. Two cattle ranchers hurried out the door. A third settled into a chair near the back as if getting ready to watch a show.

She clutched the embroidered bag to her chest and approached one of the gilded cages. The teller leaned backwards as if he could avoid her

"I would like to see Robert Millard," she said.

"I'm sorry, ma'am," the teller said. "Mr. Millard sees people only by appointment."

Behind the teller, another man—this one rotund and officious—watched with ill-disguised interest.

"He'll see me," Roz said.

"Ma'am—"

Artistic Photographs

"Tell him it's about his daughter." She said that last loud enough for the entire bank to hear it.

The teller frowned at her and was about to tell her what everyone knew: that Mr. Millard didn't have a daughter. But the officious man in the back understood a problem when he saw it.

"Come with me, ma'am," he said as he let himself out of the cage.

He led her through a carpeted hallway, past oak doorways with names emblazoned in gold letters. She had to work to keep the smile off her face; the buzz of conversation behind her convinced her that the first part of her ploy worked. The bank's customers hadn't been aware that Millard had a daughter, but they were now. Even if they thought the daughter was hers.

The man stopped at the last door, held up a finger, then disappeared inside the room. She heard a faint shout, a word that most men would have considered imprudent when spoken around a lady (fortunately for Millard, she was no lady) and then the officious man appeared again.

"He'll see you now."

No announcing of her name, no asking of her name. Just a simple invitation inside. The officious man held the door for her, then left the room so quickly that she wouldn't have been surprised to see a foot on his nether regions, propelling him forward.

The man behind the desk was standing. He was tall and imposing, with a shock of gray hair and bushy gray eyebrows. He glowered at her and she resisted the urge to grin at him. But she had a role to play.

"Mr. Millard?" Again, she used the tone she had learned from his former mistress. Deep, formidable, and disapproving.

"What is this about?"

"Mr. Millard," she said, "my name is Rosalind Donnelly. My husband owns the photography studio on A Street."

"I have never been to that studio," Millard said, making it very clear what he thought of photography and her Irish last name.

"No, sir, you haven't, but your daughter has."

"I don't have a daughter."

There it was. The hypocrisy she had been hoping to avoid. She felt the outrage she had been pretending only a moment before. Roz reached into her bag, grabbed the portrait, which she had had the forethought to frame and slammed it on his desk.

"My husband tells me this is your daughter. Is that true?"

Millard looked down and his face flamed red. "Where did you get this?"

"I found my husband developing it." She crossed her arms. "Mr. Millard, we both understand that men will be men, particularly when provoked. I want you to keep your daughter away from my husband. If you do not, I'm sure I can find other portraits of her. My husband said she was quite eager to be photographed—as he puts it—artistically."

Millard grew redder as she spoke. Sweat ran down the side of his face. He continued to stare at the portrait as if he couldn't believe it existed.

"My husband is a God-fearing man, Mr. Millard. He has sworn off this practice before. It is the reason we moved to the City of Kansas which, we were assured, was a moral and decent place to make our home. Instead, we discover that young women prefer to be photographed in a state of undress."

Millard's mouth worked, but he said nothing.

"I have it on good authority that your daughter approached my husband. He did not approach her. She has led him back down a path of sin, which is between him and his God. But between you and me, Mr. Millard, is this young woman yours? Because if she is—"

"What do you want?" He forced the words out as he reached for the portrait and turned it over.

"Only your assurance that this girl will not venture near our studio again." Roz took a step forward, looming close to him, as his former mistress had done to Jack. "You do have control of your daughter, do you not?"

"She, um. She..." He reached into his breast pocket, removed a carefully folded linen handkerchief, and dabbed at his forehead. "She lives with her mother."

Roz froze as if she were in shock. "You and your wife no longer share a home?"

"My wife and I are quite happily—blast, woman! You've put me in a delicate position."

Roz's chin went up. Her entire body straightened and she forced the flush into her own face. "Are you telling me, sir, that your daughter is illegitimate?"

Maybe Roz had pushed that statement too far. But she couldn't take it back. Besides, all the morally righteous women she'd ever met were given to melodramatic turns of phrase.

"Ma'am, it was a youthful indiscretion and she—"

"Are you telling me you have had no hand in raising that child?"

"My wife knows nothing of her," he said and she could actually hear pleading in his voice.

"Well, I can assure you, Mr. Millard, that will change." Roz grabbed the portrait. She made her hand shake. "This girl is a menace to decent society. Someone must control her before she does even more damage."

She shoved the portrait into the bag and headed toward the door. He wasn't stopping her.

Dammit. He was supposed to stop her. Now what was she going to do? She couldn't very well go back to the studio. Jack had sold it just that morning.

"What do you expect me to do?" Millard's voice was soft. She almost didn't hear it.

She stopped. "Apparently nothing, Mr. Millard. Don't worry. I shall take care of this."

"I am worried, Mrs. Donnelly. A man of my reputation—"

"Should think things through before he makes a mess of them." Now she turned, slowly, hoping he would take the glee in her eyes for anger. "After all, we both know men will be men."

His gaze met hers. He seemed to be appraising her. "Yes," he said, "I guess we do."

They stared at each other for a long moment. Finally, his gaze returned to the desk, where the portrait had been.

"What, exactly, can I do, Mrs. Donnelly, to prevent you from talking with my wife?"

Roz straightened. "You should control your daughter."

"Yes, ma'am."

"But of course you will not. So this will happen again. And my husband seems to be the person she has chosen to lead down the path of inequity."

Too thick. She was going to have to stop frequenting vaudeville.

She touched her hair with a shaking hand. "My husband and I have relocated because of this problem before. I'm afraid we'll simply have to do so one more time."

She turned, hoping—praying—Millard would stop her again.

"Ma'am," he said. "I'll pay you for the portrait."

"What?" She put that frosty tone back in her voice. "My husband and I have agreed not to sell these evil things any more. If he discovers that I have done so—"

"I can't expect you to give it to me to keep it out of the wrong hands. I'll buy it from you. Call it a loan. So that you can restart your business in—"

"The West," she said. "We will be taking the next train out."

"Yes, ma'am."

"I do not take bribes, Mr. Millard."

"It's not a bribe, Mrs. Donnelly. I would like the portrait, and I am certain that you will need funds to make your fresh start."

She bowed her head. "I did not come here for this."

"I know that, ma'am."

Roz had a hunch he had done this before, paid money to keep talk of his former mistress and daughter quiet. He would do it again if he could.

"I will take your loan," she said, walking back toward him, still clutching the bag. She wouldn't relinquish that until he gave her the money. "But I will repay it as soon as I can."

"I'll draw up a note, then, ma'am," he said.

It took all Roz could do not to look at him in surprise. Apparently, he had believed her.

"So we have to pay him back?" Jack sounded indignant. He was leaning on the railing, staring down at the water of the Missouri. The paddlewheeler had left port an hour ago, with all of Roz's camera equipment, some new clothes, and a lot of money in gold coins sewn into her shift and Jack's vest.

"No, silly," Roz said. "He thinks we're heading west. I even told him what train we'd be on."

"We need new names again, just in case," Jack said.

"We need them anyway," Roz said. "I trust you've been selling the daguerreotypes."

"Not yet," Jack said. "Someone might know her. She doesn't need that stigma."

As if Jack were worried about Emmeline. "Still afraid of her mother, huh?"

"For a former sexpot, she wields a mighty umbrella."

"Well," Roz said. "She won't come after you. She'll come after me."

Jack turned toward her. "What did you do?"

Roz shrugged. "On the way out, I saw the editor of the local paper. I gave him one of the daguerreotypes and told him that the portrait was of Mr. Millard's daughter, that she had it taken so that the entire town would be scandalized and he would have to pay attention to her."

Jack seemed shocked. Roz had never seen Jack look shocked before. It gave her a heady sense of power.

"Why would you do that?" he asked.

"It's what Emmeline wanted," she said.

"Roz, you hated Emmeline."

Artistic Photographs

Roz moved away from the railing. No sense standing so close to the water when she was weighted down with gold coins, coins she hadn't—technically—stolen.

"Of course I hated Emmeline," she said with just a hint of a smile. "But she's an adult. And she did want her father's attention. Now she has it."

Jack shook his head. "Be careful what you wish for because Roz might give it to you."

She took his hand. "I'll give you what you wish for, big boy."

"All I want, my darling Roz," he said with a rakish grin, "is a little bit of your attention."

"A little bit?" she asked.

"Forget what I just said." He bundled her in his arms and lead her to their stateroom. "I don't want a little of your attention. I want all of it."

"Mmm," she said, opening the stateroom door. "What a demanding husband."

"Be happy," he said. "I could be like Millard."

"No, you couldn't," she said, pushing the door closed and grinning at her husband. "Not if you want to live."

Trains

Kristine Kathryn Rusch

In her earliest memories, Corinne saw trains. Big, black trains that belched smoke and ash, their metal wheels grinding on metal track. The old trains, not the streamlined vehicles they would become, but the trains of her childhood, the glamour trains that, a decade later, would span the continent. She always associated Silas with trains, but she didn't actually see him until she was fourteen.

She was running down the street, her long skirt twisted and her hair disheveled, escaping the house, escaping her stepfather and his roving fingers. When her breasts grew and the blood came, his fingers seemed to grow longer, more demanding, and more than once he rubbed his crotch against hers. She hadn't told anyone; he said he would hurt her if she did. And so she just endured the fingers and the rubbing until the day when she would marry, when another man would save her from all of that.

She tripped as she ran up a flight of stairs and found herself on the train platform. In the distance, she could see the billowing smoke signaling an approaching engine. She turned to run back down, but her skirt caught, sending her flying across the rails. She looked again toward the train. A man dressed in a black suit sat on the cow catcher, strumming a banjo. The sight mesmerized her; she didn't even think of getting up.

She wouldn't know until years later that she was looking at Silas.

Then someone grabbed her blouse. The fabric ripped and she pushed her hands against the wooden ties. Her stepfather had followed her. He was going to embarrass her here, in public, in front of the man with the banjo. Another hand grabbed her armpit, brushing against her breast, and pulled her against the platform. She landed on her back, sending the air through her in a whoosh as the train roared by.

No man sat on the cow catcher. She had imagined him, his banjo, everything.

And nearly died.

"You okay?"

She looked up into a soot-begrimed face. The eyes gazing down on her were green, surrounded by thick, thick lashes. "You okay?" he asked again.

"I think the wind got knocked out of me, but other than that." Her voice came out breathless and tired. He wrapped a coat from a nearby bench around her. She looked down. Some of her skin was showing through the rips in her blouse. With her left hand, she closed the front of the coat. "Thank you," she said.

"That was close."

She nodded.

He sat beside her. He smelled of coal and wood smoke. "I'm Nathan."

"Corinne," she said, and smiled her prettiest smile.

She didn't meet Silas until nearly seven years later. Nathan had left the night before on one of his many trips for the railroad. Corinne buttoned the sleeves on her dress. The bruises on her arms had faded, but were still visible. She touched the mark on her cheek. If she wore a hat, no one would notice.

She leaned against the wavy glass. He would be gone for a week. A week without his yelling or the fist that came crashing into her even when she hadn't done anything wrong. Sometimes she thought all men spoke loudest with their hands. But she knew differently. Her real father hadn't touched her at all. Her real father had been an honorable man who had died in an honorable way. She had a medal from President Lincoln to prove it.

Corinne put a basket over her arm and one of her prettiest bonnets on her head. Her gown was a bit faded and too warm, but it would have to do. Her daughter was asleep and would stay so for a few more hours. Corinne was going out; she didn't care what Nathan would say.

The morning was fresh, clear, not yet hot, although the stale-sweet odor of horses permeated the air. A horse she had never seen before was tied outside the bank; another in front of the general store. She looked at the pair as she passed. Both were dapple grays, so much alike that they seemed to be the same animal.

"Startling creatures, aren't they?"

Corinne whirled, surprised by the soft baritone. A man sat on the rough-hewn bench in front of the store, his face shaded by his wide-brimmed hat. His legs were crossed and a banjo rested on his knee.

"You surprised me," she said.

"No more than you surprise me." He took off his hat. His hair was jet-black and his skin was the color of wheat. His eyes sparkled. Their blueness seemed to match the morning sky. "But I suppose you're wearing a wedding band."

She held out her left hand. The thick gold ring seemed tarnished, binding. She could almost feel it constricting her finger.

He nodded. "I'm Silas."

"Corinne."

"It's a mite warm to be wearing long sleeves, Corinne."

She flushed and ducked her head aside so that he couldn't see. The sentence was too pointed. He knew what her sleeves were hiding. "I've been shopping," she said.

He touched her hand. His fingertips were hard but the rest of the skin was soft. She pulled away.

"A good Christian lady would stand and talk."

His eyes made her nervous. There was too much intelligence in them. He seemed to miss nothing. "I'm not a good Christian lady," she said.

Any other man would have taken that as a rebuke, but Silas seemed to hear the truth behind the words. "Then you can take the ring off," he said, "and it won't make any difference."

She smiled. "You're forward, Silas."

"And you're lonely." He stood up, grabbing his banjo by the neck. "Let me take you home and make you something to eat."

"Thank you," she said, moving closer to the door. "But I have shopping to do."

He shook his head. "Best wait for that. Mrs. Stevens died in her sleep."

Corinne froze. Mrs. Stevens, who ran the store, had been sick, but not that sick. "You were just inside?"

"Yes." He slung the banjo across his back and went down the steps, touching the flank of the dapple gray. "The banjo and I, we have a bit of magic. It makes the pain go away."

"Of course," Corinne said, following him. "Like taking off my wedding ring makes the marriage go away."

∼

Nathan arrived a week later. The back door banged open, knocking Corinne out of sleep. She huddled in the middle of the bed, knowing from the heavy footsteps that Nathan was home and Silas wouldn't share her bed anymore.

"Corinne?" Nathan's voice was loud, the diction slurred. "I'm gonna find you, you slut."

Slut. A new word. She shivered and pulled the covers up tighter. If she were a more courageous woman, she would get the gun he left for her in the bureau.

"I don't leave to have my wife sleeping with no fancy man."

She swallowed. Angry and drunk. He had almost killed her that last time. She got out of bed and smoothed her nightgown against her body, the nightgown that she had worn waiting for Silas. Her feet whispered across the scratchy wood floor as she walked to the bureau.

A light grew in the hall. Maxine cried out in her sleep. Corinne opened the bureau drawer and felt among the linens until she found the gun barrel. A man stood in the doorway, silhouetted against the light.

"Bitch."

She took a deep breath and pulled the gun out, holding it with both hands. She was shaking. "Leave me alone."

"Goddamn slu—" A sharp crack echoed and the silhouette crumpled slowly to the floor. Corinne still held the shaking gun. A wisp of smoke seemed to rise from its mouth.

"Mommy! Mommy!" Maxine was shrieking.

"Tell her it's all right, Corinne." A deep baritone, rumbling from the hall.

"Silas!" Corinne had never felt so relieved. Jesus, it had been Silas who stopped Nathan. She had been afraid that she had done it.

"Mommy!"

"It's all right, Maxy. Mommy will be right there." She set the gun back in the bureau and walked out into the hall. A lantern sat on the floor and beside it lay Nathan, blood seeping from his chest. Silas bent over him, the banjo slung across his back.

"Is he dead?" Corinne asked.

Silas nodded. He pulled the banjo around to the front and began to pick, although Corinne could barely hear the notes. "Get Maxine," he said.

She went into her daughter's bedroom. The little girl was sobbing, large whooping sounds that caught in her throat. Corinne picked her up, smelled the sleeping-child sweat mixed with fear, and stroked her daughter's hair. "It's all okay," Corinne whispered, and with each note she began to believe it.

Finally, she took Maxine out into the hall. Silas seemed surprised to see her. He touched her face, nodded, as if he recognized her calmness and said, "I have to leave."

The calm shattered. Maxine's body tensed as Corinne's did. "No," Corinne whispered. "You can't leave me now."

He studied her for a long moment. "I like you, Corinne."

"Then stay," she said.

"I can't."

She gazed at Nathan's body and then at the home which had never been a home, only a place of pain and bruises. The choice was easy. "I'll come with you."

"I usually travel alone. I've never allowed anyone to come with me before." He plucked idly at the banjo. The notes sent shivers through Corinne. Finally, he sighed. "There are three rules you have to follow. Ask no questions. Put yourself first."

"That's two," she said, afraid that her statement was too close to a question.

"Go ahead." He smiled. "Your last question before all of this starts."

She swallowed. "What's the third rule?"

"When I leave, do not follow. Wait for me to come back."

Corinne smiled and hugged her daughter closer. "I think I can do that," she said.

～

After they'd made love, Corinne lay on her side of the bed and stared at the banjo glistening in the dark. She knew that some time before dawn, Silas would creep out of bed, grab the banjo and disappear for several hours. Sometimes he left in the middle of meals and sometimes he didn't come home at all. She couldn't question him, but he had seen the look in her eyes once, just once, toward the beginning.

"I'm the only one working Nevada," he said, as if that were an explanation. "It gets tiring."

Tiring for her, too, wondering where he was and what he was doing. There always seemed to be enough money, more than enough, he told her, even if he never returned.

He always spoke as if he would never return.

She waited until his breathing was steady and even, then she got out of bed. The throw rug felt soft against her bare feet. She crossed the rug and knelt in front of the banjo. In all the time she had been with Silas, she had never touched it.

It seemed to shine even more up close, although the moonlight fell away from the banjo and across the bed. She reached out and her fingers brushed the rounded front surface. It was scratchy and hot, not like an instrument at all, but like a living thing.

"Corinne?"

She turned. The moonlight fell across Silas, his hair tousled and the sheets pooled around his naked waist. "What is it, Silas?" she asked. "What's it made of?"

His mouth fell open and he let out a small, quiet sigh. "It's magic, Corinne," he said. "It brings rest, peace, and comfort to the people who hear it."

"You never use it to give me peace," she said.

"I did once." He ran a hand through his thick hair. "When Nathan died."

"I wasn't at peace." The banjo throbbed beneath her hand. "You were going to leave."

He sighed again. "There is only one time when a body can be truly at peace, Corinne."

A glimmer of understanding flashed through her. He was talking about death. Silas had come for Nathan that night, not for her. She was about to grab the idea when she realized why

Silas had sounded so sad. She clapped both hands over her mouth. "Silas," she said. "I'm sorry. I'll never do it again. I promise. I'll never—"

He shook his head and got out of bed. He grabbed his pants and slipped them on. "I love you," he said.

She stood up and reached for him. Her fingers slipped right through his arm—or perhaps he had moved away from her as he buttoned his shirt. "I love you, too," she said. "I promise. I'll never ask another question. Just stay, okay?"

He picked up his banjo. "You'll see me again," he said.

But, as she sat alone in the darkness, she realized that he'd never said he would be back, like he always had in the past. Just a promise that she would see him again.

Although she wouldn't see him again for a long time, not for ten more years.

∽

Corinne stood in front of the crowd. Maxine hadn't wanted to come. "What do I want to see any dumb old death train for?" she had asked. She was fifteen. Corinne had been five when her mother had taken her to a presidential death train. Funny how life repeated itself, adding its own little twists as time went on.

The train slowed as it approached. Its locomotive and passenger cars were draped in black. Flags rested across it as if they mourned too. She had never realized how much a train looked like a coffin.

The train was supposed to pass slowly so that everyone could whisper their goodbyes to the president, McKinley, felled by an assassin's bullet. But, in a screech of brakes and a hiss of steam, the train stopped. The crowd seemed motionless.

A man stepped down from the platform. He was tall and reedy, a banjo slung around his back.

"Silas!" she whispered.

He saw her and smiled.

"You look the same," she said.

The years hadn't touched him, although they had added wrinkles to her eyes and a streak of silver to her hair.

"I know." He stood between her and the old man beside her, close enough, but not close enough to touch. "And I will look the same on the day you die."

"I want you beside me," she said, meaning now, meaning forever.

"I'll be there. No matter how far away you are, I'll be there." He reached out as if to kiss her and then stopped himself. His eyes turned down sadly. He pushed past the old man and started back for the train.

"Silas," Corinne said, grabbing his arm. This time, her fingers did slip through as if he weren't really there at all.

He kept moving. As the train began to chug its way to full power, Silas grabbed the metal railing beside the stairs. "Be strong," he said. "That's what I have always admired about you, Corinne. You're strong."

And then he disappeared. The train eased forward, wheels squealing, and the crowd noises filtered into her ears. Low conversation, sobbing, an occasional sigh. The old man beside her gasped. Corinne stared at the flags, standing out in sharp relief against the train's black iron sides.

The old man gasped again. She turned. His face was blue and he clutched at his chest.

"What's happening?" someone cried.

"He's dying," Corinne said. The old man collapsed on the platform. People circled around him. Corinne loosened his shirt. As his last breath rattled in his throat, he reached out to her.

Behind her, the train's whistle wailed.

She turned. Despite the pain around her heart, she did not cry as the caboose faded in the gray skies.

She knew she would see Silas one more time.

Midnight Trains

A Faerie Justice Story

Kristine Kathryn Rusch

Nights he would find himself in the Metro, just before closing. The wide tunnels emptied around 11:30 p.m. Most locals did not use the Metro late, avoided the buses that some ridiculous city planner believed could replace the trains in the wee hours, and generally, found their own ways home. Sometimes, he imagined that savvy Parisians simply stayed wherever they ended up, in some ongoing party to which he would never ever be invited.

Alex was 100% American. Nothing reminded him of that as much as Paris, which looked familiar, but always, always had an air of impenetrable mystery. Perhaps to the French, it was simply their grand city, like New York was to him—marvelous, yes, but not mysterious at all.

He shoved his hands in his coat pockets—a heavy wool great coat he'd found in some thrift shop, not that thrift shops here were anything like the thrift shops at home. Here, they smelled not of mothballs and sadness, but of cigarettes and perfume, forgotten traces of someone else's life.

He loved the coat. It warmed him and made him feel like a

local, only because he dressed like one. Only because the coat had history. He did not.

His first Christmas in Paris left him flat-footed and unprepared. No one had warned him that the city shut down over the holiday. Even some of the ATMs stopped working.

Before he left America, his friends spoke enviously of his assignment—*Imagine Christmas in Paris,* they'd say. *Imagine the City of Lights.* The City of Lights was beautiful—holiday markets, decorations everywhere, elaborate baked goods that he couldn't imagine seeing at his last job in Chicago.

He'd come here to work, and his job, ostensibly in tech, was so high-up, he had trouble finding anyone at work who wasn't a subordinate, and therefore off-limits.

He had friends in the city now, but they didn't ask him to their Christmas celebrations. He never mentioned the holiday, but one-by-one, his French friends pulled him aside to tell him why they couldn't ask him to join them. As one woman told him, *The holiday, she is for family, no?*

Only he had none. That was why the company had chosen to send him to France. That, and the fact that he spoke fluent French, although he soon learned that what he actually spoke was fluent American-flavored prissy and dated French, the kind that actually made the French wince and ask if they could practice their English instead. It was the polite French way of telling him that they didn't want to hear him mangle the language.

He mangled anyway, and tried to imitate the accents he heard. Hard for him, since he grew up in Austin, then escaped to Chicago for high school. His personal accent was a jumble of the two cities, with Chicago taking precedence when he was awake, Austin when he was exhausted. Apparently, his French was mostly Texas-flavored, which his co-workers found hysterical. Once they relaxed around him, they'd mimic him in front of him, and rather than be offended, he learned what to say, when to say it, and how it should sound.

He had arrived in April; by September, he felt as accepted as a man like him could be, and by December, he'd been a bit surprised that he received no invitations.

And that was when he learned: *Christmas, she is for families, c'est ne pas?*

It shouldn't have bothered him. He had been alone for Christmas for ten years. He was eighteen when his parents died in a terrible plane crash. He had been old enough to live alone, but too young to figure out how to do it right. A girlfriend in college (which he could afford with insurance money) had taken him to her family for every major holiday in the three years they dated.

When they broke up, he felt it not as the loss of a love, but like the loss of his parents all over again. A man without family, and this year, a man without country, away from the familiar rhythms of the commercial holiday season that he had grown up with.

His late-night walks around the city had started in August, another time when the French seemed to abandon work and their lives en masse to go somewhere else. He noted the closed businesses, the confused tourists, the occasional angry employee, left to guard the restaurant, the bar or the shop.

He got to know the sound of his own footsteps, echoing along the Seine in the Ile de la Cite, and he liked that sense of anonymity, which used to frighten him back in the States.

Back there, he used to think: *What if I died here? No one would find me for days, weeks, even. No one would care.*

Somehow Paris taught him a different attitude, a sense that nothing died, not really, and at the same time, that no one cared except in a way that interfered with their daily lives.

Maybe, someday, Alex would find someone who loved him as much as the couples who kissed on Pont des Arts bridge seemed to love each other. But not yet, and maybe not ever.

When he realized he would be alone on Christmas (*Noël est pour les familles, non?*), he checked his favorite restaurants in the area to see if they would be open. Of course, they were not. (*It is,* one kind chef told him, *the only time we escape.*)

Alex could, he was told, eat at some brasseries (except Christmas Eve, when almost everything was closed) or a few tourist spots, or in one of the train stations. Or, as in America, in any of the Chinese restaurants.

Alex decided to decide on Christmas Day. He walked everywhere, after all. He could walk then, even if it rained. He didn't mind the rain; it was so much better than the Chicago cold.

He bought some food in case he felt like staying in, and thought it done.

But he was not prepared for the silence in a city usually filled with traffic, honking horns, music in the streets, arguing couples, and the occasional singing drunk. The closed shops, the empty streets, the shuttered restaurants, brought the city home to him in a way he had never seen before.

It was as if he had gotten closer to her, only to find her abandoned by the ones who loved her the most.

Midnight Trains

The Metro stations remained open—some people had to go to work, after all—but they all ran Sunday hours, and Sunday hours meant some stations were, for all intents and purposes, closed, trains running on a whim, it seemed, rather than on a schedule.

Early in December, he went to the Galleries Lafayette, because a friend had told him he had to see the entire store festooned in light. He did, and instead of taking his usual train home, he went to the Left Bank, and stopped in the Cluny-La Sorbonne.

If someone asked, he would say it was his favorite Metro station. If they asked why, he would give them the tourist answer—because of the mosaics. They covered the station's vaulted ceiling. Most tourists adored Jean Bazaine's gigantic frieze, *Les Oiseaux*, a yellow, orange, and pink monstrosity that suggested birds in flight.

But Alex liked the historic signatures represented in mosaic tiles. Some he recognized, like Robespierre and Richelieu, and others he had never heard of.

He stared at them for hours. They receded into the darkness that marked both tunnel entrances, some illuminated only as a train went through. It was in the Cluny-La Sorbonne that he realized rats appeared the moment the station closed. He'd gotten locked in one night, and was saved only by a kind guard who took him for a dumb tourist.

He didn't want to stay with the rats—they heard the final announcement and poured from the holes in the walls, like something from a bad horror movie. Strangely, they didn't frighten him.

This station had belonged to them much longer than it belonged to humans.

Because, what he really loved about Cluny-La Sorbonne was its history. The station, then called simply Cluny, opened in 1930, and was closed in 1939 because, the official records said, it was too close to another Metro station.

The Cluny-La Sorbonne became one of Paris's Ghost Stations, a place on a map that only a few knew about. For nearly fifty years, the station remained unused. In the 1980s, city planners decided to revive it because they needed the connection—making it, in his opinion, one of the few ghosts to ever return from the dead.

The station also felt odd to him—a little cold, a little displaced, as if it never got used to its return. No ads graced its white tile walls, and the benches seemed like all others in the Metro, placed at comfortable intervals. The plainness of the walls, the ornate ceiling, the miles of track, disconcerted him on a deep level, and made him feel out of time, as if nothing could touch him here.

He would wander in cold nights, and sit, staring at the ceiling as if it held answers, the great wool coat wrapped around him. If he sat very still, the coat's faint scent of cigarettes and perfume would rise like a half-forgotten memory.

He wouldn't let himself doze—the rats had cured him of that thought—so on nights when he was most exhausted, he would stand and sway like a drunk.

Sometimes he would board a midnight train and ride it to a station near his apartment, but most often, he would sigh, give his station a fond glance, and head back out into the well-lit Parisian night.

Midnight Trains

～

He thought of going to church on Christmas Eve, but he wasn't sure when the services would start. And he knew he would have a choice of listening to Latin or French. He wasn't particularly religious, nor was he greatly interested. Much as he liked the great cathedrals of Europe, he saw them more as architectural curiosities, filled with a potent sense of history, rather than as a place to worship.

A neighbor told him of a concert to be given that night; another mentioned that some of the revues would be open; a third had winked and offered to give him the name of a proper gentleman's club.

Alex finally decided on the concert, and started his walk. He ended up in the Latin Quarter, not far from the Cluny Museum, right near his favorite Metro stop, and somehow he made a decision without making a decision—he walked down the stairs to see if the station was still open on this most unusual night of the year.

The station was open, but he was alone. A train whispered by as if inspired by the city's holiday hush. Even the announcements seemed fewer than normal, and the usually strident voices giving commands in rather harsh French seemed warmer than usual.

He huddled in his great wool coat, and then he saw her. Black hair, wedge cut, lipstick so red that it shouldn't have worked on anyone's face, let alone a face as small and delicate as hers. Her black dress with its diamond shaped neckline and nipped waist looked a bit old-fashioned. Even her stockings seemed dated. They had seams running down the back of her legs.

She held a cigarette in her left hand.

"Light?" she asked in Parisian-accented English. He had become used to that sixth sense Europeans had about him. They all seemed to know his nationality before he even opened his mouth. Even after seven months in Paris, somehow, he had not assimilated.

"No, I'm sorry," he said gently.

"Ah," she said. "It is a filthy habit that they claim will kill me. They know nothing."

She looked at the cigarette as if she were deciding whether or not to hang onto it, and then she touched its tip. It flared, glowed red, and the rich scent of expensive tobacco rose around him.

He frowned at it, wondering if it was one of those electronic cigarettes he'd heard about, but then wondered why she would ask him for a light if it were.

"I thought you needed a light," he said.

"I decided you would not mind," she said.

"Mind what?" he asked.

"Me." She smiled.

He felt dizzy. Maybe it was the cigarette smoke—maybe he had inhaled too much. Or maybe he was tired; it was the end of a very long year, after all, and he was at loose ends—not professionally, never professionally—but personally. Wondering if this was all there ever would be for him: Christmas Eves alone, in beautiful places.

"Why would I mind?" he asked, wishing he could follow her logic.

"Some do," she said.

The station remained silent. He wondered if he could check his phone for the time, and then decided against it because he considered it rude. The fact he was worried about being rude to this woman, this confusing woman, seemed strange to him.

"We probably missed the last train," he said.

She looked at him sideways. Her eyes were the color of dark chocolate, her skin smooth. Her faint perfume seemed familiar.

"You do not take the train," she said.

He frowned at her. Of course, he took the train. He took the train all the time.

Just not here. He'd disembarked here the first time, but after that, he hadn't come here at all. Not for the trains. For the signatures. The feel, the clean white tiles and the dim lights. The sense of something otherworldly.

"You've seen me here before," he said.

"Yes." Quick, with that accent. He was beginning to be able to distinguish one French accent from another, and this one had a curtness, a fillip at the end of words that he hadn't heard before.

"I'm sorry," he said. "I don't remember seeing you."

And he would. He would remember her, delicate and pretty and vibrating with an energy very similar to the trains themselves.

"I know," she said. "I did not let you see me."

He felt a chill. Was she stalking him? Was she crazy? He smiled at her, knowing the smile probably looked fake, knowing it probably seemed dismissive. He couldn't help it. He no longer wanted to stand beside her.

He was about to move when she took the edge of his coat sleeve in her right hand.

"The man who owned this," she said, "he was—how do you say?—a dreamer. Is that the word?"

How would he know what word she wanted when he didn't know what she was trying to say? He bit back the irritation. He didn't want to be near her any more.

"It's just a coat," he said.

"Ah, *mon cher*," she said. "It is not just a coat. It is history, no?"

"No," he said, and walked away. His footsteps echoed in the silence. The skin on the back of his neck crawled. She was watching him; he knew it.

He turned—

But she was gone.

∽

He vowed not to go back. On his entire walk home, the cobblestone slick with rain he had missed while underground, his breath fogging before him, he told himself he was done with the Metro, with the Cluny-La Sorbonne. He'd seen it. He had had enough.

She unnerved him. He recognized that.

The lights of the Eiffel Tower did not comfort him, so he walked to Notre Dame. He checked his phone—no calls, of course—but its clock told him that it wasn't yet midnight.

Well-dressed worshippers walked behind the large Christmas tree near the entrance. The blue lights decorating the tree startled him as they had from the beginning; he was still used to red and green and white. But Paris preferred blue—all along the Champs-Elyse, near Les Halles and in the Place de la Concorde—so very much blue.

Blue Christmas.

He almost walked around the gigantic tree himself. He could hear choral music on the night air, the harmonies pure and clear. He hesitated.

History waited for him in there, that sense of time standing still. Midnight mass at Notre Dame on Christmas Eve had to date back hundreds, maybe even a thousand years.

But it wouldn't satisfy him. Christmas Eve mass wasn't his tradition, wasn't something he really believed in, wasn't something that would touch his heart.

Like the brush of cool fingers as they touched the edge of his coat.

The man who owned this...

How had she known?

He turned, looked back down the street toward the Cluny Museum, which was impossible to see from here. He only had a sense of it, knew that it wouldn't be open, maybe not even lit. It had looked surprisingly dowdy compared to the show the rest of Paris put on in the holiday season.

But he wasn't looking at the museum. He was thinking of the Metro station. By the time he walked back, it would be closed. She would be gone.

Or would she?

He shook his head slightly, and stood, hands in his pockets, staring at the tree and the massive cathedral behind it.

This moment was almost magical enough for him. The

music, the blue lights, the worshippers crossing the ancient stone, going under the ancient arches.

He took one step forward, and a hand slipped through his arm.

He looked to his side. She was there. She wore a black coat now over her black dress, with what looked like fur trim on the wrists and neck. She looked up at him and smiled.

"I do not go into such places," she said. "They make me crazy."

Then, she patted his arm, slipped away, and walked toward the tree. Its blue lights fell across her features, altering them, making her look almost two dimensional, like the old computer images. Her fingers rose toward the branches, brushing them like she had brushed his coat.

She stepped back.

Worshippers went around her, as if she were giving off a force field. One or two frowned at her as they went by. Others gathered their coats tightly around themselves and shivered.

He watched, not certain what she was doing.

The choral music flowed high above them, the harmonies unearthly.

She came back to him, slipped her arm through his, and said, "Let's go."

∽

They walked through the quiet city. The lights made it seem like it had been abandoned mid-party. The scents of cigarettes and perfume followed them, and eventually, he realized it wasn't just his coat. The scents also came from her.

When they came to the Institut de France, illuminated in white, they turned toward the Pont des Arts bridge. In all of his time in Paris, he had never seen the bridge empty—no humans at all.

The benches in the center bore no kissing couples, the wooden slats looked slick and lonely. The day's padlocks remained on the railings, bearing the names of lovers, of happy couples and important dates. No one had cleared them off yet, and he wondered if anyone would over the holiday.

She led him up the bridge, her hands wrapped around his arm. The Seine reflected lights, mostly blue, from the holiday itself.

"You said you know my coat," he said, because he couldn't stand the sound of his heels on the wood. It sounded as lonely as he felt, even though he was walking with a beautiful woman in the most beautiful city in the world.

She led him to one of the benches, and ran her hand across it. Then she rubbed her fingers together as if testing whether or not they were wet.

She sat, then patted the wood beside her. It looked surprisingly dry.

"Your coat, like everything else in this city, has a past," she said softly. "It called to me."

He frowned, wishing she could be clear, maybe afraid that she was clear.

"It is why I watched you in the Metro," she said. "I had forgotten the coat."

Then she shook her head.

"I had forgotten the solstice. I have slept for so long."

He frowned at her. She smiled at him. The light again played on her face, only this time, it was golden light reflected off the water and the buildings on either side of the bridge. The Louvre cast the most light. Perhaps, he thought, it should, since it gave the bridge its name.

The random thoughts, his emotional distance, the remaining loneliness, they still surprised him. This beautiful woman, for all her odd talk, should have intrigued him more.

But he didn't understand her, almost as if she were speaking a different language and he only caught every other word.

"I wanted to believe I was used to iron," she said, "and then it trapped me."

She leaned her head on his shoulder for just a moment. He expected warmth. Instead, he got more perfume, more cigarettes.

"You freed me, you know."

"What?" he asked.

She shook her head. "My people—this was our holiday. Midwinter. We celebrated with lights. We put greenery in our homes. We danced, and feasted, and made love…"

He shuddered. He shouldn't have shivered when a beautiful woman spoke of sex.

"Then we lost our homes, our forests, and came to Paris." She ran a hand along his coat. "The man who owned this, he is dead now."

Alex had supposed that much. Coats like this didn't end up in thrift stores by accident.

"He died defending me. My family, we hid in those tunnels, because the Germans, they decided to do what they had always done. Take us, destroy us, make us into something more like them." She nodded toward the road they had just walked on. "Like that cathedral, with one of our trees outside."

She really was crazy. Germans, dead men, trees. She seemed to be conflating World War II with the Christian Church slowly taking over the pagan celebrations and making them part of the liturgy.

She made him nervous.

But Alex had to ask. "He died defending you?"

She nodded, then looked at Alex, tears in her eyes. "He had a pistol. He held the Germans off while my family and I escaped into the ghost tunnels. We were to leave, but the iron, it held us prisoner, changed us, trapped us. Like rats. That is how I first saw you, through the wall. I thought you were him."

God, what was he to do with her? She was against the church, so he couldn't take her to the priests there for help. And he had no idea what other place might take her in. He wasn't even sure where the homeless shelters were—if there even were homeless shelters in this city.

She clearly had escaped from somewhere—an institution, a caregiver. Someone had to be looking for her, right?

There were several hospitals close to here, one near the Louvre itself. He wondered if he could get her there. He had never had cause to use any of the medical facilities in the city before.

"But you are not him, are you?" She brushed at his coat, as if she were removing lint. "You are not even his reincarnation. Mortals have such short lives."

Alex couldn't help himself. He engaged. "What are you, if not mortal?"

Her smile was sad. "We are so lost you no longer recognize us."

She swept her hair back, then cupped his cheek. Her touch was cold.

"Lonely man," she said. "You believe forever lonely."

He tried not to move, not to betray anything with his expression. How had she known that? Was it that obvious?

It probably was. He was alone on Christmas Eve, after all. He was American. He clearly didn't belong.

It didn't take much to figure out that he was lonely, that he had no one to spend his time with.

"Because you freed me," she said softly, "I owe you."

"I don't understand," he said, "how did I free you?"

"You saw me," she said. "As me, not as what I had become. To most, I was a creature. To others, the ghost of a woman they once loved. But to you, I was myself. You saw only me."

She flattened her palm on his heart.

"It is because you have no woman and lost no woman that you saw me. It is your sadness that brought me back to life."

Like the station itself, something whispered in his head. He didn't like that thought. It made him uncomfortable. But, then, *she* made him uncomfortable.

"So," she said, "a gift to you."

She placed her red lips against his forehead. They were cold, like the rest of her.

And then, oddly, his heart lifted. Like it used to do when he was a child, when his parents were alive.

His mother used to say, *Your heart has wings.*

It had wings now.

"Sometimes," the woman before him said, "hearts shatter. They must be repaired before they work again."

Then she placed her chill forefinger under his chin, lifted his head slightly, and kissed him on the lips.

"I thank you," she said—and disappeared.

∼

He sat on the bench for a long time. Bells rang all over the city for midnight mass—Christmas Eve mass.

She had been an illusion, a figment of his overheated imagination.

He had himself convinced of that by the time he finished the long walk back to his apartment. A Christmas Eve hallucination. An undigested bit of beef, as Scrooge once said of Marley's ghost.

Who turned out to be real enough.

Alex shuddered, not certain why he was so very cold. It was warmer in Paris on Christmas Eve than it usually was in Chicago on Christmas Eve. There, he would not have walked the center of the city in a coat, without a hat or gloves.

He took off the coat, and hung it on the built-in coat hanger near the door. Then he walked into the bathroom to wash the chill from his skin. He turned on the overhead light, and saw his face in the mirror, cheeks rosy from the chill, skin a bit too pale.

But that wasn't what caught his eye.

What caught his eye was the bright red lipstick print on his forehead, with traces of the same lipstick on the side of his mouth.

She had been real.

And she had disappeared as if she had never been.

～

Oddly, he didn't return to the Cluny-La Sorbonne Metro station for nearly a year. If asked, he would not say that was by design. He still used the Metro—maybe more than he had before—but he no longer wandered into the stations by himself, no longer stood waiting for midnight trains to whoosh by him on the way to something much more important.

He had important things to do now. A wife, an infant daughter, newly born. The City of Light had become a city of warmth for him.

He ended up in the Cluny-La Sorbonne by accident on the Winter Solstice, a bouquet of winter flowers in his hand, a bottle of wine under his arm. He had been distracted; he got on the wrong train, which brought him here.

He had already called his wife to apologize for being late. His wife, so lovely, so French. She had no family either, so she helped him make one. They had met on New Year's Eve. He hadn't planned to go out, yet he couldn't stay in. He'd never been in a world-class city on a world-class holiday. It seemed churlish to avoid the celebrations.

And he didn't want to seem lonelier than he already was.

He had stumbled into her. Truth be told, he worried for a half second that she was the crazy woman from the Metro, but his wife was not tiny or crazy. She was tall and blonde and sensible. She filled his arms, and somehow, she filled his heart—the heart he once thought untouchable.

Maybe it had healed. Or maybe...

That sensation of wings returned to him whenever he thought of that moment on the Pont des Arts. A gift, the strange woman had said. A gift he had told no one about.

He was the only person inside the Cluny-La Sorbonne. The birds mosaic flew overhead. The signatures glistened. And then the announcement sounded. The station had closed. Only one exit remained open.

He turned toward the wall, expecting rats.

But there were none.

His breath caught.

He wanted to believe the city had gotten rid of them.

But he had looked up old legends in the past year. Stories of Faerie. Trapped by iron, forced to change shape in their prison. Industrialization destroyed their habitat, just like the church had stolen their power.

The Germans had searched for them. Hitler believed magic would become one of the weapons of the Third Reich. If the Faerie existed, they hid.

And sometimes, all it took was something simple to destroy a curse.

Like a man, looking at a woman, and seeing her for who she was.

Alex shook his head, smiled at his fanciful nature. His wife said he was a dreamer. Perhaps he was.

Now.

He pulled one of the white roses from the bouquet. He knew the strange woman was no longer down here, just like he knew the rats were truly gone. But he needed a token anyway.

He placed the rose on the bench near where he had first seen her.

Whoever she was, she had touched him. She had made him see a future he didn't want, one of lonely Christmas Eves that extended forever, like the Metro tunnels, midnight trains running with no one to board them.

He might have seen her, but she saw him as well.

And because she had, he saw himself more clearly.

That vision, that moment, led to this one.

"Thank you," he whispered—and then walked to the exit, holding flowers for his wife, wine for their celebration, and a little bit of hope, in the wings of his heart.

Except the Music

Kristine Kathryn Rusch

"Where *do* musicians go to die?" She rested on one elbow, her honey brown hair spilling down her arm and onto the pillow. The rest of her body was hidden by the linen duvet, which warded off the room's chill.

Max paused, his left black tuxedo pump—shined to perfection before the concert—in his right hand. The question unnerved him. She had overheard his remark earlier, made at the festival to one of the other performers: *Places like this are where classical musicians go to die.*

His cheeks warmed. He was glad he had his back to her. He slipped the pump over his sock-clad foot, then picked up the other shoe. "It was a joke."

His voice was soft, gentle, as if he wasn't the kind of man who had any malice within him. He knew that wasn't true, and he had a hunch she did as well. But he couldn't be certain of that; he knew so very little about her.

"I know you meant it that way," she said, scrunching up the pillows and pulling the duvet over her large—and not fake—breasts. "Still, it got me to wondering."

He buttoned his shirt halfway, stuffed the bow tie in the

pocket of his pants, and looked for his jacket. The room seemed smaller than it had two hours ago. Then it had seemed charming—slanted ceilings, large windows with a spectacular view of the ocean, a bed in the very center—made, which surprised him—and two antique upholstered chairs next to a curved reading lamp. A small table sat near the even smaller half kitchen. The walls were lined with bookshelves, filled floor-to-ceiling with well-read paperbacks. Until he saw those, he would have guessed that she was a weekender, like so many others in this godforsaken coastal town.

"Wondering?" he asked. "About death?"

She shrugged a pretty shoulder, then turned a lamp on the end table beside the bed. He hadn't noticed the lamp or the end table before. Of course, he had been preoccupied.

"Death is a hobby of mine," she said so calmly that it made him nervous.

He finally turned toward her. She was forty, give or take, but still beautiful in a mature way that he rarely saw outside of the major cities.

She didn't look like the typical classical music groupie. Granted, most of them were middle-aged women with too much time on their hands, but their beauty—if they once had any at all—had faded. They now had a soft prettiness or a competent intelligent look about their tired faces. Dressing up made them look like librarians, and he always sensed desperation in them.

She had stood out, even on the first night of the festival, wearing a lavender silk blouse that made her honey hair seem blond. She was statuesque, overdressed for the Oregon Coast, and yet, he had a sense then—which he still had—that she had dressed down for every one of the concerts she attended. Her hair was long, where most of the middle-aged women wore theirs too short—and she wore no makeup: she needed none.

"You seem startled," she said, and that was when he realized how ridiculous he looked. He still had his shoe in his hand, one sock-clad foot resting on his knee, his shirt unbuttoned and his pants unzipped.

A man who was trying to escape. A man who was done with this one-night stand, as pleasurable as it had been.

A man who should have known better, but had—even at the ripe old age of 45—let his penis get the best of him.

"I just never heard anyone claim they specialized in death before," he said.

"I don't specialize," she said. "I dabble."

She fumbled in the end table's only drawer, finally pulling out a cigarette with an air of triumph. Max winced. The place didn't smell of tobacco, but apparently that didn't mean anything. She hadn't tasted of tobacco either. Maybe the cigarette was of a different kind.

She lit it, and he realized he was both right and wrong: the cigarette was a different type—he just hadn't expected to smell cloves instead of marijuana.

"I wouldn't have bought the season tickets if it weren't for the Mozart on the bill." She took a long drag from the cigarette, then let the blue smoke filter slowly out of her lungs. "I so love that requiem. I think it's the best of all of them."

Max didn't; he preferred Fauré's. "Mozart never finished it. There's some argument about how much of it is his work."

"Precisely." She jabbed the cigarette toward him with the movement of a long-standing smoker. "A requiem partially composed by a dead man. Don't you find that amazingly appropriate?"

"I think it's more appropriate that I find my coat before I leave." He slid the other shoe over his foot. "Did you see where I dropped it?"

She gave him a wicked smile. "I wasn't looking at your clothes."

He gave her a wicked smile in return. No sense letting her know that she was freaking him out.

He stood, looked around the small space for the tuxedo jacket that had cost him more than she probably paid for everything in this place. He remembered this feeling; he'd had it in his twenties before he married, this sinking sensation that if he had simply taken five minutes to talk with the woman before slipping into bed with her, he would never have touched her.

Then he saw the jacket, lying in a heap on top of a fake Persian rug.

"You don't have to run out," she said.

"Actually, I do," he said, picking up the jacket in one neat movement. "I'm staying with a local family, and it would be rude to wake them just because I stayed out too late."

That shoulder shrug again, accompanied by a practiced pout. "So don't go home at all."

"I'm the celebrity," he said, with only a trace of irony. "They'll be watching for me."

As if he were a child again, and they were his parents. He hated this part of music festivals, and he didn't care how much the organizers explained it to him, he still didn't understand the lure. He felt as though the patrons, who had spent thousands of dollars supporting music in the hinterlands, had also bought a piece of him, even though none of them acted that way. They all seemed honored that a man of his skills would deign to visit their home.

He would rather have deigned to drop $500 per night for a suite at a local resort, but that money would have come out of his own pocket. And with CD sales declining precipitously and classical music going through a concurrent but unrelated slide, he had to watch his pockets closely. He still had a lot of money by most people's standards, but he also had a sense that that money might have to last him for the rest of his life.

"Poor, poor pitiful you," she said with a smile. It had been that smile, wide and warm and inviting, that had brought him here in the first place.

"Yep," he said, "poor, poor pitiful me."

And with that he slipped out the front door and into the cool fog-filled night. As he walked the three blocks back to the performing arts center—built twenty years ago with funds raised at the festival—he realized that he hadn't even learned her name.

He was out of practice. There had once been a time when he would have learned enough about her to cover himself for the rest of the festival. Now he was going to have to avoid her.

He sighed, feeling the accuracy of his earlier statement.

This really was where classical musicians went to die.

∽

The North County Music Festival drew several thousand people annually to the Oregon Coast. Max had come every year since the very first, mostly because of Otto Kennisen, the genius behind it all. Otto had taken Max under his wing when Max had been fourteen, and Max owed him for that.

The festival had grown from a tight little community of internationally known musicians who wanted a coastal vacation into one of the more respected classical music festivals in the Northwest. Although that didn't mean much anymore.

When he had started in professional music as an acclaimed prodigy about thirty years ago, the international music scene had more festivals than sense. Classical music sales were at an all-time high, and some musicians had become superstars.

Now, the music wasn't being taught in the schools or played much on the radio, and what was being played was Top 40 Classical—"acceptable" excerpts from Bach or Mozart or Beethoven, rarely the entire works, and never works by "difficult" composers like Schoernberg or Stravinsky.

Europe still loved its classical music, but it also loved its classical musicians, preferring anyone with a European pedigree to an upstart American.

Max was able to make his living touring and playing music —his CD sales were down, but not as far down as some of those former superstars—but the changes bothered him. Once, he would have toured the major concert halls in Portland and Seattle. Now, he made the rounds of the music festivals, and augmented his visits with performances with the remaining reputable orchestras.

Max stopped outside the performing arts center. He had a key—the only one granted to the performers beside the one given to Otto. Max walked around to the back door, and let himself inside.

He had lied to the groupie: he didn't have a real curfew. The guest cottage where he was staying this time had a detached entrance, and a private drive. He could come and go as he pleased. The couple who owned the place probably did keep track of him, but he didn't care. On this trip, at least, he didn't have to answer to anyone.

The performing arts center was dark. It smelled of greasepaint and dry air mingled with a hint of wood and old sweat. He loved that mixture—the smell of an empty theater, no matter what city he was in, no matter the size of the theater.

He wound his way through the curtain pulls and the old flats that lined the backstage area. The piano sat on the stage, covered in a cloth.

He crossed the stage, pushed the bench back, and sat, hands resting on the keyboard cover. After a moment, he took off the cloth, and uncovered the keyboard. He rested his fingers on the keys, but didn't depress them, simply sitting there for a moment, in the dark and silent auditorium, and closed his eyes.

He belonged here. Not on a stage, but with a piano. It was the only place he felt alive. The groupies, the concerts, the strangely worshipful perks of fame, none of them made him feel complete like these moments alone did.

He sighed once. It had been a mistake to go off with the woman, but then, he'd been making a lot of mistakes like that lately. The divorce—his second—had left him vulnerable and even more lonely than usual. He hadn't spent a lot of time with his wife—that had been one of the issues—but he had called her every night, shared the day's events, and he found had intimacy in that. His wife hadn't.

His fingers came down hard on the keys, and he found himself playing Grieg's Piano Concerto in A Minor, with the great crashing chord in the beginning that ran down the scale like a wave breaking against the shore. He'd always thought the piece appropriate to the coast, but the festival had never played it.

And he wasn't playing it now because of the sea. He was playing it because the piece helped him vent—the loud passages weren't angry, but they were dramatic, and he was feeling dramatic.

A woman who called death her hobby.

A woman who had pursued him with the single-mindedness of one possessed.

He played and played and played until he'd exorcised her. Until he felt clean again. Until he felt calm.

Then he put the cloth back on the piano, and sat in the silence for a long time, wishing for something he didn't completely understand.

∼

She was at the next concert, of course. There were two weeks' worth of concerts left until the requiem—and he had a hunch he would see her at all of them.

He wasn't playing in the first set—a Mozart trio, a Bach cantata, and an obscure chamber piece by a composer few of the musicians liked. Still, Max had come early, and he was wearing his tux.

During the Mozart, he peered out of the wings, and saw her in her customary seat, four rows back, where the light of the stage played up the shadows on her face.

Otto Kennisen came up beside Max. Otto clutched his

violin, his thick fingers strong despite his age. He was over eighty now, although he looked like a man in his fifties. He loved the music, but he lacked the stamina he'd had as a younger man. Now he only performed one piece per concert instead of all of them, and even that one piece took something out of him.

Otto's career made Max's look as if it hadn't even gotten started. Otto had been one of the superstar musicians of the 1950s and '60s, and had been in a state of semi-retirement since 1990. He loved the Oregon Coast, and now he brought the musicians he wanted to meet here, rather than going to see them.

As applause rose at the end of the Mozart, Max turned to Otto and nodded toward the woman in the fourth row. "Do you know her?"

"Which her?" Otto squinted.

"The woman with the long, honey-colored hair," Max said.

"The one you escorted out of here last night?" Otto's blue eyes twinkled. "You didn't bother to learn her name?"

Max made himself grin. "It was an oversight."

"Now you want me to correct it," Otto said.

"I want someone to before I embarrass myself."

"Again." Otto's smile was puckish.

"As if you've never done anything like that," Max said.

"At your age, dear boy, I was married with five children." Otto stared into the audience.

And with mistresses all over the globe, Max wanted to add, but didn't. Otto's attraction to women had been legendary. When he'd semi-retired, musicians the world over wondered how Otto would survive with only one country's women to choose from.

"I at least learned their names," Otto said into Max's silence.

"Well, I'm trying to learn hers," Max said, a little more defensively than he had planned.

"I believe Maria knows," Otto whispered as the next group of performers filed across the stage for the Bach cantata.

Max slipped away from him and went in search of Maria, the board chairman, and Otto's answer to everything.

~

But no one knew the woman's name. Max had gone from local volunteer to local volunteer, all of whom claimed they had no idea whom he was talking about. One of the volunteers used most of intermission to check the computer records of the ticket sales, hoping to find the woman by seat number, but there was no name, only a record that someone had paid cash for that seat for the entire festival.

He didn't think of her while he was on stage. That night, he was playing a series of piano concertos, first a Schubert, then an obscure piece by Prince Louis Ferdinand, and ending with a rather frothy Chopin work, familiar and popular with the festival audience.

Max had gotten so lost in the music that as he stood for the final bow, he realized Otto was looking at him in surprise. Usually, Max held part of himself in reserve at these smaller concerts. The venue was too intimate for him, the audience too close.

In larger halls, like the Carnegie, he could lose himself, pretend he was playing alone in his room like he used to do as a child, and when he gazed toward the audience (if he accidentally did) he would see only darkness. Here, he saw faces, and the faces reminded him that he was not by himself.

But here, he had gone to that place, that place that had made him an international sensation, and he could tell just from the quality of the applause that Otto wasn't the only person he surprised. He had taken the audience, held them in that place where only music could go—that place between simple emotion and rapture, the place that was beyond words.

It surprised him that the moment of ecstasy came this night, and surprised him even more that it had happened through him. The audience sensed it, and found that rhythmic pattern in their applause where their hands seemed to speak with one voice. They were on their feet, clapping in unison, a spine-tingling sign of affection that he had missed more than he realized.

He bowed, then rose, following the other musicians off stage, in a daze. The applause continued, stronger, and Otto shook his head as if he couldn't believe it. The festival audiences were appreciative, sometimes embarrassingly so, but never like this.

Otto sighed, then swept his bow in a come-on sign. He led the musicians back to the stage, where the applause got even louder.

Max followed, stood beside the piano, his hand on its frame, and bowed again. As he did, he felt his back muscles knot with tension. Otto would yell at him when the applause ended. They would go backstage, and Otto would remind him, as only Otto could, that Max should give more of himself in all of his performances.

Max had met Otto so young, that any criticism from that

man felt like the criticism from a parent. Max rose out of the bow, saw the audience still standing, saw the faces, saw...

...her. She was clapping like the others, only it seemed as if she believed that he had played that music just for her. Her gaze met his, and he looked away. He wondered how he had ever found her attractive.

He followed the musicians out a second time, and kept going. Even if there was going to be a third bow, or an encore, he would not be part of it.

She had shattered the illusion for him, made him remember what he hated about performance, and it saddened him.

The whole festival saddened him.

He was beginning to think he had lost his heart.

～

Max avoided her that night, but he knew that he might have to speak to her over the next few weeks. In particular, he worried about the next two concerts. One was an informal "encounter" in which Otto spread his expertise to the audience as if they were students who had never heard of classical music before. Most festivals had a version of this, the free afternoon session that existed to drum up ticket sales for the next night's performance.

The North County Music Festival had been sold out for weeks. The encounters really weren't necessary—to anyone except Otto. He claimed he lived for them, and indeed, he seemed to have more energy than usual when he bounded onto the stage, rubbing his hands together as he enthusiastically explained the motifs of the following night's Bartok.

Max's job at the encounters was to accompany the soloist,

Penelope, who had to sing little snippets of a cantata, and to illustrate Otto's sometimes esoteric points, using the music before him to illuminate the melody or the melodic inversion or the composer's little in-jokes.

Max hated these sessions more than anything: He didn't like wooing the audience. They made him feel self-conscious. On these afternoons, he felt like a pianist for hire, not an artist. Anyone could do this part of the job, so long as they'd had enough keyboard training to sight-read the classics.

He was sitting on the piano bench, staring at the Bartok score, trying to pay enough attention to Otto's lecture to catch his cue, when he realized that Otto had stopped speaking.

For a moment, Max froze, wondering if he had missed his entrance. But he had done that in the past, and Otto had laughed at him, or tapped him on the shoulder, or made some joke about musicians living in their own worlds.

But Otto said nothing. Max turned toward the audience, saw Otto clutching one hand to his throat. Penelope took a step toward him, but Otto held up one imperious finger, warning her away. Maria, the board chair, ran toward the back, grabbed a bottle of water, opening it as she brought it to the stage.

Otto took it like a man dying of thirst, guzzled the contents, set the bottle down and shuddered. Max didn't move. Otto was old, but he was a bear of a man, a pillar of the musical community, one of the foundations of the earth. Nothing could happen to Otto.

Nothing would dare.

Then Otto coughed, turned toward the musicians and grinned, and said to the crowd, "Now you understand the drama of silence. How composers use it for effect..."

And he continued with his lecture as if nothing had gone wrong.

If Max hadn't known Otto so well, Max would have thought that it had all been a ploy, but it hadn't.

When he approached Otto after the encounter, lamentably the fourth person to do so in the space of five minutes, Otto held up that imperious finger again.

"I am fine. I made the mistake of sampling some of the fine cheese that the vineyard had brought to serve with its wine, and a bit of Gouda caught in my throat. It is nothing, really."

Max made no reply. Like the good musicians, he knew the value of silence.

∽

He didn't see her at the encounter, but she was at the concert. She caught his arm during intermission, when he had tried to sneak through the lobby to get himself a glass of the excellent wine being served by the local vineyard.

"Are you going to allow dancing during the minuet?" she asked.

He had to lean toward her to understand her. Her question hadn't been one he expected; he had thought she was going to challenge him about the way he had been avoiding her.

"Dancing?" he repeated rather stupidly. "Why would we allow dancing?"

"Because a minuet is a dance. The composer intended it as a dance, not as something that a group of people listen to while seated in plush chairs, pressed against the backs like wallflowers."

Max frowned at her. She had her luxurious hair up that night, which only accented her surprising beauty and, for the first time, she wore a touch of makeup, just enough to inform him that she knew how to use it to accent her assets like most women did not.

Her face seemed familiar to him, and not because he had spent an evening cupping it between his hands. She looked like someone he had known before, or someone famous, someone highly photographed.

"Don't you think it would be fun?" She swept the skirt of her ankle length dress, revealing delicate shoes. "We could move some chairs to the side here in the lobby, leave the auditorium doors open, and let anyone who wanted to dance."

"It's against fire code," he said, wondering if that was even true. He had no idea what passed for fire code in this godforsaken town.

"But it's a crime to embalm the music like this," she said. "You treat it as if it were a museum piece instead of a living thing, a joyous thing. You take away its purpose and make it about the musicians instead of about—"

He didn't wait for the end of her analysis. He excused himself and pushed through the crowd, listening to the pretentious voices discuss pretentious topics with an astounding amount of misinformation. When he reached the concessions, he glanced over his shoulder to make sure she hadn't followed him.

He didn't see her.

He leaned against the service counter with a sense of relief. People pushed against him, trying to get food or drink during the short intermission. The staff behind the counter moved in the make-shift kitchen as if they had been digitized and programmed double-time.

"A glass of white," he said when it was his turn. The server smiled at him like she hadn't done with the others. She seemed delighted that he had deigned to speak to her.

She gave him a glass, her hand shaking, the amber liquid threatening to spill over the lip.

He took the stem, paid her despite her protests, then made his way through the crowd.

Most of the audience didn't notice him, and for that, he was relieved. A few smiled at him and moved out of his way. One elderly man raised a finger—imperious just like Otto's—obviously about to ask a question, but Max simply nodded and moved on.

It took him nearly five minutes to get backstage. He let out a sigh of relief at the plainness, the comparative silence, the lack of bodies pressing against him.

His shoulders relaxed. She wasn't back here. She couldn't be.

He wasn't sure what it was about her that frightened him. They had had a pleasant enough evening, albeit a bit strange. She wasn't really his type, but he was beginning to believe he had no type—at least not one he wanted to put up with permanently.

He sipped the white, which was even better than he had hoped, and then set it down. He needed all his faculties for the second half of the program. The Bach pieces weren't difficult—at least for Bach—but they weren't pieces he normally played; he couldn't fake his way through them.

Not that he would ever fake in front of Otto, anyway. The very idea made Max shudder.

He turned, saw Otto leaning against a heavy wood table that had clearly been used as a props table for a recent play, and frowned. Otto's face was an unusual shade of red.

The room was hot—no air-conditioning, which usually wasn't a problem on the coast—but could be when there were so many bodies in one place. Still, Otto didn't look good.

"You don't have to go out, you know," Max said softly. "Hu knows the violin part. She's been doing it for years."

Otto raised his head as if realizing Max was there for the first time. "No worries. The heat and I do not get along, but I've had Maria open the doors. The breeze should cool things down."

His voice was strong, but beads of sweat dotted his forehead.

"The audience will understand," Max began.

"The audience never understands." Otto reached into his breast pocket and removed the decorative handkerchief. He used it to blot his forehead. "To them, we are kissed by the gods, untouched by human concerns."

Max suppressed a smile. The old-fashioned way of looking at performing. He had forgotten that Otto had trained in the days when performers were gods instead of tabloid fodder.

In the concert hall, a bell pinged, signaling that the audience should return to their seats. Otto wiped his face a final time, took a deep breath and winced as if it hurt, then straightened his shoulders.

"Otto..." Max said, elongating the word, making his warning clear.

Otto waved his hand. "I am fine."

He stood up, but his knees buckled. Max hurried over to catch him. Otto was heavier than Max expected, and Max struggled beneath his weight.

"Help!" he yelled. "Someone!"

He eased Otto to the ground, loosened his bow tie, then his jacket, and finally his shirt. People scurried around him, three already on cell phones, dialing 911.

Otto's face was a lurid shade of red.

"Anyone done CPR recently?" Max asked. He had never used his training, which was two decades old.

"Move aside," someone said from behind him. He turned as Hu crouched beside him. "I have EMT training."

He didn't ask why a world-class violinist would have EMT training. He just stepped aside, like she had commanded him, watched helplessly as she worked Otto's chest, checked his mouth for blockages, and murmured words of encouragement.

Outside, a siren wailed.

There would be no proving to the audience today that their musicians were gods. The tower of strength, the most famous of them all, Otto, had fallen.

And Max felt like one of the main supports of his world had fallen too.

∼

The concert went on, of course, with Hu's bruised hands caressing the violin part. Her hair, normally braided and curled in a bun behind her head, had come undone while she worked on Otto, so she had taken it down. The blue-black strands waved, hanging free, catching on the chin rest and the neck support.

Twice Max had seen Hu shake her hair back during a rest and once he had thought he saw tears in her eyes.

No one danced to the minuet. No one would now, even if it were permitted, not with Otto hauled away on a stretcher, insisting weakly that his festival continue.

Sometimes music was an antidote, a relief after crisis, but not this time. Sonatas, perhaps, or symphonies, would have felt appropriate, but minuets were happy bits of fluff, toe-tapping music as Max's groupie had mentioned, and while the audience was attentive, they clearly did not want to tap their toes.

No one did.

By default, Max had become the one in charge—the second most famous, the most experienced, the only one with real power besides Maria. And briefly, Max had toyed with substituting a different piece of music.

But they had little left that they had rehearsed as a group. Only the minuet, a few obscure 20th Century pieces that Otto had sprinkled into the Top 40 Classical like pills stuck in dessert, and the requiem. The requiem was extremely inappropriate, even if the choir was ready—which it was not. Most of the soloists hadn't arrived yet. They would reach the coast tomorrow.

So Max had gone on stage, informing the audience that Otto wanted the festival to continue, and then introduced Hu. She normally played only in the afternoons at the encounters or as second chair to Otto, if a second chair were needed. Mostly Otto avoided any pieces with violin parts if he was not going to play.

And Hu, despite the way she had used her hands on Otto's chest, despite the problems with her hair, had acquitted herself beautifully. Her playing was the only inspired playing among the chamber musicians.

Everyone else seemed to be marking time until the concert ended. Including Max.

And finally it was done. There was applause, even a shout or two of bravo (most likely for Hu) and some sighs of relief, all from the musicians themselves. They bowed as they always did, smiled at the applause as they always did, and then trailed off the stage into the darkness beyond.

Max's wine glass still sat on the table. Otto's bow tie and handkerchief littered the floor. This was not a real theater—not the kind that Max preferred, with stage managers and a hundred employees, people who would have made the reminders of the night's trials disappear.

Instead, he bent, picked up the bow tie, pocketed it, and grabbed the handkerchief, still wet from Otto's brow.

Hu stopped beside Max, still clutching her violin. It always surprised him how small she was.

"What do you think his chances are?" Max asked.

She shrugged, but wouldn't meet his gaze. That was answer enough.

"We should go to the hospital," she said.

He wasn't sure he could take the hospital—Otto looking frail, vulnerable. Mortal. But he would miss Max if Max wasn't there.

"I'll take care of everything here, then join you," Max said.

Hu nodded and hurried off. Max stood there for a moment longer, clutching Otto's handkerchief. Every festival he had ever played had a crisis. A musician down with food poisoning; a damaged instrument; the time that a regional festival lost its venue a day into the concert series.

But those seemed small compared to this. This felt

catastrophic—the world shifting, becoming a place Max no longer recognized.

Someone touched his arm. He looked down. Maria, the board chair, stood beside him, her face wet with tears.

His breath caught. "News?"

She shook her head. "I'm just not sure what to do. The other board members have been asked if tomorrow night's concert will happen. And then there's next week."

Max's mouth went dry. If they were talking like this, then Otto wouldn't be back this evening. Max had somehow hoped...

He shook his head. Someone had to make decisions, and no one could make decisions about the music except Otto. That was why she had come to Max. Max was the only other musician she really knew at this year's festival.

"This is Otto's baby," Max said. "He'd be furious if we abandoned it now."

She bit her lower lip, another tear running down the side of her face. "But the violin solo—it's the Paganini tomorrow."

"Hu can handle it," Max said, hoping that was true. And if it wasn't, then they'd substitute. The audience would understand. The audience *had* to understand.

They weren't gods after all.

"But we need a second chair—"

"I have a friend at the Portland Symphony," Max said. "We'll see who we can find."

Maria clutched his hand, squeezed it, and let go. "Thank you," she whispered, and ran off.

He stuffed the handkerchief in his pocket and sighed. Someone had to take over the music side. It was better than hovering around Otto's bed, worrying.

Although Max was worrying already.

~

Three hours later, he returned to the performing arts center, parked, and looked at the darkened building. He had lied to himself, told himself he had come to see whether everything was in order, but he knew it was. He had worked with the stage manager the way Otto usually did, even taking Otto's violin to Otto's beach "cottage"—a small mansion on a cliff face overlooking the Pacific. The housekeeper had offered to take the instrument, but Max, knowing how precious it was, placed it in Otto's music room himself.

Then he had gone to the hospital, only to discover they had life-flighted Oscar to Portland. They didn't want to trust a world-famous violinist to the inadequacies of small-town doctors. Hu, who had waited for Max, had added her own interpretation as she drove him home.

"They don't want him to die here," she said quietly. "They're afraid they'll get blamed."

"Should they?" Max asked.

"He's eighty," Hu said, "and he's very ill. You tell me."

He didn't have to. Eighty, and Otto had had an incident at the encounter, then refused to let anyone help him. Perhaps Otto believed the immortality myth as well.

Max dropped off Hu, then committed his internal lie, heading to the Performing Arts Center to make certain everything was all right. He knew when he saw Otto in Portland tomorrow, Otto would want to know his festival was still going fine.

But really, Max thought as he unlocked the door, stepped inside, and smelled the greasepaint, he had wanted to come to the closest place to home that he had on the coast. It certainly wasn't that free-standing guest cottage up a windy road. It was here, among the empty seats and quiet stage, where the piano waited, looking lonely under the dim backstage lights.

He went to her and ran his fingers along the keys, but didn't play. He was unable to play, worried he would find only silence inside his own head.

He sat there for a long time, afraid to think, afraid to move. Afraid to acknowledge that even he had believed in Otto's immortality, in the redemptive power of a man who, with just a violin, could steal the voice of God.

∽

The drive to the hospital took forever. Max had come alone, even though he knew he should have offered some of the other musicians transportation. This was a scheduled day off—in that, they had been fortunate. If it had been an encounter afternoon, Max had no idea what they would have done.

Otto's prognosis was not good. Apparently, he had already refused treatment that would have saved his life—treatment he had needed nearly a year before.

Max had been wrong: Otto had not believed the immortality myth. He had known this was coming, and had chosen to perform during his last year instead of spend it in doctor's offices, laboratories, and hospitals, getting poked and prodded and gradually reduced of dignity.

Max learned all of this from Otto's second wife, Dani, who

seemed relieved to finally tell someone. Until now, Otto had demanded her silence.

But when she finished telling Max the news, she let Max into Otto's room, and then left them alone.

Otto had tubes up his nose and protruding from his arms. Only his eyes seemed familiar, bright and sad at the same time.

Max sat beside the bed. "You never said anything."

Otto rolled those eyes, just like he would have if Max had played a particularly emotionless set.

"My dear boy," Otto said. "If I had said anything, you would have treated me like glass. I am not glass. I am merely old."

"And ill," Max said.

"And dying," Otto corrected. "I had hoped to make it through the festival. Now you must finish it for me."

Max folded his hands together. He was supposed to leave before the end of the festival; he had no role in the final night, the night of the requiem. The piano was not required.

"The festival," Otto said, "is yours now. Forever, if you want it. I would like it to go on. And you shall get the house too. Dani does not mind. It is less hers than mine. She prefers the house in Milan, and will of course get the apartments in New York and London. This place will die without someone who loves it."

Max almost protested. He did not love it here. He had come every year for Otto.

"You'll get better," Max said.

"No," Otto said. "There is a time when people do not get better. No matter who they are."

Max wanted to take Otto's hand, but it looked frail, not like the hand that had so commanded the bridge on his violin, making it sing.

Except the Music

Otto coughed. The sound was moist, almost as if Otto were drowning. He finally managed to catch his breath. It had to be sheer force of will that kept the moistness from his voice. "There is no cure, you know. Except the music."

Max wasn't sure what Otto was referring to. "Otto, I—"

"It is not necessary to say anything more." Otto gave him a weak smile. "Save my festival. There is still a week left."

∼

One week and a lot of music. Max had never known exactly how much Otto had done. Maria coordinated everything—hiring the violinist to take second chair, picking up the additional musicians from the airport, dropping off those who had finished their stint.

Max did not listen to the rehearsals—he didn't step into that part of the job, partly because he lacked the expertise to guide others. When Max had returned from Portland, Maria had pulled him aside and asked him, shyly, if he thought it was still appropriate to do the requiem.

It made Max uncomfortable as well, but he knew Otto: Otto had planned all of the music himself. Max would not second-guess him.

And then, on Thursday, just as that night's performance ended, word came that Otto had died.

Max made the announcement to the still-gathered crowd. He could not remember what he said or how they reacted, only that he hadn't been able to keep his voice level. Otto would have said that Max had shown an unusual amount of emotion on stage.

Afterwards, Max comforted the stagehands and the board, reassured musicians that they would both perform and get paid, and helped the stage manager clean the house. When it was all over, Max locked up, alone, his hands shaking. They were the only part of his body over which he had no control.

He stood outside in the sea fog, locking up the last door. His car was the only one still in the parking lot.

"You weren't lying."

He didn't have to turn to recognize the voice. It was her—the unknown woman, the fling, the one who had so attracted and annoyed him at the start of the festival. Weeks ago.

It seemed like years.

"I'm very tired," he said.

"And not in need of comfort?" Her voice held amusement, not an offer.

He felt a surge of anger at her presumption. What could she give him, after all? The pillars of the earth had fallen, and he no longer stood on solid ground.

She put a hand on his back and he moved away, violently.

"What do you want?" he snapped.

Her eyes still sparkled in the hazy parking lot lights. "Dancing for minuets. Or corpses. For requiems."

He felt chilled. The air was damp, and she was almost invisible, lost in swirling mists of fog.

"What did you do?" he whispered.

"Nothing," she said. "It was inevitable. And you know that."

Then she stepped backwards. The fog swallowed her as if she had never been.

He reached for her—

—and found nothing.

He stood in the chill for another ten minutes, waiting for her to come back, although he wasn't sure why. He didn't even have a name to call or an understanding of who she was, or why she had deliberately provoked him.

The damp air wet his cheeks and the shaking in his hands didn't stop. He leaned against the door, but didn't open it. Nor did he go to his car.

He just stood in the fog, alone, listening to the ocean boom, and wishing for silence.

~

He almost didn't go to the festival on the final night. His performance had ended the night before. He had planned to do a solo, a favorite Chopin, but at the last minute had pulled Brian, the principal cellist, into service accompanying him in Fauré's *Élégie* for cello and piano.

That performance had been difficult enough: Max could almost imagine Otto sitting in the wings, listening for the moment when the piano became more than an instrument, the music more than notes. Max wasn't sure how well he played; the audience seemed to love it—as much as an audience could love a mournful piece of music—but he hadn't been playing for them.

He had been playing for the ghost in the wings, the one who would never again tell him how well he had done or that he had failed.

Max remembered to stand and bow at the end, and he had worked hard not to look in the first few rows for her. He was afraid if he saw her again, he would take her thin throat between his two powerful hands, and press until she could not say another word.

Ever.

Then he had gone back to the guest cottage, looked at his plane ticket, and felt the pull of somewhere else—anywhere. He had already canceled next week's performance in Texas; he had to stay for the first of Otto's memorial services, this one to be held here. There would be others—one in New York that Max wouldn't miss either, and another in Vienna, which he might have to, given his own touring schedule.

The next six months would be hard, and he would need to rest, need to think about this shuddery feeling that he now seemed to have all the time.

He went so far as to look up Hu's number, to ask her to say a few words before the requiem, to end the festival with a plea for next year's funding and to keep Otto's memory alive. But his hand froze over the phone.

For his sake, and for Otto's, he had to stay.

∽

Max wore a tux, even though he did not have to since he was not performing. Still, he walked onto the stage with all the dignity of a performer, startled to see risers where the piano normally was, and chairs all the way to the lip.

He had to stand in front of the empty chairs, where the conductor would be in just a few moments. And Max used a microphone, which he normally abhorred doing, hating the amplification of sound, the way it turned the beauty of the human voice into something almost mechanical.

He spoke of Otto as he had first seen him—a vibrant man in his fifties, who had taken a frightened boy under his wing. Max had been a prodigy, but he had been sheltered—and suddenly he was famous, touring, lauded for his immense talent at his very young age.

Age will creep up on you, Otto had told him that first day. *Become the best musician for any age.*

Max had forgotten that. He had forgotten so many things—the way that Otto had shown him that music was more than a collection of notes; it was also a history of all that had come before.

Music does not exist without the audience. It is written for the audience. The performer is merely a collaborator with the composer. And centuries from now, the greatest composers will be remembered; only the music historians will remember the greatest performers.

Max did not say that in his tribute, nor did he say much about his own experiences with Otto, preferring to speak only of Otto's dedication, and his consistent support of young, up-and-coming musicians, many of whom would soon be on the stage.

"Otto planned the requiem," Max said. "He had known this would be his last festival. He had hoped to stand in the back and listen. We must imagine him there, whispering a bit too loudly to Dani, and being the first to shout, 'Bravo!'"

And then, before Max lost his voice entirely, he shut off the mike and left the stage. Only when he got to the wings did he realize he had said nothing about next year's festival or about fundraising. The festival would have to fight that battle without him.

As the performers walked onto the stage, he took the side

stairs, just like Otto used to do, and walked toward the back. In spite of his best plans, Max looked for the woman. She was not in her seat. Some elderly man Max had never seen before leaned forward as if he had been waiting for the requiem all of his life.

Strange that she wouldn't show when she had said that she had come only for that piece. Of course, *she* had been strange. Perhaps she had finally decided her behavior was inappropriate. Perhaps she had embarrassed herself that night in the fog.

Perhaps she was gone for good.

He felt an odd pang at that thought, almost as if he had relished tangling with her again—this time, letting her know his fury at her insensitivity. But this evening was not about her.

It was about Otto, and Mozart's *Requiem,* a piece of music —as she had said—written by the dead for the dead.

Max shuddered a little as he reached the back of the auditorium. He moved to the spot near the doors, where the room's most perfect acoustics lived.

And there he listened as the orchestra swelled, and the chorus started the introduction, one of the few sections Mozart had written in its entirety, taking the Latin words from the Catholic Mass for the Dead, begging for eternal rest and perpetual light, against the darkness that would eventually befall everyone.

The words faded, but the music did not. It rose, the soprano's voice soaring like a prayer, the bass, tenor, and contralto joining, adding balance and strength.

In the past, Max had felt his soul rise for only a few performers—Otto had been one of them—but on this night, with this piece, the orchestra, chorus, and soloists seemed to be speaking as one, their power raising goosebumps on his flesh, and transforming the auditorium into a place sublime.

He had not expected it. He had expected to listen, as he had always done, trying to parse the sections that Mozart had written and those Süssmayr had finished—the acolyte never quite living up to the original.

But those considerations were beyond him. Instead, Max let the music sweep through him and soothe him, and give voice to all the complicated emotions within.

There is no cure, Otto whispered a little too loudly. *Except the music.*

Max started and looked. He felt Otto's presence as if the man were beside him. But no one was.

Except the woman.

He knew better than to ask her what she wanted. That question had led to the response that had angered him the last time.

He was going to tell her to leave; instead, he blurted, "Who are you?"

And she smiled the smile that had attracted him in the first place, wide and warm and inviting.

"It's about time you asked," she said.

To his surprise, she curtsied. No one else seemed to notice.

She rose slowly, her movements as practiced as if she had done this a thousand times before.

"I am your muse," she said. She touched his cheek lightly. She still smelled ever so faintly of cloves. "Perhaps now, you will pay attention."

And then she vanished. Literally disappeared. Max could not see her, or touch her. But he could feel her.

He could still feel her fingers on his cheek, just as he had felt Otto beside him earlier.

A shiver ran through him, and he looked at the stage. No one had noticed his conversation with the woman.

Only Otto had noticed her before. Otto, who had always had a finger on music's soul.

Otto had once told Max there was magic in music, and a touch of the angels. Only Max had mostly forgotten it—or perhaps he had never learned it, not really, not understanding how music did more than provide an evening's entertainment.

It existed for dancing—and for mourning.

It was the most basic of human expressions, and it was his gift.

Which he had mostly been ignoring, using it to achieve wealth through technical perfection, almost never letting it speak from his heart.

No wonder she had looked familiar. She had shown up at other concerts—not often—or perhaps he had just not noticed her. But she had been there on those nights when he had forgotten where he was and what he was doing, how much he was being paid, and who was listening.

She had been doing her best to stand beside him all this time, and he had treated her like a one-night stand. Over and over.

No wonder Otto had chided him.

No wonder Max had failed to respect himself.

He leaned against the cold wall, and listened to voices rising in remembrance of a great man, using the talent of other great men long dead, feeling the power that lingered, the intangible bits of memory that wove themselves into a benediction. He did not feel forgiven.

He felt renewed.

And when it was all over, he didn't leave as he had planned. Instead, he walked down the aisle, determined to find Maria, the board chair, and begin the plans for next year—to continue Otto's dreams, yes, but also to help Max start his own, whatever they might be.

Loop

Kristine Kathryn Rusch

Amelia could not believe she was actually sitting there. The log was cold and damp beneath her jeans. The trees above dripped water. Out in the mist, an owl called, followed by the faint echo of a dog barking. Laughter from the porch made her cringe.

Above the ground fog, the sky was clear. Stars twinkled and a tiny satellite made its consistent way around the heavens. Her cheeks tingled with chill.

She could still feel the controls, clutched in her left palm. The sharp plastic edges bit into her skin.

Somehow she hadn't imagined it would be like this. Somehow she had thought the device would send her into the middle of an extended memory: *she* would be sitting on the porch, Tyler's hand warm on her knee, Jeanne and Paul beside them, the smell of eggnog in the air. She had wanted to relive it all, not observe it from the side.

"More eggnog anyone?" Tyler's voice had a deep richness. It warmed her. She longed to crawl onto the porch, knock her old self out of the way, and sit beside him again.

She had tried that when she first arrived. Her hands went

through them all—and they hadn't noticed. She felt like Emily in *Our Town*: trapped in the best memory of her life, and no one saw her.

"Me," her own voice replied. It sounded higher, more confident than it did from the inside.

"Yeah, and a little more rum," Paul said.

"None for me." Jeannie's southern accent had an air of falseness. Amelia didn't remember her well. Paul had broken up with Jeanne after dating her for only a year.

A long time ago.

It had all been a long time ago.

Amelia got up off the log, brushed the water off her jeans (—how could she feel that and not her friends on the porch?—), and let herself in the back door. The kitchen was as she remembered it: done in browns and tans, filled with too many dishes, too many books and too many papers. The room smelled like turkey and pumpkin pies cooled on the counter. A calico cat—Nerdboy! She hadn't thought of Nerdboy in years—slept on an overstuffed kitchen chair.

Tyler stood over a large punchbowl filled with eggnog batter. With his right hand, he poured a steaming bowl of hot rum into the mixture. His dark hair curled over his collar, and his broad shoulders strained at his denim workshirt.

She had forgotten how slim he was, how graceful his movements. As she walked toward him, Nerdboy looked up. His tail thumped against the chair, and his ears went back. He growled.

Tyler half-turned. "What is it, Nerdie?"

She froze there, waiting for him to see her. Nerdboy growled again.

"There's nothing there, kiddo," Tyler said, and returned to

the eggnog. In the living room, the opening strains of the Elvis Presley version of "Blue Christmas" blared before someone turned the stereo down.

"Hey, you hiding in there or what?" Paul yelled.

"Coming!" Tyler ladled eggnog into three glass cups, looped his fingers through the handles, and carried them into the living room. Amelia followed. A fifteen foot Douglas fir dwarfed the room, decorated only in colored lights and clear glass balls. Elvis crooned in the background, and brightly wrapped packages huddled under the tree. Her younger self patted the couch for Tyler. He handed Paul a cup before sitting down.

Her younger self looked up and the smile froze on her face. She grabbed Tyler's wrist, nearly spilling some eggnog on his shirt. "Tyler, look. There she is again. That woman."

Tyler set his cup on the coffee table before looking up. Amelia didn't move. She wanted them to see her. She wanted *him* to see her. "Hon, it's shadows."

"No," Paul said. "I see someone too." He stepped out of the living room. Amelia walked toward him. If Paul believed, then Tyler would too. Then she could touch him again—

She squeezed the controls tightly, holding her breath as Paul walked into the darkened hallway. The machine squealed, and light shattered around her.

∽

She could see nothing for what felt like an eternity. Then the white light faded into red and green spots. The air was warm, warmer than it had been in the house. She didn't move, uncertain of where she was.

The spots cleared and she found herself in the lab. The lab was as empty as it had been when she got there hours—a day?—ago. The forlorn Christmas tree left a pile of needles on the tiled floor. The Happy Holidays banner had come loose from its nails and the middle sagged. Dirty cups sat on the worktables and gift-wrap overflowed from the wastebaskets.

It took a moment before she focused on the figure sitting in the middle of the mess. It was another version of herself—the version she had seen in the mirror that morning—fifty-six, slightly overweight, with deep, sad lines forming around her mouth, and silver hairs overpowering the black ones in her short haircut.

Something was wrong. She shouldn't be able to see herself. Not here. Not in the now. She should be *in* herself, experiencing the moment from the inside.

Perhaps that was a moment from her past. Perhaps that was what she had looked like before she had gone to the memory. Perhaps she hadn't come all the way back.

She looked down at the controls, but they were still hidden by that incredibly bright light. She couldn't feel her left hand.

Tyler would have known what to do. Tyler always test-ran the equipment, while she stayed back and monitored the progress from the Now-station. Only no one was monitoring for her. No one could see if the small red malfunction light was blinking.

It would be so easy, she had said to herself after having too much rum and eggnog alone in that big empty house. *Just a little trip back, set for only ten minutes: routine. No one would argue with routine.*

No one would even notice. No one was scheduled to return

to the lab until the day after New Year's, and that was Mark and Christy, the junior team, who would test all the equipment to see if everything was running properly for the week's experiments. Mark and Christy were grad students who had only been on the Project since Tyler died. Even if they saw the malfunction button blinking, they wouldn't know what to do about it.

Not that it mattered. No one had survived in the time stream this long. Tyler had thought it impossible to last more than a day. The government forensic experts who had autopsied him had thought some temporal distortion had killed him. They had warned her to pick the next traveler carefully—someone young with a lot of stamina and no family history of severe medical problems. Having anyone else travel would jeopardize the government funding and the Defense Department approval.

Amelia didn't know how long she had been in the stream. Tyler had never mentioned a white light.

She closed her eyes and reached for her left hand. Her fingers encountered fabric. She followed it until she felt her left wrist bone—with her right hand, as if it were someone else's wrist—then slid her fingers around to the controls. The plastic was cold. She couldn't feel any of the indented keys. She fumbled, reached, and heard an explosion loud as a clap of thunder.

∼

The sun warmed her face. Her back was wet. An odd tingling ran up her left side. Her left arm had gone to sleep. She opened her eyes and found herself staring at a sky so blue it looked like it had been painted by a child who loved bright colors.

Water lapped around her, pushing at her clothes, raising her off the ground and then retreating. A hesitant lover, uncertain of his touch. She smiled and reached for Tyler as she had every morning since she was twenty-five.

He was gone.

She sat up, memory returning. Her left arm dragged in the sand, the control fused to her hand as if she too were made of some sort of synthetic. The sand was white, the air humid. The branches on the palm trees swayed with the gentle breeze. To her left the ocean stretched as far as she could see. To her right, the beach ended in a rise that led to a modified Spanish adobe.

Amelia had never been here before.

She stood. Her arm swung heavy and useless beside her. Water dripped off her hair, and down her clothes. Her tennis shoes were soaked. That sensation bothered her most of all. She slipped off one shoe, then the other, picked them up and walked barefoot across the hot sand.

Halfway to the adobe, her feet encountered stone. The stone path led through a hedge of oversized ferns. She walked through it and stood on a rise overlooking a shaded verandah. Small groups of white wicker furniture surrounded a small swimming pool. Two large glass doors were propped open. Thin white curtains blew inside the house, revealing more white furniture and a white carpet. A serving tray bearing a glass filled with brown liquid floated by itself through the double doors. It stopped near one of the furniture groupings.

"...can't." A woman's voice floated up toward Amelia. Amelia walked down the rise beside the pool, looking for the source of the voice.

A young woman sat in one of the wicker lounge chairs, slim legs crossed at the ankles. She wore a sheer white wrap with bikini bottoms underneath. Her feet were bare. Her right hand rested on a glass table, the beverage beside her. The serving unit floated back toward the house.

"I know this isn't the most festive place to spend Christmas. But—" her voice broke "—Grandmama's funeral is tomorrow, and all the relatives will already be here."

Amelia couldn't see the phone at all, but she knew it had to be there. The young woman was speaking into the air. Amelia wondered how the young woman heard the voice on the other end. She walked closer, remaining half-hidden, uncertain if the young woman could see her.

Then she stopped. The young woman had long black hair, a narrow face, and wide dark eyes.

She looked like Tyler.

She looked exactly like Tyler.

Amelia sat on one of the wicker chairs near the pool. Her left hand bumped the edge of the chair, sending a dull ache to her shoulder. The unit squealed and light eased out of its sides. The fingers on her right hand tingled.

A lump rose in her throat. She and Tyler had never had children. On purpose. So what had brought her here, to this woman, near Christmas? It was somewhere beyond Now, somewhere in the future, judging by the devices. Had Tyler had a child he hadn't told her about? He had had so many relationships before they met.

"No, look. I'm sorry," the young woman said. "I can't talk any more." She moved her right hand slightly and sighed. The connection had been severed somehow. Then she sat forward and squinted in Amelia's direction.

"Grandmama?"

The young woman reached for Amelia.

"Grandmama?" she repeated.

The light grew brighter. Amelia reached back. Their fingers met, but did not touch. Instead, the light engulfed her, and she could no longer see.

∽

The gifts were open. Brightly colored wrapping paper lay in shreds on the floor. Paul and Tyler sat cross-legged on the hardwood floor, playing with matchbox trucks. Jeanne and Amelia's younger self leaned on the back of the couch, arms crossed, and made snide comments about boys always being boys.

Amelia stood next to Paul. His red truck skid across the floor and went through her feet. Her entire left side tingled, and the tingle had grown in her right fingers. She wanted to kneel next to Tyler and ask him what was happening. She wanted him to reassure her that everything was all right.

But everything was not all right. She was wasting away. Tyler had had the same symptoms, spread over a longer period.

She crouched, her left hand scraping the smooth wood floor. Paul started, then slid back, grabbing Tyler's arm as he moved. "There she is," Paul said.

"Where?" Amelia's younger self stepped forward. Jeanne followed.

Tyler looked up. "I don't see anything."

"Jesus," Paul said. "It looks like your mother, Amelia."

"Mother was never in this house," Amelia's younger self said.

Amelia remained still. She met Paul's gaze steadily.

"Where?" Tyler asked.

"Right next to me," Paul said.

Suddenly Tyler saw her. She recognized the light in his eyes. "My God," he said. He got up and walked around her. She stifled the urge to move with him. Then he tried to put his hand on her shoulder. She leaned into the touch, but his hand went right through her.

"My God," he repeated. "This isn't your mother, Amelia. This is you."

Amelia nodded. Tyler jumped back.

"This isn't possible," Amelia's younger self said. "I'm right here. I'm alive."

"And so is she." Tyler crouched in front of Amelia. His cheeks were flushed. "You can hear me, can't you?"

"Yes," she said.

"Yes," he whispered. "But I can't hear you." He tried to touch her again, and frowned as his hand went through her. "It's some kind of distortion field. You're not a ghost at all."

"I'm alive," Amelia said. She had to repeat it twice before Tyler understood.

"It is a distortion field. Time experiments?"

The older Tyler would have yelled at her for giving his younger self that much information, but she didn't know what it would hurt now. He had already seen her.

She nodded.

"My God," he said. "They work."

She shook her head and touched her arm. "Help me," she said. "Please. Help me."

"She's asking for help," Paul said. "Tyler—"

But Paul's voice was fading. The light had returned: brighter this time. It burned into her left hand, along her side. She cried out in pain—and then the light engulfed her.

∼

Colors flashed behind her closed eyelids. She was on a cold, hard floor. Her head ached. She sat up and rubbed her forehead with her good hand before opening her eyes.

The lab again. Her Now-self still huddled over the controls like they were her last link to sanity. She stared at her Now-self for a moment. Had she really looked that lost before stepping into the time stream? She used to pity women who looked like that after they had lost their man. Tyler had been dead six months. She still had the experiments, their house, their friends.

But they all felt so empty without him. An ache grew in her chest.

It's a dream, Tyler had said. *We're living a dream.*

She made herself get up. She swayed a bit, unused to moving without the help of her left arm. She walked around the benches to her Now-Self. Her Now-self was fiddling with the controls. Amelia remembered that moment: she only had time to return to one memory. She had to make it a good one.

Odd that she hadn't picked one with her and Tyler alone.

But she had been thinking Christmas, since it was the loneliness of the holidays that had driven her to the lab in the first place. And the best Christmas had been that first one in the country house, with Paul and Jeanne. She and Paul and Tyler had always compared the others to that one, thinking that nothing could measure up.

But it didn't really seem that special now. Perhaps it had been special because it had been the first.

Her Now-self looked up and gasped. Amelia sat on the bench across from her. Her Now-self reached out just as the air exploded around them.

∼

She couldn't get air. Her mouth was filled with water. Her right arm flailed. She opened her eyes to a blue distorted world. Underwater. She was under water. She had to reach the surface or she would drown.

She kicked up, three good strong kicks that pushed her to the air. She spit the water out of her mouth and took deep, thankful breaths. Water rippled around her. Her presence had disturbed it. She was in a pool. The pool she had seen near the adobe house. She kicked her way to the ladder on the pool's deep end, and grabbed onto the metal railing with her right hand. The tingling had progressed into her wrist. She could barely move the hand at all.

She was running out of time.

She climbed out and sat on the side, breathing heavily. The young woman was asleep in her lounge chair, left arm covering her beautiful face. Amelia knew better than to try and touch her. The people were not real but the places were, as if they were a revolving set for a cosmic play.

Amelia grabbed a towel off the stack and wiped the water from her face. The humid air almost felt cool. She wrapped the towel around her neck, and wandered inside the house.

The main room was white with white furniture: obviously

for entertaining. The back rooms had beds in them with clothes scattered about. The young woman did not live alone. A cat slept in the middle of one of the beds, and gave Amelia the evil eye as she passed.

She stopped in the only bedroom that looked as if it hadn't been used recently. The bed was an oversized four-poster like the one she and Tyler had had, with pale pink sheets under a pink and brown patterned spread. But that wasn't what drew her. What drew her were the pictures on the walls.

Some looked familiar: an early date with Tyler at a seafood place; a prize-winning photo of their first lab. But others were dream photos: her in a white wedding gown, Tyler in a black tux smiling down at her; both of them smiling in professional photography fashion at the tiny baby she held in her arms. Then baby pictures and school pictures of a young girl surrounded by family groupings with Tyler aging as he had and the temporal distortion wasting him away. He wore another tux for the young girl's wedding, looking proud and fatherly, and after that, he appeared in no more pictures even though they continued to chronicle the girl, and then her daughter—the young woman Amelia had seen outside.

She sighed and leaned on the bed. Her body was shaking. A life that she hadn't lived, complete with photographs. This had probably been her room until she died.

The shaking turned into a shudder. A life she hadn't lived. A life she could never live, even if she had married Tyler and had a child. She would die in this time stream—in this loop—and no one would know. They would just think she had disappeared.

She stared at the photos, and watched as they vanished in a blur of light.

Loop

～

She awoke to the sound of voices. Tyler was hunched over her, a frown on his too-young face. "She's back," he said.

Amelia couldn't move either arm. She wanted to sit up, but knew she didn't dare, not in front of this young Tyler, not with the chance of losing her balance.

"What's happening to you?" he asked.

She wished he could hear her. She would tell him and maybe he would find a solution. Still, it wouldn't hurt to try. "I'm trapped," she said. "I'm stuck in a loop."

He understood the part about being trapped. She had to repeat herself three times before he said: "Loop? Like in the movies?"

Not exactly, because she did move forward in each time period. She just kept visiting the same three settings. But she nodded anyway.

"Loop," he said reflectively. The tree lights winked behind him.

"I still think she's a ghost," Paul said, from somewhere behind them. "I don't care about the scar on the chin. She looks like Amelia's mother."

Tyler shook his head just a little. He smiled at her with the love she had missed. He knew her, just as she would have known him. It didn't matter that she had a younger self watching somewhere in the background.

The light was back, eating Tyler, making him disappear. The loops were shorter now. "Tyler," she said, wishing she could reach for him. She didn't want to lose him again—

—but when she came to herself she was back in the lab, propped against the large black lab table near the front of the room. The numbness had started in her feet. She looked at her arms. They seemed to be hers, except for her left hand, with the control fused to her skin.

She had jumped back too far. She had known there would be that risk. Tyler had said that when he went on trips longer than ten years he always felt depleted. But she had thought she could deal with depleted.

Her Now-self left the bench and walked over to Amelia. Her Now-self wore a ring on the third finger of her left hand. Had Amelia altered something by appearing? Or had she slipped into another life, another time? Had that trapped her?

Her Now-self's hands were shaking. They passed over Amelia's useless left hand, and her Now-self swallowed, hard. "Your control is broken," her Now-self said.

"I know," Amelia said.

But her Now-self was looking down and didn't seem to hear. Even in this place, she couldn't speak to herself.

Her Now-self set the control down. "Here," she said. "If I don't touch it, you can. Take mine."

Amelia shook her head. She couldn't move her arms. She smiled a little sadly. She would die here.

"You're the woman we saw all those years ago, aren't we?" Her Now-self asked.

Amelia nodded. She was getting too tired to speak.

"You went to see him, didn't you?" Her Now-self asked. "Just like I was going to."

Amelia smiled a little. She *had* seen him, one last time. And he had smiled at her. He loved her, no matter who or when she was.

"And it was wrong. It trapped you." Her Now-self stood. "When he—when he was alive, he made me promise to never come here by myself. He knew, didn't he?"

"He guessed," Amelia said, even though her Now-self couldn't hear.

"And all the precautions," her Now-self said quietly. "He was trying to protect me. He said, before he died, that he would always love me. And I didn't believe him. I had to see—"

Amelia nodded. The tingle filled her entire body. The light was returning, and the sound was fading. She had done this. She had made the changes, by appearing in her own past. As a ghost.

She wanted to tell her Now-self not to go, but she couldn't. She couldn't move at all.

∽

The light faded one final time. Amelia knew something supported her, but she couldn't feel it beneath the tingle in her body. As the red and green dots dissipated, she found herself on the four-poster bed in the adobe house, staring at the pictures on the wall.

They hadn't changed: she and Tyler gazing happily at each other, the baby between them; Tyler, giving away the bride. It took a moment before she understood what the photographs meant. They meant that her Now-self had heard, had understood. Her alternate self, the one who had married Tyler, born a child, and worked on the project, had set the controls aside, faced the dark and lonely house, and conquered it.

A breeze moved the curtains. The air had a fresh, salty smell here that she could have grown to love. A movement caught the corner of her eye. She tried to turn her head, but couldn't. The floorboards creaked, and the young woman in the white shift appeared at the edge of Amelia's vision.

"Grandmama," the woman said, kneeling beside the bed, "Grandmama, I miss you so."

Amelia smiled her last smile at the woman she and Tyler had helped make in a world she would never remember. "I missed you too, honey," she said as the light took her. "I missed you too."

Millennium Babies

Kristine Kathryn Rusch

Two weeks into the second semester, she got the message. It had been sent to her house system, and was coded to her real name, Brooke Delacroix, not Brooke Cross, the name she had used since she was 18. At first she didn't want to open it, thinking it might be another legal conundrum from her mother, so she let the house monitor in the kitchen blink while she prepared dinner.

She made a hearty dinner, and poured herself a glass of rosé before settling down in front of the living room fireplace. The fireplace was the reason she bought this house. She had fallen in love with the idea that she could sit on cold winter nights under a pile of blankets, a real fire burning nearby, and read the ancient paperbacks she found in Madison's antique stores. She read a lot of current work on her e-book, especially research for the classes she taught at the university, but she loved to read novels in their paper form, careful not to tear the brittle pages, feeling the weight of bound paper in her hands.

She had added bookshelves to the house's dining room for her paper novels, and she had made a few other improvements as well. But she tried to keep the house's character. It was a hundred-and-fifty years old, built when this part of Wisconsin had been nothing but family farms. The farmland was gone now, divided into five acre plots, but the privacy remained. She loved being out here, in the country, more than anything else. Even though the university provided her job, the house was her world.

The novel she held was a thin volume, and a favorite—*The Great Gatsby* by F. Scott Fitzgerald—but on this night, the book didn't hold her interest. Finally she gave up. If she didn't hear the damn message, she would be haunted by her mother all night.

Brooke left the glass of wine and the book on the end table, her blankets curled at the edge of the couch and made her way back to the kitchen. She could have had House play an audio-only version of the message in the living room, but she wanted to see her mother's face, to know how serious it was this time.

The monitor was on the west wall beside the microwave. The previous owners—a charming elderly couple—had kept a small television in that spot. On nights like this, Brooke thought the monitor was no improvement.

She stood in front of it, arms crossed, sighed, and said, "House, play message."

The blinking icon disappeared from the screen. A digital voice she did not recognize said, "This message is keyed for Brooke Delacroix only. It will not be played without certification that no one else is in the room."

She stood. If this was from her mother, her tactics had changed. This sounded official. Brooke made sure she was visible to the built-in camera.

"I'm Brooke," she said, "and I'm alone."

"You're willing to certify this?" the strange voice asked her.

"Yes," she said.

"Stand-by for message."

The screen turned black. She rubbed her hands together. Goose bumps were crawling across her skin. Who would send her an official message?

"This is coded for Brooke Delacroix," a new digital voice said. "Personal identification number…"

As the voice rattled off the number, she clenched her fist. Maybe something had happened to her mother. Brooke was, after all, the only next of kin.

"This is Brooke Delacroix," she said. "How many more security protocols do we have here?"

"Five," House said.

She felt her shoulders relax as she heard the familiar voice.

"Go around them. I don't have the time."

"All right," House said. "Stand-by."

She was standing by. Now she wished she had brought her glass of wine into the kitchen. For the first time, she felt as if she needed it.

"Ms. Delacroix?" A male voice spoke, and as it did, the monitor filled with an image. A middle-aged man with dark hair and dark eyes stared at a point just beyond her. He had the look of an intellectual, an aesthetic, someone who spent too much time in artificial light. He also looked vaguely familiar. "Forgive my rudeness. I know you go by Cross now, but I wanted to make certain that you are the woman I'm searching for. I'm looking for Brook Delacroix, born 12:05 a.m., January first in the year 2000 in Detroit, Michigan."

Another safety protocol. What was this?

"That's me," Brooke said.

The screen blinked slightly, apparently as her answer was fed into some sort of program. He must have recorded various messages for various answers. She knew she wasn't speaking to him live.

"We are actually colleagues, Ms. Cross. I'm Eldon Franke..."

Of course. That was why he looked familiar. The Human Potential Guru who had gotten all the press. He was a legitimate scientist whose most recent tome became a pop culture bestseller. Franke rehashed the nature versus nurture arguments in personality development, mixed in some sociology and some well documented advice for improving the lot nature/nurture gave people, and somehow the book hit.

She had read it, and had been impressed with the interdisciplinary methods he had used—and the credit he had given to his colleagues.

"...have a new grant, quite a large one actually, which startled even me. With that and the proceeds from the last book, I'm able to undertake the kind of study I've always wanted to do."

She kept her hands folded and watched him. His eyes were bright, intense. She remembered seeing him at faculty parties, but she had never spoken to him. She didn't speak to many people voluntarily, especially during social occasions. She had learned, from her earliest days, the value of keeping to herself.

"I will be bringing in subjects from around the country," he was saying. "I had hoped to go around the world, but that makes this study too large even for me. As it is, I'll be working with over three hundred subjects from all over the United States. I didn't expect to find one in my own back yard."

A subject. She felt her breath catch in her throat. She had thought he was approaching her as an equal.

"I know from published reports that you dislike talking about your status as a Millennium Baby, but—"

"Off," she said to House. Franke's image froze on the screen.

"I'm sorry," House said. "This message is designed to be played in its entirety."

"So go around it," she said, "and shut the damn thing off."

"The message program is too sophisticated for my systems," House said.

Brooke cursed. The son of a bitch knew she'd try to shut him down. "How long is it?"

"You have heard a third of the message."

Brooke sighed. "All right. Continue."

The image became mobile again. "—I hope you hear me out. My work, as you may or may not know, is with human potential. I plan to build on my earlier research, but I lacked the right kind of study group. Many scientists of all strips have studied generations, and assumed that because people were born in the same year, they had the same hopes, aspirations, and dreams. I do not believe that is so. The human creature is too diverse—"

"Get to the point," Brooke said, sitting on a wooden kitchen chair.

"—so in my quest for the right group, I stumbled on thirty-year-old articles about Millennium Babies, and I realized that the subset of your generation, born on January 1 of the year 2000, actually have similar beginnings."

"No, we don't," Brooke said.

"Thus you give me a chance to focus this study. I will use the raw data to continue my overall work, but this study will focus on what it is that makes human beings succeed or fail—"

"Screw you," Brooke said and walked out of the kitchen. Behind her, Franke's voice stopped.

"Do you want me to transfer audio to the living room?" House asked.

"No," Brooke said. "Let him ramble on. I'm done listening."

The fire crackled in the fireplace, her wine had warmed to room temperature, bringing out a different bouquet, and her blankets looked comfortable. She sank into them. Franke's voice droned on in the kitchen, and she ordered House to play Bach to cover him.

But her favorite Brandenburg Concerto couldn't wipe Franke's voice from her mind. Studying Millennium Babies. Brooke closed her eyes. She wondered what her mother would think of that.

∼

Three days later, Brooke was in her office, trying to assemble her lecture for her new survey class. This one was on the two world wars. The University of Wisconsin still believed that a teacher should stand in front of students, even for the large lecture courses, instead of delivering canned lectures that could be downloaded. Most professors saw surveys as too much wasted work, but she actually enjoyed it. She liked standing before a large room delivering a lecture.

But now she was getting past the introductory remarks and into the areas she wasn't that familiar with. She didn't believe in regurgitating the textbooks, so she was boning up on World War

I. She had forgotten that its causes were so complex; its results so far reaching, especially in Europe. Sometimes she just found herself reading, lost in the past.

Her office was small and narrow, with barely enough room for her desk. Because she was new, she was assigned to Bascom Hall at the top of Bascom Hill, a building that had been around for most of the university's history. The Hall's historic walls didn't accommodate new technology, so the university made certain she had a fancy desk with a built-in screen. The problem with that was that when she did extensive research, as she was doing now, she had to look down. She often downloaded information to her palmtop or worked at home. Working in her office, in the thin light provided by the ancient fluorescents and the dirty meshed window, gave her a headache.

But she was nearly done. Tomorrow, she would take the students from the horrors of trench warfare to the first steps toward U.S. involvement. The bulk of the lecture, though, would focus on isolationism—a potent force in both world wars.

A knock on her door brought her to the 21st century. She rubbed the bridge of her nose impatiently. She wasn't holding office hours. She hated it when students failed to read the signs.

"Yes?" she asked.

"Professor Cross?"

"Yes?"

"May I have a moment of your time?"

The voice was male and didn't sound terribly young, but many of her students were older.

"A moment," she said, using her desktop to unlock the door. "I'm not having office hours."

The knob turned and a man came inside. He wasn't very tall, and he was thin—a runner's build. It wasn't until he turned toward her, though, that she let out a groan.

"Professor Franke."

He held up a hand. "I'm sorry to disturb you—"

"You should be," she said. "I purposely didn't answer your message."

"I figured. Please. Just give me a few moments."

She shook her head. 'I'm not interested in being the subject of any study. I don't have time."

"Is it the time? Or is it the fact that the study has to do with Millennium Babies?" His look was sharp.

"Both."

"I can promise you that you'll be well compensated. And if you'll just listen to me for a moment, you might reconsider—"

"Professor Franke," she said, "I'm not interested."

"But you're a key to the study."

"Why?" she asked. "Because of my mother's lawsuits?"

"Yes," he said.

She felt the air leave her body. She had to remind herself to breathe. The feeling was familiar. It had always been familiar. Whenever anyone talked about Millennium Babies, she had this feeling in her stomach.

Millennium Babies. No one had expected the craze, but it had become apparent by March of 1999. Prospective parents were timing the conception of their children as part of a race to see if their child could be the first born in 2000—the New Millennium, as the pundits of the day inaccurately called it. There was a more-or-less informal international contest, but in the United States, the competition was quite heavy. There were other races in every developed country, and in every city. And in most of those places, the winning parent got a lot of money, and a lot of products, and some, those with the cutest babies, or the pushiest parents, got endorsements as well.

"Oh, goodie," Brooke said, filling her voice with all the sarcasm she muster. "My mother was upset that I didn't get exploited enough as a child so you're here to fill the gap."

His back straightened. "It's not like that."

"Really? How is it then?" She regretted the words the moment she spoke them. She was giving Franke the opening he wanted.

"We've chosen our candidates with care," he said. "We are not taking babies born randomly on January 1 of 2000. We're taking children whose birth was planned, whose parents made public statements about the birth, and whose parents hoped to get a piece of the pie."

"Wonderful," she said. "You're studying children with dysfunctional families."

"Are we?" he asked.

"Well, if you study me, you are," she said and stood. "Now, I'd like it if you leave."

"You haven't let me finish."

"Why should I?"

"Because this study might help you, Professor Cross."

"I'm doing fine without your help."

"But you never talk about your Millennium Baby status."

"And how often do you discuss the day you were born, Professor?"

"My birthday is rather unremarkable," he said. "Unlike yours."

She crossed her arms. "Get out."

"Remember that I study human potential," he said. "And you all have the same beginnings. All of you come from parents who had the same goal—parents who were driven to achieve something unusual."

"Parents who were greedy," she said.

"Some of them," he said. "And some of them planned to have children anyway, and thought it might be fun to try to join the contest."

"I don't see how our beginnings are relevant."

He smiled, and she cursed under her breath. As long as she talked to him, as long as she asked thinly veiled questions, he had her and they both knew it.

"In the past forty years, studies of identical twins raised apart have shown that at least fifty percent of a person's disposition is apparent at birth. Which means that no matter how you're raised, if you were a happy baby, you have a greater than fifty percent chance of being a happy adult. The remaining factors are probably environmental. Are you familiar with DNA mapping?"

"You're not answering my question," she said.

"I'm trying to," he said. "Listen to me for a few moments, and then kick me out of your office."

She wouldn't get rid of him otherwise. She slowly sat in her chair.

"Are you familiar with DNA mapping?" he repeated.

"A little," she said.

"Good." He leaned back in his chair and templed his fingers. "We haven't located a happiness gene or an unhappiness gene. We're not sure what it is about the physical make-up that makes these things work. But we do know that it has something to do with serotonin levels."

"Get to the part about Millennium Babies," she said.

He smiled. "I am. My last book was partly based on the happiness/unhappiness model, but I believe that's too simplistic. Human beings are complex creatures. And as I grow older, I see a lot of lost potential. Some of us were raised to fail, and some were raised to succeed. Some of those raised to succeed have failed, and some who were raised to fail have succeeded. So clearly it isn't all environment."

"Unless some were reacting against their environment," she said, hearing the sullenness in her tone, a sullenness she hadn't used since she last spoke to her mother five years before.

"That's one option," he said, sounding brighter. He must have taken her statement for interest. "But one of the things I learned while working on human potential is that drive is like happiness. Some children are born driven. They walk sooner than others. They learn faster. They adapt faster. They achieve more, from the moment they take their first breath."

"I don't really believe that our entire personalities are formed at birth," she said. "Or that our destinies are written before we're conceived."

"None of us do," he said. "If we did, we wouldn't have a reason to get out of bed in the morning. But we do acknowledge that we're all given traits and talents that are different from each other. Some of us have blue eyes. Some of us can hit golf balls with a power and accuracy that others only dream of. Some of us have perfect pitch, right?"

"Of course," she snapped.

"So it only stands to reason that some of us are born with

more happiness than others, and some are born with more drive than others. If you consider those intangibles to be as real as, say, musical talent."

His argument had a certain logic, but she didn't want to agree with him on anything. She wanted him out of her office.

"But," he said. "Those with the most musical talent aren't always the ones on stage at Carnegie hall. There are other factors, environmental factors. A child who grows up without hearing music might never know how to make music, right?"

"I don't know," she said.

"Likewise," he said, "if that musically inclined child had parents to whom music was important, the child might hear music all the time. From the moment that child is born, that child is familiar with music and has an edge on the child who hasn't heard a note."

She started tapping her fingers.

He glanced at them and leaned forward. "As I said in my message, this study focuses on success and failure. To my knowledge, there has never before been a group of children conceived nationwide with the same specific goal in mind."

Her mouth was dry. Her fingers had stopped moving.

"You Millennium Babies share several traits in common. Your parents conceived you at the same time. Your parents had similar goals and desires for you. You came out of the womb and instantly you were branded a success or a failure, at least for this one goal."

"So," she said, keeping her voice cold. "Are you going to deal with all those children who were abandoned by their parents when they discovered they didn't win?"

"Yes," he said.

The quiet sureness of his response startled her. He spread his hands as if in explanation. "Their parents gave up on them," he said. "Right from the start. Those babies are perhaps the purest subjects of the study. They were clearly conceived only with the race in mind."

"And you want me because I'm the most spectacular failure of the group." Her voice was cold, even though she had to clasp her hands together to keep them from trembling.

"I don't consider you a failure, Professor Cross," he said. 'You're well respected in your profession. You're on a tenure track at a prestigious university—"

"I meant as a Millennium Baby. I'm the public failure. When people think of baby contests, the winners never come to mind. I do."

He sighed. "That's part of it. Part of it is your mother's attitude. In some ways, she's the most obsessed parent, at least that we can point to."

Brooke winced.

"I'd like to have you in this study," he said. "The winners will be. It would be nice to have you represented as well."

"So that you can get rich off this book, and I'll be disgraced yet again," she said.

"Maybe," he said. "Or maybe you'll get validated."

Her shoulders were so tight that it hurt to move her head. "'Validated.' Such a nice psychiatrist's word. Making me feel better will salve your conscience while you get rich."

"You seem obsessed with money," he said.

"Shouldn't I be?" she asked. "With my mother?"

He stared at her for a long moment.

Finally, she shook her head. "It's not the money. I just don't want to be exploited any more. For any reason."

He nodded. Then he folded his hands across his stomach and squinched up his face, as if he were thinking. Finally, he said, "Look, here's how it is. I'm a scientist. You're a member of a group that interests me and will be useful in my research. If I were researching thirty-year-old history professors who happened to be on a tenure track, I'd probably interview you as well. Or professional women who lived in Wisconsin. Or—"

"Would you?" she asked. "Would you come to me, really?"

He nodded. "It's policy to check who's available for study at the university before going outside of it."

She sighed. He had a point. "A book on Millennium Babies will sell well. They all do. And you'll get interviews, and you'll become famous."

"The study uses Millennium Babies," he said, "but anything I publish will be about success and failure, not a pop psychology book about people born on January first."

"You can swear to that?" she asked.

"I'll do it in our agreement," he said.

She closed her eyes. She couldn't believe he was talking her into this.

Apparently he didn't think he had, for he continued. "You'll be compensated for your time and your travel expenses. We can't promise a lot, but we do promise that we won't abuse your assistance."

She opened her eyes. That intensity was back in his face. It didn't unnerve her. In fact, it reassured her. She would rather have him passionate about the study than anything else.

"All right," she said. "What do I have to do?"

First she signed waivers. She had all of them checked out by her lawyer—the fact that she even had a lawyer was yet another legacy from her mother—and he said that they were fine, even liberal. Then he tried to talk her out of the study, worried more as a friend, he said, even though he had never been her friend before.

"You've been trying to get away from all of this. Now you're opening it back up? That can't be good for you."

But she wasn't sure what was good for her any more. She had tried not thinking about it. Maybe focusing on herself, on what happened to her from the moment she was born, was better.

She didn't know, and she didn't ask. The final agreement she signed was personalized—it guaranteed her access to her file, a copy of the completed study, and promised that any study her information was used in would concern success and failure only, and would not be marketed as a Millennium Baby product. Her lawyer asked for a few changes, but very few, considering how opposed he was to this project. She was content with the concessions Professor Franke made for her, including the one which allowed her to leave after the first two months.

But the first two months were grueling, in their own way. She had to carve time out of an already full schedule for a complete physical, which included DNA sampling. This had been a major sticking point for her lawyer—that her DNA and her genetic history would not be made available to anyone else—and he had actually gotten Franke to sign forms that attested to that fact. The sampling, for all its trouble, was relatively painless.

A few strands of hair, some skin scrapings, and two vials of blood, and she was done.

The psychological exams took the longest. Most of them required the presence of the psychiatric research member of the team, a dour woman who barely spoke to Brooke when she came in. The woman watched while Brook used a computer to take tests: a Rorschach, a Minnesota Multiphasic Personality Interview, a Thematic Apperception Test, and a dozen others whose names she just as quickly forgot. One of them was a standard IQ test. Another was a specialized test designed by Franke's team for his previous experiment. All of them felt like games to Brooke, and all of them took over an hour each to complete.

Her most frustrating time, though, was with the sociologist, a well-meaning man named Meyer. He wanted to correlate her experiences with the experiences of others, and put them in the context of the society at the time. He'd ask questions, though, and she'd correct them—feeling that his knowledge of modern history was poor. Finally she complained to Franke, who smiled, and told her that her perceptions and the researchers' didn't have to match. What was important to them wasn't what was true for the society, but what was true for *her*. She wanted to argue, but it wasn't her study, and she decided she was placing too much energy into all of it.

Through it all, she had weekly appointments with a psychologist who asked her questions she didn't want to think about. *How has being a Millennium Baby influenced your outlook on life? What's your first memory? What do you think of your mother?*

Brooke couldn't answer the first. The second question was easy. Her first memory was of television lights blinding her, creating prisms, and her chubby baby fingers reaching for them, only to be caught and held by her mother's cold hand.

Brooke declined to answer the third question, but the psychologist asked it at every single meeting. And after every single meeting, Brooke went home and cried.

∼

She gave a mid-term exam in her World Wars class, the first time she had ever done so in a survey class. But she decided to see how effective she was being, since her concentration was more on her own past than the one she was supposed to be teaching.

Her graduate assistants complained about it, especially when they looked at the exam itself. It consisted of a single question: *Write an essay exploring the influences, if any, the First World War had on the Second. If you believe there were no influences, defend that position.*

Her assistants tried to talk her into a simple true/false/multiple choice exam, and she had glared at them. "I don't want to give a test that can be graded by computer," she said. "I want to see a handwritten exam, and I want to know what these kids have learned." And because she wanted to know that—not because of her assistants' complaints (as she made very clear)—she took twenty of the exams to grade herself.

But before she started, she had a meeting in Franke's office. He had called her.

Franke's office was in a part of the campus she didn't get to very often. A winding road took her past Washburn Observatory on a bluff overlooking Lake Mendota, and into a grove of young trees. The parking area was large and filled with small electric and energy efficient cars. She walked up the brick sidewalk. Unlike the sidewalks around the rest of the city, this one didn't have the melting piles of dirty snow that were reminders of the long hard winter. Instead, tulips and irises poked out of the brown dirt lining the walk.

The building was an old Victorian style house, rather large for its day. The only visible signs of a remodel (besides the pristine condition of the paint and roof) were the security system outside, and the heat pump near the driveway.

Clearly this was a faculty-only building; no classes were held here. She turned the authentic glass door knob and stepped into a narrow foyer. A small electronic screen floated in the center of the room. The screen moved toward her.

"I'm here to see Dr. Franke," she said.

"Second floor," the digital voice responded. "He is expecting you."

She sighed softly and mounted the stairs. With the exception of the electronics, everything in the hall reflected the period. Even the stairs weren't covered in carpet, but instead in an old-fashioned runner, tacked on the sides, with a long gold carpet holder pushed against the back of the step.

The stairs ended in a long narrow hallway, illuminated by electric lights done up to resemble gaslights. Only one door stood open. She knocked on it, then, without waiting for an invitation, went in.

The office wasn't like hers. This office was a suite, with a main area and a private room to the side. A leather couch was pushed against the window, and two matching leather chairs flanked it. Teak tables provided the accents, with round gold table lamps the only flourish.

Professor Franke stood in the door to the private area. He looked at her examining his office.

"Impressive," she said.

He shrugged. "The university likes researchers, especially those who add to its prestige."

She knew that. She had published her thesis, and it had received some acclaim in academic circles, which was why she was as far ahead as she was. But very few historians became famous for their research. She doubted she would ever achieve this sort of success.

"Would you like a seat?" Franke asked.

She sat on one of the leather chairs. It was soft, and molded around her. "I didn't think you'd need to interview every subject to see if they wanted to continue," she said.

"Every subject isn't you." He sat across from her. His hair was slightly mussed as if he had been running his fingers through it, and he had a coffee stain above the breast pocket of his white shirt. "We had agreements."

She nodded.

"I will tell you some of what we have learned," he said. "It's preliminary, of course."

"Of course." She sounded calmer than she felt. Her heart was pounding.

"We've found three interesting things. The first is that all Millennium Babies in this study walked earlier than the norm, and spoke earlier as well. Since most were firstborns, this is unusual. Firstborns usually speak *later* than the norm because their every need is catered to. They don't need to speak right away, and when they do, they usually speak in full sentences."

"Meaning?"

"I hesitate to say for certain, but it might be indicative of great drive. Stemming, I believe, from the fact that the parents were driven." His eyes were sparkling. His enthusiasm for his work was catching. She found herself leaning forward like a student in her favorite class. "We're also finding genetic markers in the very areas we were looking for. And some interesting biochemical indications that may help us isolate the biological aspect of this."

"You're moving fast," she said.

He nodded. "That's what's nice about having a good team."

And a lot of subjects, she thought. Not to mention building on earlier research.

"We've also found that there is direct correlation between a child's winning or losing the millennium race and her perception of herself as a success or failure, independent of external evidence."

Her mouth was dry. "Meaning?"

"No matter how successful they are, the majority of Millennium Babies—at least the ones we chose for this study, the ones whose parents conceived them only as part of the race—perceive themselves as failures."

"Including me," she said.

He nodded. The movement was slight, and it was gentle.

"Why?" she asked.

"That's the thing we can only speculate at. At least at this moment." He wasn't telling her everything. But then, the study wasn't done. He tilted his head slightly. "Are you willing to go to phase two of the study?"

"If I say no, will you tell me what else you've discovered?' she asked.

"That's our agreement." He paused and then added, "I would really like it if you continued."

Brooke smiled. "That much is obvious."

He smiled too, and then looked down. "This last part is nothing like the first. You won't have test after test. It's only going to last for a few days. Can you do that?"

Some of the tension left her shoulders. She could do a few days. But that was it. "All right," she said.

"Good." He smiled at her, and she braced herself. There was more. "I'll put you down for the next segment. It doesn't start until Memorial Day. I have to ask you to stay in town, and set aside that weekend."

She had no plans. She usually stayed in town on Memorial Day weekend. Madison emptied out, the students going home, and the city became a small town—one she dearly loved.

She nodded.

He waited a moment, his gaze darting downward, and then meeting hers again. "There's one more thing."

This was why he had called her here. This was why she needed to see him in person.

"I was wondering if your mother ever told you who your father is. It would help our study if we knew something about both parents."

Brooke threaded her hands together willing herself to remain calm. This had been a sensitive issue her entire life. "No," she said. "My mother has no idea who my father is. She went to a sperm bank."

Franke frowned. "I just figured, since your mother seemed so meticulous about everything else, she would have researched your father as well."

"She did," Brooke said. "He was a physicist, very well known, apparently. It was one of those sperm banks that specialized in famous or successful people. And my mother did check that out."

Your father must not have been as wonderful as they said he was. Look at you. It had to come from somewhere.

"Do you know the name of the bank?"

"No."

Franke sighed. "I guess we have all that we can, then."

She hated the disapproval in his tone. "Surely others in this study only have one parent."

"Yes," he said. "There's a subset of you. I was just hoping—"

"Anything to make the study complete," she said sarcastically.

"Not anything," he said. "You can trust me on that."

∽

Brooke didn't hear from Professor Franke again for nearly a month, and then only in the form of a message, delivered to House, giving her the exact times, dates, and places of the Memorial Day meetings. She forgot about the study except when she saw it on her calendar.

The semester was winding down. The mid-term in her World Wars class showed her two things: that she had an affinity for the topic which she was sharing with the students; and that at least two of her graduate assistants had a strong aversion to work. She lectured both assistants, spoke to the chair of the department about teaching the survey class next semester, and continued on with the lectures, focusing on them as if she were the graduate student instead of the professor.

By late April, she had her final exam written—a long cumbersome thing, a mixture of true/false/multiple choice for the assistants, and two essay questions for her. She was thinking of a paper herself—one on the way those wars still echoed through the generations—and she was trying to decide if she wanted the summer to work on it or to teach as she usually did.

The last Saturday in April was unusually balmy, in the seventies without much humidity, promising a beautiful summer ahead. The lilac bush near her kitchen window had bloomed. The birds had returned, and her azaleas were blossoming as well. She was in the garage, digging for a lawn chair that she was convinced she still had when she heard the hum of an electric car.

She came out of the garage, dusty and streaked with grime. A green car pulled into her driveway, next to the ancient pick-up she used for hauling.

Something warned her right from the start. A glimpse, perhaps, or a movement. Her stomach flipped over, and she had to swallow sudden nausea. She had left her personal phone inside—it was too nice to be connected to the world today—and she had never gotten the garage hooked into House's computer because she hadn't seen the need for the expense.

Still, as the car shuddered to a stop, she glanced at the screen door, wondering if she could make it in time. But the car's door was already opening, and in this kind of stand-off, fake courage was better than obvious panic.

Her mother stepped out. She was a slender woman. She wore blue jeans and a pale peach summer sweater that accented her silver and gold hair. The hair was new, and had the look of permanence. Apparently her mother had finally decided to settle on a color. She wore gold bangles, and a matching necklace, but her ears were bare.

"I have a restraining order against you," Brooke said, struggling to keep her voice level. "You are not supposed to be here."

"I'm not the one who broke the order." Her mother's voice was smooth and seductive. Her courtroom voice. She had won a lot of cases with that melodious warmth. It didn't seem too strident. It just seemed sure.

"I sure as hell didn't want contact with you," Brooke said.

"No? Is that why your university contacted me?"

Brooke's heart was pounding so hard she wondered if her mother could hear it. "Who contacted you?'

"A Professor Franke, for some study. Something to do with DNA samples. I was to send them through my doctor, but you know I wouldn't do such a thing with anything that delicate."

Son of a bitch. Brooke hadn't known they were going to try something like that. She didn't remember any mention of it, nothing in the forms.

"I have nothing to do with that," Brooke said.

"It seems you're in some study. That seems like involvement to me," her mother said.

"Not the kind that gets you around a restraining order. Now get the hell off my property."

"Brooke, honey," her mother said, taking a step toward her. "I think you and I should discuss this—"

"There's nothing to discuss," Brooke said. "I want you to stay away from me."

"That's silly." Her mother took another step forward. "We

should be able to settle this, Brooke. Like adults. I'm your mother—"

"That's not my fault," Brooke snapped. She glanced at the screen door again.

"A restraining order is for people who threaten your life. I've never hurt you, Brooke."

"There's a judge in Dane County who disagrees, Mother."

"Because you were so hysterical," her mother said. "We've had a good run of it, you and I."

Brooke felt the color drain from her face. "How's that, Mother? The family that sues together stays together?"

"Brooke, we have been denied what's rightfully ours. We—"

"It never said in any of those contests that a child had to be born by natural means. You misunderstood, Mother. Or you tried to be even more perfect than anyone else. So what if I'm the first vaginal birth of the new millennium. So what? It was thirty years ago. Let it go."

"The first baby received enough in endorsements to pay for a college education and to have a trust fund—"

"And you've racked up enough in legal fees that you could have done the same." Brooke rubbed her hands over her arms. The day had grown colder.

"No, honey," her mother said in that patronizing tone that Brooke hated. "I handled my own case. There were no fees."

It was like arguing with a wall. "I have made it really, really clear that I never wanted to see you again," Brooke said. "So why do you keep hounding me? You don't even like me."

"Of course I like you, Brooke. You're my daughter."

"I don't like you," Brooke said.

"We're flesh and blood," her mother said softly. "We owe it to each other to be there for each other."

"Maybe you should have remembered that when I was growing up. I was a child, Mother, not a trophy. You saw me as a means to an end, an end you now think you got cheated out of. Sometimes you blame me for that—I was too big, I didn't come out fast enough, I was breach—and sometimes you blame the contest people for not discounting all those 'artificial methods' of birth, but you never, ever blame yourself. For anything."

"Brooke," her mother said, and took another step forward.

Brooke held up her hand. "Did you ever think, Mother, that it's your fault we missed the brass ring? Maybe you should have pushed harder. Maybe you should have had a c-section. Or maybe you shouldn't have gotten pregnant at all."

"Brooke!"

"You weren't fit to be a parent. That's what the judge decided on. You're right. You never hit me. You didn't have to. You told me how worthless I was from the moment I could hear. All that anger you felt about losing you directed at me. Because, until I was born, you never lost anything."

Her mother shook her head slightly. "I never meant that. When I would say that, I meant—"

"See? You're so good at taking credit for anything that goes well, and so bad at taking it when something doesn't."

"I still don't see why you're so angry at me," her mother said.

This time, it was Brooke's turn to take a step forward. "You don't? You don't remember that last official letter? The one cited in my restraining order?"

"You have never understood the difference between a legal argument and the real issues."

"Apparently the judge is just as stupid about legal arguments as I am, Mother." Brooke was shaking. "He believed it when you said that I was brought into this world simply to win that contest, and by rights, the state should be responsible for my care, not you."

"It was a law suit, Brooke. I had an argument to make."

"Maybe you can justify it that way, but I can't. I know the truth when I hear it. And so does the rest of the world." Brooke swallowed. Her throat was so tight it hurt. "Now get out of here."

"Brooke, I—"

"I mean it, Mother. Or I will call the police."

"Do you want me at least to do the DNA work?"

"I don't give a damn what you do, so long as I never see you again."

Her mother sighed. "Other children forgive their parents for mistakes they made in raising them."

"Was your attitude a mistake, Mother? Have you reformed? Or do you still have law suits out there? Are you still trying to collect on a thirty-year-old dream?"

Her mother shook her head and went back to the car. Brooke knew that posture. It meant that Brooke was being unreasonable. Brooke was impossible to argue with. Brooke was the burden.

"Some day," her mother said. "You'll regret how you treated me."

"Why?" Brooke asked. 'You don't seem to regret how you treated me."

"Oh, I regret it, Brooke. If I had known it would have made you so bitter toward me, I never would have talked to you about our problems. I would have handled them alone."

Brooke clenched a fist and then unclenched it. She made herself take a deep breath and, instead of pointing out to her mother that she had done it again—she had blamed Brooke—Brooke said, "I'm calling the police now," and started toward the house.

"There's no need," her mother said. 'I'm going. I'm just sorry—"

And the rest of her words got lost in the bang of the screen door.

∼

An hour later, Brooke found herself outside Professor Franke's office. She ignored the small electronic screen that floated ahead of her, bleating that she didn't have an appointment and she wasn't welcome in the building. It was a dumb little machine; when she had asked if Professor Franke was in, it had told her he was. A good human secretary would have lied.

Apparently the system had already contacted Franke for he stood in his door, waiting for her, a smile on his face even though his eyes were wary.

"Everything all right, Professor Cross?"

"I never gave you permission to contact my mother," she said as she came up the stairs.

"Your mother?"

"She came to my house today, claiming I'd nullified my restraining order by contacting her. She said you asked her for DNA samples."

"Come into my office," he said.

Brooke walked past him and heard him close the door. "We did contact her, as we did all the parents, for DNA samples. We were explicit in expressing our needs as part of the study, and that they had every right to refuse if they wanted. In no way did we ask her to come here or to tell her that you asked us to contact her."

"She says it came from me and she knew I was involved in the study."

"Of course," he said. "One of the waivers you signed gave us permission to examine your genetic heritage. That includes parents, grandparents, living relatives if necessary. Your attorney didn't object."

Her attorney was good, but not that good. He probably hadn't known what that all entailed.

"I want you to send a letter, through your attorney or the university's counsel, stating that I in no way asked you to contact her and that you did it of your own volition."

"Do you want me to apologize?" he asked.

"To me or to her?" she asked.

He drew in his breath sharply and she realized for the first time that she had knocked him off balance.

"I meant to her," he said, "but I guess I owe you an apology too."

Brooke stared at him for a moment. No one had said that to her before.

"Look," he said, apparently not understanding her silence. "I should have thought it through when your mother said she didn't allow such confidential information to be sent to people she didn't know. I thought that was a refusal."

"For anyone else it would have been," Brooke said. "But not for my mother."

"She's an interesting woman."

"From the outside," Brooke said.

He nodded as if he understood. "For the record, I didn't mean to cause you trouble. I'm sorry I didn't warn you."

"It's all right," Brooke said. "Just don't let it happen again."

∼

Except for receiving a copy of the official letter Franke sent to her mother, Brooke didn't think about the study again until Memorial Day weekend. The semester was over. Most of her students successfully answered the question on her World Wars final: *Explain the influence World War I had on World War II.*

One student actually called the World War I the mother of World War II. The phrase stopped Brooke as she read, made her shudder, and hoped that not every monstrous mother begot an even more monstrous child.

Professor Franke sent instructions for Memorial Day weekend with the official letter. He asked her to set aside time from mid-afternoon on Friday to late evening on Monday. She was to report to TheaterPlace, restaurant and bar on the west side of town.

She'd been to the restaurant before. It was a novelty spot in what had once been a fourplex movie palace. The restaurant was in the very center, with huge meeting rooms off to the sides. The builders had called it a gathering place for organizations too small to hold conventions. Still, it had everything—the large restaurant, the bar, places for presentations, places for seminars, places for quiet get-togethers. There were three smaller restaurants in what had once been the projection booths—restaurants that barely seated twenty. One of the larger rooms even showed live theater once a month.

Cars were no longer allowed in this part of town, thanks to a Green referendum three years before. Someone had tried to make exception for electric vehicles but that hadn't worked either as the traffic cops said it would be too hard to patrol. Instead, the light rail made several stops, and some enterprising entrepreneur had built underground tunnels to connect all of the buildings. Many people Brooke knew preferred to shop here in the winter; it kept them out of the freezing cold. But she found the necessity of taking the light rail annoying. She would have preferred her own car so that she could leave on her own schedule.

She walked from the light rail stop near the refurbished mall to TheaterPlace. On the outside, it still looked like a fourplex: the raised roof, the warehouse shape. Only up close did it become apparent that TheaterPlace had been completely gutted and remodeled, right down to the smoke glass that had replaced the clear windows.

A sign on the main entrance notified her that TheaterPlace was closed for a private party. She touched the door anyway—knowing the party was theirs—and a scanner instantly identified her.

Welcome, Brooke Cross. You may enter.

She shuddered slightly, knowing that Franke had programmed the scanner to recognize either her fingerprints on the backside of the door or her DNA. She felt like her mother, worried that Franke had too much information.

The door clicked open and she let herself inside. A short dark haired woman she had never seen before hurried to her side.

"Professor Cross," the woman said. "Welcome."

"Thanks," Brooke said.

"Just a few rules before we get started," the woman said. "This is the last time we'll be using names today. We ask you not to tell anyone who you are by name, although you may tell them anything else you wish about yourself. Please identify yourself using this number only."

She handed Brooke a stick-on badge with the number 333 printed in bold black numbers.

"Then what?" Brooke asked.

"Wait for Professor Franke to make his announcement. You're in the Indiana Jones room, by the way."

"Thanks," Brooke said. She stuck the label to her white blouse and made her way down the hall. All of the rooms were named after characters from famous movies, and the décor in all of them except the restaurants was the same: movie posters on the wall, soft golden lighting, and a thin light blue carpet. The furniture moved according to the function. She had been in the Jones room before for a faculty party honoring some distinguished professor from Beijing, but she doubted the room would be the same.

The double doors were open and inside, she heard the sound of soft conversation. She stopped just outside the door and surveyed the room.

The lights were up—not soft and golden at all—but full daylight, so that everyone's faces were visible. The Jones room was one of the largest—the only theater, apparently, whose dimensions had been left intact. It seemed about half full.

There were tables lining the wall, with various kinds of foods and beverages, small plates to hold everything, and silverware glimmering in the brightness. People stood in various clusters. There were no chairs, no furniture groupings, and Brooke knew that was on purpose. Small floating serving trays hovered near each group. Whenever someone set an empty glass on one, the tray would float through an opening in the wall, and another tray would take its place.

Something about the groupings made her nervous and it wasn't the lack of chairs or the fact that she didn't know anyone. She stared for a moment, trying to figure out what had caught her.

No one looked the same; they were fat and thin, tall and short. They had long hair and beards, no hair, and dyed hair. They were white, black, Asian and Hispanic or they were multiracial, with no features that marked them as part of any particular ethnic group. They were incredibly diverse—but none of them were elderly or underage. None of them had wrinkles, except for a few laugh lines, and none of them seemed younger than twenty.

They were about the same age. She would guess they *were* the same age—the exact same age as she was. It was a gathering of Franke's subjects for this study: all of them born January 1, 2000. All of them thirty years and 147 days old.

She shuddered. No wonder Franke was worried about this second half of the study. Most studies of this nature didn't allow the participants to get to know each other. She wondered what discipline he was dabbling in now, what sort of results he was expecting.

A man stopped beside her just outside the door. He was

wearing a denim shirt, a bolo tie, and tight blue jeans. His long blond hair—naturally sunstreaked—brushed against his collar. He had a tan—something she had rarely seen in her lifetime—and it made his skin a burnished gold. He had letters on his name badge: DKGHY.

"Hi," he said. His voice was deep with a Southern twang. "I guess we just go in, huh?'

"I've been steeling myself for it," she said.

He smiled. "Feels like they took away my armor when they took my name. I'm not sure if I'm supposed to say, 'Hi. I'm DKG—whatever-the-hell the rest of those letters are.' Or if I'm not supposed to say anything at all."

"Well, I don't want to be called 333."

"Can't say as I blame you." He grinned. "How about I call you Tre, and you can call me—oh, hell, I don't know—"

"De," she said. 'I'll call you De."

"Nice to meet you, Tre," he said, holding out his hand.

She took it. His fingers were warm. "Nice to meet you, De."

"Where do y'all hail from?"

"Right here," she said.

"You're kiddin'? No travel expenses, huh?"

"And no hotel rooms."

He grinned. "Sometimes hotel rooms can be nice, especially when you don't get to see the inside of them very often."

"I suppose." She smiled at him. He was making this easier than she expected. "Where're you from?"

"Originally Galveston. But I've been in L'siana a long time now."

"New Orleans?"

"Just outside."

"Some city you got there."

"Yeah, but we ain't got a place like this." He looked around. "Want to go in?"

"Now I do," she said.

They walked side-by-side as if they were a couple who had been together most of their lives. Neither of them looked at the food, although he snatched two bottles of sparkling water off one of the tables, and handed one to her. She opened it, glad to have something to carry.

A few more people came in the doors. She and De went farther into the room. Bits of conversation floated by her:

"...never really got over it..."

"...worked for the past five years as a dental hygienist..."

"...my father wanted to take us out of the country, but..."

Then there was a slight bonging sound, and the conversation halted. Franke stood in the very front of the room, where the theater screen used to be. He was easy to see because the floor slanted downward slightly. He held up his hands, and in a moment there was complete silence.

"I want to thank you all for coming." His voice was being amplified. It sounded as if he were talking right next to Brooke instead of half a room away. "Your assignment today is easy. We do not want you sharing names, but you can talk about anything else. We will be providing meals later on in various restaurants—your badge I.D. will be listed on a door—and we will have drinks in the bar after that. We ask that no one leave before midnight, and that you all return at noon tomorrow for the second phase."

"That's it?" someone asked.

"That's it," Franke said. "Enjoy yourselves."

"I have a bad feeling about this, Tre," De said.

"Me, too," Brooke said. "It can't be this simple."

"I don't think it will be."

She sighed. "Well, we signed on for this, so we may as well enjoy it."

He looked at her sideways, his blue eyes bright. "Want to be my date for the day, darlin'?"

"It's always nice to have one friendly face," she said, surprised at how easily she was flirting with him. She never flirted with anyone.

"That it is." He offered her his arm. "Let's see how many of these nice folks are interested in conversation."

"Mingle, huh?" she asked, as she put her hand in the crook of his arm.

"I think that's what we're meant to do." He frowned. "Only god knows, I 'spect it'll all backfire for the weekend's done."

∼

It didn't backfire that night. Brooke had a marvelous dinner in one of the small restaurants with De, a woman from Boston, and two men from California. They shared stories about their lives and their jobs, and only touched in passing on the thing that they had in common. In fact, the only time they discussed it was when De brought it up over dessert.

"What made y'all sign up for this foolishness?" he asked.

"The money," said the man from Los Gatos. He was slender to the point of gauntness, with dark eyes and thinning hair. His shirt had wear marks around the collar and was fraying slightly on the cuffs. "I thought it'd be an easy buck. I didn't expect all the tests."

"Me, either," the woman from Boston said. She was tall and broad shouldered, with muscular arms. During the conversation, she mentioned that she had played professional basketball until she was sidelined with a knee injury. "I haven't had so many tests since I got out of school."

The man from Santa Barbara said nothing, which surprised Brooke. He was a short stubby man with more charm than he had originally appeared to have. He had been the most talkative during dinner—regaling them with stories about his various jobs, and his two children.

"How about you, Tre?" De asked Brooke.

"I wouldn't have done it if I wasn't part of the university," she said, and realized that was true. Professor Franke probably wouldn't have had the time to convince her, and she would have dismissed him out of hand.

"Me," De said, "I jumped at it. Never been asked to do something like this before. Felt it was sort of important, you know. Anything to help the human condition."

"You don't really believe that," Santa Barbara said.

"If you don't believe it," Los Gatos said to Santa Barbara, "why'd you sign up?"

"Free flight to Madison, vacationer's paradise," Santa Barbara said, and they all laughed. But he never did answer the question.

∽

When Brooke got home, she sat on her porch and looked at the stars. The night was warm. The crickets were chirping and she thought she heard a frog answer them from a nearby ditch.

The evening had disturbed her in its simplicity. Like everyone else, she wanted to know what Franke was looking for. The rest of the study had been so directed, and this had been so free form.

Dinner had been nice. Drinks afterward with a different group had been nice as well. But the conversation rarely got deeper than anecdotes and current history. No one discussed the study, and no one discussed the past.

She lost De after dinner, which gave her a chance to meet several other people: a woman from Chicago, twins from Akron, and three friends from Salt Lake City. She'd had a good time, and found people she could converse with—one historian, two history buffs, and a librarian who seemed to know a little bit about everything.

De joined her later in the evening, and walked her to the rail stop. He'd leaned against the plastic shelter and smiled at her. She hadn't met a man as attractive as he was in a long time. Not since college.

"I'd ask you to my hotel," he said, "but I have a feelin' anything we do this weekend, in or out of that strange building, is going to be fodder for scientists."

She smiled. She'd had that feeling too.

"Still," he said, "I got to do one thing."

He leaned in and kissed her. She froze for a moment; she hadn't been kissed in nearly ten years. Then she eased into it, putting her arms around his neck and kissing him back, not wanting to stop, even when he pulled away.

"Hmm," he said. His eyes were closed. He opened them slowly. "I think that's titillatin' enough for the scientists, don't you?"

She almost said no. But she knew better. She didn't want to read about her sex life in Franke's next book.

The rail came down the tracks, gliding silently toward them. "See you tomorrow?" she asked.

"You can bet on it," De said. And there had been promise in his words, promise she wasn't sure she wanted to hear.

She brought her knees onto her lawn chair, and wrapped her arms around them. Part of her wished he was here, and part of her was glad he wasn't. She never let anyone come to her house. She didn't want to share it. She had had enough invasions of privacy in her life to prevent this one.

But she had nearly invited De, a man she didn't really know. Maybe De really wasn't a Millennium Baby. Perhaps a bunch of people weren't. Perhaps that was what the numbers and the letters meant. She had spent much of the evening staring at them, wondering. They appeared to be randomly generated, but that couldn't be. They had to have some purpose.

She shook her head and rested her cheek on her knees. She was taking this much too seriously, like she always took things. And soon she would be done with it. She would have bits of information she hadn't had before, and she would store them into a file in her mind, never to be examined again.

Somehow that thought made her sad. The night was beginning to get chilly. She stood, stretched, and made her way to bed.

∽

The next morning, they met in a different room—the Rose room—named after the character in the 20th century movie *Titanic*. Brooke hoped that the name wasn't a sign.

There were pastries and coffee against the wall, along with every kind of juice imaginable and lots of fresh fruit, but again, there were no chairs. Brooke's feet hurt from the day before—she usually stood to lecture, but not for several hours—and she hoped she'd get a chance to sit before the day was out.

She was nearly late again, and hurried inside as they closed the doors. The room smelled of fresh air mixed with coffee and sweat. The group had gathered again, the faces vaguely familiar now, even the faces of people she hadn't yet met. The people toward the back who saw her enter, smiled at her or nodded in recognition. It felt like they had all bonded simply by spending an evening in the same room. An evening and the promise of a long weekend.

She shivered. The air-conditioning was on high, and the room was cold. It would warm up before the day was out; the sheer number of bodies guaranteed that. But she still wondered if she was dressed warmly enough in her casual lilac blouse and her khaki pants.

"Strange how these places look the same, day or night."

She turned. De was half a step behind her, his long hair loose about his face. He still wore jeans and his fancy boots, but instead of the denim shirt and bolo tie, he wore an understated white open collar shirt that accented his tan. Somehow, she suspected, he seemed more comfortable in this. Had he worn the other as a way of identifying himself or a way of putting others off? She would probably never know.

"The people look different," she said.

"Just a little." He smiled at her. "You look nice."

"And you're flirting."

He shrugged. "I always believe in using my time wisely."

She smiled, and turned as a hush fell over the crowd. Franke had mounted the stage in front. He seemed very small in this place. A few of his assistants stood on either side of him.

"Here it comes," De said.

"What?"

"Whatever it is that's going to make this cocktail party stop." He was staring at Franke too, and his clear blue eyes seemed wary. "I've half a mind to leave now. Want to join me?"

"And do what?"

"Dunno. See the sights?"

It sounded like a good idea. But, as she had said the day before, she had signed up for this, and she didn't break her commitments. And, she had to admit, she was curious.

She bit her lower lip, trying to think of a good way to respond. Apparently she didn't have to.

De sighed. "Didn't think so."

The silence in the room was growing. Franke stared at all of them, rocking slightly on his feet. If Brooke had to guess, she would have thought him very nervous.

"All right," he said. "I have a few announcements. First, we will be serving lunch at 1 p.m. in the main restaurant. Dinner will be at 7 in the same place. You will not have assigned seating. Secondly, after I'm through, you're free to tell each other your names. We've had enough of secrets."

He paused, and this time Brooke felt it, that dread she had seen in De's eyes.

"Finally, I would like everyone with a letter on your name badge to go to the right side of the room, and everyone with a number to go to the left."

People stood for a moment, looking around, waiting for

someone to go first. De put a hand on her shoulder. "Here goes nothing," he said. He ran his finger along her collarbone and then walked to the right.

"Come on, folks," Franke said. "It's not hard. Letters to the right. Numbers to the left."

Brooke could still feel De's hand on her skin. She looked in his direction, seeing his blond head towering over the small group of letters who had gathered near the pastries on the far right wall.

She took a deep breath and headed left.

The numbers had gathered near the pastries too, only on the left. She wondered what Franke's researchers would make of that. Los Gatos was there, his hand hovering between the cinnamon rolls and the donuts as if he couldn't decide. So was one of the twins from Akron, and the woman from Boston. Brooke joined them.

"What do you think this is?" Brooke asked.

"A way of identifying us as we run through the maze."

Brooke recognized that voice. She turned and saw Santa Barbara. He shrugged and smiled at her.

She picked up a donut hole and ate it, then made herself a cup of tea while she waited for the room to settle.

It finally did. There was an empty space in the center of the carpet, a space so wide it seemed like an ocean to her.

"Good," Franke said. "Now I'm going to tell you what the badges mean."

There was a slight murmuring as the groups took that in. Boston, Santa Barbara, and Los Gatos flanked Brooke. Her dinner group, minus De.

"Those of you with letters are real Millennium Babies."

Brooke felt a protest rise in her throat. She was born on January 1, 2000. She was a Millennium Baby.

"You were all chosen as such by your state or your country or your city. Your parents received endorsements or awards or newspaper coverage. Those of you with numbers..."

"Are fucking losers," Los Gatos mumbled under his breath.

"...were born near midnight on January 1, but were too late to receive any prizes. You're here because your parents also received publicity or gave interviews before you were born stating that the purpose behind the pregnancy wasn't to conceive a child, but to conceive a child born a few seconds after midnight on January 1 of 2000. You were created to be official Millennium Babies, and failed to receive that title."

Franke paused briefly.

"So, feel free to make real introductions, and mingle. The facility is yours for the day. All we ask is that you do not leave until we tell you to."

"That's it?" Boston asked.

"That's enough," Santa Barbara said. "He's just turned us into the haves and the have-nots."

"Son of a bitch," Los Gatos said.

"We knew that the winners were here," Boston said.

"Yeah, but I assumed there'd be only a few of them," Los Gatos said. "Not half the group."

"It makes sense though," Santa Barbara said. "This is a study of success and failure."

Brooke listened to them idly. She was staring at the right side of the room. All her life, she had been programmed to hate those people. She even studied a few of them, looking them up on the net, seeing how many articles were written about them.

She had stopped when she was ten. Her mother had caught her, and told her what happened to the others didn't matter. Brooke and her mother would have made more of the opportunity, if they had just been given their due.

Their due.

De was staring at her from across the empty carpet. That look of dread was still on his face.

"So," Santa Barbara said. "I guess we can use real names now."

"I guess," said Los Gatos. He hitched up his pants, and glanced at Boston.

She shrugged. "I'm Julie Hunt. I was born at 12:15 Eastern Standard Time in..."

Brooke stopped listening. She didn't want to know about the failures. She knew how it felt to be part of their group. But she didn't know what it was like to be with the winners.

She wiped her damp hands on her pants and crossed the empty carpet. De watched her come. In fact the entire room watched her passage as if she were Moses parting the Red Sea.

The successes weren't talking to each other. They were staring at her.

When she was a few feet away from him, he reached out and pulled her to his side, as if she were in some sort of danger and he needed to recognize her.

"Comin' to the enemy?" he asked, and there was some amusement in his tone. "Or'd they give you a number when you shoulda had a letter?"

The lie would have been so easy. But then she would have had to lie about everything, and that wouldn't work. "No," she said. "I was born at 12:05 a.m. in Detroit, Michigan."

One of the women toward the back looked at her sharply. Anyone from Michigan might recognize that time. Her mother's lawsuits created more than enough publicity. Out of the corner of her eye, Brooke saw Franke. She could feel his intensity meters away.

"Then how come you made the crossin', darlin'?" De's accent got thicker when he was nervous. She had never noticed that before.

She could have given him the easy answer, that she wanted to be beside him, but it wasn't right. The way the entire group was staring at her, eyes wide, lips slightly parted, breathing shallow. It was as if they were afraid she was going to do something to them. But what could she do? Yell at them for something that was no fault of their own? They were the lucky ones. They'd been born at the right time in the right place.

But because they hadn't earned that luck, they were afraid of her. After all, she had been part of the same contest. Only she had been a few minutes late.

No one had moved. They were waiting for her to respond.

"I guess I came," she said, "because I wanted to know what it was like to be a winner."

"Standing over here won't make you a winner," one of the men said.

She flushed. "I know that. I came to listen to you. To see how you've lived. If that's all right."

"I'm not sure I understand you, darlin'," De said. Only his name wasn't De. She didn't know his name. Maybe she never would.

"You were all born winners. From the first moment. Just like we were losers."

Her voice carried in the large room. She hadn't expected the acoustics to be so good.

"I don't know about everyone else in my group, but my birth time has affected my entire life. My mother—" Brooke paused. She hadn't meant to discuss her mother "—never let me forget who I was. And I was wondering if any of you experienced that. Or if you felt special because you'd won. Or if you even knew."

Her voice trailed off at the end. She couldn't imagine not knowing. A life of blissful ignorance. If she hadn't known, she might have gone on to great things. She might have reached farther, tried harder. She might have expected success with every endeavor, instead of being surprised at it.

They were staring at her as if she were speaking Greek. Maybe she was.

"I don't know why it matters," a man said beside her. "It was just a silly little contest."

"I hadn't even remembered it," a woman said, "until Dr. Franke's people contacted me."

Brooke felt something catch in her throat. "Was it like that for all of you?"

"Of course not," De said. "I got interviewed every New Year's like clockwork. What's it like five years into the millennium? Ten? Twenty? That's one of the reasons I moved to L'siana. I'm not much for attention, 'specially the kind I don't deserve."

"Money was nice," one of the women said. "It got me to college."

Another woman shook her head. "My folks spent it all."

More people from the left were moving across the divide, as if they were drawn to the conversation.

"So'd mine," said one of the men.

"There wasn't any money with mine. Just got my picture in the newspaper. Still have that on my wall," another man said.

Brooke felt someone bump her from behind. Los Gatos had joined her. So had Santa Barbara and Boston—um, Julie.

"Why'd this contest make such a difference to you?" one of the letter women asked. She was staring at Brooke.

"It didn't," Brooke said after a moment. "It mattered to my mother. She lost."

"Hell," De said. "People lose. That's part of living."

Brooke looked at him. There was a slight frown mark between his eyes. He didn't understand either. He didn't know what it was like being outside, with his face pressed against the glass.

"Three weeks after I was born," Los Gatos said, "My parents dumped me with a friend of theirs, saying they weren't ready for a baby. I never saw them. I don't even know what they look like."

"My parents said they couldn't afford me," Santa Barbara said. "They were planning on some prize money."

"They abandoned you too?" the woman asked.

"No," he said. "They just made it clear they didn't appreciate the financial burden. If they'd won, I wouldn't've been a problem."

"Sure you would have," De said. "They just would've blamed their problems on something else."

"It's not that simple," Brooke said. Her entire body was sweating despite the chill in the room. "It was a contest, a race. A lot of people didn't look beyond that. There were news articles about abandoned and abused babies, and there were a disproportionate number born in December, January, and February of 2000, because parents wanted to split some of the glory."

"You can't tell me," De said, "that something as insignificant as the time we were born determines our future."

"It does," Brooke said, "if we're brought up to believe it does."

"That bear out, Professor Franke?" De said.

Brooke turned. The professor was standing close to them, listening, looking both bemused and perplexed. Apparently he had expected some kind of reaction, but probably not this one.

"That's what I'm trying to determine," Franke said.

"And I'm askin' you if you determined it," De said.

Franke glanced at one of his assistants. The assistant shrugged. The entire room full of people was crowded around Franke, and was silent for the second time that day.

"This part of the study is experimental," he said. "I'm not sure if answering you will corrupt it."

"But you want to answer me," De said.

Franke smiled. "Yes, I do."

"It's an experiment," Brooke said. "You can always throw this part out. You might have done that anyway. Isn't that what you told me? Or at least implied?"

Franke glanced from her to De. Then Franke straightened his shoulders, as if the gesture made him stronger. "I believe that Brooke is right. My studies have convinced me that something becomes important to a child's development because that child is told that something is important."

"So us losers will remain losers the rest of our lives," Los Gatos said.

Franke shook his head. "That is not my conclusion. I believe that when something becomes important, you chose how to react to it." His voice got louder as he spoke. His professor's voice. "Some of you wearing letters have not done as well as expected. You've rebelled against those expectations and worked at proving you are not as good as you were told you were."

A flush colored De's tan cheeks.

"Others lived up to the expectations and a few of you, a very small few, exceeded them. But—" Franke paused dramatically. "Those of you who wear numbers are financially more successful as a group than your lettered peers. You strive harder because you feel you have something to overcome."

Brooke felt Los Gatos shift behind her.

"I think it goes back to the parameters of the study," Franke said. "Your parents—all of your parents—wanted to improve their lot. They all had drive, therefore most of you have drive. We've found a biological correlation."

"Really? Wow," Santa Barbara said.

"But there's more than biology at work here."

"I'd hope so," De said. "I'd hate to think you can determine who I am by reading my genes."

Franke gave him a small smile. "Your parents," Franke said, "all chose a contest as the method of improving their lives. A lottery, if you will. And most of them failed to win. Or if they succeeded, they discovered Easy Street wasn't so easy after all. You numbered folk have realized that luck is overrated. The only thing you can trust is work you do yourselves."

"And what about those of us with letters?" one of the twins from Akron asked.

"You learned a different lesson. Most of you learned that luck is what you make of it. You might win the lottery, but that doesn't make you or your family any happier than before." Franke looked at Brooke. "There were a lot of studies, some of them prompted by your mother, that showed how many unsuccessful Millennium Babies were abandoned or mistreated. But the successful ones had similar problems. Only no one wanted to lose the golden goose as long as it was still golden. Many of those abandonments were emotional, not physical. People became parents to become rich or famous, not because they wanted children."

"Sounds like you should be studying our parents," Los Gatos said.

Franke grinned. "Now you have my next book."

And the group laughed.

"Feel free to enjoy the rest of the day," Franke said. "Over the rest of the weekend, I'll be talking to individuals among you, wrapping things up. I want to thank you for your time and participation."

"That's it?" De asked.

"When you leave here tonight, if I haven't spoken to you," Franke said, "that's it."

His words were met with a momentary silence. Then he started to make his way through the group. Some people stopped him. Brooke didn't. She turned away, not sure how to feel.

She wasn't as successful as she wanted to be, but she was better off than her mother had said she would be. Brooke had her own house, a good job, interests that meant something to her.

But she was as alone as her mother was. In that, at least, they were the same.

"So," De said. "Is your life profoundly different thanks to this study?"

The question had a mixed tone. Half sarcasm, half serious. He seemed to be waiting for her answer.

"What's your name?" she asked.

"Adam," he said, wincing. "Adam Lassiter."

"The first man."

"If I'd missed my birth time, I'd have been named Zeb." He smiled as he said that, but his eyes didn't twinkle.

"I'm Brooke Cross." She waited, wondering if he'd guess at the name, despite the change. He didn't. Or if he did, he didn't say anything.

"You didn't answer my question," he said.

She looked at the room, at all the people in it, most engaged in private conversations now, hands moving, gazes serious as they compared and contrasted their experiences, trying to see if they agreed with Professor Franke.

"When I was a little girl," she said. "We lived in a small white house, maybe 1200 square feet. A starter, my mother called it, because that was all she could afford. And to me, that house was the world. My mother's world."

"What kind of world was that?" he asked.

She shook her head. How to explain it? But he had asked, and she had to try.

"A world where she did everything right and failed, and everyone else cheated and somehow succeeded. If she'd had the same kind of breaks your parents had, she believed she would have done better than they did. If she hadn't had a child like me, one who was chronically late, her life would have been better."

He was watching her. The crease between his eyes grew deeper.

Her heart was pounding, but she made herself continue. "A few years ago, when I was looking for my own home, I saw dozens and dozens of houses, and somewhere I realized that to the people living in them, those houses were the world."

"So each block has dozens of tiny worlds," he said.

She smiled at him. "Yeah."

"I still don't see how that relates."

She looked at him, then at the room. The other conversations were continuing, as serious as hers was with him. "You asked me if this study changed my life. I can't answer that. I can say, though, that it made me realize one thing."

His gaze was as intense as Franke's.

"It made me realize that even though I had moved out of that house, I hadn't left my mother's world."

He studied her for a moment longer, then said, "Sounds like a hell of a realization."

"Maybe," she said. "It depends on what I do with it."

He laughed. "Thus proving Franke's point."

She flushed. She hadn't realized she had done so, but she had. He leaned toward her.

"You know, Brooke," Adam said softly, "I like women who are chronically late. It balances my habitual timeliness. How's about we have lunch and talk about our histories. Not just the day we were born, but other things, like what we do and where we live and who we are."

She almost refused. He was from Louisiana, and she was from Wisconsin. This friendship—if that's all it was—could go nowhere.

But it was that attitude which had limited her all along. She had been driven, as Franke said, to succeed materially and professionally on her own merits. But she had never tried to succeed socially.

She had never wanted to before.

"And," she said, "you get to tell me what you learned from this study."

"Assumin'," he said with a grin, "that I'm the kinda man who can learn anything a'tall."

"Assuming that," she said and slipped her hand in his. It felt good to touch someone else, even if it was only for a brief time. It felt good.

It felt different.

It felt right.

Without End

Kristine Kathryn Rusch

The sun, high in the hot August afternoon, sent short shadows across the neatly trimmed grass. A small clump of people huddled in a semicircle, close but not touching. The coffin, in the center, sat on a platform covering the empty hole.

Dylan placed a rose on the black lacquer surface, and stepped back. A moment, frozen in time and space.

A hand clutched his shoulder. Firm grip, meant as reassurance. He turned. Ross nodded to him, mouth a thin line.

"She was a good woman," Ross whispered.

Dylan nodded. The minister was speaking, but he didn't care about the words, even though the rest of the group strained forward.

"She would have found this silly," Dylan said, and then stopped. Ross's expression had changed from one of sympathy to something else—confusion? Disapproval? Dylan didn't know, and didn't really want to find out. Outside he was calm. Inside he felt fragile, as if his entire body was formed of the thinnest crystal. One wrong look, a movement, a shadow on the grass, would shatter him into a thousand pieces.

A thousand pieces. Shards, scattered on the kitchen floor.

Geneva, crouched over them, like a cat about to pounce. *Look, Dylan,* she said. *To us, a glass shattered forever. But to the universe, possibilities. A thousand possibilities.*

He stared at the black box. He could picture Geneva inside as she had looked the night before: black hair cascading on the satin; skin too white; eyes closed in imitation sleep. Geneva had never been so still.

He wondered what she would say if she stood beside him, her hand light on his arm, the summer sun kissing her hair.

For just a moment, trapped in space and time.

∽

Stars twinkled over the ocean. Dylan stood on the damp sand, Geneva beside him, her hand wrapped in his and tucked in his pocket—the only warm thing on the chilly beach. Occasionally the wind would brush a strand of her hair across his face. She would push at her hair angrily, but he liked the touch, the faint shampoo smell of her.

She was staring at the waves, a frown touching the corners of her mouth. "Hear it?" she asked.

He listened and heard nothing except the pulse of the ocean, powerful, throbbing, a pulse that had more life than he did. "Hear what?"

"The waves."

In her pause, he listened to them crash against the sand, the heart of the pulse.

"It's so redundant," she said.

"What is?" He turned, his attention fully on her. She looked like a clothed Venus, rising out of the sand, hair wrapped around her, eyes sparkling with unearthly light.

"Sound is a wave, a wave is sound. We stand here and listen to nature's redundancy and call it beautiful."

He leaned into her, feeling her solidness, her warmth. "It is beautiful."

She grinned at him. "It's inspiring," she said, and pulled her hand out of his pocket. She walked down to the edge where the Pacific met the Oregon coast. He didn't move, but watched her instead, wishing he could paint. She looked so powerful standing there, one small woman facing an ocean, against a backdrop of stars.

He went through her papers for the university, separating them into piles with equations and piles without. The cat sat on the piles without, watching the proceeding with a solemnity that suited the occasion.

Dylan's knowledge of physics and astronomy came from Geneva. He had had three semesters in college, a series called Physics for Poets (hardly any equations), and by the time he met her, most of his knowledge was out of date.

(If you knew as little about women, Geneva once said, *I'd be explaining to you what my clitoris is.)*

His specialty was philosophy, not so much of the religious type, even though he could get lost in the Middle Ages monkish romanticism, but more a political stripe: Descartes, Locke, Hegel, and John Stuart Mill. He liked to ponder unanswerable questions. He had met Geneva that way—one afternoon, wind off the lake,

Wisconsin in the summer, sitting on the Union Terrace, soaking up the rays and pretending to study. Only he wasn't even pretending, he was arguing basic freshman philosophy: if a tree falls in the forest, and no one hears it, does it make a sound? Geneva had been passing at the time—all legs and tan and too-big glasses on a too-small nose.

Of course, she said, *because it makes a disturbance and the disturbance makes a wave, and that wave is sound.*

He didn't remember what he said in response. Something intriguing enough to make her sit and argue until the sunset turned the lake golden, and the mosquitoes had driven the other students away.

From that moment on, he and Geneva always talked that way. The philosophy of physics. The physics of philosophy. He got the education without the equations and she, she felt free enough to explore the imaginative side of her science—the tiny particles no one could see, the unified theories, the strings binding the universe.

There's something out there, Dylan, she would say, *and it's more than we are.*

He knew that, as he held her papers, in her sunlit office just past their den. In her crabbed writing, on those dot-matrix computer sheets, was the secret to something.

If he could touch that, he could touch her. And if he could touch her, he might be able to hold her.

Forever.

~

The campus bar was full of people impossibly young. Dylan grabbed his frosty mug of beer and sat across from Ross, watching the people intermingle. A different university, a different time. Now the students wore their hair short, and the professors wore theirs long. Dylan sipped, let the foam catch him full on his upper lip, and let the sound of co-mingled voices and too-loud music wash over him.

"I worry about you," Ross said. His beer was dark and warm. Its color matched the tweed blend of his blazer. "You've locked yourself up in that house, and haven't gone anywhere in weeks. You don't have to get her papers in order before the end of the term, Dylan. The department just wants them on file."

Dylan shook his head. He wasn't always working. Sometimes he wandered from room to room, touching her clothes, the small sculpture she had brought back from Africa, the pieces of Inuit-carved whalebone they had found in Alaska. "I'll get it done," he said.

"That's not the point." Ross pushed his beer aside, ignoring it as a bit of foam slopped out. He leaned forward, and would probably have touched Dylan's arm if Dylan had been the kind of man who permitted it. "She's dead, Dylan. She's gone. She was a spectacular woman, but now you have to get used to living without her."

Dylan stared at Ross's hand, outstretched on the scarred wooden table. "But what if she isn't really dead? I can feel her sometimes, Ross, as close to me as you are."

"That's part of grieving," Ross said. "You're in the habit of feeling her presence. It's like a ghost limb. You know it was there; you know what it felt like, and you can't believe it's gone."

"No." Dylan's fingers were frozen to the side of the mug. He pulled them away. "She was working on space-time equations, did you know that?"

Ross removed his hand from the tabletop, the odd expression—the one Dylan had seen at the funeral—back on his face. "Of course I knew that. We have to report on her research twice a term."

"She said she was close to something. That we thought about time wrong. That we were looking for beginnings and endings, and they weren't important—and possibly not even probably. She said we were limited by the way we think, Ross."

"It's not a new area," Ross said. A cocktail waitress went by, her tray loaded with heavy beer mugs. Patrons ducked and slipped into each other to stay out of her way. "We've been exploring space-time since Einstein. Geneva was going over very old ground. The department was going to re-examine her position if she hadn't taken a new angle this term."

"Her angle was new." Dylan wiped his hands on his jeans. "It was new from the beginning. She said the problem was not in the physical world, but in the way our minds understood it. She said—"

"I know what she said." Ross's voice was gentle. "It's not physics, Dylan. It's philosophy."

Dylan's entire body tensed. "I didn't change her, Ross. She was thinking this way when we met, when she was an undergraduate. She said that our limitations limited the way we looked at the universe, and she's right. You know she's right."

"We already know about space-time," Ross said. "About the lack of beginnings and the lack of endings. We know all that—"

"But we still think in linear terms. If we truly understood relativity, time would be all encompassing. We would experience everything at once."

"Dylan," Ross said, his voice soft. "Linear times keeps us sane."

"No," Dylan said. "That's why ancient maps had dragons on them, and why no one believed that the world was round. Why Galileo got imprisoned for showing the universe didn't work the way the church wanted it to. You all got upset at her because she was showing you that your minds were as narrow as the ancients', that you have your theories of everything and think you can understand it all, when you don't take into account your own beings. She is doing physics, Ross. You're just too blind to see it."

Dylan stood up. The conversation around him had stopped, and the short-haired, too-young students were staring at him. Ross was looking at his hands.

Dylan waited, breathing heavily, a pressure inside his chest that he had never felt before. Ross finally looked up, his round face empty of all emotion. "The anger," he said. "It's part of grieving too."

∽

They first tried it in her dorm room, shutters closed on the only window, lights off so that the posters of Einstein were hidden, so that only the glow-in-the-dark stars on the ceiling remained. They crowded, side by side, on her narrow bed, after removing their clothes in the dark. He could smell her musk, feel the warmth of her, but as he leaned into her body, she moved away.

"We can't touch," she said. "Defeats the purpose."

So they lay there, staring up at the bright pink and green

stars. And she began speaking softly, her voice no more than a murmur in his ear.

She told him what she liked to do with him, how he tasted, how soft his mouth was, how sensitive his ear. She worked her way down his body, never touching him, only talking to him, until he thought he could wait no longer. And then she was on top of him, wet already, nipples hard, and within a few seconds, they had worked their way to mutual orgasm—the best he had ever had.

She rolled back beside him, and sighed. "Intellectual foreplay," she said. "It really works."

～

Ghost limb. From the moment Ross mentioned it, Dylan felt not one but dozens of ghost limbs throughout the house. Here, in the bedroom, done in designer pink by the previous owner *(all we need is a big bow on the bed, and it'll be perfect—for eight-year-old girls,* Geneva said). Something they were going to remodel when the money allowed. The small side room, well heated, well lit, filled with boxes and scraps of Christmas wrapping: he saw babies in there. First the little boy, cherubic face puckered in sleep. Then a little girl, all wide-eyed and exploring, Geneva in the raw. Future ghosts, possibilities lopped off with the branch that was Geneva.

One night he woke in the dark, confident that he had just missed her. Her scent lingered; the energy of her presence electrified the space. He knew, just a moment before, that she had been there—Geneva, alive, bright, and dancing with ideas.

He got up and went into the living room. The cat followed

him, sleepy and dazed. Together they stared out the wide living room window at the street. A long streetlight illuminated a patch of concrete. The light's reflection made the neighboring homes look gray and indistinct. Ghost homes, full of possibilities.

The cat got bored and leapt from the sill, but when Dylan closed his eyes, he could still see her, outlined in red shadow against his eyelids. Even though she was alive, moving, and breathing, the cat too left ghosts.

It flashed across his mind, then, the possibility—and as quickly as it appeared, it was gone. But he knew it was there. He knew he would find it, and then he would no longer be alone, among the ghosts.

~

"Dammit. The little shit!" Geneva's voice rose on the last syllable, so Dylan knew she wasn't upset, just inconvenienced. He came out of his office to find her standing by the front door, hands against her hips. "Cat's out," she said.

He glanced out the door. The cat sat on the porch huddled against the rain, acting as if the world had betrayed her by getting her wet. He picked her up and carried her inside, closing the door with his foot.

Geneva reached beyond him and locked the bolt.

"There's no need," he said. "Door's closed."

Geneva grinned at him. He dropped the cat and she scampered into the living room, pausing at the end of the couch to clean the vile wetness off her fur.

"Little shit," Geneva said again. She was staring at the cat fondly. "She figured out the door. I came out here in time to see her grasp the knob in both paws and turn."

"Cats can't do that," he said.

"No. *Dogs* can't. Cats think differently." She kissed him lightly on the nose. "Imagine, being trapped by your mental abilities. A cat can get out of a man-made trap. A dog can't."

Then she smiled as if she had solved the riddle of the universe, went back into her office, and closed the door.

∼

He had chalk on his hands. Facing all those clean, bright students, he felt rumpled and old. Most of them sat before him because his elective brought them three credits. Only a handful liked to grasp the elemental questions as much as he did. He rubbed his hands together, saw chalk motes drift in the fluorescent light.

"The Deists believed in a clockmaker god," he said, leaning against the metal lip of the blackboard. "A god who invented the world, then sat back and watched it play, like a great ticking clock. Jefferson believed in Deism. Some say that was why he became a great political philosopher—he believed that God no longer intervened in his creation, so the creation had to govern itself."

Dylan paused, remembering Geneva's face when he had discussed this with her, so many years ago. None of the students had her sharpness, her quick fascination with things of the mind. He waited for someone to raise a hand, to ask why those who believed in God the clockmaker didn't believe in predetermination, but no one asked. He couldn't go into his long explanation without prompting, and he didn't feel like prompting himself.

He waved a hand, almost said, "Never mind," but didn't. "Read chapters thirteen and fourteen," he said to those blank faces, "and write me a paper about the contradictions in Deistic philosophy."

"By tomorrow?" someone asked.

"Four pages," he said tiredly. "I'm letting you out early." They looked at him as if he had betrayed them. "You can do four pages. It's not the great American novel."

He grabbed his books and let himself out of the room. The hallway was quiet. It smelled faintly of processed air, and looked cleaner than it did when filled with students. Down the stairs, he heard a door slam. A moment later, a woman appeared on the staircase.

She was tiny, blonde, her hair wrapped around her skull like a turban. When she looked up, he recognized her. Hollings, from psychology.

"What are you pondering so seriously?" she asked.

He studied her for a minute, then decided to answer truthfully. "If God were a watchmaker, like the Deists believed, and if he abandoned his watch, which they did not believe, wouldn't that leave a vacuum? Wouldn't that vacuum have to be filled?"

Her mouth opened slightly, revealing an even row of perfect white teeth. Then she closed it again. "A watchmaker makes a watch and gives it to someone else. Presumably the watch owner maintains the watch."

"That assumes a lot of watches—and a lot of watchmakers."

"Indeed it does." She smiled and walked away.

He watched her go, wondering if the exchange had

happened or if he had imagined it. He thought no one besides Geneva would engage in flip philosophies.

Perhaps he was wrong.

Perhaps he had been wrong about a lot of things.

∽

They lay on their backs on the public dock. Below them, Devil's Lake lapped at the wood, trying to reach them. In the distance, they could hear the ocean, shushing its way to shore. The Oregon night was cool, not cold, and they used each other for warmth.

Above them, in the Perseids, meteors showered at the rate of one per minute. Dylan oooed his appreciation, but Geneva remained unusually silent. She snuggled closer and slipped her hand in his. It was thinner than it used to be. He could feel the delicate bones in her palm.

"I wonder," she said, "if that's going on inside of me."

He tensed. She didn't talk about the cancer much, and when she did, it often presaged a deep depression. "You wonder if what's going on inside of you?"

"If somewhere, deep down, two tiny beings are lying on the equivalent of a dock on the equivalent of a lake, watching cells die."

"We're watching history," he said. "The cells are dying inside you now."

"But who knows how long it takes the message to reach those two tiny beings on the lake equivalent? If the sun died now, we wouldn't know for another eight minutes. So to us, the sun would still be alive, even though it was dead."

Her words sent a shudder through him. He imagined himself, talking to her, listening to her response, even though she was already dead.

"We think about it wrong, you know," she said, breaking into his reverie. She was alive and breathing, and snuggled against him. He would know when she died.

"Think about what wrong?"

"Time. We act as if it moves in a linear fashion, straight from here on as if nothing would change. But our memories change. The fact that we have memories means that time is not linear. String theory postulates twenty-five dimensions, and we can barely handle the three we see. We're like cats and dogs and doors."

"And if we could think in time that wasn't linear, how would it be?"

He could feel her shrug, sharp shoulder bones moving against his ribcage. "I don't know. Maybe we would experience everything at once. All our life, from birth to death, would be in our minds at the same time. Only we wouldn't look at it as a line. We'd look at it like a pond, full of everything, full of us."

Her words washed over him like a wave, like tiny particles he could barely feel. "Geneva." He kept his voice quiet, like the lapping of the water against the dock. "What are you saying?"

She sat up then, blocking his view of the meteor showers, her face more alive than it had been in weeks. "I'm saying don't mourn for me. Mourning is a function of linear time."

"Geneva," he said with a resolution he didn't feel. "You're not going to die."

"Exactly," she said, and rested her head on his chest.

He pulled open the heavy oak doors and went inside. The chancel smelled vaguely of candle wax and pine branches, even though it wasn't Christmas. A red carpet ran down the aisles between the heavy brown pews. The altar stood at the front like a small fortress. He hadn't been inside a church since he was a teenager, and inside this one now, he felt small, as if that former self remained, waiting for a moment like this.

A ghost limb.

He smiled just a little, half afraid that the minister would find him, and order him out. He sat in a back pew and stared at the altar, hoping the words would come back to him. He ran through the rituals in his mind. Standing up for the opening hymn, watching the choir process, listening to the readings, singing more hymns, and then the offering—and the music.

>...as it was in the beginning
>is now and ever shall be
>world without end.
>Amen.
>Amen.

World without end. He picked up a hymnal, stuck in the back of the pew, and thumbed through it. They listed the Doxology, but not the year it was written, nor the text it was written from. Surely it didn't have the meaning that he interpreted. When it came to the church, the hymn probably meant life ever after. Not time without end. Not beginnings without endings, endings without beginnings. Not non-linear time.

He stood. He had never been in this church before, of that he was certain. So the ghost limb he brought with him applied to the Presbyterian church in Wisconsin, the one in which he was raised, where they too sang the Doxology, where a red carpet ran down the aisle, where the altar rose like a fortress.

Then a memory came, as clear and fresh as a drop of spring water. He couldn't have been more than eight, sitting beside his father on Christmas Eve, listening to the way that God had sent his only son to earth, to have him die for our sins.

And why, Dylan asked, *if God had a son, why didn't God have a father?*

Because God is the father, his father replied. And no matter how much probing Dylan did, he couldn't get at a better answer

The beginnings of a philosopher—the search for the deeper meanings. Not being satisfied with the pat, the quick, the easy answer. That path had led him away from the church, away, even, from God, and into Geneva, whom he felt understood the mysteries of the universe.

He wouldn't find Geneva here. She felt that the church destroyed thought. He didn't know why he had come looking in the first place.

∽

Bare feet on the deck, cat behind her, hat tipped down over her eyes. Geneva wasn't moving. Geneva, frozen in sunlight.

"How'd it go?" he asked.

The cat leapt off the chair, rubbed her soft fur against his legs, demanding attention. He crouched and scratched her back, all the while watching Geneva.

"They imprisoned Copernicus," she said, not moving. "Newton too. They kicked Einstein out of Germany, and made Socrates drink hemlock."

"It didn't go well, then," he said, sitting on the deck chair beside her.

She tilted her hat up, revealing her green eyes. They shone in the sun. "Depends on your point of view. If they accepted me, I probably wasn't on enough of an edge."

He didn't know how to respond. He was secretly relieved that she hadn't gotten the post-doc. MIT was an excellent school, and an even better research facility, but she would have been in Boston, and he would have been in Oregon. Together only on breaks and during term's end.

"Did you ever think of working on your theories on your own time?" he asked.

"And give those stupid committees the pap that they want?" She sat up then, and whipped her hat off her head, letting her black hair cascade around her shoulders. "You ever think of becoming a Baptist?"

"Geneva, it's not the same."

"It is too the same. People become arbiters of thought. In your area, the church still holds. In mine, it's the universities. This is an accepted area of research. That is not. Scientists are children, Dylan, little precious children, who look at the world as if it is brand new—because it is brand new to them. And they ask silly questions, and expect cosmic answers, and when the answers don't come, they go searching. And if they can't ask the silly questions, if they get slapped every time they do, their searches get smaller, their discoveries get smaller, and the world becomes a ridiculous, narrow place."

She plopped her hat back on her head, swung her tanned legs off the deck chair and stood up. "I can make you come without even touching you. Just the power of our minds, working together. Imagine if the right combination of minds, working together, break through the boundaries that hold us in our place in the universe. We might be able to see the Big Bang at the same moment we see the universe's end. We might be able to see the moment of our birth, this moment, and every other moment of our lives. We would live differently. We would be different—more than human, maybe even better than human."

Her cheeks were flushed. He wanted to touch her, but he knew better.

"It's steam engine time, that's all it is," she said. "A handful of minds, working together, change our perception of the world. Does a tree falling unobserved in the forest make a sound? Only if we believe that a tree is a tree, the ground is the ground, and a sound a vibration. Only if we believe together."

"And someone who doesn't believe gets denied a post-doc," he said.

"It's the twentieth-century equivalent of being forced to drink hemlock," she said, and flounced into the house.

∽

He hadn't turned on a light yet. Dylan sat in the dark, watching the fuzzy grayness slip over the entire living room. The cat slept on a corner of the couch. Geneva's papers were piled on the coffee table, on the end tables, in the corner. He had been sitting in the dark too much, thinking perhaps that was when her ghost would arrive.

A light flipped on in the kitchen and he jumped.

"Jesus Christ, don't you use lights anymore?"

Ross. Ross had let himself in the back door. Dylan took a deep breath to ease the pounding of his heart. He reached up and flicked on a table lamp.

"In here," he said.

Ross came through the dining room door, and stared at the living room. The cat curled into a tighter ball, hiding her eyes from the light.

"We need to get you out of here," he said. "How about a movie?"

Dylan shook his head. He didn't need distractions now. He felt like he was very close. Her papers held little that was illuminating, but his memories—they were like a jigsaw puzzle, leaving gaps, creating bits of a picture. As if she had given him the answer out of order, and he had to piece it together. Alone.

"Okay," Ross said, slumping into the sofa. "How about a beer?"

The cat sat up and looked at Ross, then jumped off the couch. Dylan wished he could be as rude.

"I want to be alone, right now," he said.

"You've been alone since the end of August. Lock yourself up in here long enough, and you'll never get over her."

"I don't want to get over her," Dylan said.

Ross shrugged. "Wrong choice of words. You got your own life, and the last thing Geneva would have done was to want you to stop living because of her."

"I'm still living," Dylan said. "I'm still thinking."

"Not good enough." Ross stood, grabbed Dylan's coat off the back of a chair, and held it out.

Dylan looked at it and sighed. Then he rubbed a hand over his face. "Sit down," he said.

Ross sat, still holding Dylan's coat. He rested on the edge of the couch, as if he were about to jump up at any point.

"When Geneva and I went to Alaska, some friends of ours took us to a glacier. We went up in the mountains, saw this fantastic lake, filled with ice bergs, and at the edge of the lake, the tip of the glacier. A boat took us right there, and we could see geologic history being made."

"I remember," Ross said. His tone was dry—*get to the point, Dylan*—and he clutched the coat tighter. "You told me when you got back."

"But I didn't tell you about the exhibit. One of those museum things, where they showed you how the glacier has traveled in the last hundred years or so. It receded so much that the point where we stood at the edge of the lake had been glacier only a hundred and fifty years before. That sucker was moving fast. Geneva stayed inside, where it was warm, but I went back out, and put my feet where that glacier had been a hundred years ago. And if I closed my eyes, I could feel it. I knew what it was like in the past; it was as if it was still there, only half a step away, and I could get to it, if I took the right step."

Ross leaned back on the couch, the coat covering him like a blanket. "When Gary died," he said, "I used to go in his bedroom and pick up one of those models he worked so hard on. And if I held it just right, at the right time of night, I could feel his little warm hand under mine. Dinah would just watch me, she wouldn't say anything, and I used to think she was jealous—Gary shows up for Ross, but not me kinda thing. But she was worried about losing me too. She was afraid I would never come out of it. I still miss him, Dylan. I see another man with a six-year-old boy and it knocks the wind out of me. But I survived, and I moved on, and we have Linny now, and she's precious too."

"You're telling me this is another phase?"

"No." Ross was twisting the coat sleeve in his hands. "I'm telling you I finally know how she felt. Dylan, give yourself a chance to heal. Geneva will always be part of your past, but not part of your future."

"What makes you so sure," Dylan asked, "that they're all that different?"

∾

Geneva rested on her stomach, knees bent, feet crossed at the ankles. She held a blade of grass between her fingers, and occasionally she would blow on it, trying to make a sound. The summer sun was hot, and the humidity was high. Wisconsin in the summer. Dylan couldn't wait to leave.

"Did you know that Mormons marry not just for life, but for all eternity?"

"You saying we should incorporate that into our vows?" Dylan rolled on his back, feeling the grass tickle his shoulders.

"I wonder if we won't be doing that already." She put her thumbs to her mouth, a blade of grass stretched between them. As she blew, it made a weak raspberry sound. "I mean, if you look at an event like you look at a pebble, falling into a pond, the action will create ripples that will stretch out from the pebble. Each event has its own ripple, independent of another ripple—"

"Unless they collide," Dylan said with a leer.

"Unless they collide," she repeated, ignoring his meaning. "But who is to say that once a pebble gets dropped, you can't go back to the same spot and watch it get dropped over and over again. You can in video tape, why not in life?"

"Because life doesn't have rewind and fast forward," he said.

"Who says? Time is just perception, Dylan."

He rolled to his side, kissed her bare shoulder, and draped an arm across her back. From his perspective, the blade of grass between her fingers looked ragged and damp. "So you're saying you might perceive that you're marrying me for eternity, and I might perceive that I'm marrying you for Wednesday. So I could turn around and marry someone else for Thursday—"

"Only if you get a divorce first." She threw away the blade of grass. "Legalities, remember? Other people's perceptions."

"—and you would still think you're married to me forever, right?"

"I think I heard about a court case like that," she said, leaning her head into him. Her hair smelled of the sun. He kissed her crown.

She turned, so that she was pressed flush against him, warm skin against his. "But when you say you'll love me for eternity, you mean it, right?"

He leaned in, his face almost touching hers. He couldn't imagine life without her. "When I say I'll love you forever," he said, "I mean it with all my heart."

∽

The dean's office was on the second floor of Erskine Hall, where the senior professors resided. Dylan used to aspire to walk up that staircase every day. Then he would have had tenure, been able to stay in Oregon until he retired. He used to imagine that he and Geneva would buy a beach house. They would work in the city, then drive the hour to the beach each weekend. They would sit outside, on a piece of driftwood, staring at the point where the sky met the ocean. Geneva would contemplate the universe, and Dylan would contemplate her.

Dreams. Even dreams were ghost limbs. Moments, frozen in time and space.

He walked down the narrow corridors, past the rows of crammed offices, filled with too many books and stacks of student papers. The dean's office was a little larger, and it had a reception area, usually staffed by upperclassmen. This time, though, the receptionist was gone.

He knocked on the gray metal door. "Nick?"

"Come on in, Dylan, and close the door."

Dylan did as he was asked, and sat on the ancient upholstered chair in front of Nick's desk. Students probably felt like they'd walked into hell's anteroom when they came here. Everything was decorated early '70s, in browns and burnt orange.

Nick was a white-haired man in his late fifties, face florid with too much food and stress. "I'm sorry about Geneva," he said. "She had spirit. I never expected to outlive someone like her."

Dylan made himself smile. "My mother said she was like a flare, brief but beautiful."

"You don't believe that," Nick said.

Dylan took a deep breath. "You didn't call me in here to talk about Geneva."

"Actually, I did. Indirectly." Nick stood up, and shoved his hands in his pockets, stretching out his pants like a clown's, and making his potbelly poof out. Geneva used to call him Chuckles when he did that, a comment made all the better by the fact that the gesture meant Nick was going to say something difficult. "Word is that you've been acting a bit erratic lately. Letting classes out early, missing meetings, spouting spontaneous philosophy in the halls."

"Doesn't sound like the crime of the century," Dylan said, then bit his lip. Defensive. He couldn't get defensive.

"No, and it's not even all that unusual—except for you, Dylan. You were always consistent and quiet. I'm not saying you're doing anything wrong, but your wife just died. I wanted you to take the term off, but you insisted on working, and I'm not sure that was such a good idea."

Dylan stared at him for a moment, uncertain how to respond.

It begins with little complaints, Geneva once told him. *Maybe your clothes are a little unusual, or you don't conduct class according to the right methods. Then, one day, you wake up and find you've been imprisoned for your beliefs.*

He opened his mouth, closed it again, and thought. The classes meant nothing this term. The students, merely full-sized reminders of how much time had passed since he had sat in their chairs, since he had met Geneva.

"You're right," he said. "I think I should take a leave of absence, maybe come back next fall term."

Nick turned, pulled his hands out of his pockets, and frowned. Obviously he hadn't expected Dylan to acquiesce so easily. "Sure it won't leave you alone too much?"

Dylan smiled and shrugged. "I'm not sure I'm really alone now," he said.

~

Toward the end, she had shrunk to half her size, her skin so translucent, he could see her veins. The hospital room had deep blue walls, a bed with restraints on it, and a television perched in the corner. The restraints were down, the television off, and the window open, casting sunlight against the awful blue.

Dylan sat beside the bed every day, from the moment visiting hours began until the moment they ended. At noon on August 23, she opened her eyes and found his. Her gaze was clear for the first time in three days, for the first time since he had brought her to the hospital.

"Dylan?" Her voice was no more than a rasp.

He took her too-small hand. It no longer fit just right in his. "I'm here, Geneva."

"You know those two tiny beings on the lake equivalent?" Each word was an effort. He leaned forward so that he could hear her. Her grip was tight in his. "I think in about eight minutes, they're going to see a supernova."

She closed her eyes. He couldn't hear her breathing. He pushed the nurse call button, once, twice, then three times.

The grip in his hand tightened. Geneva was looking at him, a small smile on her face. "Don't mourn, Dylan," she said. "Forever, remember?"

"I remember," he said, but by that time, she had loosened her grip on his hand. The nurses came in, with their equipment and needles, pushing him aside. He watched as they checked her, as they looked under her closed eyelids, and felt for her pulse. One of them turned to him, and shook her head. He shoved his hands in his pockets and walked out of the room, a much poorer man than he had been when he entered.

∼

On All Hallow's Eve, he packed his car to the light of the single streetlight. During the afternoon, he had taken the cat over to Ross's, explaining that he was going on a short trip, and wasn't sure when he would be back. He waited until dark, packed the car, and headed west.

He had awakened with the idea, the jigsaw puzzle complete in his mind. He knew how to find her, and how they could be together, forever, as she had said. As he drove over the Coast Range, the puzzle became clearer; the answer seemed right. Steam engine time, she had said. But who would have thought that a philosophy professor would be the first to ride the rails?

Geneva had. She knew that philosophers were used to broad concepts of the mind.

He pulled into the public beach at Lincoln City, grabbed a blanket and a cooler from the back of the car, and walked to the loose sand. He was careful to sit on a driftwood log, untouched by high tide.

Geneva called the point where the sea met the sky infinity. In the dark, it seemed even more vast than it did in the day. He put the blanket on the sand, set the cooler to the side, and leaned on the driftwood log.

He managed to arrive on the dark side of the moon. The night sky was full of stars, points of light, points of history. To their friends, these stars could be dead, but to him, they lived, and twinkled, and smiled for one last show. His mind could grasp each point of light, see it for what it was, and for its pattern, feel the backdrop of blackness against it and beyond.

The ocean spoke to him in its constant roar, and beneath it, he heard Geneva's voice talking about sound and waves, waves and sound. *Inspiring,* she had said, and so it was.

The edge of the universe was just beyond his imagination. The whole universe was within his grasp. He didn't want to see the Big Bang or the end of everything. He didn't want to see all of time, nor all of time and space. Only those points of light that were Geneva, from her birth to her death and back again. He wanted to hold all of those points in his mind at the same time, to be lying with her on the dock at the same time he sat here alone, to be holding her hand in the hospital while they played at intellectual foreplay in her dorm. He wanted his mind to be like the sky, holding history, the future, and infinity at the same time.

Geneva.

She was out there, in time and space, each moment of her existence a moment for him to hold.

He cast his mind into the inky blackness—

And felt the barriers break.

Newsletter sign-up

Be the first to know!

Please sign up for the Kristine Kathryn Rusch and Dean Wesley Smith newsletters, and receive exclusive content, keep up with the latest news, releases and so much more—even the occasional giveaway.

So, what are you waiting for?
To sign up for Kristine Kathryn Rusch's newsletter go to kristinekathrynrusch.com.
To sign up for Dean Wesley Smith's newsletter go to deanwesleysmith.com.

But wait! There's more. Sign up for the WMG Publishing newsletter, too, and get the latest news and releases from all of the WMG authors and lines, including Kristine Grayson, Kris Nelscott, Dean Wesley Smith, *Fiction River*, *Smith's Monthly*, *Pulphouse Fiction Magazine* and so much more.

To sign up go to wmgpublishing.com.

About the Author: Dean Wesley Smith

Considered one of the most prolific writers working in modern fiction, with more than 30 million books sold, writer Dean Wesley Smith published far more than a hundred novels in forty years, and hundreds of short stories across many genres.

At the moment he produces novels in several major series, including the time travel Thunder Mountain novels set in the Old West, the galaxy-spanning Seeders Universe series, the urban fantasy Ghost of a Chance series, a superhero series starring Poker Boy, and a mystery series featuring the retired detectives of the Cold Poker Gang.

His monthly magazine, *Smith's Monthly*, which consists of only his own fiction, premiered in October 2013 and offers readers more than 70,000 words per issue, including a new and original novel every month.

During his career, Dean also wrote a couple dozen *Star Trek* novels, the only two original *Men in Black* novels, Spider-Man and X-Men novels, plus novels set in gaming and television worlds. Writing with his wife Kristine Kathryn Rusch under the name Kathryn Wesley, he wrote the novel for the NBC miniseries The Tenth Kingdom and other books for *Hallmark Hall of Fame* movies.

He wrote novels under dozens of pen names in the worlds of

comic books and movies, including novelizations of almost a dozen films, from *The Final Fantasy* to *Steel* to *Rundown*.

Dean also worked as a fiction editor off and on, starting at Pulphouse Publishing, then at *VB Tech Journal*, then Pocket Books, and now at WMG Publishing, where he and Kristine Kathryn Rusch serve as series editors for the acclaimed *Fiction River* anthology series.

For more information about Dean's books and ongoing projects, please visit his website at www.deanwesleysmith.com and sign up for his newsletter.

For more information:
www.deanwesleysmith.com

facebook.com/deanwsmith3
patreon.com/deanwesleysmith
bookbub.com/authors/dean-wesley-smith

About the Author: Kristine Kathryn Rusch

Kristine Kathryn Rusch has sold more than 35 million books. Generally, she uses her real name (Rusch) for most of her writing. Under that name, she publishes bestselling science fiction and fantasy, award-winning mysteries, acclaimed mainstream fiction, controversial nonfiction, and the occasional romance. Her novels have made bestseller lists around the world and her short fiction has appeared in eighteen best of the year collections. She has won more than twenty-five awards for her fiction, including the Hugo, *Le Prix Imaginales*, the *Asimov's* Readers Choice award, and the *Ellery Queen Mystery Magazine* Readers Choice Award.

Publications from *The Chicago Tribune* to *Booklist* have included her Kris Nelscott mystery novels in their top-ten-best mystery novels of the year. The Nelscott books have received nominations for almost every award in the mystery field, including the best novel Edgar Award, and the Shamus Award.

She writes goofy romance novels as award-winner Kristine Grayson.

She also edits. Beginning with work at the innovative publishing company, Pulphouse, followed by her award-winning tenure at *The Magazine of Fantasy & Science Fiction*, she took fifteen years off before returning to editing with the original anthology series *Fiction River,* published by WMG Publishing. She acts as series editor with her husband, writer Dean Wesley Smith, and edits at least two anthologies in the series per year on her own.

    To keep up with everything she does, go to kriswrites.com and sign up for her newsletter. To track her many pen names and series, see their individual websites (krisnelscott.com, kristinegrayson.com, retrievalartist.com, divingintothewreck.com, pulphouse.com).

kriswrites.com

facebook.com/kristinekathrynruschwriter
patreon.com/kristinekathrynrusch
bookbub.com/authors/kristine-kathryn-rusch

The Make 100 Kickstarter Series

Dean Wesley Smith's Make 100 Challenge

The First Thirty-Three
The Second Thirty-Three
The Final Thirty-Four

Colliding Worlds

A Science Fiction Short Story Series

by Kristine Kathryn Rusch and Dean Wesley Smith

Vol. 1, Vol. 2, Vol. 3, Vol. 4, Vol. 5, Vol. 6

Crimes Collide

A Mystery Short Story Series

by Kristine Kathryn Rusch and Dean Wesley Smith

Vol. 1, Vol. 2, Vol. 3, Vol. 4, Vol. 5

Fantasies Collide

A Fantasy Short Story Series

by Kristine Kathryn Rusch and Dean Wesley Smith

Vol. 1, Vol. 2, Vol. 3, Vol. 4, Vol. 5

Also by Dean Wesley Smith

THE POKER BOY UNIVERSE

Poker Boy

The Slots of Saturn: A Poker Boy Novel

They're Back: A Poker Boy Short Novel

Luck Be Ladies: A Poker Boy Collection

Playing a Hunch: A Poker Boy Collection

A Poker Boy Christmas: A Poker Boy Collection

Ghost of a Chance

The Poker Chip: A Ghost of a Chance Novel

The Christmas Gift: A Ghost of a Chance Novel

The Free Meal: A Ghost of a Chance Novel

The Cop Car: A Ghost of a Chance Novella

The Deep Sunset: A Ghost of a Chance Novel

Marble Grant

The First Year: A Marble Grant Novel

Time for Cool Madness: Six Crazy Marble Grant Stories

Pakhet Jones

The Big Tom: A Packet Jones Short Novel

Big Eyes: A Packet Jones Short Novel

THUNDER MOUNTAIN

Thunder Mountain

Monumental Summit

Avalanche Creek

The Edwards Mansion

Lake Roosevelt

Warm Springs

Melody Ridge

Grapevine Springs

The Idanha Hotel

The Taft Ranch

Tombstone Canyon

Dry Creek Crossing

Hot Springs Meadow

Green Valley

SEEDERS UNIVERSE

Dust and Kisses: A Seeders Universe Prequel Novel

Against Time

Sector Justice

Morning Song

The High Edge

Star Mist

Star Rain

Star Fall

Starburst

Rescue Two

COLD POKER GANG

Kill Game

Cold Call

Calling Dead

Bad Beat

Dead Hand

Freezeout

Ace High

Burn Card

Heads Up

Ring Game

Bottom Pair

Also by Kristine Kathryn Rusch

THE FEY SERIES

The Original books of The Fey

The Sacrifice: Book One of the Fey

The Changeling: Book Two of the Fey

The Rival: Book Three of the Fey

The Resistance: Book Four of the Fey

Victory: Book Five of the Fey

The Black Throne

The Black Queen: Book One of the Black Throne

The Black King: Book Two of the Black Throne

The Qavnerian Protectorate

The Reflection on Mount Vitaki: Prequel to the Qavnerian Protectorate

The Kirilli Matter: The First Book of the Qavnerian Protectorate

Barkson's Journey: The Second Book of the Qavnerian Protectorate

(coming 2023)

THE RETRIEVAL ARTIST SERIES

The Disappeared

Extremes

Consequences

Buried Deep

Paloma

Recovery Man

The Recovery Man's Bargain

Duplicate Effort

The Possession of Paavo Deshin

Anniversary Day

Blowback

A Murder of Clones

Search & Recovery

The Peyti Crisis

Vigilantes

Starbase Human

Masterminds

The Impossibles

The Retrieval Artist

THE DIVING SERIES

Diving into the Wreck: A Diving Novel

City of Ruins: A Diving Novel

Becalmed: A Diving Universe Novella

The Application of Hope: A Diving Universe Novella

Boneyards: A Diving Novel

Skirmishes: A Diving Novel

The Runabout: A Diving Novel

The Falls: A Diving Universe Novel

Searching for the Fleet: A Diving Novel

The Spires of Denon: A Diving Universe Novella

The Renegat: A Diving Universe Novel

Escaping Amnthra: A Diving Universe Novella

The Court-Martial of the Renegat Renegades

Thieves: A Diving Novel

Squishy's Teams: A Diving Universe Novel

The Chase: A Diving Novel

Maelstrom: A Diving Universe Novella

Standalone Science Fiction Novellas

The Tower

The End of the World

G-Men

The Gallery of His Dreams

Recovering Apollo 8

September at Wall & Broad

Writing as Kris Nelscott

THE SMOKEY DALTON SERIES

A Dangerous Road

Smoke-Filled Rooms

Thin Walls

Stone Cribs

War at Home

Days of Rage

Street Justice

AND

Protectors

~

Writing as Kristine Grayson

The Charming Trilogy, Vol. 1

The Charming Trilogy, Vol. 2

The Fates Trilogy

The Daughters of Zeus Trilogy

Also from WMG Publishing

FICTION RIVER
Kristine Kathryn Rusch & Dean Wesley Smith,
series editors

Unnatural Worlds
Edited by Dean Wesley Smith & Kristine Kathryn Rusch

How to Save the World
Edited by John Helfers

Time Streams
Edited by Dean Wesley Smith

Christmas Ghosts
Edited by Kristine Grayson

Hex in the City
Edited by Kerrie L. Hughes

Moonscapes
Edited by Dean Wesley Smith

Special Edition: Crime
Edited by Kristine Kathryn Rusch

Fantasy Adrift

Edited by Kristine Kathryn Rusch

Universe Between
Edited by Dean Wesley Smith

Fantastic Detectives
Edited by Kristine Kathryn Rusch

Past Crime
Edited by Kristine Kathryn Rusch

Pulse Pounders
Edited by Kevin J. Anderson

Risk Takers
Edited by Dean Wesley Smith

Alchemy & Steam
Edited by Kerrie L. Hughes

Valor
Edited by Lee Allred

Recycled Pulp
Edited by John Helfers

Hidden in Crime
Edited by Kristine Kathryn Rusch

Sparks

Edited by Rebecca Moesta

Visions of the Apocalypse
Edited by John Helfers

Haunted
Edited by Kerrie L. Hughes

Last Stand
Edited by Dean Wesley Smith & Felicia Fredlund

Tavern Tales
Edited by Kerrie L. Hughes

No Humans Allowed
Edited by John Helfers

Editor's Choice
Edited by Mark Leslie

Pulse Pounders: Adrenaline
Edited by Kevin J. Anderson

Feel the Fear
Edited by Mark Leslie

Superpowers
Edited by Rebecca Moesta

Justice

Edited by Kristine Kathryn Rusch

Wishes
Edited by Rebecca Moesta

Pulse Pounders: Countdown
Edited by Kevin J. Anderson

Hard Choices
Edited by Dean Wesley Smith

Feel the Love
Edited by Mark Leslie

Special Edition: Spies
Edited by Kristine Kathryn Rusch

Special Edition: Summer Sizzles
Edited by Kristine Kathryn Rusch

Superstitious
Edited by Mark Leslie

Doorways to Enchantment
Edited by Dayle A. Dermatis

Stolen
Edited by Leah Cutter

Chances

Edited by Denise Little & Kristine Kathryn Rusch

Dark & Deadly Passions
Edited by Kristine Kathryn Rusch

Broken Dreams
Edited by Kristine Kathryn Rusch

Fiction River Presents

Fiction River's line of reprint anthologies.

Fiction River has published more than 400 amazing stories by more than 100 talented authors since its inception, from *New York Times* bestsellers to debut authors. So, WMG Publishing decided to start bringing back some of the earlier stories in new compilations.

VOLUMES:
Debut Authors
The Unexpected
Darker Realms
Racing the Clock
Legacies
Readers' Choice
Writers Without Borders
Among the Stars
Sorcery & Steam
Cats!
Mysterious Women
Time Travelers

To learn more or to pick up your copy today, go to www.FictionRiver.com.

Pulphouse Fiction Magazine

Pulphouse Fiction Magazine, edited by Dean Wesley Smith, made its return in 2018, twenty years after its last issue. Each new issue contains about 70,000 words of short fiction. This reincarnation mixes some of the stories from the old *Pulphouse* days with brand-new fiction. The magazine has an attitude, as did the first run. No genre limitations, but high-quality writing and strangeness.

For more information or to subscribe, go to www.pulphousemagazine.com.

Hearts Collide, Strange Romance, Vol. 2
Copyright © 2024 by Kristine Kathryn Rusch and Dean Wesley Smith
Published by WMG Publishing
Cover and layout copyright © 2024 by WMG Publishing
Cover design by WMG Publishing & Alex Hale
Cover art copyright © grandfailure/Depositphotos

"The Secrets of Yesterday"
Copyright © 2024 by Dean Wesley Smith
First published in *Smith's Monthly* Issue #1, October 2013
Published by WMG Publishing

"Cucumber Party"
Copyright © 2024 by Dean Wesley Smith
First published in *Smith's Monthly* Issue #11, August 2014
Published by WMG Publishing

"After the Dance"
Copyright © 2024 by Dean Wesley Smith
First published in *Smith's Monthly* Issue #18, March 2015
Published by WMG Publishing

"In the Shade of the Slowboat Man"
Copyright © 2024 by Dean Wesley Smith
First published in *Smith's Monthly #22*, WMG Publishing, July 2015

"Roses Around the Moment"
Copyright © 2024 Dean Wesley Smith
First published in *Stories From July*, WMG Publishing, 2015

"The Lady of Whispering Valley"
Copyright © 2024 Dean Wesley Smith
First published in *Stories From July*, WMG Publishing, 2015

"That Old Tingling: A Marble Grant Story"
Copyright © 2024 by Dean Wesley Smith
First published in *Smith's Monthly* Issue #39, December 2016
Published by WMG Publishing

"An Immortality of Sorts"
Copyright © 2023 by Dean Wesley Smith
First published in *Smith's Monthly* Issue 41#, February 2017
Published by WMG Publishing

"Smile"
Copyright © 2024 by Dean Wesley Smith
First published in *Smith's Monthly* Issue 42#, March 2017
Published by WMG Publishing

"Something in My Darling"
Copyright © 2024 by Dean Wesley Smith
First published in *Smith's Monthly* Issue #50, June 2021
Published by WMG Publishing

"Name-Calling"
Copyright © 2024 by Kristine Kathryn Rusch
First published as an Amazon Short on Amazon.com in 2005
Published by WMG Publishing

"Something Blue"
Copyright © 2024 by Kristine Kathryn Rusch
First published in *Black Cats and Broken Mirrors*, edited by Martin H. Greenberg and John Helfers, DAW, June, 1998
Published by WMG Publishing

"Canopy"
Copyright © 2024 by Kristine Kathryn Rusch
First published in Sirius Visions, Fall 1994
Published by WMG Publishing

"Artistic Photographs"
Copyright © 2024 by Kristine Kathryn Rusch
Published by WMG Publishing

"Trains"
Copyright © 2024 by Kristine Kathryn Rusch
First published in *Asimov's Science Fiction Magazine*, April, 1990
Published by WMG Publishing

"Midnight Trains"
Copyright © 2021 by Kristine Kathryn Rusch
First published in *A Fantastic Holiday Season: The Gift of Stories*, edited by Kevin J. Anderson and Keith J. Olexa, Wordfire Press, 2014
Published by WMG Publishing

"Except the Music"
Copyright © 2024 by Kristine Kathryn Rusch
First published in *Asimov's*, April/May 2006.
Published by WMG Publishing

"Loop"
Copyright © 2024 by Kristine Kathryn Rusch
First published in VB Tech Journal, November, 1995
Published by WMG Publishing

"Millennium Babies"
Copyright © 2024 Kristine Kathryn Rusch
First published in *Asimov's Science Fiction Magazine*, January, 2000
Published by WMG Publishing

"Without End"
Copyright © 2022 by Kristine Kathryn Rusch
First published in *The Magazine of Fantasy & Science Fiction*, April, 1994
Published by WMG Publishing

This book is licensed for your personal enjoyment only. All rights reserved. This is a work of fiction. All characters and events portrayed in this book are fictional, and any resemblance to real people or incidents is purely coincidental. This book, or parts thereof, may not be reproduced in any form without permission.

Milton Keynes UK
Ingram Content Group UK Ltd.
UKHW011822140624
444031UK00010B/146/J